The De

Paul Finch is an ex-cop and journalist turned best-selling author. He first cut his literary teeth penning episodes of *The Bill*, and has written extensively in horror and fantasy, including for *Dr Who*. He is also known for his crime/thriller novels, of which there are twelve to date, including the Heckenburg and Clayburn series. Paul lives in Lancashire with his wife and business-partner, Cathy.

Also by P. W. Finch

The Wulfbury Chronicles

Usurper
Battle Lord

The Thurstan Wildblood series

The Devil's Knight

THE
DEVIL'S
KNIGHT

P. W. FINCH

CANELO

DK Penguin Random House

First published in the United Kingdom in 2025 by

Canelo, an imprint of
Canelo Digital Publishing Limited,
20 Vauxhall Bridge Road,
London SW1V 2SA
United Kingdom

A Penguin Random House Company
The authorised representative in the EEA is Dorling Kindersley Verlag GmbH. Arnulfstr. 124,
80636 Munich, Germany

A CIP catalogue record for this book is available from the British Library.

Print ISBN 978 1 80436 221 1
Ebook ISBN 978 1 80436 220 4

This book is a work of fiction. Names, characters, businesses, organizations, places and events are either the product of the author's imagination or are used fictitiously. Any resemblance to actual persons, living or dead, events or locales is entirely coincidental.

Cover design by kid-ethic

Cover images © Shutterstock. Knight figure © Satine Zillah

Printed and bound in Great Britain by Clays Ltd, Elcograf S.p.A.

Look for more great books at
www.canelo.co | www.dk.com

I

For my Mum and Dad,

who are finally reunited

...*it is evident who are the children of God, and who are the children of the Devil: whoever does not practice righteousness is not of God, nor is the one who does not love his brother.*

John 3:7–10

June, 1189

The king was dying. He'd never admit it, but it was as plain as the sweat seething on his ashen face. Rarely the most graceful of horsemen, he now slumped sideways in the saddle, one gloved hand on his reins, the other hanging lifeless, a lump of wood rather than flesh. He'd removed his helmet and pulled back his coif, the hair beneath a tangled red-grey mop. His mouth was slack, his eyes glazed. Brownish suds stained the front of his tabard where he'd vomited, obscuring the three Plantagenet lions.

'My liege!' William Marshal shouted, galloping along the rutted track to join him. 'The road to Chinon is clear... *God's blood, Henry!*'

'How dare you... address me so,' the king replied, with a chuckle that caused him to wince.

Marshal glanced in the direction of Le Mans. The royal escort was coming in slow pursuit, the rags and tags that remained of it. Two knights, four men-at-arms, one squire. Like the king, all were coated with grime.

'How many?' Marshal asked, grabbing out to steady his liege, who, with eyelids fluttering, seemed ready to topple.

'A handful,' one of the knights replied, drawing rein. 'But Richard is with them.'

Marshal chewed his lip, pondering.

The knight who'd spoken was Thurstan Wildblood, a surname that matched his reputation. It didn't go unnoticed by Marshal that Wildblood's own lions were spattered crimson, as were the mail-coat and leggings that he wore underneath the tabard, though he himself was uninjured. The longsword hilt at his hip was slick with gore, the small piece of cloth that he always kept tied around it sopping.

'William des Roches,' Marshal said, addressing the other knight. 'Take our sovereign lord to Chinon. Be swift. He can't be caught in the open. Wildblood, you will stay with me. There are words we must have with Duke Richard.'

Wildblood nodded. He wore a cylindrical helm, gashed and dented many times, but had lifted its visor. The unshaved face beneath was pale and even featured, the eyes cool and grey. He seemed untroubled by the prospect facing them.

As the king and his retainers lumbered on, Marshal and his chosen man waited in the hazy heat, the summer fields of Touraine stretched out on every side, parched and yellow, chirping with grasshoppers, broken only by stands of dusty greenery.

'This is no way for a glorious reign to end,' Marshal muttered.

'The next reign can end before it's begun,' Wildblood replied. 'Just say the word.'

'You'd rather live under that wastrel, John?'

'They're all the Devil's spawn.'

'I'm not so sure. John would lose everything his father's built within two or three years.'

'And Richard would fritter it away on war.'

Marshal was amused. 'Without war, what would *you* be, Wild-blood? What would any of us be?'

More dust arose as three riders cantered into view a hundred yards ahead. All were mounted on warhorses and carried lances and shields. The one in the middle wore a mail-shirt, leather trews and hunting boots, and an iron cap instead of a helmet. It was the Hot Duke himself, as Marshal referred to him. That very morning, when the rebels' assault on Le Mans commenced, Richard had watched from the rear, more prepared to use up those contingents loaned to him by Philip of France than his own forces, but on hearing that his prize had escaped the burning city, he'd led the pursuit himself, angry and frustrated.

Those on either side of him were better armed, fully mailed and helmed, clad in flowing surcoats, the one on the left in shimmering blue and gold, the one on the right in white and green.

Some thirty yards off, they reined up.

Duke Richard – now called 'Lionhearted' after his heroics at Château Taillebourg – stood tall in his stirrups. He was similarly handsome to his father, or at least, as his father had *once* been. Chiselled and square-jawed, and of the same shape: squat but solid, with a broad chest and large sloping shoulders implying explosive strength. His neck was thick, his head large and leonine. Though whereas Henry had been a close-cropped redhead in his youth, Richard was like his mother: wild and tawny.

'Stand down, Marshal!' he commanded. 'This chaos can end here. And every one of us will benefit.'

'Except your father, my lord,' Marshal replied.

'My father is the cause of all this. My father and his perpetual preference for that simpering brat of a brother of mine…'

'Your father is the king!' Marshal interrupted. 'And I am his loyal servant, and I will not see violent hands laid upon him.'

Richard eyed his adversaries. The king's eldest surviving son excelled at war. It wasn't just the Hot Duke's personal courage. He had leadership skills, too, along with tactical awareness. Even now, he'd be weighing up the strengths and weaknesses of the vying parties, estimating the consequence of battle.

Both Marshal and Wildblood, as members of the *Familia Regis*, the elite royal guard, wore the official insignia, the golden prancing lions on scarlet. To the duke at least, Wildblood, of average height and build, would be indistinguishable from so many others. But William Marshal, as knight-commander of that company and King's Champion to boot, was a different matter. At three inches over six feet and almost half as wide, he was a great bear of a man, the most feared knight in Christendom.

'These men are Vulgrin of Grouville and Aimar of Genzac,' Richard called. 'Personal retainers, and two of my best fighters. I charge you to stand aside, Marshal. If you refuse, we'll have no choice but to cut our way through.'

'Vulgrin of Grouville and Aimar of Genzac,' Marshal said to Wildblood. 'I've heard of Genzac… Grouville, not so much. Can you handle them both? Because Richard will need to be mine.'

3

'I dare say so,' Wildblood replied.

'Father is at no physical risk from me, Marshal,' Richard called again. 'You of all people ought to realise that.'

'You're a sweet man, my lord, is that it?' Marshal replied. 'You'd never stain your sword with innocent blood?'

The duke's face reddened. 'Father needs only to approve my marriage with Alys Capet, and declare in public that I, and *only* I, am heir to all his lands and titles... and the war is over.'

'None of that is possible if the king wills against it. Waste no more of your breath issuing demands from the King of France, sire... and no more of our time.'

If Duke Richard had any weakness, it was his temper.

With a roar, he kicked his horse forward, his companions lurching into motion with him, all three lances levelled.

Marshal and Wildblood lowered their own shafts and spurred their beasts.

–

When it came to the dash and clash of battle, Thurstan Wildblood was all about instinct.

Barely even thinking about his actions, he veered off the road onto open ground on the right. Genzac and Grouville broke away from their overlord to copy the manoeuvre. Ordinarily, it would have been surprising. The purpose of bodyguards was to guard. But Duke Richard being the man he was, he doubtless considered that he didn't need this.

As the parties closed, Wildblood hunched behind his shield, a ball of tensile muscle locked tight under his thick iron weave. To ride out two blows simultaneously would be difficult but not impossible, and it could only help if he reduced the target area he allowed them. He thus veered further and further to the right. His opponents sought to copy him, but at full gallop this was difficult. Genzac, on their far right, had one option now, to strike Wildblood on the shield, and so to compensate he angled his lance to the left, into the pathway of his comrade. Grouville swore and swerved and lost his own focus on the rider filling his vision.

Hooves thundering, steeds snorting and spraying sweat, Wildblood was into them, and with a clatter like hammer on anvil, struck Grouville in the middle of his helmet.

Grouville's own spear-tip missed entirely as he hurtled backward, neck unhinged, shield and lance flying free. Genzac landed a fierce blow, but only on Wildblood's shield – and from side-on – his weapon shattering mid-shaft, and the knight himself almost thrown by the recoil.

Through them and clear, Wildblood's horse slid to a halt on the bone-dry ground, and he wheeled it around, spurring it back into a second charge. Grouville took his lance full in the chest as he stumbled groggily to his feet. He was mailed under his mantle of blue and gold, but the speed of the collision and the mountain of man and horse muscle behind it was sufficient to drive it home.

Grouville tottered, transfixed, blood gouting from his gagging mouth.

Genzac cursed as he fought to gain control of his animal and urge it forward, drawing the longsword from the scabbard on his belt. Wildblood opted for the chain-mace coiled among his saddlebags. He twirled it round his head as his horse hit a third furious gallop.

They clashed over the corpse of the fallen Grouville, Genzac hacking madly at Wildblood's shield. The blows were fearsome, steel chewing layers of painted hide, slicing timber. Wildblood was jolted elbow to shoulder, but he held his guard. When his adversary tired, Wildblood slashed down with his six pounds of spiked iron and then upward again, catching Genzac's shield top and bottom, splitting it across the middle.

Casting the broken limewood aside, Genzac thrust repeatedly, stabbing at Wildblood's shield, punching through it – but only by inches, and all the time wearing himself out. When Wildblood struck again, Genzac was too exhausted to fend off the spiked head as it whistled down and stove in the crest of his helm. The knight crumpled on his saddle, ruby droplets spurting from his eye-slits. Wildblood threw his mace down, drew the razor-sharp bone-handled knife that he always kept sheathed at his back, and reining his horse in close, rammed it under the lower rim of his opponent's helm, driving it through the aventail and deep into flesh and cartilage.

Aimar of Genzac's sweat-drenched horse lurched away, its rider tilting from his saddle, a rope-thick crimson stream gurgling from his punctured windpipe, before dropping to the ground.

As Wildblood dismounted to retrieve his mace, he glanced leftward to the road, where Duke Richard's horse also lay dead, the broken shaft of a lance jutting upward from its chest. The duke himself, longsword wielded in two hands, but filthied from head to ankle, bellowed with rage as he retreated on foot. William Marshal rode slowly after him, his own blade drawn, his warhorse rearing, threatening to hammer the nobleman's skull and brains to pulp with its flailing, iron-shod hooves. It was no contest, and by the time Wildblood had regained his saddle, the duke had voluntarily disarmed and sunk to his knees in submission. Marshal, ignoring his opponent further, cantered onto the open ground, though he reined in sharply when he saw the corpses of the slaughtered knights. He lifted his helmet, shaking out his dark, sweaty mane.

'Richard's mount?' Wildblood asked.

Marshal seemed distracted. 'I slew it on the first pass.'

'You slew his mount?' Wildblood was taken aback; to strike an opponent's horse instead of the opponent himself was expressly against the code. And that was unlike his knight-commander.

'I didn't want to,' Marshal said. 'But I had to unhorse him without killing him. I see you had no such compunction.'

'They came here in pursuit of our king. We couldn't allow that.'

Marshal regarded the younger man carefully. 'You're a fair hand with steel, Wildblood. I saw that the moment you joined us. You fear nothing, and you serve the king loyally. Which is all to the good. But the road to war, which we so often ride, need not be a road to damnation.'

Wildblood had heard such before. He didn't discount it entirely, though it contravened everything he'd learned at his father's court.

Chivalrous law imposed limits on the blind fury of battle. This was in keeping with holy scripture, though to Wildblood's mind, scripture was for monks cossetted behind monastery walls. Scripture was for those who preached redemption through pain and knew none themselves. Scripture was for those who believed there was light at the end of this tunnel.

But all that said, William Marshal commanded here, so the younger knight nodded and hung his mace among his bags.

'What did you say to the duke?' he asked as they rode away.

'He challenged me to dismount,' Marshal replied. 'To fight him on foot. I told him I had no time for games… that I would keep my advantage. He said that in that case I should kill him. I told him the Devil could kill him, and probably would in due course.'

'Might have been better for both of us if you'd done as he asked, my lord.'

'Aye. It might.'

The king died.

The inevitable came on July 6, three days after he was bought back to Chinon Castle on a litter, having been forced to attend peace talks with his son, Richard, and Richard's usual ally of convenience, King Philip of France, where he was presented with terms he considered outrageous. With a vast army, the combined levies of Aquitaine, Poitou and all the French king's dominions, now encircling what remained of his own paltry force, his reinforcements broken at Tours, and no strength left in his own ailing body, King Henry had agreed to everything. But the final blow had fallen after his return to Chinon, where he'd studied a scroll presented to him by the rebels that listed all those complicit in taking arms against his interests, and there in the middle of it was the name of his youngest and favourite son, John.

King Henry, England's second of that name, never spoke another word.

Wildblood became aware of the monarch's passing when he stood on Chinon's gatehouse battlements that fateful morning. A dawn mist

7

blanketed the River Vienne. The dark woods both south and north of it sparkled with the breakfast fires of Richard's army. There'd been no attempt to storm the fortress, but then there'd been no need. Of course, the citizens of Chinon were grateful for that. Wildblood was, too, if he was honest. With less than forty crossbows from the garrison remaining, and fewer knights and men-at-arms than when they'd departed Le Mans, resistance would not have lasted. But when he heard the sound of the gates being opened below, and leaning through an embrasure, saw a handful of servants, cloaked and hooded, carrying sacks and hurrying away along the road, accompanied by a couple of crossbowmen, he realised that the matter was finally settled.

A short time later, he was warming his hands by a brazier, an aged sentry sitting on the other side of it, staring at nothing, when Marshal came up.

The royal champion stood huddled in his scarlet cloak, gazing across the river at the many camps slowly stirring to life.

'I never understood why the king came south from Le Mans,' Wildblood commented. 'Most of the barons of Normandy still support him. He could have raised a new army there.'

When Marshal turned, his eyes were moist. He signalled with a click of his fingers to the sentry, who, muttering complaints, rose and traipsed away along the battlement walk.

'With henchmen like that, it's a miracle it didn't end days ago,' Wildblood said.

'At least he's still here,' Marshal replied. 'There are many others I can name who aren't. But to answer your question… Henry knew his time was short. And he wanted to come home.'

'Was it quick in the end?'

Marshal wiped at his eyes with his fingertips. 'He passed in his sleep, which is a kind of mercy. But I don't think anyone really thought it quick. All these years of betrayals and back-stabbing.'

'Like I said… Devil's spawn.'

'The issue now,' Marshal said, 'is delivering this news, and the crown, to Richard.'

Wildblood grunted. 'It's the only course now that John has shown his colours.'

'And because the realm must endure.'

'So, who is this honour bestowed upon?'

Marshal sighed. 'In all the battles and sieges I've fought, Wildblood, I've never yet sent any man to do something I wouldn't do myself.'

He produced Henry's crown from under his cloak and placed it on the nearest merlon. It was wrought from gold of course, but unadorned and unremarkable. And sore in need of a polish.

'You could stick that thing on a shelf in some peasant's hovel and it would barely be noticed,' Wildblood said.

'Henry was never given to extravagant displays.'

'And yet so much blood shed for the sake of it.'

'Our station is not to question, Wildblood.'

'When do you depart?'

Marshal shoved the crown into a hessian sack and hung it from his belt. 'The longer we have no king, the greater our trouble.'

'Good.' Wildblood nodded, checked the longsword at his waist and pulled on his gauntlets. 'As it happens, I have nothing else to do this morning either.'

Marshal eyed him incredulously. 'Are you mad?'

'You're my captain. Where you go, I follow.'

The royal champion shook his head. He looked bewildered. 'There's an eerie strangeness in you, Thurstan Wildblood. You seem to embrace these horrors, even when you yourself are under threat.'

'Strange is our world, Will. Yesterday, Richard was in the wrong. Today, he's in the right. Who can say where he'll be tomorrow?'

BOOK ONE

LAND OF DEMONS

CHAPTER 1

1191, Palestine

The city's walls had mostly withstood the bombardment, though many parts were fissured and blackened by smoke and fire. For all that, the blistering Levantine sun still glared from the high battlements, glinting off the helmets and spearpoints of the hundreds of soldiers crowded along them, gazing down in silence on the prisoners, who – ragged, filthy and chained together like animals – were brought out from the east-facing gate, trudging past the siege machines and snaking in double-file between the huts, tents and pavilions.

Most limped or leaned on each other, many bearing poorly band-aged wounds.

'You think the king intends to do it?' the lad asked, pale faced.

There was no doubt in Thurstan Wildblood's mind about that. He adjusted his mail coif, where – along with the grit and bristles – it chafed at his sun-reddened neck. 'The problem when you're a serial bluffer, Pandulf, which seems to be the way of this Sultan Saladin… you must always be prepared to have your bluff called.' He turned in his saddle. '*Ramon!*'

Ramon la Hors, Knight-Captain of the *Familia Regis*, cantered forward.

'Take them to the top of that ridge.' Thurstan indicated the great rise of rocky ground to the north, which the locals knew as Ayyadieh. 'So their friends can see them.'

The knight-captain nodded, wheeling his animal round.

'They're mounted and armed already.' The lad looked beyond the bulwark of trenches and fences of stakes, and across the corpse-littered plain of Arab-el-Ghawarneh to the Ayyubid horde. They were just less than half a mile away, but his eyes bulged as he scanned the thousands of horsemen mustering there, the ever-colourful livery of their nobles visible even amid clouds of swirling dust, their multiple prayer-banners fluttering in the desert wind. 'If we proceed with this, they'll charge.'

'I imagine that's the plan, young Pandulf.'

Pandulf was only sixteen years old, and easily shocked. 'The *plan*?'

'You know Richard,' Thurstan said. 'He likes a battle. He's been denied one thus far. A real one. And that isn't sitting well with him.'

The siege of the great port city of Acre had been under way for nearly two years when Philip of France and Richard of England, arrived with their huge armies. Originally prosecuted by the ousted King Guy of Jerusalem, the siege up to that point had made negligible progress, constant attempts to escalade the fortress failing at huge cost, similar losses incurred when what remained of the Christian army of Outremer had then to turn and defend itself against Sultan Saladin's massive relief force. But everything had changed thanks to these fresh cohorts from Europe, particularly those under Richard of England, who'd refortified the Christian camp east of the city, and assailed Acre's walls with his trio of pet mangonels, *Siege Cat*, *God's Sling* and *Evil Neighbour*. Within days, the city had fallen. But now, two immense armies – perhaps thirty thousand strong apiece – faced each other across the plain where so many men had already died.

Pandulf turned in his saddle. From this position, they could clearly see the host of armoured horsemen waiting behind King Richard. For the most part, they were knights, but there were also companies of mounted men-at-arms, and though the majority were English and Norman, having arrived with their overlord seventy-four days ago, there were many others drawn from all corners of Christendom, not to mention the military orders of the Temple and the Hospital. Only their horses stirred, pawing the dirt with their hooves, flicking their manes at flies. Their riders, for all that they broiled in their mail and leather, waited in disciplined silence.

It was the king who set that example.

Richard had suffered as many privations on this harsh campaign as his men. He'd been ill for several days on first arriving, though even then he'd controlled operations from his sickbed, but now he'd regained his strength and vigour. He sat astride his warhorse resplendent in glimmering mail, the Plantagenet lions shining like gold on his scarlet shield and surcoat, his longsword at his hip, his battle-axe in hand. The visor was lifted on his cylindrical helm, his handsome, bearded face a picture of studied concentration.

'Why don't they just return it?' the lad wondered. 'It can't have meaning for them.'

He referred to the True Cross, which King Guy had carried before him when he marched his army out of his capital four years ago to meet Sultan Saladin of Egypt – or Salah al-Din Yusuf ibn Ayyub, to use his real name – and suffered a crushing defeat on the Horns of Hattin. After some brief negotiations with Richard, the sultan had promised to return the Cross in exchange for the garrison of Acre. But nothing even resembling that potent symbol had materialised thus far.

'You think they actually possess it?' Thurstan asked his squire.

'If not, why claim they do?'

'To grind our infidel noses into the blood-soaked sand. Why else?'

'If that's the case, it had the opposite effect.'

Thurstan was amused by that, though on principle he never showed such emotions in front of his men. But Pandulf, for all his inexperience, wasn't wrong. The slaughter at Hattin, and the theft of Christendom's holiest artefact, had aroused the ire of Europe, bringing one of her greatest warriors to this sacred land. Richard had even brought Mategriffon with him, named after the Greek word for 'terror', a vast, timber fortress, taller than the walls of Acre itself and equipped not just with catapults and ballistae, but with an undercarriage and wheels, so that it could be towed from one corner of the battlefield to the next, which the Saracens had initially regarded with horror and awe.

Saladin's policies thus far hadn't cowed anyone.

'They seek an upper hand… any upper hand,' Thurstan said. 'And to that end, a lie about the Cross is as good as a truth. If such a treasure ever existed, it was likely lost in the chaos at Hattin. Broken up, carried off in fragments.'

If Pandulf was shocked to hear such doubts expressed about the fabled relic's authenticity, he didn't voice them. Having been squired to Thurstan Wildblood for a month now, he clearly knew better.

'The same goes for that two hundred thousand gold bezants,' Thurstan said, suspecting that this was the more likely reason why Richard was looking for a fight today. Ever the pragmatist, the king had demanded a cash ransom in addition to the relic, and thus far, though the sultan had agreed, he'd showed no sign that he would pay it. 'Anyway, enough talk.'

A rider had detached from King Richard's presence, and came cantering across the low hummocks at the southern tip of Ayyadieh. Glancing to the top of the ridge, Thurstan confirmed that the first hundred or so prisoners had been arrayed in an extended line and forced to their knees at crossbow point. Some wailed, some wept. Most, to their credit, were resigned to their fate, and simply prayed. Their captors were other members of the *Familia*, knights and men-at-arms, all now waiting at their hostages' backs with swords drawn or axes hefted.

'Return to the camp,' Thurstan told his squire. 'If the Saracens break through, go into the city.'

'I'm your squire, lord. I should stand by you.'

'This war won't end today. You'll have many opportunities to show how brave you are. But not here and not now.'

The lad nodded, turning his horse around.

'Knight-Commander!' The messenger from the king halted close by. 'His Highness authorises you to proceed with the executions.'

Thurstan nodded. Fifty yards south, a phalanx of great lords sat horsed beneath a panoply of rippling banners: King Guy at the front, with Count Conrad and Duke Leopold behind. There were fathers of the Church too: the papal legate, Archbishop Ubaldo, Bishop Hubert, Archbishop Gerhard, all these men of God looking on sternly, not a hint of clemency among them.

Thurstan kept his usual lid on any feelings of scorn. He'd long wielded steel for popinjays like these. So often, they used other men to commit their crimes for them. But at the same time, they feared those men. And there were gains to be made there. He spurred his animal up the rugged path to the crest of the ridge. As he reached the top, Knight-Banneret Bertrand du Voix, also mounted, approached him.

'My lord, you shouldn't participate.' His red-bearded face was drawn and thin.

'I have my orders,' Thurstan replied, dismounting and handing his reins to a man-at-arms.

Bertrand dismounted alongside him. 'You'd willingly share in this dishonour?'

'Dishonour?'

The banneret indicated the kneeling prisoners. Many more of them, two thousand at least, marshalled into batches of several hundred each, now waited in their chains on the west-facing slope. By their dogged aspect, they knew they'd be hustled up into position the moment the first group had been despatched.

'These men surrendered in good faith,' Bertrand said quietly. 'Thurstan, by all the rules of chivalry...'

'There are no rules for *these*,' Thurstan replied.

'Didn't Christ extend the hand of friendship to pagans?'

'At Hattin, they slew every Templar and Hospitaller they captured. Those men, too, had surrendered, but their heads were still piled into pyramids for the vultures to pluck out their eyes.'

'And do two mortal sins make something virtuous?'

Steel rasped as Thurstan drew his longsword. 'All wrongs must be righted. If they didn't want to die, they shouldn't have made war on us. Rejoin the king, Bertrand. When the charge comes, ensure our gonfalon flies high.'

Bertrand looked sad as he climbed back into the saddle and steered his mount down the path.

Thurstan turned to the prisoners. The nearest glanced fearfully round, the eyes darting in his haggard, nut-brown face, but still barely seeing Thurstan's steel as it flashed in the sun. His severed head tumbled.

Next along stood Knight-Serjeant Ivan de Vesqui, a hulking, black-haired brute whom Thurstan had always felt enjoyed the carnage of war more than was good for any man. De Vesqui grinned, a row of white, wolflike teeth splitting his scarred, wind-scoured face, and with a single blow of his axe, sundered his own prisoner's skull. All along the line, *thunking* impacts sounded as the *Familia* struck hard with blades and maces. Howls of anguish rolled across the plain. Thurstan eyed the distant horde, which suddenly was advancing. Initially with caution, in separate, disorderly companies, but eventually all together, the earth quaking, the clamour of their horns, drums and cymbals affrighting the air.

He loosened a rag from his harness and wiped down his blade as he watched.

The first line of prisoners was unchained and kicked downslope. The next row were forced into their place. On lower ground to the right, Richard came galloping around the southern end of the ridge, the great three-lion standard flying alongside him as Bertrand du Voix slotted it into his pannier, the huge host of knights at their rear snapping visors down, raising shields.

Thurstan turned to where his men rained further killing blows on the helpless.

Ramon la Hors stood near. By his unsullied mantle, he himself hadn't participated.

'Complete the executions,' Thurstan said, signalling for his horse. La Hors nodded, unperturbed. The commander sheathed his sword, stepped into his stirrup and threw himself up into the saddle. 'All the prisoners must die, Ramon. Those are the king's orders.'

Again, La Hors nodded. He still seemed unperturbed.

–

Apollonius was a five-year-old roan which Thurstan had acquired on first being elevated to the rank of knight-commander by Richard one year earlier. It was flat in the belly and huge in the chest and shoulder, and at full gallop could outrace a peregrine falcon. That wouldn't be so easy today. When Thurstan joined the charge, he was far to the rear and had to thrust his way forward, jostling other riders out of his way. Richard's vanguard had ploughed into the infidels long before he was anywhere near, the clash and clang of arms resounding on the scorching air, even over the thunder of hooves and baying of battle-horns.

When he entered the fray, it was much as he'd expected: the thick press of men and beasts now breaking apart, dozens of Saracen warriors already unhorsed by Richard's initial charge. There were almost no soldiers braver than these men of Mohammed, and they too were driven by a zealous adherence to their faith, but when it came to close, mounted combat, the Christian heavy cavalry was more than a match for them. The Ayyubids were famous for their disciplined infantry, archers and spearmen, who fought with great organisation but in a cavalry battle like this were useless. They also boasted regiments of horse-archers, and possessed their own lordly caste, who, like the knights of Europe, rode to war in the saddle and led companies of armed retainers raised from their own lands. But all these groups, though skilled with weapons, were often lightly armoured, donning a fine mesh for mail, their steeds fleet-footed mares rather than brutish stallions like Apollonius.

Just ahead, amid a deafening chaos of dust and horse-sweat, Richard and those *Familia* knights assigned to ride as his personal *mesnie*, were wreaking furious execution, the king himself cleaving shields and forearms with his battle-axe, crushing helmets, parting necks from shoulders. Bertrand rode next to him, the royal standard steady in its pannier and soaring overhead, the knight's own longsword drawn and glimmering with gore.

Thurstan met his own first opponent head on – a Berber horseman, coming fast on his Arabian grey. By the gold-and-purple plumage under his mail and the prayer-pennon fluttering from his lance, he was no common soldier. His shield was a circular slab of timber, faced with ox-hide, bossed with iron. The spike of a steel helmet poked from his turban.

But as they joined, Thurstan arced his longsword upward, sending his adversary's lance askew, and with a single backhand, sliced his larynx. Another rode at him, again helmed and shielded, this one wielding one of those great curved blades the Muslims knew as *scim-itars*. Thurstan fended it off with his shield, then drove his sword into the unprotected face, the lethal steel piercing flesh and bone, puncturing the brain beneath.

'*Wildblood!*' someone shouted, straining himself hoarse over the din.

It was James of Avesnes, a knight of Flanders and a brawling, battle-hardened warrior of great fame. He halted his steed alongside Thurstan. He was grimy with blood and grit, and bled from his mouth, where several teeth had been knocked free, but he was laughing. 'A good day on the tiltyard, is it not?'

Nearby, a Christian knight was struck from his saddle by a well-aimed lance. No sooner had he fallen than two Muslim footsloggers were onto him, stabbing at his face and throat with their daggers. Thurstan spurred Apollonius forward. One of them went down under bone-shattering blows from the battle-steed's hooves. The other tried to duck away, but Thurstan wheeled and struck from behind, slashing down hard, shearing into the fellow's shoulder, lopping arm from torso in a cloudburst of blood. He reined up again, sweating, panting, wiping crimson spray from his eyes.

'God's bread, Avesnes!' he shouted. 'What kind of tournaments do you attend?'

Avenes riposted with a bellow of laughter, and urged his horse forward, hitting a fresh gallop as a new target came into view.

'Sire!' Thurstan cantered up to Richard, who had halted and now leaned on the pommel of his saddle, chest heaving under his mail. 'Are you wounded?' The king shook himself, to show that he wasn't. 'I think they've broken,' Thurstan said.

In truth, he wasn't sure. By his estimation, three or four thousand Christian horsemen had ridden out from Acre that day. Sultan Saladin had fielded at least that number, and who knew how many more he was deploying beyond the veil of dust and blood, though wherever Thurstan looked now, the Saracen horse were falling back.

'He didn't come out himself, you notice.' Richard raised his visor. 'That weaselly sultan of theirs.'

Thurstan was tempted to reply that crowned heads seldom did, the main reason being that most of them understood how, if they were lost, the cause was lost. Though as always with Richard, different rules seemed to apply. The reckless courage he so often displayed was ill-advised to many, but his presence in the front line was an inspiration to his men.

Sensing that the charge had achieved its aim, other knights now approached, their mounts picking through the debris of spent weapons and broken corpses. Garnier de Nablus, Grandmaster of the Hospitallers, a wiry, bearded bald-head, was first, followed by Count Robert of Dreux. Grandmaster Garnier had lost his helmet and been cut across the forehead; even now, the *clairet* streamed down his face and beard, dripping onto the white cross emblazoned on his black tabard. He irritably wielded a bunched corner of his cloak in his efforts to mop it away.

'The field is ours, my liege?' Count Robert wondered.

Richard pivoted on his saddle. On all sides, horsemen careered about, exchanging blows, but most of those in close proximity were Christians.

He nodded. 'Have our trumpeters sound the recall. But if they approach again, we charge again. And again. You understand, my lords? Pass it through your ranks. They need to know that Acre is ours. Now *we* control the sea-gate to Palestine...'

'*My noble lords!*' Bertrand du Voix, who as a simple banneret, had been waiting a few yards away, spurred his horse forward, levelling the royal gonfalon, couching it as a lance. '*My liege, beware... beware!*'

They turned as one and saw a fresh company of Ayyubid horsemen advancing at speed, *scimitars* drawn. By their heavier mail-coats, kite-shaped shields and plumed helms engraved with Arabic verse, the aventails of which came to just beneath their gleaming gimlet eyes, these were Mamluks, Saladin's elite corps.

Thurstan kicked his horse into a frenzied counter charge. In seconds, he sensed others alongside him, Richard at their fore. It was this sudden clarity of vision that enabled him to pinpoint the tasselled javelin thrown from the rear of the Mamluk squadron, his eyes fixing on it as it lofted towards them, arcing down. Thurstan's shield was intact, but for some reason he had no time to adjust its position. The missile's thudding impact knocked the wind from his chest, struck his pelvis like a hammer blow.

And then there was that searing, burning pain as steel penetrated muscle and bone.

He struck at the shaft as it jutted outward, but his strength was draining fast, and suddenly he was swaying in the saddle, and Apollonius, sensing his trouble, swerved from its target, alarmed. As Thurstan fell from his mount, the rest of his comrades rumbled past, calling on Saint Michael and Saint George.

But as he descended into darkness, he heard only one voice clearly.

It was Bertrand.

'A priest!' he cried. 'In God's name, bring a priest!'

CHAPTER 2

Thurstan threw off his cloak and levered himself up from the straw-stuffed bedroll. The interior of the tent was stifling and reeked of sweat, cheap wine and rotten breath. There was no sound from his companions. They slept, though normally there'd be a chorus of grunts, snorts, nightmare-induced whimpers.

Too fuddled to work out why he was awake, let alone on his feet, he stumbled to the entrance, pushed the flap aside and stepped out.

By his groggy estimation, it was the early hours. The searing heat of the day had not yet arrived, but clouds had come in from the sea, so it wasn't cold either. The camp lay silent and still, though the air was rancid with the stink of those hacked, dismembered forms left out on the plain of Arab-el-Ghawarneh and not yet eaten by vultures or jackals.

For reasons he couldn't comprehend, Thurstan's feet took him out that way. They were bare, but the sand and grit beneath them felt strangely soft. He wore only a pair of leather breeches but had brought his cloak and drew it about himself. When he passed through the outer defences, the sentries were no more than motionless shapes in the darkness.

He was stiff, sore, wearied to his marrow, but ahead saw lights on the battlefield – an array of writhing, reddish blots. Bonfires? Even from this distance, he could smell the smoke. Cremation pyres were more likely. But when he came closer, he saw that they were lighted braziers encircling a vast banquet table, some fifty yards in length, with many individuals seated along it. He could even distinguish the stooped outlines of scurrying servants bringing food and drink.

The knight still had no idea why he was out here. No one had called him. There was no business he must attend to. Who these people were, dining in the midst of death, he couldn't fathom, but he wasn't invited to their feast, so why proceed? But proceed he did.

'*Knight-Commander!*' A roaring, resonant voice assailed him.

Thurstan straightened, squared his shoulders.

'Knight-Commander Wildblood… you are most welcome!'

He entered the circle of braziers, but the light they cast wavered, and the air was thick with their smoke, the acrid smell hard on his nose and throat.

'Knight-Commander!' That voice again: deep, bass. 'Join us. Make a place for this gallant fellow.'

Thurstan was ushered – in fact, steered; firm hands taking his elbows – to the far end of the table, where, on a great ecclesiastical throne, carved all over with beasts and flora, the immense figure of a bishop was seated. It was no bishop Thurstan recognised, but his status was evident from the blood-red vestments adorning his colossal frame, and the crimson mitre on his huge, anvil-shaped head.

'Come, come!' The bishop beckoned with several fingers at once.

Thurstan descended bewilderedly onto a stool at his host's left-hand side. The bishop had a reddish, porcine face, great slab-like jowls where cheeks should be, a large, flattish nose and small, amber-coloured eyes set closer together than could ever be natural. Despite this, he was all *bonhomie*. When he laughed, it was hearty and infectious.

'You are most welcome!' He had no accent, neither French nor English nor anywhere in between, but his voice was thunderous. 'Food and drink for our honoured guest!'

'You… you must have me for someone else, your grace.'

'I doubt that.'

'But I don't know you…'

'I am Belphagor.' The bishop rested his cheek on his immense left hand and arched a bushy, red eyebrow.

Thurstan's mind remained blank. He could barely remember what he'd done the day before, let alone those many episcopal princes he'd met during his varied travels.

A huge wooden trencher was placed in front of him, on top of which a massive cut of meat simmered in rich gravy. A bowl of steamed vegetables was placed alongside it, and then a huge chunk of bread. Another servant put down a goblet foaming with wine, and an even larger-sized pitcher, from which to replenish it.

The knight's hollow stomach groaned, his mouth filling with spittle, yet he was hesitant. He glanced along the table, where, by an oily, greenish light cast from a succession of ornate candelabra, he saw that similar delectable treats were being fallen on with gusto by innumerable other guests. Again, none were recognisable. In addition, they wore a range of costumes: everything from the heraldic livery of high nobility and the ornate robes of the merchant class to the leather and homespun of the everyday field-hand. Thurstan peered at those closest, but they were indistinct, too shaggy with unkempt hair, too dirty and slobbery, too buried snouts-first in their succulent repast.

'Eat! Drink!' Bishop Belphagor said in friendly but domineering fashion. 'Be one with us!'

'Your grace, I'm—'

'You're wondering why you're here?' The prelate sat back, his heavy hands hanging loose over the ends of the arms of his throne. 'To answer that, I must first share solemn tidings, Thurstan Wildblood of House Aelfricsson…'

Thurstan was even more bewildered. 'Aelfricsson' was an archaic name that his family line had dispensed with in his father's time.

'It is my responsibility,' the bishop said, 'to warn you that this most glorious endeavour is doomed to fail.' He'd adopted an ominous tone, yet his hefty, hoglike features remained indifferent. 'Your masters have assembled the finest fighting force that ever left Christian lands. The pick of the knights of Europe and the Levant are gathered here. Even your common men are unmatched in their zeal and discipline. And yet this mighty force, this army of God is already fragmenting.'

'I don't understand, your grace…' Thurstan shook his head, though partly to clear it; the heady, smoky atmosphere was seeping into him, muddying his thoughts. 'We… we captured the city.'

'A remarkable feat. But so long as your leaders squabble, this victory will not be capitalised on. Sooner rather than later, the initiative will be seized by the pagans. Even now, Conrad of Montferrat leaves your host, returning to his power base in the north.'

Thurstan was shocked. 'Count Conrad has the best soldiers in all of Outremer. He defeated Saladin at the battle of Tyre before Richard even arrived…'

'And now he takes home those troops who won that battle. All ten thousand.'

On the table, Thurstan's meal was congealing with uncommon speed. He'd little enough appetite anyway, he realised, but this news was apt to knock him sick. Ever since arriving in the East, he'd feared that Count Conrad, whose huge contingent were among the best trained, best equipped and most experienced at desert fighting in the whole Christian army, would resent having to serve alongside King Guy of Jerusalem, because Conrad considered that he had the better claim to that title. Fears that the count would abandon the mission before it was complete had affected everyone. In his worst dreams though, Thurstan had never considered that it might happen so early in the campaign.

'There's more, I'm afraid…' Briefly, Bishop Belphagor was distracted by a nun, who appeared alongside them to arrange what looked like a pan of glowing coals on a raised wrought-iron stand. 'Philip of France has also departed.'

Thurstan knew about this. It had happened several days ago, but the French monarch had left his host behind, under the command of the elderly Duke Hugh of Burgundy.

'Alas, Philip was never a warrior,' the bishop opined. 'The pains of this arduous expedition were already proving too much. His army stays, but for how long do you think the flower of French chivalry will serve under the King of England?' Again, he arched a thick, red-bristled eyebrow.

Thurstan couldn't answer. Richard was known and admired across all the equestrian classes of Christendom, but the French saw him mainly as a foe. A chivalrous foe, a heroic foe. But still a foe.

'Others will follow,' the bishop said. 'Duke Leopold for one. It wasn't a clever move of your monarch, throwing the Babenberg banner down from the walls of the city because the duke showed the temerity to erect it there. Granted, a duke is only a duke, hardly a king… you agree? But did the Germans not play their part in the siege? Did their blood not spill alongside Richard's own followers'?'

Thurstan hadn't considered it wise either, castigating the leader of the German forces in front of the entire army.

'The Church of Jesus Christ faces a catastrophe if steps aren't taken to reverse these fortunes…' The bishop broke off to poke the glowing coals with a long-handled tool.

'Why put this case to *me*, your grace?' Thurstan asked. 'I'm no great lord. I'm a third son. I'll never even inherit my family title. I'm nothing, a household man…'

'But you are strong in spirit and pure in heart.'

'That settles it, your grace. You definitely have the wrong man.'

The bishop laughed again, the smoggy air reverberating. 'You undervalue yourself, Wildblood. You are a warrior through and through. You were knighted at the age of seventeen while fighting for King Henry during the Great Rebellion…'

'My father was always loyal to King Henry. I served in father's household.'

'You served with distinction. As you did later in Ireland. You then went on to win countless tournaments.'

'Only because I was never pitched against William Marshal.'

'Pah.' The bishop waved that away. 'A man who's had his day. At the end of King Henry's life, you engaged two of Duke Richard's deadliest knights in single combat… and slew them both.'

'For which Richard has never forgiven me.'

'He kept you in the *Familia Regis*. He promoted you to the rank of knight-commander.'

'He was tying me to his horse's tail. Keeping those he mistrusted closer than those he trusted.'

'Maybe, but he's come to see your value since, has he not? Not least because you are dutiful. You obey his every order without question.'

'Some would say that isn't always a good thing.'

'In wartime, duty is all.' Belphagor leaned towards him. 'But so is strength, so is courage. Both of which you possess in abundance.'

'I don't understand. What can I do that I don't do already?'

The bishop's nostrils expanded as he breathed deep of the greasy, smoke-befouled air. 'You can become your king's talisman, his supreme weapon, a champion who, when he takes the field, is the guarantor of victory.'

'No knight can do that. Even William Marshal didn't win every fight...'

'Forget the Marshal!' A first hint of impatience, sharpened nubs of bone showing where normal men had teeth. 'He was your mentor in the *Familia*, I understand. Your esteemed leader. The officer who commended you to the king for the role of knight-captain. William Marshal has long shown probity, but what he's always been short on, Wildblood, is ruthlessness, and only ruthlessness will turn this war. And that, my friend, is *your* strength...'

'King Richard can be ruthless...'

'King Richard has one eye on his own kingdom... and especially on his holdings in France. Even more so now that Philip is returning home. *You*, however, suffer no such preoccupations.'

Thurstan regarded the nun who waited alongside them. He'd rarely seen one as well-shaped, despite her monastic regalia, or maybe because of it. Her habit and scapular were cinched at the waist by a rope of beads, which accentuated her generous bosom and round hips. Though she wore both veil and wimple, uncombed straggles of straw-blonde hair hung down. Her nose was petite, her mouth full and red. She stared sidelong at him with eyes as blue as honed steel.

'I can't replace the Lionheart,' Thurstan replied, distracted.

'But you can bolster his power until it's irresistible,' the bishop said. 'By the example you set on the field, by the cohorts of enemies you slay. By your implacable hostility to the enemies of God, you can be a figurehead to which all Christian men will rally...'

'Lord-Bishop, I'm only a man...'

'For now.' The bishop's toothy grin split his ogre-like face. 'But with my blessing, you can be so much more.'

'Your... *blessing*?'

'You will rule every battlefield.'

The knight was again distracted by the nun's beguiling gaze. His loins stirred, his breath coming short. 'I... Lord Bishop, I...'

'Say the word.'

It can hardly hurt, Thurstan reasoned, entranced.

The cerulean eyes glimmered with unashamed promise. It had been so long since he'd lain with a woman. His words diminished to a whisper. 'Bless... bless me, Father.'

Her hand snaked onto his shoulder, then the back of his neck, then into his mat of dark hair, which she softly ruffled. With an oath, Thurstan pulled her onto his lap. Her curves melded into his muscle-hard frame as she engulfed his mouth with her own, her hands entwined in his locks, knifepoint fingernails pricking his scalp. Her tongue slithered between his lips, and he shuddered at the heat of lust that speared through him. So much so, that when he glimpsed the colossal, crimson-clad form leering over them, eyes aglow with flame, drool fizzling through his tusks, the knight barely even flinched.

Not even when he sensed the bishop's hand roving around his back.

Until he spied the implement gripped in it.

Thurstan's eyes snapped open. He struggled to be free, but the lascivious creature wrapped him like a cat, silken and soft, yet unyielding as iron.

He watched with disbelief as the inverted, white-hot cross impressed into his lower right side, burning through his leather breeches, sizzling into flesh and bone. His protracted cry of pain was lost amid the gibbers and howls of the animal courtiers, and the rolling, booming laughter of Bishop Belphagor.

CHAPTER 3

'He's here! Knight-Captain Ramon… he's here!'

Thurstan was vaguely aware of the excited voice. His head throbbed and his limbs felt leaden, but he appeared to be lying face-down in sand.

What sounded like hooves thundered up.

'Does he live?' A different voice. Ramon la Hors, perhaps.

'He's in poor condition, but he lives.' The first voice again. Pandulf.

Thurstan sensed others arriving. Someone dropped to their knees.

'Quickly…' It was Bertrand du Voix. 'Get some water.'

Hands assisted Thurstan over onto his back, then up into a sitting posture. He blinked in the fierce sunlight. La Hors watched him from horseback, Ivan de Vesqui drawing rein alongside. Others were also present, some standing, some kneeling.

'My lord…' Bertrand held a waterskin to his lips.

Thurstan drank thirstily. He ran a limp hand through his damp, gritty hair. Beyond his companions, he spied the arid landscape, its far distance hazed by heat and swirls of yellow dust.

'The banquet?' he said. 'What happened to the banquet?'

Pandulf and Bertrand exchanged looks.

'Still feverish,' La Hors commented.

Bertrand touched Thurstan's shoulder. 'Cooler than he was. Much.'

De Vesqui chuckled. 'You could have fried eggs on him yesterday.'

'Banquet, my lord?' Pandulf asked.

Thurstan gazed at the lad's ever earnest face. 'The bishop?'

'Which bishop?'

Thurstan sipped more water. 'Said his name was… Bel… Bishop Belphagor?'

With a crashing of hooves, another rider arrived. It was James of Avesnes. 'So, you found him?' He sounded vindicated. 'I told you he'd be all right. That filth in his veins... I knew it wouldn't take long to work its way out. Not the way he was sweating.'

Thurstan tried to rise, but turned dizzy.

'Don't get up, lord,' Pandulf cautioned. 'You've been ill.'

'Where am I?'

'Outside the camp.'

Thurstan turned to look behind him, seeing the outer defences, the roofs and peaks of various flimsy structures, and beyond those, the great sandstone walls of Acre.

'You must've walked out last night while you were delirious,' Bertrand said.

'Some of the sentries saw you,' Pandulf added. 'They said they hailed you, but you paid them no heed.'

Thurstan frowned. 'There was a banquet...'

The lad looked troubled. 'My lord... what banquet?'

Thurstan struggled to his feet. He turned in a tottery circle, but there was no sign in any direction of a feast table, or even a litter of discarded food or cutlery.

'There was a table... there were servants, guests.'

'And a bishop called Belphagor?' De Vesqui sounded amused.

'You were feverish,' Pandulf replied. 'Your wound was deep. You've been raving for days.'

'Days?' Thurstan was shaken by that. 'How many?'

'Three.'

'*Three!*' The knight-commander whirled back to the camp, finally recognising the great bustle taking place there, the men and animals hurrying, the tents coming down. 'What's happening?'

'We're moving out,' La Hors said. 'The king's orders.'

'Then we have things to do.'

'My lord...' Pandulf almost dared to sound disapproving, 'you need rest.'

'Don't be absurd, boy!'

'Put him on my horse.' De Vesqui slid from his saddle.

'Your horse be damned, Knight-Serjeant. I can walk back, I'm not a child.'

Avesnes barked with laughter. 'There's no doubt he's alive and well and back to his usual charming self.' Thurstan shot him a look, but the aged warrior ignored it. 'I knew a single javelin couldn't do for you, Wildblood. More's the pity, eh? *Hah...*'

He spurred his horse away, cantering towards the camp.

'At least tell me if we won the battle?' Thurstan said to La Hors as he limped in pursuit.

The knight-captain mused as he rode. 'The king considers it a draw, my lord. Though in truth it was more a skirmish than a battle.'

'A skirmish?'

'Several hundred casualties apiece. Probably a few more among the infidels, which is why they seem to have pulled back.'

Thurstan glanced again across the plain. All he saw was blowing dust. 'So, where are we moving out to?'

'South. We march on the port of Jaffa.'

Again, Thurstan was shocked by the speed of events. They said he'd been ill. He didn't feel ill now, only weak and hungry. He walked with a limp because his right hip ached, but for the most part he'd recovered from whatever ailment had stricken him.

'Muster the men, Captain. Strike the tents and load the wagons.'

The knight-captain galloped on ahead, De Vesqui riding next to him.

'Are you sure you're well?' Bertrand asked. He walked, leading his horse by the reins. 'We extricated the javelin from your hip on the field. That wound was deep.'

'Clearly not as deep as you thought.'

'We thought you'd die. These last three days, it's been touch and go.'

'We're here to serve the Lord, Bertrand. We shouldn't be surprised if from time to time he bestows his blessings on us...' The words faded on Thurstan's tongue as he remembered the 'blessing' that he himself had received.

A fantasy, though. A figment of his fevered brain. And yet even then he couldn't help wondering where such an abomination had come from. The finer details of the dream were already fading, as dreams were wont to. Yet, strangely, the atmosphere of that terrible feast lingered: the darkness, the decadence and decay, the gluttony all around him, the rankness of the air, the globular and bestial Bishop Belphagor, draped in his blood-red vestments…

'My lord?' Pandulf said, concerned that his master had half-stumbled.

'It's nothing. Any wound will have an aftereffect. Bertrand… the road between here and Jaffa will be dangerous. Go into the camp, ensure everyone's in full harness.'

Bertrand mounted up and rode on.

'I think you're right about that, my lord,' Pandulf said.

'About what?'

'The road to Jaffa. Apparently, it's a three-week march, and it's all open coast. The king still hasn't had the battle he wanted. But he's confident he'll have it in the next few days.'

CHAPTER 4

Even in the dimness of the tent, it was clear that the wound on Thurstan's right hip resembled an inverted cross. But that wasn't the only strange thing about it. Though it hurt to press it with his fingertips, it had already knitted itself closed. Crude sutures were still in evidence, but there was no seepage, no blood, no pus.

'Curious, is it not?' Pandulf said.

Thurstan pulled his leather breeches over the top of it and re-belted them. 'Did someone cauterise it?'

'I cleaned it a couple of times. But hot iron wasn't used. We might have if it had festered. But as you can see, it's healed well.'

Thurstan was perplexed. After only three days, the wound should still be open and suppurating. 'The steel went deep, you say?'

'The javelin tip was bloodied to eight or nine inches.'

That should have killed me, Thurstan told himself. If not straight away, in due course. Even through the hip, it should have pierced his bowel.

'How are you feeling, my lord?' the lad asked.

'I'm fine, for Christ's sake! Are you my squire or my betrothed?'

Pandulf averted his eyes. 'Forgive me, lord.'

Thurstan felt an immediate flicker of regret. Quick anger was not his normal way. He much preferred his quieter, steelier approach. As both his father and William Marshal had demonstrated, that always brought greater respect. And it was sheer folly to let the matter of his wound gnaw at him. Evidently, it had been clean, which had accounted for the quick healing. While he told himself again that the encounter with Bishop Belphagor had been a dream, nothing more. Fever, sickness. Easily explained.

'Don't be concerned, lad,' he said.

Pandulf nodded and swallowed. It was understandable to Thurstan why he was uneasy.

Originally squired to a knight of Exeter, the lad had arrived in the first wave of English soldiers, under the leadership of the late Archbishop Baldwin of Canterbury, a full year before Richard and Thurstan. But his master had died in the same futile attempt to storm the city that had killed the archbishop, both men consumed in a blazing siege tower, leaving the lad destitute around the camp and begging for scraps. He was a half-starved scarecrow by the time Thurstan came ashore, spotted him, enquired about his status, and took him as his own trainee. The last thing Pandulf would think he needed now was to lose another master.

The knight rose to his feet. 'Bring my armour.'

Pandulf passed him his felt doublet, which he pulled over his head, and his felt sleeves, which he laced at the shoulder. After that came the mail leggings, which Thurstan climbed into, looping the support straps over his shoulders, then his thick animal-hide boots, which he fastened behind the knee. Next, came his mail-coat, then his leather hauberk, which he belted at the waist, and finally a clean tabard – crimson, of course, the three golden lions prancing on the front.

'I want *you* in full kit, too,' Thurstan said. 'And fully armed. If you're lacking anything, take it from my personal store.'

The lad nodded warily. 'What do you think our chances are, lord, now that King Philip and Count Conrad have abandoned us?'

Thurstan spun around. 'Count Conrad?'

The lad's mouth made a perfect O. 'You didn't know...'

No... I did, Thurstan realised dully. 'I *did* know.' He sank back onto his stool, memories of the banquet flooding back again. 'But that's... *that's* not possible.'

'I don't understand.'

Bishop Belphagor... Before Thurstan knew it, he was saying it aloud. 'Belphagor?'

'Forgive me, lord...' the lad looked sheepish, 'but we don't think there's any churchman in the army who bears that name.'

'He told me Count Conrad would abandon us.'

35

'In your fever-dream, you mean?'

It *was* a dream, Thurstan reminded himself. That was all. A nightmare in fact, in which his worst fears had taken physical form. Yes, those fears had now been confirmed… but it was still only a dream. No one but a fool would contemplate anything else. If there was no one who cared in the heavens, why would anyone care in the caverns under the Earth.

'Maybe you overheard it being discussed?' Pandulf suggested. 'While lying in a stupor.'

That also was possible, Thurstan supposed. 'Do we happen to know whether the count's departure will be permanent?' he asked.

'He says he won't serve under Richard as long as Guy of Lusignan is destined for the crown of Jerusalem.'

Thurstan pulled his coif over his head. 'Guy of Lusignan already wears that crown.'

'That is King Richard's position. But Count Conrad argues that Saladin now rules in Jerusalem, and so the Lusignan claim is forfeit.'

'Either way, it makes it difficult.' Thurstan sheathed his two blades, the bone-handled knife at his back, and his longsword in its scabbard. 'Pack everything up.'

He went out into the chaos of the camp, and shielding his eyes against the glare and flying dust, shouted for his banneret.

Bertrand du Voix rode up. 'My lord?'

'Is Captain Mercadier aware this will be a battle march?'

'I've advised him. He says he welcomes the chance to grapple with the Infidel.'

Thurstan had expected nothing less.

Mercadier was captain of the *Familia Regis* infantry, and though a yeoman by birth, an experienced soldier of irreverent, impertinent disposition. Richard had only appointed him after he and his band of *routiers* – sometime mercenaries, sometime common outlaws – had captured and looted seventeen castles across the Aquitaine, the king taking the view that any fellow of such resourcefulness was better on your side of the fence than the other, no matter how villainous his nature.

Bertrand looked concerned. 'You have reservations?'

'Let's just say we're on one of two roads. They lead either to glory or destruction.'

'At least if it's the latter, it's guaranteed salvation.'

Thurstan's thoughts strayed again to Bishop Belphagor in his blood-red raiment, with his wild booming laughter... and said nothing.

CHAPTER 5

There was no doubt in Thurstan's mind. In Acre, they were abandoning a valuable position.

The king would leave a garrison behind to secure the port, but given their recent reduction in numbers, that would be a miniature force. With the larger army on the move, there'd be no need for this vast encampment, which extended all along the eastern side of the city, and then stretched for miles along the south-lying beaches, which had allowed the men to bathe regularly, and cool breezes to keep the worst of the heat, the flies and the stink of the battlefield at bay. In addition, the Bay of Acre had provided an expansive shallow-water anchorage, as evidenced by the ships of the royal fleet, which were still dotted to the far horizon, though for the first time since they'd arrived here, several were now on the move, sails and banderoles billowing as they hove southward along the coast. Yes, there were various reasons why abandoning this location was ill-advised, but it was still the obvious next step. Jerusalem lay fifty miles inland from here, and over the harshest terrain. Acre was simply too far from their objective to use as anything other than a base camp.

When Thurstan found King Richard, he was on raised ground, in company with King Guy, Count Robert, Duke Hugh, and Bishop Hubert of Salisbury, the latter who, since the death of Archbishop Baldwin, had assumed religious leadership of the English contingent. The august group pored over a table spread with maps, the king himself looking relaxed in a loose, russet tunic, leather trousers and hunting boots. 'We follow the old Roman road from Syria to Egypt,' he said. 'According to King Guy, the lie of the land is good, the road intact and clear of scrub. It follows the shoreline, so we'll have a natural defence from the west. But our formation will be the key to our success. Mark you, my lords, break apart or become disorganised, and we'll be easy pickings.'

There were grunts of agreement. This much at least they all understood. Thurstan eyed the army's senior men with interest, as he waited a respectful distance away with several other of the lesser field-commanders.

King Guy had been tall and handsome in his youth; the truth be told, he wasn't much past forty now, but he'd prematurely aged and stooped due to all the troubles he'd known, his hair and beard run to grey, his face permanently stiff with dejection. Less downcast was Count Robert of Dreux, the most loyal of all Richard's Norman barons, an experienced and successful campaigner. Though blinded in one eye and stricken with a permanent limp thanks to past wounds, his mere presence commanded respect. His manner was curt but not uncivil, his face hard and pitted like stone.

'It's vital we learn from mistakes,' Richard said. 'At Hattin, the army of Jerusalem inflicted defeat on itself by marching away from water through intense heat.'

King Guy reddened but said nothing.

'We, therefore,' Richard said, 'will march only in the early morning, starting out before sunrise, and will receive a constant supply of fresh water from the fleet, who even now are scouting along the coast for suitable landing places.'

'Sire, won't our progress be slow?' Duke Hugh wondered.

Thurstan regarded him with interest. As King Philip of France's deputy, Hugh of Burgundy, a peevish older fellow, rather short on teeth, ought to have known better.

'You're already aware, my lords, that at least part of the purpose of this march is to draw Saladin into a confrontation,' Richard said. 'The longer we are on the road, and the longer he is unable to stop us simply by launching harassment attacks, the likelier that is. You look uneasy, my Lord of Burgundy? The plain fact is that up until now this war has been waged in disorderly fashion. Persistent futile assaults on the city walls with ill-prepared, half-hearted forces cost us dear.'

King Guy reddened again.

'For that reason and from this point,' Richard said, 'when we march, we march in three parallel columns. On the landward side, infantry. Saladin will harry us with his horse-archers. They're among the best in the world and will seek to target our knights and their steeds. Therefore, we will shield them with our footmen, who quite simply must endure, but who also, if they proceed in alternating companies of crossbows and polearms, can, in the event of a large cavalry attack, throw up a quick defensive wall.'

It would be an onerous task for those foot-soldiers, Thurstan thought. They'd be suffering the brunt of those arrow attacks as it was, but it was correct that the army's prime fighting force was its heavy cavalry, and they must be preserved. It wasn't as if the infantry couldn't take it. There were many professional companies among them, particularly the crossbows, who for the most part were trained men-at-arms drawn from innumerable great households. Even the others, the peasant spearmen, were a hardy breed, having made it all this way to the Holy Land without the protection of the king or his barons.

However, Bishop Hubert looked shocked. He was a shortish, rotund man, with plump, pleasant features and a penchant for simple monastic wear rather than lordly regalia.

'Forgive me, sire… Would it not be wiser to counter cavalry with cavalry?'

'We will, my lord bishop,' the king replied. 'When their real cavalry takes the field. In the meantime, our cavalry will occupy the inner column. They will neither attack nor counterattack under their own volition. Instead, they must await our signal, which will be sounded by two trumpets at the rear, two in the centre, and two at the front.' The king addressed the small group of lesser captains standing close by, though he didn't deign to look at them. 'Grandmaster Robert, as our first elite corps, your Templars will form the vanguard.'

'My liege,' the leader of the Knights Templar replied.

'Grandmaster Garnier… as our second elite corps, your Hospitallers will form our rearguard.'

'Of course, sire.'

'As our third elite corps... Did I see Thurstan Wildblood over there?'

Thurstan stepped forward, hand on sword-hilt. He bowed. 'My liege.'

The king gave him half a glance. 'As Knight-Commander of our *Familia Regis*, you will occupy the centre of the column and protect our standard.'

Again, Bishop Hubert seemed discomforted. It was often said that his plump, boyish looks disguised a calculating mind, but clearly, he was no tactician. 'Sire... even, with my limited experience of war, I know the most likely place for attack is the front or rear. Would it not be better to place *all* our ablest fighting men at one or both of these points?'

The king smiled to himself. 'Saladin will be fearful of us reaching Jaffa, which as you've no doubt heard, is a highly rewarding location. He may even be fearful of us reaching Haifa and Ceasarea, which are less than half that distance and little more than empty ruins. This means that at some point he will – *will*, not may – come at us with his entire host. This then is not just an order of march, but an order of battle.'

And in that respect, Thurstan thought, *it's an excellent strategy.*

When the Ayyubids finally rode at them in full strength, they would come from the east. All that Richard's well-marshalled force would need do was execute a single left-hand turn, and with gaps opening between the separate companies of foot, the Christian cavalry could charge to meet them... also in full battle order.

'All other mounted companies will be distributed along our line,' Richard said. 'In the forward section, all knights of the Angevin domain... these under you, King Guy. Behind those, the knights of England and Normandy... these under you, Count Robert.' He turned to Duke Hugh. 'In the rear section, all French knights, all knights of Outremer and other nations under you, my lord.' He surveyed them. 'Any questions?'

'What of the seaward column, sire?' Count Robert asked.

'The seaward column will be used for baggage and artillery, and as shelter for our religious brethren, but also for rest and recuperation

41

for our infantry. Of us all, they will suffer most regular contact. They must therefore be rotated continuously.'

Count Robert nodded his approval.

'My lords...' The king adopted a solemn tone. 'Doubtless, you're concerned that without Count Conrad, we have fewer men than before. I would argue that we are still a strong, cohesive force. But the truth is that these Ayyubid devils outnumber us maybe ten to one, and those odds will steepen the more time passes. We *must* bring them to open battle, where, with our heavier cavalry, we'll have the advantage. If we can destroy the bulk of Saladin's army in one fight, it will take him time to raise another... buy us space not just for further reinforcements to arrive from Europe, but maybe in which to make an assault on Jerusalem before this year is out.'

The nods and mutters remained muted, but the more they mulled it over, the more sense it made to them. Count Conrad's defection had come as a bitter blow, but the only alternative was to sit on their arses at Acre, hoping, more through optimism than realistic expectation, that the arrival of new companies from Europe would mirror the speed with which Saladin could summon extra levies from North Africa.

Thurstan remained impassive as he weighed things up.

'Something troubles you, sir knight?' Richard asked.

Thurstan shook himself from his thoughts, surprised to find the king watching him, the other lords having now been dismissed.

'Forgive me, sire.' Thurstan bowed again. Richard had a reputation for being a soldier's king, whom any man could speak plainly with. But in truth there was no such creature. 'I was wounded three days ago. I'm just back on my feet.'

'I understood you were at death's door. You seem to have recovered astonishingly well.'

'I fear the men exaggerated my condition.'

'I'm glad to hear it.' Richard scrolled his maps. 'You're presumably aware that since those self-interested jackanapes Conrad and Philip departed, we've also lost our German contingent under Leopold?'

'I hadn't heard that, my liege, no.' Again, Thurstan was shaken. Though the bulk of the German and Hungarian soldiery had turned home on the death of their emperor in Armenia, while more had departed on the slaying of his son during the first few days of the siege, Leopold was another notable loss.

Another that Bishop Belphagor foresaw.

For a figment of diseased imagination, that crimson-clad brute of a churchman had demonstrated a remarkable gift for prophecy. Again though, Thúrstan reminded himself, this was something he'd been concerned might happen. Another secret fear that had been preying on him.

'Leopold and his people left the camp before this morning's cock-crow,' the king said. 'All together, it means we are significantly down on numbers. As such, we need every man who can wield a sword. You're fit to fight, I trust?'

'I'm always fit to fight, my liege.'

Richard half-smiled. His blue eyes roved the seascape. More and more galleys were headed south. 'When William Marshal was young they called him the "New Lancelot". In combat, he could not be bested. But he picked his battles prudently. He wouldn't fight at all unless he saw reason for it. You, on the other hand...'

'I will fight whenever and wherever you command me, sire.'

The king nodded appreciatively. He might not have been his knight-commander's friend, but there was no denying that he prized loyalty. 'Ready your men, Wildblood. We march at dawn.'

CHAPTER 6

'If you think it's a foolhardy plan, why didn't you speak up?' Bertrand asked.

'Perhaps because I value my life,' Thurstan replied, wondering why such an answer wasn't obvious.

Both were mounted and picking their way over a sloping, rugged landscape covered with spiny scrub. Insects trilled, while overhead the sun hung molten in a steel-blue vault. The two knights basted in their mail and leather and pulled repeatedly at their water bottles.

'You didn't need to use those exact terms,' Bertrand said.

'Well… to start with, I don't think it is foolhardy.'

'You just said we have a mountain to climb before Jerusalem can be ours.'

'We do.' Thurstan watched carefully as he guided Apollonius over the scorched rock. 'But if there's anyone who can manage that, it's the Lionheart.'

He drew rein, forcing Bertrand to do the same.

Below them, the coastal plain ran flat to the turquoise sheet of the Mediterranean. On the plain itself, lumbering ponderously south-ward, but stolidly maintaining the three parallel columns the king had devised two days ago, was the entire host of the Pilgrimage. It numbered perhaps eighteen thousand men, so great palls of dust swirled over it, but myriad heraldic banners still flew, chain-mail and spear-tips glinting. Drummers beat out a steady march, and the progress, while slow, was continuous. Flotillas of galleys kept pace offshore.

'*This* is our best option, Bertrand,' Thurstan said, impressed by the rigid phalanx of men and horses. Again, rowboats were coming

44

beachward loaded with barrels. King Richard was a stranger to this parched land, but, instinctively it seemed, he understood its requirements.

'Make no mistake, Bertrand, the road will be long, but if we'd taken the inland route to Jerusalem – which I understand is shorter – we'd have been far from water and faced many ambush points.'

He didn't bother to mention that it would have taken them past Nazareth. Bertrand would have sought it for that reason alone, as would numerous others. So many were here purely for spiritual upliftment. Not so Thurstan of course. He was here because it was war, and war was what he did, though that didn't mean he was unconcerned about surviving.

'They'd have broken us for certain,' he said. 'Even this way you'll need to look to your work many times before the journey ends. Which of course, as a sword of the *Familia Regis*, you are sworn to.'

'My thanks, Commander. I appreciate that reminder.'

They rode on, descending and ascending as the ground fell into narrow, thorn-filled canyons, and then rose again, all the while scanning the heat-hazed ridge to the east.

'Would you leave this company if you could?' Bertrand asked.

'What makes you think I can't?'

'You once told me that King Richard keeps you in post as punishment.'

Thurstan pondered. 'It was a belief I briefly held. But the king had similar reason to punish William Marshal, and *his* leave to depart was granted.'

'And yet here you still are.'

'You'd have me ride out on comrades?'

'But the Marshal…'

'When the Marshal resigned, it was peacetime.'

'Aye, because he knew there were wars to come. Wars in which he wanted no part.'

Thurstan ran a gloved finger around the inside of his coif. His bearded face dripped with sweat. 'Whether I wanted to or not, duty forbids it.'

Bertrand seemed dissatisfied. 'Your devotion to duty astounds me, Thurstan. You ordered the killing of those prisoners last week when you didn't want to. I saw it in your eyes.'

Thurstan was unaware that he'd given any such sign. It irked him.

'Those prisoners were still the enemy,' he said. 'And trained warriors to boot. If we'd freed them, they'd have rejoined their allies and fought us again. If we'd kept them in prison, they'd have used up our food.'

He had no doubt that he was correct.

In war, you faced many dilemmas. Especially as the occupying force, when all those around you, the entire population even, might become foes at the drop of a hat. Richard had passed that harsh order out of necessity. There'd been vengeance intended too. For the murders of the Templars and Hospitallers at Hattin. A firm lesson had needed to be taught. But necessity had trumped most other consider-ations.

Though if so, he wondered, why was discomfort niggling at the edge of his thoughts?

That discomfort's even got a shape, has it not? Red in colour? Wearing a mitre?

He fought the idea down. He'd learned his warlike ways in the service of his father, Earl Ranald of Radnor, and specifically, Hugh de Lacy, one of the fiercest, coldest knights in the whole bachelry of England, and had done many dishonourable deeds to enforce their control over vassals. It was less dishonourable by far to strike hard in the name of the king, a leader divinely chosen.

Divinely? Indeed? So, you can bow to that word after all? When it suits you.

Bertrand was still talking. 'Christ would have found another way...'

'Mother of God,' Thurstan retorted. 'Christ is the reason we are here, doing the things we are doing. Or had you forgotten?'

Bertrand's face creased with disquiet. Thurstan knew that his banneret believed in the gospels and creeds to the letter. He was by far the most religious-minded of all the knights in their company, as evidenced by the gold crucifix with the ruby centrepiece that he wore under his mail and clutched to his heart when praying for guidance.

'We made a vow,' Thurstan said. 'To reclaim the Holy Places? Whatever means we employ, is that not a worthy end?'

'No doubt.' Bertrand urged his beast forward. 'Yet this army is crammed with nobility who make self-interest an artform. This last week alone three have abandoned us. One because it was too hot for him, another because he can't be the next king of Jerusalem... another because his flag was thrown down from a wall.'

'So, because they are fallible, should we be too?'

'I'm not saying that.'

'Good.' Thurstan raised a hand, bringing the pair of them to a halt. He lowered his voice. 'Because we're about to be tested.'

Directly below, in a gully, the sun glared from the steel cuirasses of a hundred or so turbaned horsemen, waiting patiently, each with a heavy quiver of arrows on his back, and a double-curved bow by his side.

–

The two scouts galloped down from the high ground, blowing wildly on horns.

The word had passed the length of the army by the time the Saracen light-horse commenced their attack, they and other squadrons emerging from defiles all along the coastal hills, swooping past the pilgrims' infantry line rather than engaging it, crying out '*Allahu Akhbar!*' and loosing as many arrows as they could.

Thurstan and Bertrand were now back with the rest of the *Familia*, who, like the other mounted companies, had pulled their helmets into place and hefted their large, kite-shaped shields. There was maybe forty yards of open ground between the infantry column and the cavalry, so, though the Christians' horses were the Saracen archers' prime objective, they were difficult targets even for marksmen. In addition, the Christian infantry were resisting as they marched, their crossbows loosing return missiles, often with deadly accuracy, hitting the Saracen steeds if not the archers, and bringing many of them down.

All the while, Richard's advance continued at its stoic pace.

Thurstan's own six hundred rode uncomplaining through the swirling dust and kiln-like heat. The knights of the *Familia Regis* were recruited from all over Christendom, though mainly from Plantagenet lands. They were mostly younger sons, but of a dangerous disposition. The basic requirement for inclusion in the handpicked corps was a royal invitation, and that wasn't extended to warriors of common-garden valour. And skill with arms was never enough on its own. The *Familia* were expected to be loyal to the point of obsessiveness. Where their royal master rode, they rode. Where he fought, they fought. The *Familia Regis* had been the king's special guard since the twenty or so knights chosen as personal shield to Duke William the Bastard during his conquest of England, but at the Lionheart's side, this often meant they were the first into battle, and the last out. All that said, the king, in his own inimitable fashion, had today insisted on riding at the head of the army, alongside the Knights Templar, his presence ensuring there was no panic in the vanguard, which might have seen the entire host break into a forward gallop.

As he pondered all this, Thurstan's shield was struck repeatedly by arrows, while one or two even glanced from his cylindrical helm.

And yet he continued to be distracted, plodding along in the heat, convinced that if their force had been the size it was supposed to be, no such piecemeal attacks would be launched, and thus brooding on those great noblemen who'd abandoned them – Count Conrad in particular, because his loss to the army had been huge. In addition, of course, the knight couldn't help but wonder again about the starker warning issued in his dream by the mysterious Bishop Belphagor: namely that Richard himself would lose interest in the campaign once Philip of France had returned to his kingdom. There was no doubt that once Philip was home, he'd commence making mischief in the realm of his rival. How long could Richard tolerate that?

This mighty force, this army of God is already fragmenting...

So had spoken the maleficent Belphagor. An imaginary being perhaps, though an odious, overbearing image of him remained in Thurstan's mind.

The initiative will be seized by the pagans...

Beyond the bulwark of Christian infantry, the Saracen horse were in retreat, leaving many corpses of their own. But this was only the start of it. The first trickle. The floodtide would follow anon.

–

They pitched camp roughly in the same formation as they marched, which Thurstan considered an excellent appreciation of the dangers here.

Portable timber breastworks, behind which the crossbowmen could stand, were erected along the landward perimeter. Scouts were no longer needed, all eyes fixed on the inland skyline, where increasing numbers of mounted bowmen visibly prowled. Every so often, a pack of them would sally down onto the flatland and swerve by, loosing arrows, but always were greeted by hails of crossbow bolts. Meanwhile, more rowboats brought fresh water to the beach.

But if the drink was good, the food was poor. In the section of camp reserved for the *Familia Regis*, Thurstan and his fellow officers sat under a canvas awning, while Pandulf served them iron bowls into which he'd ladled measly portions of thin turnip gruel. There was bread too, but it was dry and stale. It came from the king's kitchen, which the *Familia* had full access to, so the poor quality was already a sign of the privations they'd soon be facing.

'How now, pretty fellows,' Captain Mercadier said in his Occitan-flavoured French.

He shoved his way into their company, plonking his stool between Ramon la Hors and Ivan de Vesqui. As an infantryman he wore a surcoat rather than a tabard, but was at least as filthy and sweat-stained as the rest. While the broken stalk of an arrow hung from the left shoulder of his mail-coat, it clearly hadn't penetrated.

He removed his helm, the head beneath grizzled and balding, the face straggly-bearded and deeply scarred. He grunted thanks as Pandulf handed him a bowl and spoon but pulled a face on tasting the fare. 'God's breath. This slop wouldn't suit a rat.'

Thurstan lifted a skillet from the fire, in which several strips of bacon sizzled.

'Ah, yes.' Mercadier helped himself to two of the strips. 'Generous of you to share your vittles, my lords. I expect you consider it the least you can do, seeing as you don't share the danger.' He treated them to an ugly, brown-toothed grin.

'You don't think we have trouble enough eating this rubbish without sights like that?' Thurstan asked him.

'Forgive me, lord. I always forget that I belong on the fringes of this company.'

'You belong wherever the king commands you to be,' Bertrand said, unamused by the commoner's usual impudent banter.

'And if you die out there...' La Hors shrugged, 'well... you die.'

'That's often the way of it,' Mercadier grunted. 'The infantry do the dying, while noble lords do the dining. Speaking of dying, Knight-Commander, we had one killed today and four wounded.'

Thurstan considered. 'How bad are the wounded?'

'Only one is serious. He's in the king's hospital tent.'

'The fatality?'

'I've arranged burial. Chaplain Gustave will say prayers.'

'Tomorrow, switch to the seaward column for rest and recovery,' Thurstan said.

Mercadier nodded graciously, though as always there was an under-current of insolence. He pulled a disgusted face. 'God's bowels! Bacon? More like shoe leather.'

'And yet you've already consumed two portions,' Bertrand observed.

De Vesqui chuckled. 'You should conjure your friend Belphagor, Lord Thurstan. He can lay on a feast, can he not?'

Mercadier looked from one to the other. 'Belphagor?'

'Some fellow called Belphagor.' De Vesqui chuckled again. 'Commander Wildblood had us search the camp for him.'

'That's a lie!' Pandulf stated. 'My lord never asked anyone. *I* put the question out.'

'God's bread!' Thurstan said, frustrated that the matter had risen again, but determined to make light of it. It wouldn't do to show the rest of these rogues how distracted he himself had been because of it. 'Even out here? On the edge of nowhere? With death stalking us daily? It was a dream. Nothing more.'

Mercadier yanked with rotted teeth at another rasher of equally rotted bacon. 'Anyone here who dreams of Bishop Belphagor, I pity them.'

A brief silence followed.

'You know such a churchman?' Bertrand asked.

'Learned about him in our village chapel.' Mercadier clucked with disapproval. 'Am I alone in that?'

No one replied.

'Don't keep us in suspense,' La Hors said with interest. 'Who is he?'

'Who else...? The Bishop of Hell.'

Another silence greeted this, before De Vesqui gave a guttural chuckle. 'Hell has a bishop?'

Mercadier became thoughtful. 'There are seven honorary titles in Hell. Or so I was taught during catechism. Lucifer, of course, is the King of Hell. Asmodeus and Beelzebub are the Princes of Hell. Mammon, Leviathan and Astaroth are the Grand Dukes, and Belphagor is the Bishop.'

'You're lying,' Pandulf said, visibly unnerved.

Mercadier glanced at him. 'Anyone who serves pigswill like this, boy, needs to mind his manners.'

'I've never heard of Bishop Belphagor,' Bertrand said.

'Two years ago, my lord, I'll wager you'd never heard of Salah al-Din Yusuf ibn Ayyub either, but who do you think's coming to nail arrows into your lily-white hide, eh?'

Thurstan wanted to intervene, to dismiss such prattle and call them to silence. But he didn't. He couldn't. Despite everything, he too wanted to know more, and yet he wasn't going to ask about it himself. He was damned if he was.

Damned?

Bertrand got to his feet. 'Curious thing to memorise, Mercadier. The names and ranks of devils.'

The captain of infantry shrugged. 'Life in our village was boring, my lord. When we weren't ploughing, planting or reaping. We had no tournaments or pageants to distract us. No beautiful ladies singing love songs, no troubadours to entertain us during feasts.'

'You talk too much for a man who's lost a comrade today.' Bertrand tossed his bowl to Pandulf and walked off.

'Wasn't he your comrade, too?' Mercadier called after him.

'Enough!' Thurstan stood. 'Now that you've eaten, my lords, repair to your billets and sleep. We'll be on the march before dawn.' The rest of them nodded and stood. 'Ivan de Vesqui,' Thurstan said, deciding that now was a good time to retaliate against his brutish underling for his raising of the matter in the first place. 'Pick four men, those in your opinion who are least in need of rest. Patrol the rear of the infantry line in case any Saracen horse break through.'

De Vesqui's smirk faded. 'For how long, my lord?'

'The remainder of today.'

'And when do I sleep?' The burly knight-serjeant was lacking in deference at the best of times, but his tone now was a viper's hiss.

'When I say. But take an extra ration of water. You're going to need it.'

De Vesqui regarded his commander icily, before nodding his compliance.

Thurstan walked away through the encampment, his thoughts already elsewhere.

Like as not, he'd heard the name Belphagor before without realising – God alone knew he'd paid only middling attention during the endless religious services he'd attended before deciding that faith in some invisible, omnipotent power was faith in nothing – and it had been summoned up from the depths of his mind through his struggle with fever. There was no mystery there. Nothing remotely worth pondering.

On the beach he stood and faced out to sea.

The water was bustling – many craft now headed south – but briefly it reminded him again of the lake at home. That soft, serene body of water nestling among soaring, pine-clad fells. Not *his* birth-home of course. Son to Earl Ranald, the most belligerent marcher-lord in the realm, he'd grown up on the wild Welsh borders, where internecine warfare had raged. But Gwendolyn's home: the place that would soon lie closer to his heart than any other. The peace of walking lakeside with her, the joy of entwining their bodies in the cool, still waters… neither could be quantified in terms of happiness. It seemed like another world now, another life even.

In truth, it was both.

No man, it seemed, was allowed more than a few moments of genuine pleasure in this life. A time would come when he'd need to beat that knowledge into himself, to kill off any fanciful hope that similar bliss might somehow come his way again.

He stripped off his mail and strode into the sea in his breeches. The water was warm as it lapped his thighs, the occasional heavier wave invigorating as it hit him from the ships wallowing past. He felt again at the inverted cross etched into his right hip. Only a few days later, it barely even hurt any more.

'My lord!' Pandulf called from the water's edge.

Thurstan glanced round. 'I told you to get some sleep.'

'My lord…' The young face looked sheepish. 'My lord… The Bishop of Hell?'

God's bowels…

'You attach importance to the words of some *routier* scum?'

'But how could Captain Mercadier have known this evil thing came to you as a bishop?'

'No evil thing came to me. It was a dream, a phantasm… born of sickness and a strong suspicion that certain fair-weather friends would desert us.'

'But the fact you dreamed of a *bishop*…'

'Our bishops are hardly pillars of virtue, lad. Why wouldn't I dream of one in evil guise?'

Pandulf remained worried. 'Bishop Hubert isn't like that. Perhaps tell him… Or even the king.'

'Tell them what precisely? That I had a vision as I lay dying?'

'You're not dying now. Far from it. And it was only a few days ago.'

Thurstan struggled to contain his anger. And his own growing concern.

'You don't consider it strange?' the lad asked.

'I know my own strength, Pandulf... So, no, I don't. I've been wounded before.'

A clangour of renewed combat sounded from the far side of the camp. Gruff shouts and the blasts of horns greeted it as reserve infantrymen were called into the defensive line. Thurstan saw clouds of dust erupt above the thatch and canvas rooftops. 'Grab some rest while you can.'

'There's one other thing, my lord.' Again, the lad seemed nervous. 'I'm sure you don't need me to tell you this...'

'Whatever it is, you're right... I don't.'

'You should beware Knight-Serjeant de Vesqui.'

Indeed?

It was definitely true that Thurstan didn't need to be told this. Like Mercadier, Ivan de Vesqui had come to the *Familia Regis* when Richard took the crown. He too had been one of the aggressive young heir-apparent's many followers from the Aquitaine. Unlike Mercadier, de Vesqui was a knight, though this hadn't stopped him raiding and pillaging in the name of whichever master he'd served, or simply for his own gain. And yes indeed, his reputation for ferocity on the battlefield was legend.

'You're new to the *Familia*, Pandulf,' Thurstan said. 'We are not the king's honour-guard for nothing.'

'I understand that, my lord, but my previous master knew de Vesqui well. He called him "a dark and deadly man".'

'That's his role here, lad.' The knight thought again, unavoidably, on Bishop Belphagor. 'That's all our role.'

CHAPTER 7

By the fifteenth day of the march, the inland hills were levelling out. At the same time, a great tract of woodland, comprised mainly of pine and cedar, descended onto the coastal plain. The Roman road cut through it but was cluttered with leaves, acorns and twigs. According to those who'd served in this region, it was called the Wood of Arsuf, but though they hadn't seen any skirmishers for a day or so now and might have expected an attack, it was not dense enough to provide for an effective ambush. Even so, significant numbers of *turcopoles*, mounted archers of Turkish origin, who had come to the Levant to serve as mercenaries, were despatched upslope as roving packs of flanking guards.

Meanwhile, the army, which by necessity had reformed into a narrower, lengthier column, proceeded in near silence, only whispers of wind stirring the overhead canopy. They scanned the sun-dappled glades with eyes like hawks but saw nothing move.

Despite the scant cover, Thurstan wondered if this was an opportunity missed by their foe, though of course Saladin's greatest strength lay in his battalions of fast-moving cavalry, which, lightweight or not, would have limited manoeuvrability in confines like these. Nevertheless, the air remained thick with tension, every man taut, their mounts whickering and nudging at each other.

'Something feels imminent,' Bertrand said under his breath.

'Aye.' Thurstan nodded ahead of them.

Through breaks in the trees, palls of yellow dust smeared the azure sky.

Bertrand paled. 'That must be many, many horses.'

'I'd say that's *all* their horses.'

The banneret gripped his gold-and-ruby crucifix and muttered prayers, as word passed down the column that Richard's *turcopoles* were returning with news of a vast Ayyubid host mustered beyond the wood's southern edge, its numbers apparently limitless.

Mortal eyes could not see from one end of it to the other.

–

Saladin's army was arrayed as professionally as Thurstan had ever seen.

First of all, the enemy had ensured they occupied the higher ground, facing down towards the trees. There were indeed more of them than a single man could initially count, but they'd been deployed in three enormous divisions. On the left resided a great block of heavy cavalry: Mamluks, glimmering in the sun in their mail-coats and aventails and their conical helms. The middle was occupied by a deep formation of infantry, mostly spear and pikemen, with squads of archers at the rear. Even from a distance, these were less well-armoured, and some weren't armoured at all, wearing belted smocks and turbans; by their ebony faces, they were Berber tribesmen, likely Nubians or Sudanese. On the right meanwhile, a more disorganised force of calvary was visible, mail and cuirasses glinting, but also sporting livery in a range of vibrant colours, as if, like their European counterparts, they sought to stand out on the battlefield. These, Thurstan heard William des Preaux – one of his knights who knew the Levant, including several of its languages – mutter, would be the sultan's levies from Arabia, Egypt and Mesopotamia. They'd comprise contingents of warriors serving emirs under feudal obligation. There'd be many great fighters among them, desert cavaliers eager to impress their masters.

But across the entire front of Saladin's army, providing an impregnable protective screen, lay several unbroken lines of horse-archers. For all the Mamluks' fabled ferocity, these lightly armed but highly mobile units were still the sultan's most lethal weapon. Not least because there were so many of them. They would open the account as they so often did. Saladin meanwhile was located in the very centre, though on higher ground than the rest, not clearly visible, though his huge banners, again sporting verses from the Koran, fluttered amid a forest of similar but smaller pennons flown by his numerous captains.

Pandulf for one seemed staggered that the bulk of the Christian army continued to march on as if this immense horde was no obstacle at all.

'They'll run over us in rivers,' he stuttered.

'Eyes front,' Thurstan instructed as they proceeded. 'Show fear and they'll sense it. It will give them courage.'

'But how can we match a force like that?'

'Numbers aren't everything, young Pandulf,' William des Roches said, riding to their rear. He was another of the *Familia*'s senior men; like Thurstan, he had first served in the *mesnie* of their former king. 'His Highness knows what he's doing.'

The king meanwhile, though he'd spent most of the march from Acre at the spear-tip of the army, had now fallen back to ride in the heart of his household. He sat astride his warhorse only a few yards ahead, but if he overheard the conversation, he gave no sign, sitting upright in the saddle as though without a care in the world.

'Ramon,' Thurstan said.

La Hors urged his mount forward. 'My lord?'

'My regards to Captain Mercadier, who will shortly be leaving us.'

La Hors nodded and turned his animal around.

Up ahead, Thurstan spied a dim but jagged outline. The ruined coastal fortress of Arsuf, no doubt.

When he'd first heard there was a strongpoint not far south of the wood, he'd wondered if Richard might seek to incorporate it into his battleplan. But by all accounts, the fort was little more than rubble, and besides, the king was determined to have his all-out fight.

'What's stopping them?' Pandulf wondered, still mesmerised by the multitude crowning the high ground.

'They aren't facing Guy de Lusignan,' Thurstan replied. 'This time it's the one called Lionheart.'

'With an army that size, why would they worry?'

'They worry because their leader is no more a fool than ours. Saladin knows this can't possibly be as easy as it looks.'

For all that, Thurstan understood his squire's concern. The Ayyubids were not just superior in numbers, they were *vastly* superior, three times the size of the pilgrim army, the *turcopole* scouts having estimated them to be somewhere between fifty and sixty thousand strong. In that regard, it was almost unnatural the way they simply waited, the majority of their infantry seated with legs crossed, their cavalry mounted but watchful and silent as the intruders in their land continued to emerge from the woods, traipsing north-to-south in orderly if complacent fashion.

Though it only appeared complacent to an untrained eye.

All Thurstan's life, he'd ridden to war. Even as a young squire, he'd been thrust into the action. But for much of it, especially along the Welsh March, it had been clandestine. Sporadic, scattered. Small bands stalking and ambushing each other in marshy woods and mountain passes, wild chases and fierce but fleeting mounted clashes. But then, in the middle of it all, had come the Great Rebellion of 1173, a period of immense battles, during which he'd come to understand broader strategic thinking.

As such, today at least, the king couldn't be faulted.

Richard's apparent disregard for the enemy's strength wasn't just a calculated insult, it was also a lure. The previous night, during the war council in the royal pavilion, he'd explained how he sought to create the false impression that his reduced force would be relying on the same tactics as previously: throwing up an infantry guard, behind which the bulk of the Christian host would hope to maintain their course. With luck, this would lull Saladin into unrealistic confidence.

But there was more to follow.

As the rest of the pilgrim army marched, companies of spearmen diverted from the main column, advancing several hundred yards onto the sloped plain, there forming schiltrons: compact squares with spears turned outward, hedgehogs of armoured footmen placed roughly equidistant from each other, perhaps a hundred yards of open space between each one. They didn't even form a solid defensive line, which should be an additional temptation for the Ayyubids. Although what Saladin would not know was that crossbowmen were concealed within these blocks of polearms, so that when the Saracen horse attacked, they'd be riding into thickets of darts and quarrels. If, as hoped, this drove them in disorder down the alleys between the schiltrons, Richard's own cavalry would charge, all of his knights unleashed in a single shockwave.

There was one potential weakness, of course. As always.

'My liege,' Thurstan said, kicking his mount forward. 'When we strike...'

'You're advising that I ride further to the rear?' Richard shook his head. 'My reputation demands that I lead. As you know perfectly well, but as always, Wildblood, your concern is appreciated.'

A warning cry sounded along the column.

From the high ground, the Ayyubids were advancing. At first it was sluggish, like some great unwieldy machine. But as they descended, they picked up pace. The horse-archers surged in front, to the raucous accompaniment of kettledrums, cymbals, gongs, and of course to a belly-deep chorus of roaring voices.

Richard rode on, unconcerned. The majority of his army did the same, at a steady pace. Only the schiltrons stood firm, shields over their heads, hedges of pikes, halberds and spears jutting on all sides. They looked formidable, but doubtless there'd be sweat and fear inside, and much muttering of prayers.

'Eyes front,' Thurstan said sternly. 'Whatever happens out there doesn't concern us. Not yet.'

The ground shuddered as battalions of descending horse broke into a gallop. The din of their hooves was terrifying, the discordant music hellish.

'Dear Christ,' Pandulf muttered.

'Eyes front!'

Some forty or fifty yards short of the schiltrons, the Muslim cavalry slowed its pace and commenced swamping the formations with arrows. Many of these volleys rattled harmlessly away, or embedded themselves in the hide-covered limewood shields, failing to penetrate. Meanwhile, the crossbows shot back through narrow gaps, in all cases having pinpointed their targets first, and immediately scored hits on riders or their mounts.

Only on the north side of the field, where the Mamluks, eager for battle, were putting undue pressure on the light horsemen in front, were the Saracens now joining hand-to-hand with the polearms. And they weren't having it their own way, the pikemen behind the shields thrusting hard with their steel-tipped shafts, plunging them into man and horseflesh alike. Very soon, though, all along the line, Saladin's horse archers having failed to knock the schiltrons down like the packs of cards they'd expected, were being pushed from behind as the ever greater weight of arms bore downhill. Even as Thurstan watched, those advance squadrons were forced past the schiltrons and down the corridors between them.

'Sire, do we charge?' Garnier de Nablus asked, having ridden along the column. He'd lifted his visor and was sweating hard. The livid scar across his forehead had thickened into a bright red band.

'Only when I give the word,' Richard replied simply.

The Lionheart's coolness in combat was well known. To Thurstan's eye, it was his most admirable quality, although it put the nerves on edge.

The footmen of the *Familia Regis* were now playing their part, their own schiltron feathered with arrows and taking a severe battering from the Saracen horse, who'd finally engaged with them. It was a solid block of men, maybe two hundred strong, but completely encircled. Many of their spearheads were lopped and it was anyone's guess how many bolts their crossbowmen had left. They would fight to the last. That much was certain. They were *Familia Regis*. But it would still be over quickly if their outer shell gave.

'Halt,' Richard said, the command passing like wildfire along the column, every man and beast grinding to a standstill. 'Left turn.'

That order too rippled through the ranks, the men swinging around.

At a simple word from their king, every soldier in the army, whatever his rank, stood ready. Swiftly and efficiently, shields were hefted, swords loosened in scabbards, axes lifted from leather sheaths. Richard himself opted for the latter, the war-axe he'd wielded since his youth, which was notched from more battles and skirmishes than any man could count, resting at his right shoulder.

In front of them, the schiltrons were engulfed. On the north flank, two had collapsed, those who'd manned them scampering every which way, Saracen riders cantering in pursuit. But across the rest of the battle-front, the enemy vanguard was a chaotic mob, forced in disorder far down the passages between the formations, significant numbers of men and animals suffering spear or crossbow wounds.

'Is my royal household ready to engage, Knight-Commander?' Richard asked.

'Ready and correct, my liege,' Thurstan replied.

The king looked to his right, where De Nablus watched him eagerly. Duke Hugh of Burgundy hovered there too. A shout then went up on the army's north flank.

They turned, and saw that, right at the far end of their battleline, the Knights Hospitaller had broken from their ranks and were charging the enemy. The destruction of the schiltrons directly to the fore of them had become too much.

The king's mouth tightened with irritation.

'Give the order.' He slammed down his visor.

Garnier de Nablus and Hugh of Burgundy galloped madly back to their companies, the word travelling ahead of them. There was a brazen blasting of battle-horns.

Six in total. The signal they'd all been awaiting.

The pilgrims charged.

CHAPTER 8

Under a sky blotted out by arrows, the mounted forces clashed in a maelstrom of hacking, slashing blades, spear-shafts splintering, angry cries turning shrill as steel sliced flesh.

King Richard rode deep into the enemy, striking to either side with his axe, cleaving heads and helms, rearing his steed to land crushing hoof-blows. Thurstan and his officers were close behind, lances lowered, colours billowing, a flying wedge of the hardiest knights in the *Familia Regis*, spearing the heart of their enemy. Those disorderly companies facing them were obliterated, but behind these came forward units of Saracen infantry, plus squadrons of heavier cavalry, among them Mamluks, who had veered across the field to get to the English king and now surged down the shallow slope, manes flying, clots of torn earth spinning.

Spittle flew, blood and horse-sweat sprayed. The crash of blade on blade and axe on mail could have knocked a man dizzy. Pandulf had no sooner rammed his lance through the trunk of a horse-archer than he took a sword to the shield, which bit clean through. He drew his own sword but was half-thrown when his beast collided with a vast, bearded fellow hooking at him with a bill. The beard went down under Pandulf's steed. Even so, the beast stumbled, Pandulf clasping her sinewy neck as he clung on.

In front of Pandulf, Bertrand fought with the royal banner lofted in his left hand and a spike-headed mace in his right, bludgeoning his way through foe after foe, pummelling helms, crushing crania so that brains and gore splurged from eye-sockets.

Further ahead, Thurstan and the king wreaked more ruin, cantering in circles as they struck down and around them. Shrieking their fear and rage, the infidels rallied, flocking forward with shields raised, hurling missiles. But the two commanders forged through, scattering all opponents, battering down their guard, splitting shields, sundering skulls.

Pandulf strove harder at his stirrups only to catch an impact on the side of his head, which tore his visor away and toppled him sideways. The battlefield, slimy with gore, rushed to meet him.

The lad lay groggy, head throbbing. His helmet had saved his life. But to be prone in the midst of such mayhem was to invite death. He levered himself upright, head swimming. His stomach lurched. Even standing, the field swayed – as an ominous shape bore upon him: a dismounted Mamluk, bellowing, his torn-open face a mask of blood.

Pandulf stumbled into retreat, tripped, landed on his buttocks and crab-crawled backward. The gruesomely wounded figure lurched in pursuit – and was hit with thunderous force in the side of the neck, the bolt driven so deep that its bodkin point emerged on the other side. The Mamluk slumped to his knees, a crimson shower bursting from his lips.

'Won't win your spurs on foot, young Pandulf!' With a gap-toothed laugh, Captain Mercadier reloaded his crossbow. 'No fame and fortune down in the dirt with us.'

Pandulf glanced past him. The cavalry charge had pushed past the schiltrons, which had now broken open, their survivors surging out, driving spears and knives into their tormentors. Mercadier loosed another shaft, striking a horse-archer's chest as he galloped towards them, *scimitar* twirling.

'Not that we don't do our bit, eh? Eh?' Mercadier clapped Pandulf's shoulder. 'Best find your animal, boy. More killing to do yet.'

–

From what Thurstan could see, the Saracen host had fallen back on itself like a wave repelled, its vanguard broken as the pilgrim knights drove on and on.

The opposition clearly hailed from many nations: Anatolia to the Levant to North Africa. But he showed no discrimination as he ploughed through them. Those horsemen who rallied to face him, he engaged sword-to-sword, always cutting them down, but now he faced that great press of infantry. It was the same for the rest of Richard's cavalry. They had the advantage, horses against men, but heavy trappers weren't always protection enough, and the noble brutes were slashed and gashed as they forced through hedges of spears and pikes. Apollonius was driven to mania, hacking and clubbing with his iron-shod hooves, yet streaming with blood from multiple wounds. Thurstan's own sword-arm was caked with gore. And yet, in the midst of the dust-thick chaos his eye fell on something he couldn't believe.

He swiftly drew rein.

Far leftward, above the madness of flying blades and broken helms, on raised ground at the heart of the melee, an immense horseman sat proud on a destrier of astounding size. The black beast, seventeen hands at the withers, reared and reared as its rider clutched its reins. Yet, this was no warrior. Thurstan lifted his visor, eyes fixed on the flamboyant garb of a mighty episcopal prince. Vestments instead of mail, a mitre instead of a helmet, all in deepest crimson, the robes and cloak billowing in the hot wind.

The knight's thoughts spun. There was no doubting who or what he was seeing. He could even hear him, the outlandish figure bellowing his approval at the blood and destruction, gazing with particular intensity, it seemed, at Thurstan himself.

'Christ's holy name,' the knight breathed.

Abruptly, Apollonius sagged beneath him, his shrieks of rage replaced by frantic squeals. Thurstan lurched from the saddle, landing with crunching impact on his right shoulder, rolling onto his back. Shaken and sickened, he scrambled to his feet, peering with dull disbelief at his fearless stallion as it twitched and shuddered, scarlet froth surging from its muzzle. A broken spear haft jutted between its forelegs.

At first, the knight was too deadened to feel anything. But soon, the blood in his veins simmered again, and when he sensed the wall of spears and shields closing from all sides, it turned to brimstone.

He felled the first two with a single stroke of his longsword. A third and fourth drove at him, but he severed both spear shafts with a

64

backhand, slamming the boss of his shield into the teeth of one, the full length of his blade into another.

More advanced from left and right, from front and behind. He spun in a blur, fending, parrying. Where his shield failed, his mail proved adequate, swords and axes failing to hew, and always in response, he launched steel into mouths or gullets, smashed faces, hacked crania open to the brains. They fell like sticks, the air misted red, riven by screams of horror. More and more of them lunged in, but Thurstan slew and slew, clearing gore-soaked paths on all sides.

In every direction, mayhem reigned. A French man-at-arms fell, clutching his crotch, where an arrow had sunk to its feathers. As he lay curled, infidel blades rained on him, but Thurstan went into them bull-like. His shield hung in half, so he tossed it, and, clasping his sword two-handed, scythed them down in showers of blood and excrement. Next, came a towering, ox-like specimen, though as he closed, a lightning forehand lopped his wrist, a reverse blow parting his skull at the hairline.

'God's breath, Wildblood!' A mounted figure loomed through the carnage. It was Richard, patterned with gore, axe-blade dripping. He raised his visor. 'You fight like a man possessed!'

Thurstan lifted his own visor. 'They killed my horse, sire.'

Richard's nostrils flared. 'Despair not, there'll be riderless steeds aplenty at the end of today.'

He steered his beast away again.

'Lord Thurstan… Lord Thurstan…'

Pandulf tottered forward, coated in grime, visor missing.

'You're unhorsed?' Thurstan said. The lad shook his head, white-faced.

Thurstan turned frontward. More footmen advanced. 'Stay behind me!' he told his squire.

To his left, a longsword stood upright in a corpse. He yanked it free.

Twin blades twirling, the knight-commander sheared his way through in a haze of blood. Pandulf staggered in pursuit. Even when adversaries came from behind, they were dead men. Thurstan sensed them, spun, clove the first between the eyes, the second across the jugular.

Ahead now, the slope steepened and yet the Saracens fell back.

Richard was only fifty yards away, his mount rearing, an Ayyubid shield clutched between its bared teeth, its hooves clattering on heads like iron hammers. Count Robert, bleeding copiously from a face wound, roared his men onward as they flooded past him uphill.

'My lord!' Pandulf cried a warning.

A mounted Mamluk rode at him with lance levelled. Thurstan smashed the shaft down, its tip striking the earth, pitching the rider from his horse.

Another Mamluk came on foot. Thurstan clove him from shoulder to breastbone.

Another and another, it was always the same.

But as Thurstan advanced, Pandulf could only stagger and vomit, tripping over, dropping to his knees.

'Pandulf!' someone yelled.

The lad glanced up, eyes stinging with sweat. Bertrand was still mounted, though a broken spear impaled his saddle. The royal gonfalon bellied over his head.

'Where's Thurstan?'

The lad gestured uphill. Bertrand rode pell-mell.

Lower down the field, the remaining infidels had formed defensive blocks, but now were assailed from all sides. Some threw down their arms and sought quarter.

Receiving none.

CHAPTER 9

The air was still, the sky grey with heat and dust. Corpses lay thick as leaves, ruby rivers trickling between them. When Thurstan spotted Ramon la Hors and Ivan de Vesqui, he was seated on the ground, his back against his fallen horse, one arm draped over its flank. His deputies' beasts picked their way forward over stiffening forms too numerous to count.

'So, my lord,' La Hors said. 'You live.'

Thurstan regarded them bleakly. 'You sound disappointed.'

'Merely surprised. We lost sight of you in the fray.'

'We hear you slew a hundred men,' De Vesqui said.

'So few?' Thurstan frowned. 'I strived for more.'

'I see Apollonius fell.' Ramon La Hors was notorious for his icy indifference to the pain of others... In fact, for his strange lack of emotion in almost any situation, but for once – maybe just *this* once – there was a hint of sympathy.

'I'm sure he's not the only comrade we lost today,' Thurstan replied.

'This is true. The Lord of Avesnes fell also.'

Thurstan glanced up. 'Where?'

La Hors pointed south.

Thurstan got awkwardly to his feet. He wasn't wounded but had been beaten and bruised severely. Also, the ache in his hip had flared a little, though it wasn't an encumbrance. 'Pandulf!' he called. 'Pandulf... where are you?'

'Here, lord.' The squire approached, stumbling and pale-faced, averting his eyes from the heaps of butchered meat and bone. He led two horses by their reins. One was his own, Daedalion, the other a larger animal, a grey, though it was bloodstained and skittish. 'I found you a mount. In a subdued state, I fear…'

'He'll do.' Thurstan took the animal by the reins, then swooped down for the sword near his feet. It was so caked with blood and ordure that he had to check that it was his from the aged scarf tied around its hilt, before swinging himself up by the stirrup. He turned to La Hors and De Vesqui. 'Scour the field. Gather what men of ours remain. We need a headcount. All wounded are to be taken to the king's hospital forthwith. Pandulf…' He threw the lad his helmet. 'Don't forget my saddle or the rest of my equipment.'

'Erm… no, my lord.'

—

James of Avesnes lay amid a whole band of fallen Mamluks, his face and throat ribboned by steel. When Thurstan arrived, a handful of others were gathered: Bertrand, Robert Sable, Grandmaster of the Temple, and Count Robert of Dreux with a couple of his Norman knights. Already bloodied and bedraggled, they looked additionally dejected by the loss of this most personable warrior.

As Thurstan dismounted, more horsemen approached.

It was the king, in company with Duke Hugh and Bishop Hubert. The latter, also in mail, clambered from his horse and knelt beside the fallen knight, where he donned a stole and commenced a quiet *Pater Noster*.

Richard stayed mounted, his hard, handsome features streaked with dirt. 'By all that's holy, this was a costly day.'

'Is it officially ours, my liege?' Count Robert enquired.

Richard nodded. 'The sultan is routed. What remains of his rabble fled into the hills.'

'I can organise pursuit,' Count Robert said. 'Say the word.'

'No.'

Duke Hugh looked surprised. 'If they aren't annihilated, my lord, they'll confront us again.'

'They've lost heavy too,' Richard said. 'They won't confront us before we reach Jaffa.'

Thurstan gazed out over the sprawling crimson wreckage. The majority of those ghostly figures drifting there, either seeking out friends or purloining whatever they could, were knights and clergy. It was difficult, if not impossible, to make an accurate estimate, but he guessed that seven thousand pilgrims lay strewn, though there were many more infidels, with perhaps more of the latter to follow. Those who lay groaning and twitching might receive succour from the victors depending on the mood the king was in… ordinarily. But they wouldn't be a priority when he had so many maimed of his own. He'd be in no mood to tarry, either, so the best they could hope for once he'd vacated this scene, was that their countrymen would come for them quickly.

Before the jackals and the vultures did.

'I see you replaced your destrier?' the king said, after despatching the others to organise burial parties and Bishop Hubert to sing the funeral rites.

Thurstan nodded. 'I have, sire. My thanks.'

The king looked thoughtful. 'I seem to remember an occasion when someone slew *my* horse from under me.'

Thurstan was unsure how to respond, though just now honesty seemed like the best course. 'I considered that a dishonourable act too.'

'I was more temperate in my response than you.'

Thurstan knew to choose his next words carefully. Richard had never previously mentioned the incident on the road to Chinon. The fact he'd promoted Thurstan afterwards rather than executed him had seemed so much like a miracle that the knight had long suspected some secret ulterior motive, half-expecting that his new liege lord would strike in the future, hitting him with some unexpected but long premeditated act of vengeance. In truth, Thurstan himself had never really understood why he'd gone with William Marshal to hand Richard the crown. Death had been a very possible outcome, though in truth the knight had only partially feared that. Richard, even Richard the Hot Duke, had admired warriors, especially those who respected rank and followed orders. There'd been at least an even chance he'd pardon the pair of them. And if he didn't, would it have mattered? Thurstan didn't feel much different in that regard, even now. Death would come on the edge of a sword at some point. And all he'd be losing was more of *this*.

'Forgive my ire, lord,' he finally said. 'It was unbecoming.'

Richard sighed. 'At least we're on the same side now. I'd sooner my knights lay waste to our enemies than each other.' He turned. 'Bertrand du Voix?'

Bertrand bowed. 'My liege?'

'There are many here dying we must speak with before they pass. Ride with us. Ensure the royal flag is seen.'

Bertrand mounted up and unfurled the standard.

Thurstan was left alone with his thoughts, which again, inevitably, were invaded by the Red Bishop. Even here, amid this sea of waste and human ruin, that ghastly thing had appeared. Or maybe it shouldn't be a surprise.

This is the perfect place to find a devil.

Already though, the mental picture was fading, the reality of what he'd thought he'd seen less and less certain. What *was* certain was that here, at his feet, lay the mangled form of James d'Oisy of Avesnes, a long-term friend and comrade. That was an image that would stay in his mind as though branded there. As did all those images of slain friends (and foes, if he was honest with himself). He pivoted around, gazing across piles of slaughtered men and beasts.

There wasn't a hummock to be seen, let alone the demonic bishop who'd perched himself there. Yet it was increasingly less easy to purge these worrisome thoughts.

Again, that question: where else would a devil prefer to be? Where else would his influence be found than among men bent on killing each other like cattle? Killing each other crazily, in a fog of blood and shit?

He fought down growing tingles of fear as he heard his name called.

'Lord Thurstan? My lord?'

Pandulf trudged towards him, leading his horse and laden with kit.

'You performed courageously,' Thurstan said stiffly. 'I'm proud of you.'

'I'm not proud of myself, lord.' Pandulf still looked sickly pale.

'You're alive. If nothing else congratulate yourself for that.'

CHAPTER 10

King Richard was under no illusions about the state of his army. They'd borne through the hard journey and its climactic battle heroically, but they now needed rest. Three days later, they found that the port of Jaffa matched this need perfectly.

A relatively insignificant port on the Palestine coast, it had never been massively fortified. What few ramparts there were had been destroyed on Saladin's orders before the Ayyubid garrison fled, but the mud-brick town within remained intact, while the central keep – first constructed in the time of Vespasian, a typically grim and austere Roman monument – remained at the heart of it. For all this, Jaffa still had an aura of magic and mystery. Here, it was said, St Peter was sent a vision in which a herd of mismatched animals, the unclean rubbing shoulders with the clean, came down from Heaven all wrapped in a single blanket, implying to him that even the Gentiles were now to be saved.

But if that wasn't enough, the relative unimportance of this place and the subsequent lack of a large and permanent military presence meant that the lush parkland on its outskirts, acres and acres of citrus and olive groves, orchards and pasture, all watered by channels cut from a tributary of the River Yarkon, was pristine. At the same time, news of their advance had arrived ahead of them, and an army of a different sort had inundated the area: wagon-trains of Greek, Jewish and Arabic merchants, bringing food, drink… and women.

There'd been cohorts of women at Acre. Richard had not forbidden them to follow in the army's wake, as they so often would during wars in Europe, because he didn't wish to sew discontent among his troops, but he'd declared that no food or drink could be spared for them which had dissuaded many from making the trip.

As such, the canvas city now set up between the palm trees along the seafront – its bawdy pleasures openly advertised on gaudily painted boards – was the most gratifying sight to greet the troops' eyes in many a long day. It might have seemed contradictory for men who avowed they were on a mission from God, but if pressed on the matter, as they regularly were by the priests and bishops among them, they pointed out that Jesus himself had supped among sinners.

Though the king and his senior counsellors found quarters in the keep, the *Familia Regis* claimed a shady orange grove only five minutes' walk from a large, open-fronted pavilion located on the edge of a broad white-sand beach, from where a wily Levantine called Saul provided wine and barley beer. The *Familia* christened it *The Gateway to Jerusalem*, which within a few days had become *The Gateway*. Needless to say, Saul also managed a stable of voluptuous, dusky beauties, which made his establishment particularly popular.

Pandulf, who'd never lain with a woman, not even a village girl during his youth in the Forest of Arden, had no such yearning. He'd drunk wine and beer before, but it felt like small recompense after Arsuf, where he'd driven his blade into men whose names he didn't even know. He knew that he shouldn't feel as shamed by these things as he did, and was determined not to show it, but those lurid impressions of dead and dying faces filled his dreams. He doubted that a few cups of wine would scour off his guilt.

But there were other things on his mind, too.

Worse things.

It felt like a betrayal, walking beside a turquoise sea or kneeling on carpeted stone and praying in the cool interiors of the city chapels now unbarred by the newly arrived clergy, because it felt like time wasted when he could have been doing something more useful. He was grateful the fighting was done, but an urgent concern nagged at him.

Five days after they'd arrived in Jaffa, with his master away reconnoitring Ascalon, the next major city along the coast, he took the path from the camp of the *Familia Regis* to *The Gateway*.

73

The sun was setting when he reached the tavern, its interior ablaze with red light. Like Pandulf, those others present wore everyday clothes, wine-stained in many cases. Bertrand and William des Roches were among them. Bertrand even ordered him a cup of wine, which Pandulf accepted with subdued gratitude.

Hesitantly, the lad outlined his concern, regardless that it might make him seem foolish.

They didn't exactly bray with laughter but snickered and waved him away.

'I know how it seems, my lords,' he said. 'But what do you actually think?'

Bertrand adjusted the painted doxy on his lap. 'What do you want me to say, Pandulf? It's all a big mystery because Lord Thurstan *isn't* a fiend with sword in hand? Everyone knows he is.'

Pandulf shook his head. 'But not like this. This was different.'

'Different, how?' William des Roches wondered. He had two women in attendance, one on his arm, one around his neck, but seemed more interested in quaffing.

'To start with, he wielded *two* swords. And he fought proficiently with both at the same time. *More* than proficiently. Against separate opponents. I saw it with my own eyes.'

William signalled for a refill. 'You're new to this company, Pandulf. And you're new to Thurstan Wildblood. You think he'd be knight-commander if he couldn't use a sword? Or even two?'

'But, my lords... a few short days ago, he was dying.'

'Plainly not,' Bertrand said.

'At the very least, he should be crippled by pain.'

'That, I will concede, is impressive.'

'It's not impressive, it's impossible.'

'You can be certain of only one thing, Pandulf,' Bertrand said. 'Thurstan Wildblood will die in battle. At some point. We all of us share that destiny. The best any of us can hope for is to die well. In which case it's a good thing he possesses these skills, is it not? To push back that date as far as possible?'

Pandulf shook his head. 'Thurstan Wildblood won't die in battle.'

William frowned. 'What are you talking about, boy?'

'That fever-dream,' the squire said. 'In which Bishop Belphagor told him he'd rule every battlefield.'

'What are you trying to say... the Devil came to your master while he was wounded?'

'*A* devil. Maybe not *the* Devil.'

Bertrand snorted through his wine. 'The Bishop of Hell, no less.'

The various women present, few if any of whom spoke French, could only watch on, bored, but now showed more interest. Like as not, the sudden emphasis on 'Devil' was something they understood. All good Levantines, Christian, Jew or Muslim, knew about the cursed valley of Hinnom – or Gehenna, as it was also known – where legions of children had once been burned alive in sacrifice to the Lord of Darkness.

'The Bishop of Hell,' Pandulf said. 'That thought doesn't chill you to the bone?'

'Thoughts of devils always chill me,' Bertrand replied. 'That's why I'm here on pilgrimage. To make up for my misspent life. But I've never seen a devil yet. Nor met a single man who has.'

'They don't come to Earth, Pandulf,' William said.

'Maybe in dreams, they do.'

'Dreams are fancies. They don't mean anything.'

'So, devils can't use their evil powers for the destruction of Man?' The squire was bewildered. 'That's contrary to everything I was taught.'

'Even if it's true, why turn Thurstan into Hercules?' Bertrand asked. 'He's a pilgrim too. A Christian warrior. How could that serve Lucifer's plan?'

'I don't know,' Pandulf said, equally puzzled, 'but you weren't there, my lords. I've never seen anything like it. Such a force of death... That can't be a good thing, whoever he fights for. And what about his wound? I saw that for myself... it was an upside-down cross, for Heaven's sake!'

'Depends which angle you viewed it from, no?' William chortled. 'Change position, and maybe it was God who guided that javelin.'

Before anyone could refute this, a shadow fell over them.

Thurstan stood in the tavern doorway, still wearing his mail, cloak and tabard, his longsword at his hip, his helmet under his left arm.

'My lord?' Bertrand got to his feet.

'Ascalon is no more.' Thurstan came forward, begrimed with dust. He pushed back his coif, revealing hair turned ratty with sweat. 'Get me wine. My mouth tastes like salt.'

Bertrand signalled to the counter maid, and she provided a brimming goblet, which Thurstan drained in a gulp.

'Ascalon's no more?' William sounded incredulous.

Only now did that message strike home. Ascalon wasn't just a stronghold of age-old renown, but the capital of one of the most important seigneuries in the Kingdom of Jerusalem. Saladin's recapture of it after Hattin had been a major coup for the sultanate.

'Not one stone stands on another.' Thurstan pushed his goblet across the counter for more. 'Saladin got there before us.'

'He destroyed his own fortress?' Pandulf asked, astonished.

'I imagine so there was no danger we might occupy it,' William said.

Thurstan grunted in the affirmative as he drank again.

'But to destroy his own fortress?' Pandulf said. None of them, save Thurstan, had yet set eyes on the coastal bastion, and in truth even Thurstan hadn't seen it before it was a heap of rubble. But they'd all heard about it.

A former Canaanite city of legendary defensive strength, it was further fortified by great powers from all the ages, from Alexander to King Herod, the Romans, and finally the Fatimids, who'd added cyclopean battlements and towers. It had guarded the main road between Egypt and Palestine for centuries, and its strategic importance could not be overstated. And now they'd found it levelled.

'Why would he do such a thing?' Pandulf said. 'Surely it was more valuable to him than that?'

'Not as valuable as the reinforcements he's obviously bringing up from Egypt,' Bertrand replied. 'He can't afford to let us cut them off.'

'The war isn't over?' The squire was dazed by the thought.

Thurstan looked at him. 'What made you think it was?'

'I thought... I...'

'You thought one bloodbath would be enough? Welcome to the real world. On which subject: the less nonsense you spread about Bishop Belphagor, the less inclined I'll be to have you horsewhipped out of camp.' Thurstan eyed the others. 'You fools weren't listening to that?'

Bertrand gestured. 'We mocked.'

'We belittled the mere notion,' William said.

'What do you think we're doing here, Pandulf?' Thurstan asked the squire. 'You express disbelief that, just because we've destroyed one army, Saladin has gone in search of another. You didn't think that would happen? When we put steel to the people of Acre? To these Muslims, we are all the Devil incarnate.'

'Then it's a good thing *we* know better,' Bertrand said.

Thurstan eyed him. 'Is it?'

Bertrand straightened. 'It doesn't matter what Saladin thinks. I'm a soldier. My job is to fight... but only those who can stand up to me.'

'Very noble,' Thurstan replied. 'But the helpless die in war too. None of you were there in Meath, in Ireland, when Hugh de Lacy asserted his power. You'd sing a different tune if you were. The point I'm making, gentlemen, is that when you do the Devil's work, you take on the Devil's mantel... At least in the eyes of those you're doing it to. You hear me, Pandulf? There's no real Devil here. Men can do terrible things without the Evil One standing at their backs.'

—

Richard was surprised about the demolished fortress rather than angry. He had never realistically felt that Saladin was finished at Arsuf. The sultan had too much to lose. But perhaps the king had hoped that, aside from the Ayyubid force now occupying the Holy City itself, there'd be no other army to fight for a couple of years. How soon the sultan could bring his new legions up from Egypt was open to question, but the mere fact this was the plan would eat into the pilgrims' resources.

'We need to rebuild Ascalon,' he said in the council chamber in Jaffa's keep. 'If nothing else, a citadel and a curtain wall.'

This met with a mixed response from the other leaders. The churchmen in particular clamoured for an immediate march on Jerusalem. Archbishop Ubaldo of Pisa and Bishop Philip of Beauvais had hoped to celebrate Mass on Christmas Day in the Church of the Holy Sepulchre, they said. Only Bishop Hubert of Salisbury recognised that Richard's more circumspect approach was the one least likely to see them all destroyed, though even he was hesitant to dispute with the papal legate.

Thurstan, having delivered the message, withdrew and let the arguments rage.

His mind was still occupied by the dressing down he'd given to his men, and as was increasingly the case, that cursed figment of a tortured imagination. Glimpsing that red phantom again in the fray at Arsuf had shaken him, but he'd been in a crazed state, and in the midst of blood-drenched chaos; it might have been odd if he *hadn't* witnessed the strange and unreal amid such horrors. It was also true that he'd fought uncommon hard that day even by his own standards; no wonder Pandulf had been shocked. But he'd been enraged by the felling of Apollonius.

Though... a horse?

A horse could bring a man to such madness?

Of course, when something couldn't be fathomed, it made no sense to dwell on it. So, he pushed his thoughts away. Far away. To a green valley with a lake in it, the pine-clad slopes reflecting in its mirror-like surface. And then the milk-white beauty of Gwendolyn as the Sisters of Cupthorne closed the wickerwork casket over it, Mother Turilda's knotty old hands clasped around his, so that he wouldn't be praying alone.

The pain of fallen friends – Apollonius, James of Avesnes – was immense.

But Thurstan Wildblood knew worse.

CHAPTER 11

Three days after his return from Ascalon, Thurstan was visited by Robert Sable, Grandmaster of the Knights Templar. Sable was a hard–bitten, humourless man, his hair shorn to stiff, grey bristles, his features stern and striated as though carved from sun–blistered wood. But Thurstan had heard it said that while rigid and prudish, he understood war.

The grandmaster rode his horse to *The Gateway*, where he drew rein disapprovingly. Thurstan and Bertrand were seated on an outside bench, mugs of wine in hand. They watched as he eyed the knights and men–at–arms, they too stripped to civilian garb and seated in the shade of palms, drinking, or in some cases stripped entirely and laughing as they frolicked in the waves with naked, giggling women. In contrast, Sable and the two mounted Templars with him were resplendent in their clean mail and white surcoats emblazoned with the red cross.

It was no surprise to see his disapprobation. The Templars and Hospitallers were monk–like in their vows of chastity and sobriety, and while the rest of the army had relaxed in Jaffa, the two military orders had passed the time cleaning their equipment, honing their weapons and drilling, which was impressive to hear about, though Thurstan felt no guilt. He too commanded an elite regiment. Like the Templars, the *Familia* enjoyed that status because its members were better trained and better equipped, but also because they were comprised solely of sworn swords… As in, oath–sworn to those who commanded them rather than to some vague notion about waging a war in Christ's name.

'Commander Wildblood.' Sable removed his helmet but refrained from dismounting. 'You are summoned to the royal presence.'

Thurstan drained the dregs from his cup. 'Am I in need of escort?'

'I am summoned too,' Sable replied, 'but I'd speak with you in private before we go.'

'I need to make myself presentable. We can call by my private quarters. It's through the orange groves here. Leave your men behind, if you please.'

Sable spoke quietly to his two knights, both of whom wheeled around and returned the way they'd come. Sable dismounted and took his horse by the bridle. They walked side-by-side along the path through the groves. Thurstan was half-expecting some reprimand for the libidinous nature of his camp, but to his surprise, Sable had more practical concerns.

'The leadership is becoming fractious,' he said.

Thurstan nodded. 'It was to be expected.'

'As commander of Richard's *Familia Regis*, where do you stand?'

'Lord Robert... you can't seriously be asking if my support for Richard is wavering? Not when I lead his personal household?'

'Trust me, Wildblood... We face a similarly difficult choice.'

It wasn't a choice where Thurstan was concerned. But he understood what the Templar meant. The senior churchmen were now contesting the king's plans to delay the march on Jerusalem. In normal times, the military orders would be staunchly loyal to the Pope's man, Archbishop Ubaldo. But in Europe, the Templars' powerbases were nearly all located on Plantagenet lands, where they enjoyed huge liberties. To make an enemy of Richard Plantagenet would be an error. In addition, if Robert Sable was truly a capable soldier, he ought to understand that Richard's strategy was the more sensible.

'The word is that Richard plans to hold off until the next campaigning season,' the Templar said.

Thurstan mulled that over. The weather was still hot and dry, but they were deep into September, and he already knew enough about the Levant to recognise that poorer conditions might be imminent. If that wasn't reason enough to delay, Ascalon's new defences were still unbuilt.

When he mentioned this, Sable remained grim. 'There is more to it. We heard this morning that Richard also seeks a truce. There's even a rumour that he's despatched a ship to bring Countess Joan from Cyprus.'

Thurstan was surprised. Countess Joan was Richard's younger sister, formerly the Queen of Sicily but though widowed now, still a famously beautiful woman, whom he doted on. 'A truce by marriage?'

'Not with Saladin, I'm sure,' Sable replied. 'Maybe his brother, Safadin. But a truce like that could hardly be a short-term arrangement, I'm sure you agree?'

Thurstan thought it through. 'First of all, Richard must know that this Safadin would never consent, as it would involve converting to Christianity. Most likely, it's a ploy to buy time.'

'The bishops aren't convinced.'

Thurstan felt a pang of irritation. 'With Ascalon a ruin, the Saracen horde coming from Egypt could just as easily attack us here at Jaffa as unite with Saladin at Jerusalem. Surely, their graces can be made to understand the danger we face?'

'Archbishop Ubaldo and his two main supporters, Archbishop Gerhard and Bishop Philip, are not the sort who can be made to understand anything if it's against their interests.'

'The last thing we need now is a battle on two fronts,' Thurstan said, 'which is what would happen if Saladin arrives here at the same time as his reinforcements.'

'Saladin will not leave Jerusalem at present.' The Templar seemed convinced of that at least. 'He has no need. Scouts returned this morning, having reconnoitred the city. He's rebuilt those walls and towers he damaged after Hattin. The bishops are concerned that Richard feels it can't be taken.'

'They think he's opened peace talks because he knows we can't win?' Thurstan shook his head. 'That isn't the Richard I know.'

'I agree, but there are other concerns. Archbishop Ubaldo fears that Richard's thoughts are straying to Europe. Specifically, the return of Philip of France to Paris.'

Thurstan didn't even like to ponder this. There was no doubt in his mind that the French king would cause trouble on Richard's borders the moment he returned there. 'You must know that I'm only a soldier, Grandmaster...'

'As we all are.'

'Except that I have less political influence than you. In any case, as you are sworn to Christ, I am sworn to Richard. Wherever he goes, the *Familia* goes too, and I will command it. Even if it means the abandonment of the Pilgrimage.'

Sable was thoughtful. 'I understand that. Perhaps though, as his closest sword, you might seek to prevent this... Might counsel him that the abandoning of the Pilgrimage, as you put it, would be akin to abandoning his soul?'

Thurstan had no doubt that Richard would think this exact same thing. An oath was an oath. For a paragon of knightly virtue, it would be anathema to do as Philip of France had and walk away from fellow Christians in conflict with pagans. And yet Philip of France was a sly dog, and when all this was over, when Richard returned home, he might find nothing awaiting him there.

This army of God is fragmenting... the Church of Jesus Christ faces a catastrophe.

—

Jaffa's keep was in the centre of the town, and encircled by a walled complexity of yards, stable blocks and barrack houses, the latter currently occupied by the Count of Dreux's Norman contingent, who had been chosen to perform guard duties.

Thurstan and Sable dismounted inside the main gate, handing their reins to a pair of grooms, and there met Garnier de Nablus, of the Hospitallers. In contrast to Sable, Thurstan knew De Nablus as an affable fellow, though at present he looked serious, even grave.

'My lords,' he said, 'we won the battle... But we need to be cleverer if we wish to win the war.'

In the main building, they handed over their longswords to a prissy, well-dressed concierge, who then led them up several flights of stone stairs. They heard the uproar from the council chamber before they reached it.

It was a long, spacious room, the shutters on its tall arched windows flung open to admit air and light. When they entered, all those in attendance stood around in groups, engaged in heated debate. King Richard, clad unglamorously in leather breeches and an open linen shirt, moved stiffly from one knot of men to the next, Bishop Hubert fluttering in agitated attendance. The king wasn't quite as red-faced as some of those others, though frustration was visibly growing on him.

Thurstan's heart sank. Robert of Dreux was deep in argument with his brother, Bishop Philip of Beauvais. Hugh of Saint Pol disputed with Bishop Adelard of Verona, King Guy with Humphrey de Toron, formerly one of his own loyal barons.

This army of God is fragmenting…

At the farthest end of the room, Archbishop Ubaldo and a small group of clerics sat on stools. The archbishop was a hefty man in his fifties, his sagging features reddened and roughened by excessive good living. Alongside him perched his deputy, Archbishop Gerhard of Ravenna, a lean, hawk-like man, dark skinned and dark haired. Behind them, somewhat surprisingly, stood Duke Hugh of Burgundy, which was not a good sign.

Richard saw the three newcomers and threaded towards them.

'Grandmaster Robert,' he said. 'Grandmaster Garnier. You're aware of the impasse we've reached here? The situation is simple. Though I hold senior rank, this Pilgrimage is a joint enterprise, and I can't in good conscience impose my will on so august a gathering of princes. We must have consensus to proceed, but archbishops Ubaldo and Gerhard are the main impediments.'

'The Duke of Burgundy as well, sire?' Sable asked.

Richard snorted. 'The French have been looking for this opportunity. Why fight on when their sovereign has left? Why suffer hardship in the name of their hated rival, the King of England?'

De Nablus eyed the French contingent with irritation. 'In the absence of King Philip, they overestimate their influence.'

'Which will be made clear to all,' Richard replied, 'if you two gentlemen, as senior members of the Church's military arm, can bring Ubaldo to our corner.'

Sable looked unhappy. 'Lord king, you're aware that we too have concerns?'

The king's expression hardened. 'And yet, as seasoned field-commanders, you surely understand my position better than most?'

They could hardly deny it.

'Then do as I ask, my lords. Advise their excellencies that if we make an ill-prepared march on Jerusalem and leave our main camp insecure, we invite destruction.'

The grandmasters undertook their assignment with no great enthusiasm.

They genuflected in front of the papal legate, who graciously allowed them to kiss his episcopal ring. At first, he heard them out politely, but was shaking his head before they had finished.

Thurstan, watching, was unsurprised. The interests of the Church supposedly aligned with the interests of mankind. And they did, when it suited the Church. Then of course, there were situations like this, when the senior churchmen present had no grasp of either the military or political predicament. Ultimately of course, though he was loyal to Richard, this was his overlord's problem, not his own. And not just because he himself was no more than a functionary bound to obey orders, but because he had no personal beef with God's vicars on Earth.

It wasn't a churchman who'd taken Gwendolyn's life less than one year after she and Thurstan had married.

'My lord archbishop!' the king said, approaching Archbishop Ubaldo. 'For all our sakes, you must divest yourself of these illusions!'

The rest of the gathering fell silent.

'Lord king,' Bishop Hubert said. 'Archbishop Ubaldo is Rome's agent. Even in this barbarous place, he is God's representative...'

'And I am God's Fist,' Richard retorted. 'And in this place especially, God's Fist trumps all powers on Earth.'

The silence persisted, everyone rapt.

The king eyed them all. 'The success or failure of the Pilgrimage may hinge on decisions you reach today. You know my position: if we march on Jerusalem before we are prepared, at the wrong time of year, we risk undoing all our achievements.'

Uncertain mumbles greeted this.

'I haven't finished!' the king thundered. They cowered.

Richard's tawny hair and beard had grown thick and mane-like since he'd arrived on these shores; his handsome, hard-carved features were deeply tanned. But now there was really something of the lion about him. He'd come a long way from the brave but angry young man Thurstan had first met on the road to Chinon.

'I make one more plea... on behalf of this army we've brought from the other side of the world, many of them common men from villages and market towns, men who have wives and families to go home to, hopefully richer and scoured of sin, but the same men who will lie en masse in unmarked graves if we misjudge our position.'

Archbishop Ubaldo licked his lips nervously.

'My noble lords,' the king said, addressing the whole room. 'Set, if you will, the wisdom of waging a proper military campaign with all contingencies planned for, against the folly of marching like some raucous, drunken rabble, like Peter the Hermit and his peasant mob, to our inevitable doom.' Richard eyed the archbishop again. 'Then consider on whose shoulders the blame will lie if the latter comes to pass.'

–

'Do you consider I was too harsh with them?' Richard asked.

Thurstan's gaze roved the heady blue haze of the Mediterranean. 'Can one ever be too harsh with bishops?'

A smile touched the king's lips as they strolled the keep battlements. 'You understand why we are playing for time?'

'Of course, sire. It's a ruse. Your proposed treaty, I mean.'

'We'll certainly gain nothing from it,' the king replied. 'Why would Saladin give us anything when the advantage will shortly turn in his favour? You see, it's no longer just a theory that new forces will come from Egypt. Our scouts report a huge army mustering at Rafah. Similar in size to the army we vanquished at Arsuf, which, as you're probably aware, has not been entirely vanquished.'

The sun beat on Thurstan's head as he absorbed all this.

'It's not a lie when I say we need extra time,' Richard said. 'But we don't need this time to restore Ascalon. Rebuilding the fortress will help, but if Saladin's new army is as large as reported, it won't make much difference. Ascalon can be the strongest castle in the East, but no garrison we put there could ever be large enough to come out and waylay these new armies of devils if they opt to march around it. What we need… is Conrad of Montferrat.'

Thurstan bit his lip. He ought to have known that Richard would not give up on Jerusalem. But without Count Conrad, he lacked the forces to capture it. This was the crux of his dilemma. Because Count Conrad would not come here while King Guy still lurked in the camp.

'You must send a reliable man to speak with Conrad on our behalf,' the king said.

'As you wish, my liege.'

'No one else must know.'

'Of course not.'

'*No one*, you understand? The army is riddled with spies.'

'I understand.'

Richard walked on. 'Whoever you choose, he must put our case to the count, explain our position… the Pilgrimage is in peril, but if we capture Jerusalem, that will change.'

'Forgive me, sire,' Thurstan ventured. 'But it might strengthen my emissary's position if he knew… do you intend to offer Conrad the crown of Jerusalem?'

Richard sighed. 'I can't do that. But maybe we can put it to a vote.' He blew out a breath, as if this very idea reviled him. 'But first we must get that recreant, Montferrat, here… with his whole army. By any means we can.'

CHAPTER 12

With hindsight, King Richard would likely not have opted to march on Jerusalem as late in the year as autumn, but the situation was forced on him by two simultaneous events. One entirely predictable, the other less so.

Firstly, though the negotiations with Saladin's brother, Al-Malik al-Adil Sayf ad-Din Abu-Bakr Ahmed ibn Najm ad-Din Ayyub, Al-Adil, to his own people, or Safadin as the Christians knew him, had been courteous, involving much feasting and hawking, the great Muslim dignitary had not been fooled by the Christians' playing for time and had graciously rejected the offer of marriage to Countess Joan. Secondly, shortly before Allhallowtide, Bertrand du Voix returned from his journey to Count Conrad's northern stronghold of Tyre with news that under no circumstances would Conrad rejoin the Pilgrimage while Guy of Lusignan remained in Richard's camp. Not even to participate in an election.

Bertrand, for one, didn't understand the king's attitude. 'Why doesn't Richard just meet his demands? What's so important about Guy de Lusignan? He's a broken man.'

'If the decision was mine, I'd do just that,' Thurstan replied. 'But Richard would argue that he did not come all the way here to throw down a fellow Christian king… while the bishops prefer Guy *because* he is weak.'

Richard himself was less surprised. 'I should have guessed,' he said, on receiving the news. 'Why would Montferrat give up his position of strength? He has one ambition, the Crown of Jerusalem, and the best way he can get it is to let his two main opponents, Saladin of Egypt and Richard of England, tear each other to pieces.'

But though he understood it, he nevertheless was now forced to act quickly, his contingency plan to win the war before Saladin could bring his fresh forces from the south. In that regard, Richard could only hope that winter in the Levant would be kinder than it was at home.

It wasn't.

—

The army wasn't ready to march until mid-November. The blazing sunshine and hot dry wind disappeared as storms descended from the north-east. Daytime temperatures plummeted and teeming rain fell. If the road from Jaffa to Jerusalem had ever been laid with Roman stone, there was no trace of it now, and so axels broke, the wheels of supply carts becoming lodged in mud, whole teams of men and horses required to haul the vehicles loose. Even the chaises transporting the bishops and their entourages became mired and often were left useless by the roadside. In a very short time, the lesser ranks among the clergy were reduced to walking.

Even before the tempest commenced, there'd been problems. Long sections of route were torturously narrow, a footpath winding through defiles or along canyons strewn with loose, heavy boulders. It was a challenge from the outset to march in formation. Thus, they straggled out lengthily, huge gaps appearing, which was of particular concern to Thurstan.

Injuries mounted daily, everything from blistered feet to sprained ankles. It was a problem that worsened the further they got into November. Food stocks were by this time sodden, sacks of fodder and flour turned green with mildew, fruit rotted to pulp, beef and bacon turned rancid. As the wind grew fiercer and colder, huge numbers of men already wet-through, fell victim to coughs and fevers.

However, the real problems came in late-November, on an open stretch of plain, where for the first time they encountered human opponents: roaming bands of horse-archers, who galloped up and unleashed hails of arrows.

The building of secure camps became near impossible. The surrounding country held little timber or brush with which to construct bulwarks, so once night fell, individuals set up their tents wherever they could, and with no time to make defences. As the rain pelted them, this whole business became an ordeal in itself. It was especially a problem at night, when the new-arrived packs of mounted assailants would single out those smaller, thrown-together encampments, and ride through them without warning, torching the tents and wagons, spearing the occupants.

At a place called Ramleh, several hundred mounted bowmen, accompanied by an equal number of Mamluks, came down from high ground, intent on driving a wedge into the army's vanguard.

Richard, in his own typical fashion, led the counter charge, but as they were strung out thinly, the king and those Templars who rode with him were initially outnumbered. In response, Thurstan led a furious gallop from further down the column, all the knights of the *Familia Regis* with him. Even then, they were inferior in numbers. It lasted almost two hours, a wild, disorganised melee, horsemen ranging across the open muddy ground as they clashed repeatedly.

'That was horrendous,' Bishop Hubert said, afterwards. He'd ridden forward into the van, which Thurstan had restored to full strength by bringing forth the *Familia* to take the places of those Templars lost.

Thurstan said nothing as they trundled wearily along the rutted road.

Several broken arrows hung from his hauberk. His visor was loose, the left side of his cheek slashed, the old wound on his hip aching abominably.

'Do you hear me, Wildblood?' the bishop persisted.

'I hear you, Lord Bishop. Did you expect me to disagree?'

'In Heaven's name, we almost lost the king.'

'Indeed we did. And it may not be the last occasion. That was a small taste of what awaits us at Jerusalem.'

Bishop Hubert, whose pudgy features had thinned, much of the excess flesh now hanging loose, seemed distraught. 'I don't see how this is possible. Not after Arsuf...'

'The king told you how it would be possible. Everything he said has come to pass.'

'I was not set on this plan to embark before we were ready.'

'Nor did you speak against it, your grace. If you'll pardon me for saying.'

Bishop Hubert made no reply; he was honest enough not to deny what they both already knew. He was Richard's man, but it would have been quite a challenge for him to side against the papal legate.

To Thurstan's mind, Mother Turilda, Prioress of Cupthorne Abbey, was the only member of the high clergy he would ever trust. The rest were ruthless and reptilian in their scheming. But Bishop Hubert Walter of Salisbury was a complex exception. It had never been intended that this lesser son of a minor landowner would lead the English Church contingent on the Pilgrimage, but as deputy to the more aristocratic Archbishop Baldwin, it had fallen to him to take charge when his superior was killed. Thurstan knew that Bishop Hubert's loyalty to Richard stemmed from the likelihood that he'd be elevated to archbishop himself if he ever made it back home. It went as read therefore that he was intelligent, another schemer, but he lacked haughtiness, recognising other men for their talents, even common men, and talking to them as equals. Not so much a friend – one should never make that mistake with any of the great episcopal princes – but a companion of sorts.

Again though, his lack of soldierly acumen was painfully exposed.

'Even if we fail to take Jerusalem,' he said, 'we can't give up.'

'We can't?' Thurstan replied.

'Think on it, Wildblood. Barbarossa's death before he even got here, and Philip's rank cowardice have gifted this whole mission to Richard the Lionheart. Look what he stands to gain if we succeed. And look how much he loses if we fail.'

'For what it's worth, your grace, the king never thought that retaking Jerusalem was beyond us. Just that we weren't ready to undertake such a feat. Not yet.'

'That's a good thing. If we're forced to retreat, we can try again...'

'But since then, we've lost a host of additional men, supplies and horses. If we retreat now, the enemy will pursue us, forcing us to fight more and more actions. We might return to Jaffa and refit, but that will take longer now than it needed to. And then consider that Jaffa itself is indefensible. Even Ascalon remains half-built... If even that. And what of the manpower we've wasted?'

'Miracles have been known, Wildblood.'

'Then pray for one.'

–

Similar encounters with the enemy occurred continuously over the next few days, the bands of Ayyubid irregulars becoming ever more numerous the closer their enemy drew to Jerusalem.

Several times more, King Richard put himself in danger. Near a village called Saris, a sizeable Mamluk force galloped recklessly into the van. The king led a direct charge in response. The weather yet again, which had worsened as December dragged on, had created huge empty spaces in the column, so as before, the Lionheart found himself surrounded by fanatical opponents. Those few members of the *Familia* in close attendance, Thurstan and La Hors among them, fought furiously, but only after ten frantic minutes, as more and more knights from further back galloped forward, did the enemy retreat.

In the last days before Christmas, when the advance guard reported back that they'd come at last within sight of the Holy City, any joy or relief was tempered by the news that the plain in front of it was spangled with the fires of Ayyubid encampments, and that squadrons of Saracen horse were everywhere. It was almost as though the victory at Arsuf had never happened.

Richard received this information on Christmas Eve, sitting wrapped in a damp blanket to one side of a meagre campfire. His face was lean and drawn, his beard grizzled and hair hanging damp and stringy. All around him, from inside the jumble of sagging, rain-sodden tents, or beneath the bellies of wagons and carts, came coughs and wheezes, moans of pain, desperate prayers.

Bishop Hubert sat opposite, wrapped but shivering.

'So close and yet so far,' the prelate muttered.

'I wonder what it looks like?' said a filthy wretch of a monk who was nameless to the rest of them, for this was the way of it now, the lordly rubbing shoulders with the base.

'In 1099, when the city was first captured,' another said, 'I heard that great numbers died assailing the ramparts. Yet those who had simply laid hands on that sacred stonework, even if they got no more than halfway up the scaling ladder, died happy... For after all that hardship, they had reached Christ's capital.'

'Damn fool story,' Count Robert grunted. 'Good job they didn't all think that, or the escalade would have failed.'

'My lords, my lords!' came an urgent voice. 'I must speak with the king!'

A newcomer arrived in the firelight, his mail gleaming, the white chevrons on his sea-blue surcoat unfeasibly clean. Thurstan recognised Henry, the Count of Champagne, a young, enthusiastic French knight, and a distant nephew of the king. Disgusted by Philip's abandonment of his countrymen's cause, he'd switched his allegiance to his uncle shortly after Acre.

'Sire...' Count Henry dropped to one knee. 'News from Jaffa.'

'Speak,' the king said.

'I've ridden from there on receipt of word from Ascalon,' Count Henry said. 'Saladin's reinforcements are dispersed.'

'Dispersed?' Richard got stiffly to his feet. 'How so?'

Count Henry rose too. Several others did also.

'My liege, the same bad weather that assails you here has been causing chaos all down the coast. Innumerable rivers and streams have burst their banks. Flash floods have washed away bridges and whole sections of road. The Ayyubid replacement army is in disarray. Many are leaving to find safer billets for the rest of the winter.'

Richard glanced from one man to the next. 'How much ground had they made before this catastrophe?'

'None, sire. They hadn't even commenced their northward march.'

'God be praised,' Count Robert muttered.

'Saladin's reinforcements won't be coming?' Bishop Hubert asked.

'They'll still come, your grace,' Count Henry replied. 'But not until spring at the earliest.'

The bishop's once chubby features broke with joy. 'Sire, this means...'

'Silence,' Richard said. 'Knight-Commander, send word. The army must prepare to march.' He turned to the others. 'My noble lords, you'll be pleased to hear that at first light we return to Jaffa.'

There were more than a few mutters of relief, but others looked shocked.

'Bishop Hubert,' Richard said, 'you will furnish their excellencies, archbishops Ubaldo and Adelard with this intelligence. I'm sure they and their entourage are in such a state by now that they'll have no objection.'

Bishop Hubert nodded.

'My lords,' the king said, 'God has chosen to spare us. We still have an enemy in front, stronger than we expected. But *no* enemy behind. That means we have the whole winter to rebuild. When next we come this way, we'll come as the disciplined force that crushed Saladin before, and one that will be ready and able to crush him again.'

When he strode to his royal tent, there was a new spring in his stride.

'You asked for a miracle, Wildblood,' Bishop Hubert said. 'It seems you have one.'

CHAPTER 13

As the pilgrim army trekked back towards Jaffa, the elements continued to pummel them, the rain and sleet unyielding. A deep dejection spread among the troops, though its origins lay with the French, in particular Duke Hugh, who told all and sundry that it was Richard who'd brought them to this disaster. Nearly every man present had his heart set on recapturing the Holy City, and after all the battles they'd fought just to get here, they hadn't even attempted it.

Bishop Hubert, meanwhile, told the king's inner circle that it was all the work of the French. Highly likely, Philip of France was now home and positioning himself to commence raiding into English-held territories. Maybe they should have expected that hostilities would commence on the Pilgrimage too.

'You can't mean the French are attempting sabotage?' Bertrand exclaimed, when Thurstan passed this information on.

'I think it's more a case of them winning back the Pilgrimage for France,' Thurstan replied. 'Or trying to.'

Bertrand pondered. 'Surely we'll go again? Now that we know there's no imminent threat from the south?'

There was a desperate yearning in his voice. Like all of them, he was in a roughened, raddled state, his hair a matted mop, his beard a bush, his features ingrained with dirt. But all these things he could tolerate, and worse, if they could reach their goal: Jerusalem, where their souls would be saved.

Thurstan Wildblood could only envy him such a potent belief.

'Lord king... I, and many others like me, feel the time has come to reassess.'

Duke Hugh spoke with confidence to the great assembly of nobles in Richard's royal pavilion, which, on their return to Jaffa, the king had re-erected on open land south of the city.

It was April now. Richard, looking better with colour in his cheeks, his fair hair and beard trimmed, and wearing a lengthy white gown patterned with crimson lions, reclined in his seat of judgement. The rest of the nobility had also recovered somewhat. Duke Hugh himself wore a handsome blue-and-gold-striped tabard. However, they'd only been back a couple of days, and Thurstan, though also clad in his *Familia Regis* best so to stand guard by the king's side, couldn't help but reflect on the bulk of the army, gathered outside – leaning morosely on their spears, their arms and armour still filthy. Even Jaffa offered little succour, because in the king's absence he'd ordered extensive repair-work on the city's outer walls, much of which had required timber, and so the district's luxurious orchards and olive groves had now been denuded of trees. Even the swaying palms adorning the shoreline had gone.

'Pray, my lord duke,' the king sat with fingers steepled, 'educate us.'

'The gist of my complaint, sire, concerns the manner in which you've conducted this campaign. When King Philip was forced to return home...'

'When he fled, you mean!' Count Robert of Dreux interjected.

Mumbles were heard. Some of them angry.

'We in the French portion of the army,' Duke Hugh said in a measured tone, 'have suffered greatly since our king left us.'

'You came here with seven thousand men in total,' Richard replied. 'You have four-thousand remaining. Those losses are severe, I'll grant you, but you are no more nor less decimated than any other section of our host.'

'Regardless, my lord... It rankles how many Frenchmen now dead or crippled made this sacrifice for no reason? We could have marched on to Jerusalem... We were almost in touching distance.'

This time there was silence. To Thurstan's mind, most of the nobles here would normally side with Richard, if for no other reason than they respected his military expertise. But on this matter, they were torn.

'Could we have mounted a siege?' Richard asked the duke. 'Were we in a fit state?'

Duke Hugh pivoted, playing to the gallery. 'My lords, we could have built ourselves a fortified camp in the vicinity of the city. Perhaps with your mobile fortress, Mategriffon, at the heart of it, lord-king.'

'And fed on what?' Bishop Hubert asked from among the prelates. 'Human waste pumped out through the sluice pipes in Jerusalem's walls?'

'You saw, did you not,' Richard said, 'the emptiness of the plains past Ramleh? Saladin scorched the land. You have only four thousand men remaining. How many would you have now if we'd done as you suggest?'

'And we'd still be *outside* Jerusalem's wall,' Bishop Hubert added.

The duke eyed him with irritation. 'Dress it up how you like, my lord Bishop of... *Salisbury*...' He added scornful emphasis, Salisbury being a very minor diocese compared to Pisa and Ravenna, the mitred heads of which currently sat in the front row of the Church delegation. 'But a majority of us now feel we need a change of leadership.'

Bishop Hubert got to his feet. He too had recovered much of his composure since the hard journey back. He had shaved, both his face and his tonsure, and now wore a scarlet homespun cloak over his violet Lenten robes.

'You wish to do this now?' he enquired. 'When God has granted us breathing space in which to heal our hurts?'

'It's about restoring faith in our purpose.' Again, Duke Hugh addressed the whole assembly. 'It's about remembering why we came to Outremer.' Only a muted response greeted this. He swung on the archbishops. 'Your excellencies? Surely you have a view? Richard the so-called Lionheart retreated from the battle that would have won us Jerusalem, and you say nothing!'

Thurstan eyed the senior churchmen. They'd both been present on the march to Jerusalem and had endured its privations for themselves.

They knew that Burgundy was trying to sell them a lie. The king's decision to retreat had purely been tactical.

'It is our belief, my lord duke,' Archbishop Ubaldo finally said, 'that King Richard, with his record of success…'

'Success?' the duke interrupted.

'At Arsuf he defeated an army several times larger than his own,' Count Robert reminded him.

'He won that day with all our help, not on his own,' Duke Hugh argued.

'And it is with your help, my son, that our next advance on Jerusalem will be more successful,' Archbishop Ubaldo replied, as if the matter was settled.

Duke Hugh averted his gaze. 'Not so, I'm afraid.' The pavilion fell silent. 'Forgive me, King Richard, but I can't commit myself further to an enterprise so lacking in ambition.' The duke remained po-faced, as if the momentous decision had saddened him.

'So said your king,' Count Robert replied. 'But we haven't noticed his absence.'

The duke eyed him darkly. 'You will. Go with Richard Plantagenet if you like, Count Robert, throw your men away for no gain. I value mine more highly… which is why later today I'll be taking them to a place of safety.'

'By any chance, the court of Count Conrad of Montferrat?' Richard asked.

There was a long, penetrating silence. It was no surprise to anyone. Even without Count Conrad's usual machinations, his domain was the obvious refuge for those at odds with Richard. Bishop Philip of Beauvais, for one, had already departed for Tyre.

'We men of France are leaving,' Duke Hugh said simply. 'The rest of you… You'll die in this place. And it will all be the fault of Richard of England.'

–

'We have ourselves quite the predicament, don't you agree, Wild-blood?'

Thurstan could hardly disagree. 'We are down to twelve thousand men in total, sire. So... yes, without doubt.'

The king mopped his brow as they rode at the head of the column. To their right, the sea washed gently on the narrow, empty beach. Inland, it was another tale of hot, rocky scrubland.

'Our numerical inferiority is the reason I now feel we must expedite the rebuilding of Ascalon's walls,' Richard said. 'The few hundred currently working there won't be enough.'

Thurstan couldn't fault the logic. But even so, he wondered, was it wise to split the army again? Granted, only a thousand had been left behind in Jaffa, but it had still been an unusual decision.

'May I speak plainly, sire?'

'Of course.'

'We're building new castles at Ascalon and Jaffa. But, at some point Saladin will come against us in such numbers that...'

'They'll fall?'

'They may, they may not... but none of this is taking us closer to our prize.'

Richard nodded. 'I'll be blunt with you, Wildblood. As things stand, we can't win this war. We're now a mere fraction of the force we need.'

Thurstan said nothing. Another attempt to appeal to Count Conrad ought to be more humiliation than any king could bear, let alone Richard, Since their return to Jaffa, the king had personally met with Conrad at a halfway point up the coast, but again had been rebuffed. And yet, rumours now held that he intended to hold his proposed election for the Crown of Jerusalem without Conrad's compliance, which would reduce him even more in the eyes of his fellow noblemen. It was all the more remarkable then, that Richard himself raised the matter.

'Do you consider it advisable that we hold this coming election?' the king asked.

'It's not my place, sire...'

'You're a senior soldier, and therefore a tactician. Your opinion is valued.'

Thurstan hesitated. 'I believe… it will show that you have gone as far as any man could to accommodate a useful underling, without actually bending to his will.'

'Some might say we have already bent to his will.'

Again, Thurstan was hesitant. 'There are longer term benefits to be gained.'

'Such as?'

'Conrad will win the election, sire. He'll then be crowned King of Jerusalem and will rejoin the Pilgrimage.'

'And what do you think about that?'

'I think it would be for the best, as it will remove most of our problems.'

'It's a shame you believe that, Wildblood. Because I don't.' Richard's voice hardened. 'Count Conrad will not be content with the crown of Jerusalem. At present, that crown is meaningless anyway so long as Saladin holds the Holy City. You understand that Conrad is not just sitting, biding his time in Tyre?'

'I've heard that while we were away, he made an effort to gain control of Acre.'

'That's correct. As his pretext, he used some trouble there, which his spies had stirred up between Genoese and Pisan sailors wintering in the city, but thankfully my castellans were able to restore order.'

'I've also heard that many of those new arrivals, those companies from Europe who ship into Acre now, are being convinced by his agents to join him at Tyre.'

The king nodded. 'Our estimate is that, for several months now, roughly half of those new pilgrims who arrive here to swell our ranks, are swelling Count Conrad's instead.'

'And now he has the French as well,' Thurstan said.

'That's the most important thing, I fear. That fact alone persuades me we have a more dangerous enemy than Saladin. It's heartbreaking, is it not, that with Islam massing its forces, we Christians are again at each other's throats?'

'Sire, if Conrad seeks to make himself leader of this Pilgrimage, an election at Ascalon will play into his hands. If the majority of your army cast lots in his favour…'

'It will be a great vote of confidence in him, I agree. A rival leader will finally have emerged... This one also wearing a kingly crown.'

They rode in silence. There was no doubt in Thurstan's mind that this new threat to the success of the campaign was the greatest one they faced yet.

'One might even say,' Richard remarked, 'that it would be fortunate for us if something happened to Count Conrad of Montferrat. Don't you agree?'

'Of course, my lord.' Thurstan stared forward. 'I hope it does.'

'You only *hope*?'

Thurstan thought long and hard. Compared to Muslims and Jews, Christians had special protection in the eyes of Heaven. That said, the actions of some Christians were beyond the pale.

'Count Conrad has enemies across this whole region,' he replied. 'I'd say the chances that something awful might happen to him are quite high.'

'So would I,' Richard replied. 'Much sooner rather than later, in fact.'

'Forgive me, sire... if something *were* to happen to Count Conrad, his seat would be vacant, his army leaderless. That wouldn't necessarily be a good thing.'

Richard seemed unconcerned. 'I'm sure there'd be another who'd step into his place. A suitable candidate might be my nephew, Henry of Champagne. He is well known to Conrad's wife, Isabella. And being unmarried himself, and the owner of vast estates in the east of France, and a capable warrior who could easily hold Tyre on Countess Isabella's behalf, he would be ideal. Of course, there are reasons why I'm having this conversation with *you* in particular, Wildblood.'

'I'm your servant, lord-king. Command me.'

'I don't think I need to do that, do I? Tell me about your men. There must be one or two you'd consider wasted on the rebuilding work at Ascalon?'

'A couple of fellows spring to mind who'd be better employed elsewhere.'

'Then they are heading the wrong way. And so are you.'

The knight nodded, awaiting further instructions.

'When you return to your billet at Jaffa,' Richard said, 'you will find a locked trunk under your bedding. The only key that can open it is buried in the sand underneath, several inches down.'

Thurstan made to turn his animal around, but again the king spoke.

'If there's any kind of man I'll *never* trust, Wildblood, it's one who carves his meat neatly, who cuts it into clean, tidy strips.' His voice was low, emotionless. 'There are some joints that just need to be butchered, to be laid on the banquet table bloody.'

CHAPTER 14

Pandulf was startled. 'We're detaching from the army?'

'No.' Thurstan checked that his waterskins were full and the bolsters among his saddlebags packed with adequate rations. '*I'm* detaching from the army. You will remain here and provide a squire's service to Bertrand.'

Bertrand looked up from beside the fire, where he'd been fastening a new thong to his crucifix. 'I don't need a squire, my lord.'

'You have one, nevertheless.'

The army was camped along the roadside under the overhang of a sea-facing cliff. Spring was well advanced, so with each new day, the heat intensified, hence this noontime break from marching. They would resume at first light, though by then Thurstan would be gone.

Pandulf still looked confused. 'Where are you going, my lord?'

'On important business. That's all you need know.'

'You'll miss the election.'

'I doubt that one vote less will change the outcome. You have full command, Bertrand.' Thurstan took his horse's reins. 'Ramon! Ivan!'

The knight-captain and his serjeant cantered into view. Their animals too were laden with kit and supplies.

'A few weeks,' Thurstan told the others, swinging up into the saddle, and riding northward along the road, his two deputies following.

'De Vesqui and La Hors go with him, and we stay here?' Pandulf sounded mystified.

'I wouldn't ask any further questions if I were you, lad,' Bertrand replied.

One time, Thurstan had prayed a lot. For example, after the death of his young mother from that grotesque and bloody flux, during which, over a period of several days, she'd coughed out great fragments of her own lungs, with only her infant son to crouch beside the sweat-sodden bed and cling to her quivering hand, while downstairs his father's household riotously feasted.

He'd been a child of course, so perhaps it had been gullible of him, expecting the High and Mighty One to suddenly recall one of his more insignificant creatures from that Realm of Eternal Night. After all, in the whole history of mankind, God had only done that with His own precious son. Why extend the favour to some flyspeck beneath His notice? To the sole offspring of a brutal marcher baron, a minor man in real terms though the ender of countless other lives and one surely destined for the Pit himself? It had been sheer folly expecting anything else. But then folly was often found in those who were very young and very impressionable.

Such betrayals of everything Thurstan had once believed in made it easier to embark on missions like this one.

'I must admit, my lord,' Ramon La Hors said, 'I never imagined that you of all people would embark on a quest like this.'

'I suppose I'm flattered.' Thurstan eyed the arid landscape around them.

They'd deliberately taken a route inland, to minimise their contact with other travellers. They were visibly armed and mailed so to dissuade any would-be robbers, though they wore no household colours, just old, ragged mantles whose faded insignia meant nothing. Their agreed story was that they were English men-at-arms who'd lost hope that they'd ever see Jerusalem, and so were returning to Acre, from where they'd take ship to Europe.

'You're mad, Captain La Hors,' De Vesqui chuckled. 'Commander Wildblood's the deadliest killer among us. What is it they say among the rank and file… that there's "a hole where his soul should be"?'

'Even so, my lord,' La Hors said, 'you're an upright man, are you not?'

'Too many men have died to let this jackanapes, Conrad of Montferrat, capsize the Pilgrimage,' Thurstan replied, taking a swallow of water.

'You're certain the king won't betray us?'

Thurstan glanced at him. 'You have reason to think he might?'

'I can name four knights who trusted his father when they shouldn't have.'

De Vesqui guffawed. 'And then, when they dipped their swords in Archbishop Thomas's brains, he denied they were acting on his orders... hung them out to dry.'

'Count Conrad is no Thomas Becket,' Thurstan replied. 'Besides, we carry royal gold, do we not?'

La Hors patted the sack of twenty bezants clinking on his horse's flank. De Vesqui carried similar, though Thurstan's sack was larger, seeing as it contained another twenty for each of them, to be paid once the work was done. In addition, there was a further twenty for each on their return to King Richard's court. It wasn't the perfect safety net, but riches of this sort could never be easily explained unless they'd originated from some wealthy patron.

'In my experience, the trick is to do the job quickly, and care nothing for who says what,' De Vesqui said. 'The grander the target, the more chaos when he falls. They'll be too busy seeking a replacement to be asking who or why.'

'You're a genuine beast, Knight-Serjeant,' La Hors replied. 'You don't fear for your immortal soul?'

De Vesqui mused. 'Killing a Christian prince? My soul will be in peril, I don't deny it. But not for long. All we need do then is kill a few more Saracens, no? That's what the Holy Father says.'

'We might win an indulgence for killing Count Conrad,' Thurstan added. 'He's working against God's wishes.'

La Hors gave a sly smile. 'I wonder do you really believe that?'

Thurstan said nothing, but in his mind it was simple. Count Conrad had betrayed them all. And the balance of the war had changed because of it. In so many ways, Conrad of Montferrat, as King of Jerusalem, would be the rightful man to lead the Pilgrimage. A lawfully anointed ruler, a supreme soldier. But he wasn't Thurstan's overlord. In fact, his very existence was now a threat to Thurstan's overlord. There could only be one response to that. Was it right, was it wrong? Thurstan didn't care. The games these noblemen played were beyond morality, anyway.

'You fought in the Great Rebellion, did you not?' La Hors asked.

'You know I did,' Thurstan replied.

'I hear you slew a mighty number. And you only a stripling.'

'We have our duty, Knight-Captain.'

'And that's the justification?'

'Performing one's duty needs no justification.'

'Which brings me back to my former question.' La Hors was clearly enjoying himself. 'Do you really believe that? Something about your manner, your knightly bearing, the way you treat your underlings... tells me you don't.'

'And what do *you* feel about it, La Hors?' Thurstan retorted. 'You're a knight too. You swore chivalrous vows.'

To his surprise, La Hors took the question seriously. 'I struggled with it once. In the early days. Wreaking mayhem in the name of whatever master I served seemed contrary to the code. But in the end... You become immune, do you not?'

Thurstan was about to reply when, on a barren summit maybe half a mile east, he spied a figure on a horse, apparently watching them.

A sizeable figure even from this distance. Clad in heavy, crimson robes.

'Christ's name,' Thurstan breathed, his blood running cold. Without a word, he put spurs to his horse's flanks, goading it into a furious gallop.

De Vesqui and La Hors gave immediate pursuit. As the land tilted upward, Thurstan shielded his eyes against the sun. The figure was still there, wavering in the haze. The next thing, he was pounding along a dry gully, at the end of which, the gradient steepened dramatically. With grunts of effort, his horse ascended it.

'My lord?' La Hors called, close on his tail.

Sweat filmed Thurstan's vision. He wiped it away but briefly had lost sight of the sentinel figure. It ought to be just over the rise. But when he came onto the summit, it was nothing but dust and broken stones. He turned the animal around, riding first to one side, then the other, aware that La Hors and De Vesqui were with him.

'My lord?' La Hors asked again, breathless.

Thurstan circled the hilltop, taking in the vista on every side. He saw the odd isolated building, even patches of greenery, but no other signs of life.

It was possible there was a hidden ravine below, where someone might hide? He felt certain there wasn't. And yet still he saw that figure. On its black horse. In its crimson brocade. With a crimson mitre on its head.

'Were we being watched?' La Hors asked. 'Someone shadowing us?'

Thurstan shook his head. 'It's nothing. A mirage. We need to press on.'

He descended the slope. As he did, he heard them talking together.

'Is he ill?' De Vesqui wondered.

'Being cautious, I fancy,' La Hors replied. 'So should we be. When you're doing the Devil's work, you take no chances.'

CHAPTER 15

Three weeks later, as they crossed into the County of Tripoli, that region once known as Lebanon, to which the ancient port of Tyre was the main entry, even the landscape looked different. It was a flat coastal plain, but verdant, similar to Jaffa with its quilt-work of vineyards and olive groves.

'The land of milk and honey,' La Hors remarked. 'It really exists.'

The towns and villages on the road seaward all had the air of prosperity, each one a thriving market crammed with hagglers of every race and creed.

It was interesting, Thurstan thought. The people hereabouts would credit all their privilege to Count Conrad. Popular leaders could do that: claim responsibility for every stroke of good fortune and no one would question it. Everything about this place, certainly compared to the deserts surrounding Acre, or the harsh, sun-bleached mountains on the road to Jaffa, would owe to the administrative talents and innate beneficence of Count Conrad.

What better candidate, they must think, for kingship of this land?

His exceptional military skills only added to that. When Saladin, buoyed by his victory at Hattin, had arrived that following December, the count had met the sultan in open battle, inflicting a heavy defeat on him. Even now, Count Conrad was ready to resume hostilities. En-route through Tripoli, they passed many of those castles and keeps belonging to his barons. Mostly, they were built from solid stone and all in an excellent state, their battlements manned by what looked like companies of professional soldiers, multiple flags rippling from their towers.

In so many ways, Count Conrad was the future for a Christian Levant.

But orders were orders. As they joined the main road to Tyre, hundreds of newly arrived pilgrims, some of them monks and nuns, but the majority men under arms, including knights of many nationalities, flocked along it in an air of celebration.

'Makes your piss boil,' De Vesqui said quietly. 'That all our hopes rest with village idiots like these. Do they even know they're going the wrong way?'

'No doubt,' La Hors replied. 'And it's an easy choice for them, isn't it? Go to Richard's camp in the teeth of the war, or spend your days here, drinking and wenching? Either way you can claim you're doing God's work.'

'By this time tomorrow they'll have no choice in the matter,' Thurstan said. 'There'll be only one place they can go, because all else will be chaos.'

–

Tyre itself, though more of an island than Acre, was not dissimilar in outward appearance. It was joined to the land by a broad, paved causeway, and sheltered behind ancient sandstone walls, but even then, it sprawled impressively against the cerulean seascape. Originally built by the Phoenicians but strengthened since by a varied host of conquerors, it was said to be impregnable.

They passed into it through the great arched portal that was the eastern gate, among the hordes of newcomers. Inside, it was the usual tale of narrow streets, stinking of sweat, dung and rancid food, and teeming with people, but in due course, following the written instructions Thurstan had found in his tent at Jaffa, they located an inn called *The Seven Stars*.

It was tucked away in a backstreet close to the Cathedral of the Holy Cross, where the following morning, a Sunday, Count Conrad, in his usual fashion, would walk in company with his wife, Countess Isabella, and a single bodyguard, Sancho Martin, the so-called Green Knight, to the morning Mass.

The inn's windows were shuttered against the noon sun, while its rabbit warren of rooms and passages were dark, crowded and rowdy. They might have felt self-conscious, armed and carrying their essentials in kitbags, but most of the guests here were leaderless troops not yet assigned to the vast military camps spread across the plain to the north, and thus were at ease, guzzling cheap wine and cramming their mouths with hummus or shawarma. When Thurstan asked a serving girl for a man called Cyrus, a swarthy fellow appeared, rubbing his hands on a cloth. He was sturdy and wore a leather apron, but his dark eyes and rich blue-black beard and moustache implied that he was a Turk.

'You are Cyrus?' Thurstan asked.

'I am,' the fellow replied in accented French. 'And before you think to treat me like a servant, I own this establishment.'

'We are…'

'I know who you are. So please don't trouble me with your comical false names and identities. Come this way.'

He led them up a creaking back staircase, into a spacious chamber which, while it wasn't luxurious – its walls cracked, its ceiling dangling with cobwebs – was carpeted, contained several mattresses and opened through a pair of shuttered doors onto a timber veranda. The muggy heat from the port swam in, along with the clamour and stench, but it gave good vantage over the cathedral plaza.

Cyrus tucked his cloth into his belt. Then froze, as he felt the edge of Thurstan's bone-handled knife at his throat.

'You may not require to know who we are, friend,' the knight said, 'but we certainly require to know who you are.'

The Turk's dark-eyed gaze flirted from man to man. The brightly honed steel pressed on his Adam's apple. 'I told you. My name is Cyrus.'

'And who is Cyrus? And why would he be helping the likes of us?'

'Does the name Cemil mean anything to you?' Sweat glinted on Cyrus's forehead. 'Or the name Kalkan?'

'We're more interested in the name Cyrus,' Thurstan said.

'I am a Kalkan. It's my family name. And Cemil was my brother. He was a captain in the *turcopole* cavalry.'

'Go on.'

'Four years ago, his company fought in Count Conrad's army. During the battle for the city. They were close comrades.'

'And what changed?'

'My brother and nine of his men were captured by the Ayyubids.'

'The Ayyubids were defeated that day.'

'This is true. Count Conrad took many prisoners of his own. As is normal, a hostage-exchange was considered. But in my brother's case the stakes were high. The armies of Islam hold a particular contempt for the *turcopoles*.'

De Vesqui snorted. 'And you wonder why?'

'Don't be fooled into thinking the Muslim world unified,' Cyrus retorted. 'There are many divisions. Some sects within Islam hate each other even more than they hate you. In addition, Count Conrad was a gracious lord. Both to Christians and Muslims alike.'

'But not so much after the battle of Tyre?' Thurstan said.

'The prisoner exchange failed,' Cyrus replied. 'The Ayyubids offered my brother and his nine *turcopoles* for a similar number of high value prisoners in Count Conrad's dungeon.'

'And let us guess,' La Hors said, 'Count Conrad wasn't in the mood for that?'

'His true colours came through,' Cyrus explained. 'The *turcopoles* weren't so important to him. Not when the alternative might be treasure.'

'And the Ayyubids wouldn't pay?'

'They refused to offer gold, but in compromise, demanded fewer prisoners in return… and still Count Conrad said no. It was gold or nothing. His price went up.'

'Which I'm guessing was the end of your brother?' Thurstan said.

'His captors took him and his men to the far side of the battlefield, and nailed them naked to X-shaped crosses, after which they were covered in honey, so the ants could make a long, slow feast of them.'

'Jesus, Mary and Joseph.' Even De Vesqui seemed startled. 'You people do that to each other?'

'I told you the hatred runs deep,' Cyrus said. 'And now it runs deep for me. So, if you plan to destroy Saladin's power in this land, then who am I to stand in your way?'

'And if Count Conrad dies in the process, all the better, eh?' La Hors said.

Cyrus shrugged.

'Well,' Thurstan put his knife away, 'we can't promise you ants, Cyrus Kalkan. But we can promise you that he'll die.'

Cyrus nodded, breathing more easily. 'Your horses are in our stable?'

Thurstan nodded.

'I'll move them after dark,' the innkeeper said. 'There's a stable nearer the cathedral. You know this place?'

'We can find it.'

'You should familiarise yourself this evening, while all is calm.' He moved to the veranda and pointed down. 'From the stable, it's a short gallop along this road to the gate we call the Roman Gate. It is rarely used, but it is only barred. There is no key. I have arranged that from mid-morning tomorrow, it will be left open. All you need do when you flee the scene is collect your horses, which will be waiting for you, saddled, and leave by the Roman Gate. From there, it is a narrow path around the wall to the causeway, but you must travel at speed...'

'That way we can be attacked from overhead,' La Hors objected.

'As I say, be swift. I doubt the word will travel quickly enough for the sentries on the battlements to impede you, but it may reach the main gate in time for it to be closed. Stop for no one, even when you're across the causeway. From there, ride east into the uplands. At this time of year, it is dry... You'll leave few tracks.'

'If anyone does pursue, they'd better be ready to meet their God,' De Vesqui grunted.

'So long as your Count Conrad has met his Devil,' Cyrus replied.

–

That evening, they strolled nonchalantly. The roads and alleys still thronged, so they went unnoticed. They surveyed the Roman Gate, a tall arched portal, somewhat neglected but which was, as Cyrus had said, located at the end of a single passage, perhaps seven hundred yards as the crow flew from *The Seven Stars.*

After that, they toured the plaza, the Cathedral of the Holy Cross, an awesome structure of white stone, built by Archbishop William of Tyre in the style of the great basilicas at Canterbury and Chartres, sitting at its west end. The plaza itself, which was paved and roughly square, about two hundred yards by two hundred, and ringed by shops and taverns, was the airiest place in the city they had so far seen, but like everywhere else, was crowded with visitors, many newly arrived soldiers.

'The word on the street,' La Hors said, 'is that the Duke of Burgundy and his men haven't made it this far. Apparently, they've lodged themselves at Acre. The fickle duke is sickening with something.'

'The Lord works in mysterious and helpful ways,' De Vesqui said.

'Maybe so,' La Hors replied, 'but these adventurers could give us a problem.'

Thurstan didn't immediately respond. When he'd opened the trunk left for him in Jaffa, the several documents in there had contained a detailed plan of action, most likely drawn up by Guy de Lusignan's agents. Everything had been allowed for, except the possibility the occupants of Tyre might get in their way.

'We must trust to it being a Sunday morning,' he said. 'The churchgoers will be here, I grant you, but the bulk of these *routiers* will be sleeping off a heavy night's drinking.'

Despite this, they circled the square, reconnoitring for any further military posts, where members of Count Conrad's city guard might be on duty in the morning.

There were none.

Again, it was a sign of the count's overweening confidence. The majority of his forces, and they numbered *more* than ten thousand by now, were camped north of the city, under his very able general, Hugh of Tiberias, the Prince of Galilee. Since Hattin, that title was nominal rather than meaningful, though Tiberias was another whose famous military talents were being wasted here in the north.

If nothing else, that thought encouraged Thurstan. The war was in the south, not here. It was good to be reminded that Count Conrad's personal ambition was damaging the cause.

On the subject of excellent men, there was also the matter of Sancho Martin, Count Conrad's personal champion and bodyguard. A Spaniard by birth and already illustrious in his homeland, he'd come to the East alone and without fanfare, but quicky won renown, not just for his flowing emerald livery, but for his performance on the battlefield. In the struggle outside the city, Martin had so caught the eye that Saladin himself had sent an emissary, offering him a fortune if he would convert and fight for the armies of Islam.

Thurstan considered. They'd already agreed that when they went out on the morrow, La Hors would be armed with a crossbow. Martin, if he was on bodyguard duty, would likely be wearing mail. But if he was heading for the cathedral, he'd also be unhelmeted. A clean headshot wasn't always easy, but the real problem was that Thurstan didn't want to kill any more Christians unless it was unavoidable.

'You must leave Sancho Martin to me,' he finally said.

For once, neither La Hors nor De Vesqui raised any objection.

CHAPTER 16

The baronial apartments were strewn with broken furniture. Tapestries and other woven hangings had been pulled from the whitewashed walls and scattered across the rush-covered floors. Fire blazed in the huge hearth, but only because a rather fine chair – heavy of frame, carved in the Italian style – had been thrust into it. There was a table too, though this was covered with smashed crockery, while a carving knife stood upright in its polished surface.

Thurstan felt this place should be familiar, an impression enhanced by the glimpses he had through the arrow-slot windows of wooded hillsides grey with rain.

A tolling bell jolted him awake. He rolled over, grabbing for the hilt of his sword, to find himself restricted by the folds of his bedding. His eyes opened properly.

La Hors stood by the open shutters, gazing across the vista of flat-topped roofs. The great basilica blotted out half the sapphire sky. The day's heat was already seeping in.

'Shithole of a place,' De Vesqui grumbled, disentangling from his own bedroll. 'Hot as hellfire during the day, cold at night as a dead woman's crotch.'

'We won't ask how you know about that, Knight-Serjeant,' La Hors said.

Thurstan, wearing only leather breeches and an open shirt, joined him by the casement. 'How is it?'

'Quiter than yesterday.'

'Not for long, with that bell ringing. Ready yourselves. It's time.'

The Mass was to be said by Bishop Philip of Beauvais. De Vesqui had opined how delicious it would be if the traitorous bishop's favourite to break Richard's power in the Levant were to die on his own church steps. Preferably in front of his eyes.

Thurstan pondered. It would certainly enforce the message that there were consequences for treachery. But there'd be something maleficent about it too. It was a dark enough deed they were doing without finding glee in it. Ultimately, of course, it wouldn't matter to Count Conrad.

They checked that their horses awaited them in the small stable near to the plaza's south-east entrance, and that they were saddled, then loaded the beasts with all remaining items of essential kit, and having concealed a purse crammed with bezants in the straw, as was promised to Cyrus, Thurstan's mind moved to the business of despatching Count Conrad, whom they set eyes on from the adjoining street.

He was walking arm-in-arm with his beautiful, sylph-like wife, Countess Isabella.

Everything about the count spoke confidence and competence. He was tall and lean, though not ungainly. With his black, neatly trimmed hair and beard, and piercing blue eyes, there was a hint of the devilish rogue about him. But he dressed well, always – even on the battlefield, he'd been renowned as the tidiest man present – and carried himself with agile grace.

Of more concern to Thurstan was Sancho Martin, walking close behind. According to the stories, Martin had never been bested in combat, and the number of times he'd been tried was self-evident, for his closely shorn head and darkly handsome face had been gashed repeatedly, all these injuries now hardened into white scars. He wasn't a tall man, an inch or so under six feet, but he had square shoulders and a broad, compact body. The other key difference, of course, was that where Conrad was unarmed, clad in his Sunday attire of embroidered silver cloak, scarlet ankle-length tunic and cross-banded scarlet hose, Sancho Martin was fully mailed under his bright green mantle, and wore a longsword at his hip.

'At least he's bareheaded,' La Hors observed.

'We're here to eliminate a single target,' Thurstan reminded them. 'No other Christian should die unless it's absolutely necessary.'

De Vesqui gave a sneering smile.

'You find that funny, Knight-Serjeant?'

'Necessary for us to succeed in our task, Knight-Commander… or for us to succeed and get clean away.'

Thurstan had no response. It was a valid question.

They entered the square unnoticed because all three now wore the black habits and cowls of Benedictine monks, heads bowed, hands joined in prayer. They ambled towards the basilica in reverential fashion, but on a diagonal line that would intersect with the route Count Conrad, his wife and bodyguard were taking.

Even disguised, they felt exposed. There were many others on the great square, most heading the same way, some coming to speak with the count himself, always stopping and giving a quick, curt bow before addressing him. In each case he responded warmly. But as Thurstan had already noted, Count Conrad's overconfidence that he was among friends had ensured there was no significant military presence close by.

Save one.

Down at the east end of the plaza stood a row of taverns, and now a group of men-at-arms in mail-coats and dusty yellow surcoats were arrayed around tables at the front of them, drinking and talking. It was uncertain whether they'd intervene. They probably would if Thurstan and his lackeys dallied. He mentioned this prospect as they advanced. They were now in the centre of the plaza, just in front and to the left of their intended target, who continued to be delayed by flunkies. Sixty yards ahead, the steps swept up to the basilica's towering front door. Its bell tolled continuously. As De Vesqui had hoped, Bishop Philip had appeared in the open doorway, a resplendent figure in full regalia of white alb, green chasuble and white mitre, a gold and bejewelled crozier in his white gloved hand.

Sensing that the count and his lady were hastening, Thurstan glanced sidelong at the bowed hooded heads of his compatriots. 'On my command.'

The handsome couple approached from the side, less than ten yards away.

Still, Thurstan waited.

Five yards.

'*Allahu Akhbar!*' he bellowed, pulling loose a cord at his belt, the monastic apparel falling away to reveal a white tunic, white *ghutra*, and white trousers tied at the waist with a blood-red sash, the latter a clear sign of the Order of Assassins, the most militant Islamic sect in the East.

The other two flung off their monk garb too, revealing similar costumes. La Hors had used his to conceal the crossbow, which was already loaded. He dropped to one knee and took careful aim at the men-at-arms outside the tavern.

Thurstan and De Vesqui, meanwhile, lurched for their target, weapons drawn.

But in the space of five yards, several things happened.

Countess Isabella screamed. Count Conrad halted mid-stride. Sancho Martin stepped in front of him, longsword drawn.

Thurstan, armed only with Saracen weapons, in particular a *shamshir*, parried it with two lightning-fast strokes, but instead of slashing the bodyguard's throat with a backhand, chose to hit him with a gauntleted fist. The impact on Martin's jaw was solid; he went down heavily on the paving stones. Count Conrad meanwhile ducked De Vesqui's sweeping *kilij*, and struck with his knee, trying to catch his assailant in the groin, but De Vesqui wore an iron codpiece under his breeches and retaliated by smashing the count across the head with his pommel. The count staggered – and was stabbed in his midriff by Thurstan's bone-handled knife. The lethal blade penetrated nine or ten inches before Thurstan ripped it loose.

The count dropped to his knees, his gaping mouth a glut of crimson. Thurstan struck again, but the shrieking Isabella threw herself onto his arm. He wrestled to throw her loose, while De Vesqui's second weapon, a falchion, buried itself in the count's skull. Before he could yank it free, Sancho Martin, who was back on his feet, lunged from behind. Thurstan shouted and De Vesqui ducked way, leaving Thurstan to swing in.

A slashing blow from his *shamshir* opened the fallen nobleman's jugular. The count fell face-first in a ruby cascade, while De Vesqui fought sword-to-sword with Martin. Thurstan eyed the men-at-arms, who, briefly screened by the sudden chaos of running people, were now on their feet. Uncertainly, they lumbered forward. La Hors loosed a bolt, and though seventy yards off, the closest went down to one knee, clutching his left breast, before pitching onto his face.

The others scattered, diving for cover.

'We need to go!' La Hors said as he rapidly reloaded.

Thurstan wheeled to De Vesqui, who, despite his terrifying reputation, wasn't having it all his own way, though the count's bodyguard was wobbling on his feet, a legacy of his broken, lopsided jaw. The brutish giant's sweat flew as he cut and parried, but at last he struck past his injured opponent's guard, hewing his left thigh, a stroke so fierce that the blade cut through the mail. Blood pumping freely, Martin tottered away, only to take another punch from Thurstan, this one so fierce that he was unconscious before he hit the ground.

Thurstan looked again at the count, a huge, *clairet*-coloured lake pooling around him, his weeping wife dabbled in it as she knelt there and cradled his lifeless form.

'We should take his head,' De Vesqui panted. 'To be sure.'

'We're sure! Go!' Thurstan pushed him towards La Hors, who'd launched a second bolt, dropping another man-at-arms, then glanced one final time at the church, where Bishop Philip had retreated inside, the heavy door now closed behind him. *He* was no Thomas Becket either. 'Quickly! Both of you!'

The dread garb of the Assassins was all it took for a passageway to clear before them as they fled. They retrieved their horses from the empty stable, and a few seconds later were riding hard for the Roman Gate, which stood open, as promised.

—

'These Saracen bladesmiths know their trade,' De Vesqui said, turning the *kilij* in his hand as they rode south along a hillside track.

Such had been the confusion in the city that there'd been no pursuit. They'd even had time to change back into their pilgrim knight garb and now, several hours later, were travelling slowly to give their horses respite.

'They're lighter than we're used to,' he said. 'But they work. With your speed, my lord, you should keep one of these to hand at all times.'

For the first time since they'd left Tyre, Thurstan spoke, but to La Hors, not De Vesqui. 'Didn't I tell you to spare Christian lives?'

'Where possible.' La Hors was unperturbed. 'And it wasn't. Not in that crowd, at that distance.'

Thurstan could hardly begrudge him that. In truth, given the crossbow was not a knightly weapon, and one the likes of Ramon la Hors had no cause to practise with, those had been two remarkable shots. He'd hit both targets squarely, which had proved sufficient to dissuade the rest of the men-at-arms in the plaza from following.

'Your determination to spare almost cost us, my lord,' De Vesqui said.

Thurstan cast him a sharp look.

'You could have opened that Spaniard's gullet on the first pass, but you chose to punch him instead. Which enabled him to fight us for longer.'

Thurstan said nothing. The dull ache in his hip had returned in the last day or so and seemed to intensify as he pondered the awful business of murder. It was an interesting exercise to try and fool yourself into thinking there were good ways and bad ways to carry it out. It was also fruitless.

'Is it not also the case,' La Hors said, 'that those who are helping the enemy are our enemy too? We are here in the Levant to destroy Saladin's power. To restore the Holy Places. Those among us who are hampering that should be dealt with accordingly.'

Again, it was true. Ayyubid warriors were under orders to slaughter *turcopoles* whenever they caught them. Why should the Christian militant behave differently with their own turncoats?

'Nasty business, war.' De Vesqui gave a guttural chuckle.

'Enough talk,' Thurstan said curtly.

'Yes, enough talk, Knight-Serjeant,' La Hors agreed. 'We've got our haloes to polish in case we meet someone on the road.'

De Vesqui chuckled again. 'They'd better hope we don't. We're not far enough away from Tyre yet. We meet anyone round here, Christian, Muslim, Jew… they're dead men. Isn't that right, Commander?'

Thurstan said nothing. Because this also was true.

CHAPTER 17

It was June before they returned to Jaffa, the landscape, which briefly had been filled with blossoms and greenery, drying out again, rippling in the heat. Before they entered the great encampment, they tidied themselves up and redonned their *Familia Regis* livery.

They found it a hive of activity, Thurstan puzzled to see wagons and other vehicles being packed with water barrels, sacks of grain and fodder, baskets of fruit, salted meat, and heaps of newly forged weapons, helmets and shields. Infantrymen were drilling, archers and crossbow companies practising on the butts. When he stopped a man-at-arms and asked what was happening, he was told that the king had returned from Ascalon early.

At the quarters of the *Familia Regis*, they found Bertrand, wearing mail leggings and an open leather tunic, honing his longsword on a whetstone. His gold-and-ruby cross hung at his throat.

'You've caught the sun, my lord,' he said, although he too was tanned – his reddish hair and beard burnished to a bright red-gold. He didn't seem surprised to see them, or especially pleased. As greetings went, there was little warmth.

'You're back from Ascalon earlier than expected,' Thurstan replied. 'What's happening?'

Bertrand regarded him curiously. 'You haven't heard?'

'Would I ask?' Thurstan swung down from the saddle.

'The pieces on the board have moved. Conrad of Montferrat has been murdered. They're saying it's the Order of Assassins.'

Thurstan pursed his lips. Bertrand watched him closely.

'Convenient,' De Vesqui guffawed. 'The timing couldn't be better.'

'Cut down in the main square in his own city,' Bertrand said.

'When did this happen?' Thurstan asked, ignoring Bertrand's close scrutiny.

Bertrand the penitent, the honest pilgrim, the spare conscience in case you need one.

Thurstan didn't. Or so he kept telling himself.

'We don't know for certain,' Bertrand said. 'The news arrived by ship a few days ago.'

'You seem unhappy about it?' Ramon la Hors observed.

'I'm neither happy nor unhappy, Knight-Captain,' Bertrand retorted. 'I neither disapprove... nor approve. But if nothing else, it's broken the stalemate. Or it would have.'

Thurstan frowned. '*Would* have?'

Bertrand shrugged. 'The king is leaving. Or so the rumours hold. That's why he brought us back to Jaffa.'

Thurstan was stumped. 'The king is leaving?'

'Philip of France has made an alliance with Prince John. They're planning to carve up Richard's territories in Europe.'

De Vesqui's grin faded. 'This had better not mean we don't get paid.'

'And the rest of us?' Thurstan was still stunned. '*We're* going too?'

Bertrand shrugged again. 'I imagine so, but no one's told me anything official.'

'Commander?' De Vesqui growled again. 'Our pay?'

'Perhaps if *you* were to see the king?' Bertrand said.

Thurstan nodded distractedly. Either this information was inaccurate, or it was incomplete. If Richard was departing, why was the army preparing to move? 'Is this the only news?' he asked.

'Count Henry of Champagne has ridden to Tyre,' Bertrand said. 'He was en-route to deliver the news that Conrad had won the election.'

'So now Count Henry controls Tyre?' Thurstan sought to confirm.

'In Richard's name, of course. Whether he'll be able to command Conrad's forces, I don't know. Probably not the French. They're still at Acre. We hear the Duke of Burgundy is ill and like to die.'

Pandulf emerged from between the tents. He smiled. 'Welcome back, my lord.'

Thurstan handed the lad his reins. 'Nothing has been left for me? No package or letter?'

'None.'

Thurstan's thoughts were too muddled to make sense of it. 'I'm for the keep.'

'Commander?' De Vesqui said again. Both he and La Hors had dismounted.

Thurstan lurched towards him until they were nose-to-nose. 'If you mention your pay one more time, Knight-Serjeant, I'll personally beat you senseless. Do you understand?'

De Vesqui cracked a half-smile. 'No disrespect, my lord, but you'll need to hit me harder than you hit...'

The words faltered as curved steel pressed into his ribs.

'You like these Saracen blades, do you not, Knight-Serjeant?' Ramon La Hors said quietly. 'Take care you don't become intimately acquainted with one.'

De Vesqui's eyes rolled sideways, to check that his normally reliable ally was being serious, but the cold, hard expression left no doubt.

Bertrand and Pandulf watched this exchange in silence, the squire pop-eyed with surprise. Thurstan took the reins off him and led his horse towards the pens.

'You heard about Count Conrad?' the lad asked, running after him.

'I have now. The Assassins are a ruthless band. Most of the Islamic world is terrified of them, so to us Christians they pose a particular and constant threat.'

'Apparently, they only *think* it was the Assassins. They aren't absolutely sure.'

'It *will* be,' Thurstan affirmed. 'They've killed emirs, caliphs, viziers... they draw the line nowhere. Anyone they consider a threat is fair game. Anyone.'

CHAPTER 18

By the looks of it, Richard had not just brought the *Familia Regis* back from Ascalon, but also the bulk of his army. When Thurstan rode through the camp, the activity had intensified, every household making urgent preparations. It didn't make sense, unless Richard intended to take his entire host with him back to Europe, which, if he did, would be a complete betrayal of the Pilgrimage.

When he reached the gates to Jaffa itself, thousands of logs and branches had been lashed together to form scaffolding along the perimeter where new walls were in the process of construction. Innumerable local labourers as well as the king's engineers, clambered on the skeletal structure like apes, hammering and mortaring the broken stones back into place. Thurstan didn't know how the work at Ascalon was proceeding. Hopefully equally speedily, as that would be a more crucial obstacle in the path of Saladin's reinforcements, but it seemed the majority of the workers who'd originally been assigned there had now been brought here.

Refortifying the town made sense. But why was the army moving, and where to?

It was mystifying. And also frustrating.

The secret mission he had just accomplished had been supposed to change everything in their favour. The ten-thousand-strong fighting force that had wasted its time at Tyre for almost an entire year had been expected to come here. And yet now it was *this* army that was leaving its comfortable base... while King Richard was leaving the Holy Land altogether. Or so the gossips said.

When Thurstan reached the keep, he handed his reins to a groom and strode to the main door, where two of his own men, Gui de Verneuil and Robert de Quincy, snapped to attention.

'No one may enter, my lord,' De Quincy, a Scottish knight, said.

Thurstan nodded. 'Very good. I'm glad to see you're both awake.'

Neither stepped aside. 'No one, my lord,' De Quincy said again, visibly unhappy.

'Are you mad?' Thurstan replied. 'Stand down.'

'The king will see no one,' De Verneuil grunted. He was a Breton by origin, and a surly, hulking fellow, who'd often verged on impertinence.

'Forgive us, lord,' De Quincy said. He was a younger man. 'But *you* were expressly named.'

Thurstan eyed them long and hard. Then ripped his longsword from its scabbard. The sentries responded in kind, though clearly neither wanted it.

'Infighting in the Christian camp,' came another voice. 'The very last thing we need.' Bishop Hubert ambled towards them, two monks in close attendance. 'Lord Thurstan,' he said amiably. 'Walk with me.'

'Pardon, your grace... I need to see the king.'

'No, you don't.' The bishop smiled as he passed. 'Any questions, I have the answers.'

Thurstan glared once more at the two sentries, before sheathing his sword and stalking after the bishop. They found themselves a table, where the cleric seated himself, bidding Thurstan take the bench opposite. Thurstan did so.

As was his way when he wasn't saying Mass, Bishop Hubert wore a monastic habit tied with a rope around a waist now restored to its familiar excessive girth. Even his cheeks were round and rosy. They were clearly well provisioned here at Jaffa, which made it all the more puzzling that they were leaving.

'Is it true, your grace?' the knight asked. 'Is the king departing the Levant?'

'He is.' The bishop seemed remarkably unconcerned. With a waggle of his plump hand, he sent his two attendants off. 'But not straight away. The information from England is vague. Of course, we've sought clarity. And in the meantime, His Highness has advanced his plans to take Jerusalem.'

Thurstan sat back. So, the army was not making urgent preparations because it was departing. But because the main prize was again in sight.

'Fresh troops have arrived from Tyre?' he asked.

'Not yet, but we understand they're en-route. Some of them.'

'*Some?*'

'The message from Count Henry is that several of those different factions sworn to Conrad are in a quandary. Do they continue the fight under Richard's banner, or do they consider they've discharged their duty and now head for home?'

'Discharged their duty?' Thurstan almost choked. 'They've sat on their arses for eleven months.'

'To be fair, many fought Saladin when he tried to take Tyre.'

'But we need them here.'

'Alas, many minds have been poisoned against Richard. French work, of course. Count Henry is attempting to mitigate this. He's already taken Countess Isabella for his wife...'

Despite all, Thurstan was surprised by that. 'He wasted little time.'

'We agree on that, at least. Less than a week after her husband's death. Positively indecent. But both Henry and Richard would likely argue that time is not on our side.'

'So, Count Henry of Champagne is the new King of Jerusalem?'

'The *de facto* king, one might say.'

'And what of King Guy?'

'In compensation, Richard has made him Lord of Cyprus.'

'And will he be happy with that?'

'He'll have no choice. But it's a prosperous island, and quite a prize for a man who's done nothing but fail in his life.'

'What of his knights and barons?'

'Most are hopeful Richard will restore them to their lost fiefs, so they remain.'

'Most?'

'Some feel they have no hope of advancement under a new ruler, so they go.'

Thurstan looked at him askance. 'So actually, we are weaker than before?'

'Whether we're weaker or stronger, Wildblood, the odds are now in our favour. The curtain wall at Ascalon is complete, while the king has gone one better, and captured the fortress of Darum, which is even further south and can only be a major difficulty for any forces coming north from Egypt. In addition, the road to Jerusalem is drier and firmer, most of our wounded are healed and the army is largely re-equipped.'

His monks returned, bringing baskets of bread, cheese and sliced cold meats, and two goblets of wine. The bishop tucked in. 'Eat,' he urged his guest. 'We can't let quality fare go to waste.'

'You're aware, your grace,' Thurstan said, 'that I've just returned from Tyre myself?'

'Of course. Now, eat.'

'We're in the midst of a war for the soul of Christendom, are we not? And yet the only blood befouling my blade is the blood of fellow Christians.'

There was no risk in him revealing this. The written instructions he'd received for his mission to Tyre had come from none other than Bishop Hubert himself.

The bishop eyed him coolly. 'We thought you understood our position.'

'So did I. Because now that position has seemingly changed.'

'The tides of war, Wildblood. We exert no control over them.'

'So, it was all for nothing?'

The bishop licked crumbs of cheese from his fingers. 'It's not something I care to discuss out here in the open.'

'I'd ask for shrift, your grace. But I'm not sure you're the right man to provide it.'

'Concern for your soul, Wildblood? This is something new. Have you had a "Road to Damascus" moment?'

Wildblood paused.

Had he?

Had the Red Bishop come from the Devil…? Or from somewhere else?

Again, he shook it from his thoughts. Its origins lay nowhere except in his own mind. He was unhappy at what he'd done in Tyre because to kill one of one's own was a momentous step for any man to take, whatever the reason.

'It matters not,' the bishop said. 'Someone else will hear your confession, if that's what you wish.'

'On which subject, my two accomplices…'

'*Comrades*, surely?'

'My two *accomplices* are owed additional monies. And if they don't get it, they too may become something we can't control.'

'How much are they owed?'

'Twenty bezants each. The final instalment of their agreed fee. I'd hoped it would be waiting on our return, but it wasn't.'

'No doubt the king considered that you might not return.' The bishop broke himself another lump of cheese. 'And withheld it until he knew otherwise.'

'Or maybe he hoped we wouldn't return?'

The bishop eyed him sharply. 'That isn't true. Believe it or not, the king likes you.'

'So much that he won't even speak to me.'

'A common-sense precaution. At some point the focus of blame will shift from the Order of Assassins to Conrad's other enemies.'

'So, it's for the best if he keeps a killer like me at arm's length?'

'Exactly,' the bishop said. 'Never fear. I'll arrange for payment to be made.'

'You know, your grace, when Ivan de Vesqui, an unthinking brute by almost any standards, likened what we did in Tyre to the martyrdom at Canterbury Cathedral, I dismissed it. I said that it wasn't comparable. I was wrong, wasn't I?'

Bishop Hubert said nothing, and Wildblood understood why. No churchman liked to be reminded of the murder of Thomas Becket. In the long run, the English Church gained greater influence because it happened, but it remained proof to many that the authority of God was sometimes less tangible than the authority of laymen armed with swords.

'I only hope I don't now face the same fate that befell FitzUrse, De Morville, De Tracy and Le Breton,' Thurstan said. 'Excommunication, exile, death.'

'So, it's not guilt you feel, but fear?'

'Perhaps both.'

'You needn't feel either. The king still requires you.'

'Of course. Who else will brave the boiling oil to escalade Jerusalem's walls?'

The bishop stuffed more bread into his mouth. 'It won't be you.'

Thurstan was confused.

'It isn't just the King of England who requires you, Wildblood. It's the kingdom itself. We have another special task in mind, which will take you far from Jerusalem.'

'Which innocent lamb will I need to strike down this time?'

At that, the bishop reddened. 'Listen, my friend... Conrad of Montferrat was no innocent lamb. So, get that idea out of your head.' He sat back. 'Conscience is a good thing, admirable even. But it can also eat away at a fellow, weaken him at a time when iron resolve is called for. So, save your regrets for when the battles are won.'

'What is the mission?' Thurstan asked.

'This one will be different. For one thing, I'll be accompanying you.'

'You?'

'Who else is familiar with King Guy's network of agents and informers? They're proving very useful to us, by the way.'

'So I've noticed.'

'You know the fortress al-Yuqhar?'

Thurstan didn't and said so.

'Formerly St Hildegard's Tower. It stands in the land called Edom. Far to the south-east. Once the property of Humphrey de Toron, it's now held by a certain al-Qazairi... an emir of Ayyubid origin. He was a prominent figure at Hattin, but after Jerusalem fell, he engaged in looting, even though Saladin had strictly forbidden it.'

'Sounds as though he's Saladin's problem, not ours.'

'More of a problem than you may think.' The bishop leaned forward. 'Al-Yuqhar is supposed to be impregnable. But that isn't the sole reason Saladin holds back from punishing this ne'er-do-well. It seems he's the custodian of a great treasure. Something the Islamic world is so keen to possess that, were Saladin to send forces to al-Yuqhar, Qazairi would spirit it away, maybe even donate it to the sultan's foes to win their favour.' The churchman smiled. 'You're right to look intrigued, Wildblood. There can only be one artifact of such unimaginable value to Muslims and Christians alike.'

'The Cross?'

'The True Cross. King Guy's gravest sin was not losing Jerusalem but losing the apparatus on which our Saviour was put to death. As long as Christendom possessed the Cross, our future was secure. And now these Mohammedan dogs have charge of it.'

'And you want me to retrieve what the Sultan of Egypt cannot?' Thurstan said.

'You won't be going alone.'

'No, I'll have *you* with me. How reassuring.'

Such was Bishop Hubert's enthusiasm that he refused to be insulted. 'The king has permitted us to take a proper fighting force. Not an army... that would attract too much attention, but a company of elite men. A few hundred perhaps.'

'A few hundred of the best men in the world can hardly storm the walls of an impregnable fortress,' Thurstan replied.

'Thanks to King Guy's spies, we have a map, which shows a secret entrance to al-Yuqhar. An old mining tunnel dug by the Saracens when they captured it from De Toron. They filled the tunnel once they had no further use of it. Or that's what the rest of the world believed. In truth, they only filled the entrance. We are advised that with half a day's digging, it can be cleared.'

Thurstan's thoughts drifted. So many times, he'd cast doubt on whether the True Cross existed. What had it been, a thousand years, since Christ had hung there? Surely it would have perished by now? Or if it hadn't, how could they know it was the same artefact? Bodies on crosses had adorned this landscape when the Jews were in revolt. The Romans had cut down whole cedar forests to provide timber. But if it *was* the True Cross. If by some machination of God Himself, they knew the moment they laid eyes and hands upon it that this shapeless lump of worm-eaten decay had once been soaked in celestial blood, what would that mean for the world?

What would it mean for him?

I don't believe in God. Or at least, God doesn't believe in me.

This had been his mantra since the death of his mother, and especially so since the death of Gwendolyn so soon after they were wed. First the loss of the only thing he'd ever cared about as an innocent child. And then, all those years with axe and sword in service of king and overlord, repaid by the loss of the only thing he'd ever cared about as an adult.

But the True Cross…?

If nothing else, retrieval of so valuable an artefact would be a worthier cause than others of late. Here would be a quest on a par with those Arthurian challenges he'd heard about as a youngster in his father's hall at Kingstone, when listening in wonder to the *jongleurs* who'd visit at Christmas and Eastertide.

'How far is al-Yuqhar?' he asked.

'A hundred and twenty miles.'

'Across open desert? In summer?'

The cleric remained unruffled. 'You've already performed one miracle on our behalf, Wildblood. We feel sure you can manage this one. There is one thing, however. The mission is to be kept a secret. For this reason, you may take some trusted members of the *Familia Regis*, but the bulk must stay with the king. Otherwise, questions will be asked.' He lowered his voice. 'We especially don't want word reaching archbishops Ubaldo and Gerhard.'

'I see,' Thurstan said. 'This holy prize will be England's alone?'

Bishop Hubert smiled, now with a hardness around his eyes. 'It certainly won't be Rome's.'

CHAPTER 19

At first, they travelled south along the coastal road, within a few days passing Ascalon, its new outer wall overlooking the road at close range, its battlements crammed with men-at-arms who watched them curiously, before veering inland, heading south-east.

It was high summer, and the heat, as the two-hundred-strong company trekked across the northern reach of the Negev Desert and into the hills of Judah, was like a kiln. Even though Thurstan followed Richard's own method of marching from dawn to noon and resting during the furnace of the afternoon, there was little cover to be had. It was a broken, blistered land, an endless vista of drifting sand and sun-scorched rock. Every horizon shimmered in an oily haze.

'So, this is the Holy Land,' Bertrand said, drooping in his saddle. He carried no banner. None of them did. All their colours were concealed under raggedy, sand-coloured Bedouin garb. 'More like a land of demons.'

'There's more in that than you know,' Bishop Hubert replied, grey-faced and running with sweat. 'These empty places in the East are filled with evil spirits. When Rome was Christianised, the new veneration of Christ in Eastern cities where once his followers were scourged and burned drove the monstrosities that inspired those horrors out. They lurk in the wilderness still. The hermits of old suffered horribly. Anthony the Great, they say, was taunted by the most hateful devils… and that wasn't far from here. Just past the Egyptian border.'

Thurstan planted a hand on his hip, which ached again, and gazed across the open plain. He half-expected to see a distant horseman in red, but nothing was visible, which came as no surprise. He continually fought off the notion that there was anything curious about his hip wound. He'd suffered many injuries in combat, and the majority made themselves known for years after.

Pandulf rode up beside him. 'Did you hear the bishop,' the squire asked quietly. 'My lord, do you think… Bishop Belphagor?'

Thurstan pulled at his water bottle. 'I cannot believe we are still talking about this.'

'You say it was a fever dream, but… the way you fought at Arsuf. And then…'

'And then?' Thurstan asked.

The lad swallowed, his thin face red with sunburn. 'Was it you who struck down Count Conrad?'

'If it had been, it would have been a wasted effort, don't you think?'

'Isn't that the way devils work? You give them your soul… then they trick you and laugh at you.'

'Pandulf, no one gave their soul to anyone. We are here to *save* our souls.' Thurstan glanced round at him. 'And now I have a question for you.'

The lad seemed surprised, and not a little bit pleased, though from Thurstan's perspective, it was no more than a distraction tactic. He wasn't just embarrassed to discuss Bishop Belphagor openly. The subject still nagged at him; in fact, 'worried him' would have been a more honest term.

'When are you going to fulfil your potential as a knight-in-training?'

Pandulf's face fell. 'My lord?'

'You scamper round the camp at everyone's beck and call, like a servant. You're supposed to be a squire.'

'I…' The lad looked abashed.

'I sparred with Bertrand while you were away. He said my sword work was coming on.'

'I'll need to see for myself. When I took you on, you were a waif, yes? A vagabond. Is that not so?'

'Of course, but…'

'I've invested much to take you away from all that. It's time I had a return.'

Pandulf looked dismayed to hear all this, so much so that Thurstan felt mild remorse, though it hadn't just been a reprimand. The lad *did* need to harden himself. Before he could say more though, they were both distracted.

Gradually, initially in his subconscious, Thurstan had become aware of a low, persistent rumbling, but now it grew steadily louder.

'What is that?' He turned in his saddle. 'Thunder?'

'There isn't a cloud in the sky,' Pandulf said.

Just behind them, Bishop Hubert also looked confused. Others in the column were reacting in similar fashion, those on horseback turning their animals to scan the empty terrain, those on foot halting, unharnessing weapons. The rumbling grew louder, deeper, progressively more malign, perhaps because they'd now realised there was a rhythm at the heart of it, a slow, steady, thumping beat.

Several hundred yards to the north-east, raised ground formed a low ridgeline. Thurstan spurred towards it at a canter, Bertrand on his left, Ivan de Vesqui on his right. They dismounted below the ridge, and near the top dropped to all fours, peering down into a shallow valley. The rumbling was now a clear, continuous pounding. It emanated from directly below, where a colossal host of spear-carrying footmen marched in ranked formation, lines of drummers interspersed between them.

'God's holy name!' Bishop Hubert muttered when he came up. Thurstan grabbed his shoulder and pulled him down onto his belly.

The air throbbed to the drumbeat, dust and pebbles shuddering.

'Saladin's reinforcements,' De Vesqui said. 'They've diverted inland from the coast. Probably to avoid Darum and Ascalon.'

'Maybe,' Thurstan said. 'But this force is coming from the south-east.'

'They aren't Ayyubid regulars either,' Captain Mercadier added.

They looked closer. The vast majority of the figures below were ebony skinned. Nubians then, some wearing mail-shirts, others bare-chested, but all turbaned, the sun glinting from their array of spears and sabres, and the bosses of their circular shields.

'Slave soldiers, I reckon,' Mercadier added. 'Sent up from Arabia.'

Thurstan thought about that. Saladin wasn't just relying on his own forces from Egypt. Clearly, the call for assistance had gone out across the whole Islamic world.

Meanwhile, whosoever this army was, it marched in clean, serried fashion, cohort after cohort, drums booming.

'So many,' Pandulf said, voice tremulous. 'Ten thousand, wouldn't you say?' But then he caught his master's eye, and he straightened his face and squared his shoulders. 'Though they're only footsloggers. Hardly be a threat to our heavy cavalry.'

'Doubtless,' Thurstan replied. 'But we still must send a galloper back.'

'Send him to whom?' Bishop Hubert asked. 'The king, or the garrison at Jaffa?'

Thurstan considered. 'Wherever the king is, he has the bulk of the army with him. And as Pandulf says, this force might look and sound ferocious, but on the open plain against heavy horse, they'll be leaves in the wind. I say we warn Jaffa. The defenders there are watching the coastal road. If we don't send word, they'll be taken by surprise.'

Mumbles of agreement greeted this.

'I volunteer to take the message, my lord,' Robert de Quincy said.

Thurstan appraised him. Of the two *Familia Regis* knights who'd recently defied him, he was the one who seemed most contrite. 'I have a strong, fast horse. I can cut back the way we came. It's less direct than the route these devils are taking, but once I hit the coastal road, the going will be smoother. I can drop word at Ascalon too... not just to warn the garrison, but to request extra men for the defence of Jaffa.'

'Shouldn't we return there, ourselves?' Bertrand said, still watching the river of burnished muscle and shining steel. 'We're only two hundred men. But those are our comrades at Jaffa, and even with assistance from Ascalon, they'll be understrength.'

Thurstan considered things again. They'd need to make a battle-march all the way back to get ahead of this new enemy, which in this heat would render them useless when they arrived.

'The mission we are set upon is too important,' Bishop Hubert intervened. 'We can't abandon it.'

'But your grace,' Bertrand protested, 'if Jaffa falls...'

'If it falls, it falls.' The bishop averted his gaze. 'Our main hope rests with the king anyway. Though even he may not succeed if we fail to secure the item we've been sent to retrieve.'

'What item?' Bertrand glanced at Thurstan. 'My lord, we've followed you this far on trust but look what we're up against. We can't go on and on if we don't know why.'

'I'll tell you everything when we next camp,' Thurstan said, aware of the bishop stiffening, though no verbal reprimand was made. If nothing else, Bishop Hubert was a pragmatist. He probably realised they were far enough now from the rest of the Pilgrimage to be open about their plan.

'According to the map, there's a water sign at the end of this valley,' Captain Mercadier said. 'A spring or well. Most likely these heathen half-men will have been there ahead of us. Pissed in it, done God knows what to it... but it's the only water for miles.'

Thurstan turned to the others. 'We pitch camp when the enemy's passed. Then all will be revealed.'

When they heard they were to recover the True Cross, there was initial stupefaction among the men. It was nighttime, and they sat in concentric circles around a small campfire just south of the water-hole where they'd been able to replenish their dwindling supplies. Bishop Hubert stood alongside the flames to sermonise as he passed on the good news. He'd even replaced his drab, weatherworn travelling clothes with ceremonial vestments.

Once they got over their shock, the men were delighted.

They hadn't just travelled all this way and endured such hardships to liberate the Holy Places, but to return those sacred artefacts plundered when Jerusalem fell. And this was the greatest artefact of all.

They spoke excitedly, clasping each other's hands, slapping each other's shoulders. The only ones whom to Thurstan seemed less enthused were Captain Mercadier and Knight-Serjeant Ivan de Vesqui. The latter had been a surly presence thus far. Most likely because

Ramon La Hors had been left behind to command the *Familia Regis* during King Richard's second advance on Jerusalem. Presumably, the brutish serjeant felt weaker without his usual ally. Captain Mercadier was another matter. Though widely disliked by the knights of the *Familia* for his commoner status, he was also intelligent, not just cunning but possessed of a backcountry wisdom born through hard experience. No doubt, he too wondered how true the True Cross could be, and how greatly even a genuine relic of that sort, which would surely be rotted and scabrous by now, could actively change their fortune.

'You don't believe in miracles?' Thurstan asked him.

Mercadier stood with arms folded. 'Faith can galvanise men to great things, my lord. Look at these infidels, who once were nothing but desert tribes. We don't lack for it ourselves. But, more relevantly perhaps, we lack numbers.'

'Which is why the Cross can only help us.'

'It can't do any harm. I understand that.'

More and more of the men embraced each other. At last, they felt they were on a mission from the Almighty. What surer way could there be to erase their sins?

'It may demoralise the opposition,' Mercadier added. 'If it reminds them there's nothing they have that we can't take for our own… that our God is mightier than theirs.'

Thurstan wasn't so sure about the latter, but he liked the idea that this new huge Muslim force had disembarked from its homeland, tramping north with great fanfare and menace, while a small company slipped behind it and wreaked irreparable damage.

'Wasn't it irregular soldiering like this that helped you capture all those castles in the Aquitaine?' he asked.

Mercadier mused. 'Partly, my lord. But also, that was because an awful lot of our opponents were sleeping on the job.'

'I can't promise they'll be doing that at al-Yuqhar.'

'I didn't think so.' Mercadier shrugged. 'Otherwise, why would you need two hundred of the best fighting men in England and Normandy?'

CHAPTER 20

The castle sat on a high rocky outcrop. From what Thurstan could see, it was a typically austere Norman design, rectangular, with four battlemented ramparts, each about sixty feet from the ground, five round towers, which stood about thirty feet higher, one at each corner and one in the middle of the north-facing wall. It lacked any ornamentation, the cruciform arrow slits intended for the use of crossbows by defenders, which was understandable given that al-Yuqhar, or St Hildegard's Tower, to use its original name, had first been built by King Fulk of Jerusalem, who'd completed it in the 1140s. A sure sign of its hasty construction was that it lacked an inner keep. By the looks of it, the various storehouses, stables and apartments would be located around the inside of its walls, facing into the courtyard. The current ownership of al-Yuqhar was visible via the single banner fluttering from its north-east tower, its background pale blue, Arabic writing garnishing it in handsome gold thread.

The fact that it was situated on high ground, with drop-away cliffsides to the east, north and west, gave it phenomenal vantage over the encircling terrain. The only actual access was on the south side, where the main gate was located. This was reachable by an access road, a man-made ramp, which ascended gradually and over several hundred yards, so that anyone approaching would be spotted well in advance of their arrival, and if they were foes, subjected to a bombardment of arrows, javelins and other missiles. Though only a small number of sentries were visible on the battlements, their spiked helmets and polished breastplates glinting, it was obvious to any soldier who knew his trade that anyone attempting an escalade here would be so impeded getting close to the wall that a full complement of defenders could easily have been called into action by the time they did.

'I can see why they call it impregnable.' Thurstan climbed from the high heap of rocks from behind which he'd surveyed it. 'All they need is a decent company of archers and any assault up that approach road will meet with disaster.'

Bishop Hubert shook his head. 'There's no need for us to attack up that road.'

'We hope,' Thurstan replied.

—

The reconnaissance party moved in single file, as quickly and quietly as they could... as much as that was possible with the bishop among them. As they scuttled from one heap of rocks to the next, al-Yuqhar drew closer, not a flicker of firelight on its darkened ramparts. Its north-east tower soon loomed over them, an obsidian monolith on the star-speckled sky. It was an ominous sight, but to Thurstan's mind, no bastion was ever as indomitable as it looked. When they reached the foot of the cliff, he dropped to his knees in the dune, produced a small shovel from under his dun-coloured cloak, and began digging. The others followed suit, and soon had exposed an upright fissure in the rock face.

It was a natural cleft, roughly triangular and rising to just over six feet, but it was narrow. The larger men among them, the likes of Ivan de Vesqui and Gui de Verneuil, would need to turn sideways just to get through it, though that wouldn't help the bishop with his ponderous gut. Fortunately, the narrow part of the passage only lasted three of four feet and then it opened out into empty blackness. Once in that wider space, they struck flints until they'd lit the straw-wrapped, resin-smeared heads of their torches.

It was not like an English cave. The air was dry, the floor made of sand, the walls eroded smoothly by the winds of millennia. Even then, each man's breath plumed as they processed forward two by two, ducking under sections of low ceiling, wafting through diaphanous veils of web, always with fiery shadows dancing ahead. Gradually, the route tilted upward. When the gradient became impossibly steep, they saw that steps had been cut into the cave floor, hewn from solid rock, only a thin scattering of sand covering them. Likewise, they saw wooden supports propping up an unnaturally flattened ceiling.

'They hacked their way from here,' Thurstan muttered.

'I saw the miners Count Baldwin brought to the sack of Thessalonica,' Bertrand said. 'Solid lumps of muscle, I swear. They weren't like men at all.'

'So long as they knew their trade.'

They weaved through a succession of timber pillars, before reaching the end of the passage, a barricade of timber, a mass of boards and planks nailed over one another, stretching from side to side, and floor to ceiling. Even when Thurstan shielded his torch, there wasn't a chink of light visible through it. Bertrand ran his gloved hand along the rough, uneven surface.

'The current occupants are aware of this entrance,' he said.

'Can we dismantle it?' the bishop asked.

Bertrand pressed the wood. There was no yield. He felt at the joists around its rim, all squared solidly into place. 'It's sturdy. Probably braced on the other side as well.'

'We'll need a battering ram,' Mercadier said.

De Vesqui indicated the various supports. 'There are beams all along here.'

'Careful which one you dislodge, you buffoon,' Mercadier replied. 'We don't want to bring the hillside down on our heads.'

The knight bared his teeth. 'I don't take advice from a common infantryman.'

'Nevertheless, he's right,' Thurstan cut in. 'We need to be careful down here.'

'There's another problem.' Mercadier tested the heavy slab of woodwork for himself. 'We hammer at this, the reverberations may pass up through the castle and alert them.'

Thurstan nodded. 'We need a diversion.'

Mercadier mused. 'An assault on the main gate would do that.'

Thurstan pondered. It would be risky for the assault party.

'So, we attack from the front after all?' Bertrand said, sounding uneasy.

Thurstan shouldered his way back along the tunnel. 'Whatever we do, we need to plan it properly.'

As they all of them headed back, Pandulf pushed his way to the front. 'My lord... I wish to ride in the vanguard.'

'What are you talking about?' Thurstan replied.

'When we assault the gate.'

'Out of the question.'

The lad's face fell. 'You told me—'

'There'll be no assault on the gate.'

'I don't understand.'

'Neither will the castle guards,' Thurstan said. 'At least, that's what I'm hoping for.'

–

'He's putting a lot of faith in that bandit,' De Vesqui grumbled.

The orange aurora of dawn had emerged over the bluffs to the east, but the majority of the camp had not yet slept. The knight-serjeant stood wrapped in his cloak, watching as a hundred yards outside their camp, the figures of Thurstan and Mercadier stood in private conference.

'That bandit knows what he's talking about,' Bishop Hubert said, though he couldn't help feeling uneasy about the arrangement. 'But these are sad times... when to do God's work, we must employ the wiles of criminals.'

De Vesqui snorted. 'Aren't *we* about to steal a holy artefact, your grace?'

The bishop eyed him. 'Steal it back, Knight-Serjeant. There's a difference.'

De Vesqui chuckled. 'You keep telling yourself that.'

Pandulf, who'd spent the last hour perched on the nearby ridge, now came over. 'There's no light showing on those ramparts. They're so complacent. Yet we're only a couple of weeks' march from the war itself.'

'A couple of weeks of burning desert,' De Vesqui said. 'That's barrier enough for most men.'

'Why are you complaining, boy?' Gui de Verneuil wondered. 'All this is good for us.'

'I'm not complaining,' the squire said. 'But this fellow, al-Qazairi, he's at odds with his own lord as well as ours. It seems strange that he isn't on his guard.'

'The True Cross is his bargaining chip,' Bertrand said. 'Saladin knows it will be traded over to him at some point… so he's probably biding his time. After that, what would anyone else want out here?'

Thurstan and Mercadier now headed back to camp, the blackness behind them streaked with bloody sunlight.

'We have a plan,' Thurstan said. 'Before I explain it to you, we need all the sticks we can find.'

'Sticks?' De Vesqui scoffed. 'Out here?'

'Sticks,' Thurstan affirmed. 'Dried grasses, cacti, camel dung, anything that will burn.'

The men drifted off in their ones and twos. Only the bishop remained. And De Vesqui, who hawked and spat.

'That applies to you too, Knight-Serjeant,' Thurstan said.

They interlocked glares. Then, spitting into the sand again, De Vesqui lumbered away.

'Sullen fellow,' the bishop observed.

'He values his knighthood when it suits him,' Thurstan replied. 'Considers menial work beneath his dignity. But everything else about him says gutter.'

'He'll be a hero after today.' If nothing else, that thought cheered the bishop. He smiled. 'You all will.'

Thurstan shrugged. 'Either that or martyrs.'

CHAPTER 21

Not long after first light, any sentries on the walls of al–Yuqhar who were paying attention, which seemed to be precious few, would have noticed a sole horseman galloping from the south. He'd have been difficult to identify at first, as he appeared to be wearing grimy, ragged Bedouin garb, though a sharp eye would have noticed as he drew closer, that he was girded in mail underneath.

As he ascended the ramp towards the front gate, some of those on the south-facing wall finally became interested, straightening up to watch. Especially when he drew rein in front of the main gate and flung down a large bundle of sticks, before turning his horse about and spurring it away again. As he thundered back into the haze of the desert, a second rider passed him in the other direction. This one also skidded to a halt close to the main gate, and hurled down a hefty bundle of sticks, before bolting away. Only when the third rider approached, and it was now apparent that they were working in a kind of relay, were demands for an explanation called down from the battlements. Of course, they were ignored. With the fourth rider, this one with a huge Mamluk shield mounted on his right arm, so that most of one side of his body was covered, the shouted enquiries became strident. When the fifth rider came up, also depositing a bundle of combustible materials, an arrow flickered down. It was a half-hearted shot, more of a warning. It missed and he rode away. When the sixth rider approached, also shielded, more arrows were loosed. One struck his shield but failed to penetrate, and he too rode off after throwing down his bundle.

When the seventh and eighth riders approached, both at the same time, but ten yards apart, there was a palpable sense of panic on the ramparts. Even from the riders' perspective, more and more bowmen were being called to the embrasures. They loosed arrow after arrow, but as the two riders drew near, they rode a zigzag course, and so were repeatedly missed. Only one of these men carried a bunch of sticks and grasses, which he threw on top of all the others. The other one, however, who the defenders now realised had been trailing black smoke as well as dust, carried a fire-pot, a clay jar filled with oil, burning rags stuffed into its neck. He hurled it as he wheeled his animal around, and it shattered amid the bundles of sticks, bursting into flame.

Wild shouts now echoed throughout the castle. Doubtless they were calling for water, for already the flames were taking fierce hold, licking up the face of the entrance gate. More riders galloped up, and as further arrows sleeted down, one was hit in the thigh, though he still threw on two more bundles. The one who came after him, flung another fire-pot. This one struck the gate itself and again erupted in flame.

There was now a mighty blaze there, which it wouldn't be easy for the castle's defenders to quench given that the gate itself was recessed. Any water poured down from above would spatter in the sand in front of it. They would need to improvise, which would take time. And time they didn't have.

More riders pounded up, alternately throwing bundles of fuel or further incendiaries. Fewer arrows were unleashed at them as the marksmen on the wall wafted at the thick smoke or called for water. As such, they were too distracted to notice that a new menace had now appeared on the horizon. In fact, was already well past the horizon and advancing up the ramp.

This new arrival was a small infantry company, marching behind a portable fortification, two rows of twenty overlapping shields, all nailed together, with a similar row fastened above but tilted backward creating a mobile shield-wall, which twenty men advancing side by side were just able to hold upright. All the castle defenders could see of it was a vast square object heading towards them. They launched arrows when it came within range, but their primary concern was still the fire raging below. With some ingenuity, they lowered four wineskins on ropes, though first having filled the skins with water and punched them with holes, the idea being they could swing them back and forth above the flames and douse them that way. But no sooner had they commenced this than the makeshift shield-wall dropped to the ground. The twenty crossbowmen who'd been advancing at a crouch behind its bearers, stood upright, took aim and loosed.

Three or four defenders above the gate were struck by the first volley. Two of the waterskins fell and landed away from the flames. In response, more archers crowded onto the battlements, taking potshots at their assailants. But the shield-wall was raised again, and though many missiles struck home, they failed to punch through. The crossbow men behind the shields reloaded, and when they were ready, a signal was muttered by Captain Mercadier, who stood among them. The shield-wall dropped, they rose and loosed.

Arrows flew back from all along the south-facing wall, but the crossbows focussed on those men above the gate, determined to hamper their efforts to douse the fire. Another two or three went down clutching wounds, one fell from the parapet, while the last of the two waterskins dropped. Shrieking curses, the defenders retaliated with another storm of arrows, but the shield-wall was raised again, goose-shafts thudding into it.

Once the crossbows were ready, Mercadier shouted, the shield barricade went down, and the marksmen stood and loosed. This latest fusillade visibly thinned out those remaining above the gate. A fifth waterskin had been procured, but this too was dropped.

'That's it, men, keep it up,' Mercadier growled, reaching under his harness, extricating a small square of burnished glass, holding it aloft in an easterly direction, and waggling it left to right. A second signaller was waiting amid heaped rocks beyond the low-lying land east of the castle. He sent a similar signal of his own towards the cavemouth.

–

Pandulf was waiting. There was no danger of him being seen from the south-facing battlements even if there'd been anyone posted there, as he was too well screened by the high ground at his rear. But he himself had a clear view of the second signaller.

He hurried along the tunnel, squatting and running like an ape to avoid the low-hanging sections, scaling the stairs at speed and sidling past the thirty men who, stripped of all their colours and Bedouin garb, and wearing chain-mail and helmets, were lined up against the barricade.

Thurstan waited at the front.

'The attack's in full force,' the squire panted. 'The garrison is occupied.'

Thurstan nodded. Six men-at-arms came forward, carrying a timber beam, and commenced swinging it against the woodwork. At first, it looked as though it would stand. But then it shuddered and cracked, and when other men came forward with axes and hammers, the planking splintered apart.

Thurstan snapped his visor down and went through first, Bertrand and De Vesqui close behind. They ascended another man-made passage, which brought them to a closed door. Inevitably, it was locked. Thurstan shouted and the battering ram was brought up again. The door lasted four impacts and then they were through into a paved antechamber, about twenty yards wide by twenty. No sooner had they entered than there was shouting from the stairway leading up from it. Twelve Saracen soldiers came clattering down, torches in hand, armed with sabres. Someone had heard the commotion.

With great, two-handed strokes of their longswords, Thurstan and De Vesqui felled a man each. Around them, the rest engaged.

The Saracens were well-armed and armoured, almost uniformed in their baggy, purple trousers, black leather boots, brightly polished cuirasses, and turban-wrapped helmets, but the assault party had worked themselves into a rage as they waited beyond the barricade, sweating intensely, hands balling into fists. Now they vented it in a furious onslaught. Thurstan fought with his longsword in one hand and his bone-handled knife in the other, the heavier blade hewing through steel, leather and flesh, the smaller one continuously ramming up to its cross-guard in eyes, gullets and groins.

Garishly bloodied, though not one of them had fallen, the attackers ascended the steps.

–

The castle's main gate was now engulfed in flames, but just to be sure, riders continued to weave past the crossbow company and hurl fire-pots. It was increasingly perilous, as there were so many archers on the battlements to the west and east of the gate. Two of the horsemen were struck down, one forced to hobble to safety with his left knee transfixed, the other lying dead, the shaft quivering in his heart.

The shield-wall itself was bristling, many bodkin heads having pierced it through. However, the crossbow men maintained their volley work, the rampart above the gate now devoid of defenders, save one, who hung through an embrasure, a bolt embedded in his skull. On Mercadier's command, they now angled their shots further along the battlements, both to left and right. Hugely outnumbered, they would soon have to retreat. But this had been the plan from the start.

Mercadier's orders were to keep the garrison occupied for as long as possible. To further distract the defenders, the remainder of the company had ridden up into view some distance behind, stripped of their travelling garb, sporting the livery of the English or Norman houses they served. They didn't attack – there was nothing they could attack against yet – but as they were out of range, they held their ground, the main purpose to impress upon al-Qazairi's soldiers that this was a Frankish raid, that these were Christian knights they were dealing with, which might even be a prelude to a much greater assault led by that lion-hearted devil, Richard Plantagenet.

This ensured that all those remaining garrison members who had not yet come onto the south-facing rampart did so, bringing fresh bushels of arrows.

'We're in the crucible,' a shield-man shouted. The fellow next to him had just gone down to his knees, and folded onto his back. An arrow had penetrated his throat.

'We hold as long as we can,' Mercadier retorted, though he ducked as an arrow glanced off his helmet. 'God's wrath, Wildblood, you need to strike soon.'

CHAPTER 22

As the assault party burst from the castle kitchens, they were already in the courtyard, and the glaring sunlight dazzled them. They had no idea of the stronghold's layout, which was a disadvantage, but on the other hand, they'd got inside without suffering a single loss.

They now split three ways, nine men behind Ivan de Vesqui headed for the west wall, and ten men behind Gui de Verneuil headed for the east, the idea being they'd work their way towards each other along the south-facing rampart, joining up above the gate and there take charge of the portcullis, which, after they'd lifted it, would leave the gate passage bare of obstruction. Thurstan's own squad, meanwhile, would aim for the baronial apartments, where the apprehension of al-Qazairi himself was their main objective. The garrison would doubtless fight harder now that enemies were inside, and they likely had more men, but the loss of their leader could tilt the balance against them.

But Thurstan still had two problems.

Firstly, he didn't know where the baronial apartments were. Secondly, the courtyard was extensive, and though a huge number of Saracens were on the south-facing wall, a significant number were still dashing about at ground-level, panicking, some not yet even armed or properly armoured, but all of them a potential hazard.

A huge specimen came at Thurstan first, his broad-bladed spear levelled. The knight was almost caught by surprise, but he parried the blow, before slashing his new opponent's eyes with his knife. The fellow staggered sideways, screaming, allowing Bertrand to finish him off. Pandulf hung close, determined to assist wherever he could, but providing no real assistance as his master fought in a silent but maniacal frenzy, demonstrating bewildering speed and skill.

A couple of times, opponents came directly at the squire. One was already wounded, so the boy needed only to exchange a couple of strokes before stabbing him in the throat. The second was burlier, more fearsome, but before they could close, Bertrand stepped in and felled him with such a blow that his mace stove the fellow's skull inward.

Thurstan now veered towards the open doors to a three-storey stone building in the courtyard's south-west corner. Compared to the rest of the castle's internal structures, most of those made from wood and thatch, this one looked sturdy and purposeful. Clearly, it was a residence. Two more Saracens issued from the entrance as Thurstan approached, one with a sabre, the other a halberd. He killed the halberdier with a blow to the collarbone, before lopping the legs from the swordsman.

–

Outside, Mercadier's shield-wall was now so embedded with arrows that it was becoming difficult manoeuvring it. Two more men had gone down, one dead, the other forced to stagger away. They continued to unload volleys of their own and were still hitting targets cleanly. But there weren't enough of them left to make a huge impact. At the same time, they were running out of quarrels.

When the first fire-arrow struck the shield-wall, followed by a second, and then a third, Mercadier took the leather bottle from his belt, scampering around to the front, where he splashed it with water. But almost immediately, the bottle was shot from his grasp. He scurried back to the rear. The shield-wall was lowered again. Those crossbowmen remaining loosed another flight.

More Saracens fell screaming.

With a thundering crash, what remained of the burning gate now collapsed, revealing a solid iron portcullis. More archers appeared behind it, loosing arrows through the bars. A fourth shield-man reeled backward, those remaining struggling to hold the shield-wall aloft.

Mercadier was ready to give the order to retreat when he spied flurries of movement on the western rampart. A band of mailed and helmeted knights were progressing along it, hacking and chopping at the archers. The knight at the front, from his hulking shape and size, was De Vesqui. Disarmed by a sword-stroke, he responded by grappling with his opponent, raising him bodily into the air, one hand grasping his throat, one his crotch, and flinging him from the battlements.

And this is the fellow I cheeked, the infantry captain thought.

–

Thurstan had watched from an arched window on the internal staircase leading to the castle's baronial apartment as De Vesqui's party made it to the battlements unhindered, though this was the least he'd hoped for, because at the same time, Gui de Verneuil and his men had run into heavier opposition in the courtyard. They'd still carved their way through but had suffered losses. As they now ascended to the eastern rampart, they met Saracens coming down. Blades clashed savagely as they fought on those steep, narrow steps. One of De Verneuil's knights fell, an adversary wrapped in each of his brawny arms.

Bertrand stopped alongside Thurstan, lifting his visor, breathing heavily.

Both were dabbled with blood, their mail scarred, their helmets dented.

'This is proving harder than we thought,' Bertrand said.

Thurstan didn't bother trying to deny it.

Pandulf now stumbled up to them. He'd removed his own helm as an axe had split it. He was white-faced and drenched with sweat, though he'd done his share of killing, his sword ribboned with gore. They approached the upper doorway together, but another Saracen appeared. He leapt down the remaining steps, landing on top of Thurstan. He was stocky, and the knight tottered as he wrestled with him, the pair of them falling and rolling downward. Bertrand stepped aside, and just in time – for a javelin hurtled down. He lurched on up towards the Saracen responsible. The fellow pulled a poniard, but Bertrand's mace found the bridge of his nose first, shattering it to pulp.

Below, Thurstan jumped to his feet. His assailant lay dead, disembowelled by the knight's bone-handled knife. He hurried up again, regathering his longsword.

At the top was the largest chamber they'd yet seen. There were tables and leather-upholstered chairs, rich carpets, tapestries cladding the walls.

Three figures waited at its far end, each in his own way impressive. In the middle, a bald-headed fellow with a curling black beard, was bare-chested under an open gown of blue and orange silk. He wore baggy trousers tucked into leather boots and multiple, jewel-encrusted rings on his hands. He also wielded a hefty, two-handed *scimitar*. Thurstan had no doubt that this was the troublesome emir, al-Qazairi.

The men to left and right of him were equally flamboyant, wearing colourful robes over breastplates, with steel spikes poking from the tops of their turbans. One wielded a *shamshir*, the other a *kilij*, the same implements of death that Thurstan's party had wielded at Tyre. Clearly, these were Saracen lords, Islamic versions of Christendom's landed knights. Not for nothing were they known as masters of their craft.

The Saracen knights advanced first, intent on protecting their prince.

Thurstan and Bertrand engaged them one man each.

Thurstan soon realised that his opponent, though he was in middle age, was a swordsman of skill. They thrust and parried, dancing, knocking the rich furnishings askew. The *shamshir* was lighter than his longsword, and the more likely to break, but also the more likely to find a narrow gap and penetrate. Which is why he wasted no time on chivalry. Twirling his blade round his head, he purposely left himself open. The Saracen lunged, but Thurstan caught the curved steel in his mailed fist. His opponent tried to yank it loose, but couldn't. And the longsword came down.

As the fellow sagged under a spraying ruby fountain, Thurstan spun to face the rest of their opponents.

The baronial apartment was already wrecked, Bertrand grappling chest-to-chest with his own adversary. His visor had been hacked away and his forehead cut, blood streaming into his eyes, but before Thurstan could intervene, the banneret twisted over, slamming his opponent flat on the tabletop underneath, and forcing the mace's handle down across his throat, leaning on it with all his weight. The Saracen gargled and dug his dagger into Bertrand's side but failed to pierce the mail, and with a *crunch*, his windpipe gave.

Bertrand sank onto his haunches, gasping.

Further sounds of combat turned their heads.

Thurstan was startled to see Pandulf swapping blows with the master of this house, the youth riding a table as he swiped downward with his longsword, the emir, bursting with sweat as he fended the blows off and then trying to chop the boy at the knee. Pandulf leapt, but landed badly, striking the wood with his backside, crashing to the floor, but now the other knights were coming.

The emir fled through an open door. A bare passage lay beyond. Thurstan ran in pursuit, Pandulf barging along behind him.

At the far end stood a single closed door. There, al-Qazairi found another of his colourfully clad bodyguards, whom he pushed forward to defend him. Thurstan met the fellow and in two strokes, opened his throat. Pandulf pushed past to re-engage the emir, who roared as he slashed with his *scimitar*. Pandulf parried and kicked him between his legs. Gagging, the emir staggered, colliding with the closed door. A frightened yelp sounded from behind it.

Pandulf was distracted by this, and so never saw the hard right hand coming. It smashed into the side of his jaw and sent him spinning into a wall, where he fell on his side. Al-Qazairi took aim again with his *scimitar*, only for Thurstan to lunge past and clamp his wrist. He spun and met Thurstan's mail-clad elbow full in the face. As he toppled back, his hand was slammed against the wall and the *scimitar* dislodged.

Bloodied and whimpering, the emir crumpled to his knees, hands clasped for mercy.

'You yield?' Thurstan demanded.

Al-Qazairi jabbered something, which sounded like acquiescence.

Pandulf meanwhile, back on his feet, examined the closed door, which had been fastened by several bolts. He drew them back, then, hefting his blade, banged it open.

What he saw on the other side stopped him in his tracks.

CHAPTER 23

De Vesqui and De Verneuil arrived on the rampart above the gate from opposite sides. Each man was alone, De Vesqui because he'd despatched his squad to deal with the archers on the south-west tower, De Verneuil because he'd met more determined opponents and his men were dead. He himself was wounded, a slashed shoulder leaking blood down his left arm. Even now, arrows struck the stonework around them, and so they wasted no time, lifting the trapdoor and descending the ladder into the gatehouse, where two hefty wheels controlled the raising and lowering of the portcullis. At present, these mighty mechanisms were in the charge of another duo of Saracen guards, both of whom were busy using tools to disable the chains running down through notches in the floor and thus failing to notice that they had company. De Verneuil struck off one's head with a single blow. De Vesqui clove the other's skull.

The knights took a wheel each and, with strenuous efforts, commenced turning them.

–

Outside, Mercadier watched with satisfaction as the portcullis was winched upward. He turned to the cavalry ranged across the hills behind, but they too, under William des Roches, had already seen it, and were plunging forward with lances lowered. They hit the approach ramp at full gallop, the infantrymen scampering aside as they thundered past, their hoofbeats clattering around the gate passage as they charged through it.

Inside, the courtyard was an abattoir, littered with corpses.

Numerically, what remained of the defenders was still evenly matched with the attackers. They had regrouped at the far end and were ready, bucklers raised, curved blades drawn. However, the heavy horse now arrayed in front of them was a new factor. One charge and they knew they'd be speared down and pounded into the grit. Even then, they seemed prepared to make a stand, only for an Arabic cry to ring out from the castle residence. Emir al-Qazairi, looking battered and bruised, was brought into the sunlight and shoved to his knees. Thurstan Wildblood stood at his rear, longsword blade at the side of his neck. Al-Qazairi raised his hands, shouting something again, and one by one, what was left of his men dropped their weapons.

Mercadier and his infantry now trooped in. Behind them rode Bishop Hubert. Thurstan, meanwhile, dragged the emir to his feet and pushed him at sword-point into the middle of the courtyard, where he kicked his legs from under him again. Bertrand and Pandulf also emerged. To the bemusement of those who noticed, the squire was clasping the arm of a girl perhaps a year or so older than himself. She wore a threadbare dress, a woollen skullcap, a shawl, and had worn-out leather shoes on her feet. In some ways, she was a picture of poverty. But she was also a true Arabic beauty, dusky-skinned, sun-kissed as they'd say in England, blessed with smooth, even features, long black tresses, and the most piercingly green eyes any man there had ever seen.

–

Behind the bolted upper door, the squire had expected to find a prison of some sort. He wasn't wrong in that. It was a locked room, with a narrow, barred window. But it was extremely plush, filled with rugs, wall-hangings and comfortable Eastern furniture. More surprising still had been the single occupant: this girl. She wasn't particularly well-dressed – she'd clearly been a captive for some time – but she appeared to be in decent health, so they'd obviously fed and watered her. On his entry, she'd stood stiffly against the far wall, frightened, hands clutched together in front of her.

'What the devil is this?' Thurstan had demanded, looking into the room behind him.

Pandulf hadn't been able to answer, regarding the girl with a combination of shock and fascination.

'A courtesan?'

'I don't know, my lord,' the lad had stuttered. 'But she was locked in—'

'Never mind that now.'

In the courtyard, Bishop Hubert gave the lass no more than a confused second glance before approaching Thurstan.

'This is al-Qazairi?' he asked.

'It would appear so,' Thurstan replied.

'Has he told you where the Cross is?'

'He hasn't told us anything, your grace. He doesn't speak our language.'

The bishop looked frustrated. He turned. 'Does anyone in our company speak Arabic?' He was greeted by helpless shrugs. 'Damn this!' He addressed the Saracens at the opposite end of the yard. 'Do any of you men speak French? Greek? Latin?'

'Latin,' Gui de Verneuil chuckled, having come down from the gatehouse.

De Vesqui was close behind him, his longsword glinting with blood. He too looked amused.

'We need to find the Cross!' the bishop ranted. 'That's the sole reason we're here.'

'What cross do you seek, lord?' came a low, wavering voice.

To Pandulf's surprise, it was the girl. She carefully extricated herself from his grasp and stood with hands clasped in front of her.

'*You* speak French at least?' the bishop asked.

She nodded. 'And Latin, if you'd prefer. A smattering of Greek.'

'French will suffice,' Thurstan cut in. 'Then the rest of us can understand.'

'Of course, my lord.' Her accent was stilted, very Eastern, but clearly, she was fluent.

'Who are you?' the bishop asked.

'Melinda, your grace.'

Melinda, Pandulf thought. A name he'd never heard before.

'What is your station?' the bishop said.

'I was a servant in the house of Patriarch Heraclius of Jerusalem,' she replied.

'You're a hostage?'

'I am.'

'Your days of captivity are over, child. But first, maybe you can help us. We seek the True Cross.'

She looked puzzled. 'The True Cross?'

'It's here somewhere,' Bertrand said. 'We know that for a fact.'

'If it is, I've never seen it.' She looked upset that she couldn't be more helpful.

The bishop shrugged. 'Likely it's in a dungeon somewhere. Do you speak Arabic?' When she nodded, he smiled. 'You're clearly more than just a pretty little creature, my dear. Speak to the emir… Tell him their lives will be spared if he hands over the Cross.'

The girl obeyed, addressing the kneeling captive, though he too looked bewildered.

'He says he has no such relic,' she told them.

'He lies, damn it!' the bishop snapped. 'We *know* the Cross is here.'

'Tell him that if he hands over the Cross, he and his men can leave unmolested,' Thurstan said. 'We'll take their arms but give them water and food for the journey.'

When she repeated this to the emir, he gestured helplessly.

'Emir al-Qazairi insists that he knows nothing of this True Cross.'

'Start executing them,' De Vesqui said. 'That'll loosen his tongue.'

Emir al-Qazairi spoke on, urgently.

'He insists the True Cross is not here,' the girl said.

'Tell me, girl,' Thurstan replied, 'and this time I'm asking *you*, not him… there's no relic of any value in this place?'

Again, she seemed upset to be delivering bad tidings. 'I've been given much freedom so long as I stayed inside the castle, but I've never seen anything like a relic, or even heard one discussed.'

'It's not just any relic,' Bishop Hubert said sternly. 'It's the Cross on which Our Saviour died. It may look like nothing to your eyes, child. Two pieces of ancient wood. Perhaps separate from each other.'

'I've seen nothing of the sort.'

De Vesqui prowled up to her. She backed away, Pandulf taking her arm again, partly to stop her running, partly as reassurance, though reassurance against what, he wasn't certain. She might be a foe of theirs yet.

'Do you even know what the True Cross is?' De Vesqui wondered.

She eyed him with terror – his huge bearlike shape, his scarred face and night-black mane.

'Of… of course,' she stuttered.

'Really?' Without warning, he snatched her by her free arm, turning it wrist-up. 'What's this?'

The others stared at a curious black tattoo. It was cruciform in shape, the end of each stave culminating in a T. Four further but smaller crosses were also visible, each one interspersed between the arms of the main image, the whole thing neat and symmetrical.

'You some kind of priestess?' De Vesqui wondered. 'A temple harlot? A pagan?'

The girl clamped a hand over it. 'No, my lord. No… I'm a Christian, as you are.'

The big knight snorted. 'You think we're fools?'

'My lords, please…' The girl turned to the others.

'Show me, girl.' The bishop offered his own hand.

Pandulf released the girl, and reluctantly, she uncovered the tattoo.

Bishop Hubert examined it. 'You can doff your persecutor's hat, Knight-Serjeant. She *is* a Christian. Of the Coptic faith. That is their sign.'

'So, she's a heretic?' someone muttered.

The bishop mused. 'It's true, that our true Church has no communion with the Coptic Church. Neither in dogma nor theology. But she believes in Our Lord Jesus Christ, which is something to be said in this land. In addition, if she can lead us to the Cross…'

'There is no Cross, my lord,' she said again, almost tearful. 'I'm sure I would know.'

Al-Qazairi now spoke up, with greater urgency.

'What is he saying?' the bishop asked.

'He wishes to know what we are talking about. He says he will be as helpful as possible if you'll spare him and his men.'

'Tell him that if he continues to deny us the treasure he keeps here, whatever that happens to be,' Thurstan said, 'we will search for it ourselves, and if we find it, and he's hidden it, it will be much the worse for him. Make sure he understands.'

Bishop Hubert looked irritated. 'Wildblood, you give them a way out by continuing to doubt the Cross is here. We aren't seeking any other treasure...'

'Your grace, we *supposed* it was the True Cross,' Thurstan retorted. 'All we really know is that Emir al-Qazairi is holding something of great value.'

The girl listened to this exchange fearfully. When the emir jabbered at her again, she snapped back at him in Arabic.

'So we can all understand, girl!' Thurstan said, angry.

Her cheeks tinged pink. 'I fear you've already found the thing you're looking for.'

'What are you talking about?' Bertrand demanded. 'We've found nothing.'

'You've found *me*,' she said.

Al-Qazairi seemed to understand this much at least. His eyes brightened and he nodded eagerly, offering an open hand, as if to say they could take his hostage with his blessing.

'I have a reputation...' The girl hung her head. 'Whether it's been earned or not, I can't say. For... spiritual prowess.'

There was a brief, dumbfounded silence.

'What is this?' De Verneuil demanded. 'Has this devious Eastern bastard got the True Cross or not?'

The girl shook her head. 'Not, my lord.' She switched her attention to Bishop Hubert. 'I was taken prisoner at Jerusalem. They might have killed me, but they had wounded men who were ailing, like to die. And I... I offered prayers for them.'

'And?' the bishop asked, intrigued despite himself.

She averted her eyes, shuffled her feet. 'They healed, your grace. Not all. Some were too badly hurt... But others recovered even though their deaths were expected.'

'My child, what are you telling us?'

'I had this same reputation when I was servant to Patriarch Heraclius. I cured a family member of his who was ill with fever.'

'How did you do that?'

'I prayed. Next to his bed... and he became well again. After that, the patriarch believed I had the power to work miracles.'

'Only God has the power to work miracles, child. This is verging on blasphemy.'

'Of course,' she said. 'I never made this claim, myself. And if the Lord worked through me, it was none of my doing.'

De Verneuil turned to Bertrand. 'This is madness. We've come all this way for this?'

Bertrand didn't reply immediately. 'What... what if she's telling the truth?'

'That she's a living saint? How many of those do you know?'

'They're a rare breed,' Bishop Hubert cut in. 'Do you men know of Margaret of England?'

Bertrand glanced at him. 'A name. That's all.'

'There's a story,' the bishop said, 'but that's for another time.' He swung back to the girl. 'You claim to be a healer?'

'It seems to be a talent of mine.'

'And a mystic?'

'As to that, I can't say. I have no visions, but I pray a lot.'

'You live a good, pure life?'

'I steer as close to the teachings of Our Lord as I can.'

'If your main virtue is Christian zeal, why would you be valuable to Muslims?' Mercadier demanded. 'This fellow, for example... this Qazairi? Even Saladin himself? Reputedly, you're such a prize that the sultan refrains from attacking this place in case you are harmed.'

'My prayers seem to work on their people as much as ours.'

The girl hugged herself in her shawl as they stared, lowering her head.

Pandulf in particular watched her with growing fascination.

'In one regard, it makes sense,' the bishop said thoughtfully. 'If she was just a servant, with nothing special about her... Why keep her as hostage?'

At which moment, with ear-splitting cries, two members of the garrison's dead, who clearly weren't, leapt to their feet very close to the girl, and came at her with sabres over their heads. Mercadier was first to react, shouldering his crossbow and triggering a shaft, striking one assailant in the back of the skull, pitching him onto his face. The other was almost upon her when Pandulf, acting on pure instinct, jumped in the way and repelled the first blow with his own sword. But the Saracen was skilled. In two passes, he'd disarmed the squire and then, pulling a dagger, rammed it point-first through a gap in the mail under Pandulf's right armpit.

All the lad initially felt was a heavy blow in his side, though it knocked the wind out of him more surely than any punch or kick. He tottered where he stood, suddenly confused, a desperate weakness in his legs. With vision already failing, he caught a fleeting glimpse of his assailant going again for the girl; of the girl ducking backward, finding herself in the arms of the bishop; of the Saracen howling, intending to strike them both down...

At which point, a longsword glimmered as it swept, and the fellow collapsed, his left leg chopped at the ankle. Pandulf fell too, the courtyard floor hitting hard. Alongside him, the surviving assailant twisted in agony, shrieking all the louder as Thurstan drove steel into his open mouth, twisting it through the thick tissue at the back of his throat and severing his spine.

After that, Pandulf knew nothing else.

CHAPTER 24

They huddled around the boy, most looking on, while Thurstan and Bertrand were kneeling.

Pandulf's eyes rolled as he jerked convulsively, blood gushing from his side.

'Staunch that flow!' Thurstan said, frantically unlacing the lad's hauberk.

Bertrand clamped his hand over it but was already shaking his head.

Pandulf coughed, red globules spattering. Thurstan did everything he could to drag off the squire's mail. 'Keep your hand there, Bertrand, damn your eyes!'

'Thurstan!' Bertrand stuttered. 'He can't survive a wound there.'

'He's not going to die. Not like this!'

And not after I goaded him for his unknightly behaviour.

'Mercadier!' Thurstan shouted.

The infantry captain, who had responded swiftly to the several Saracens at the end of the courtyard who'd grabbed up their weapons, by ordering his crossbow men to loose, killing them all, now hunkered down beside them. His eyes roved the fallen lad, from his milk-white face and fluttering eyelids to the ragged, puckered mouth in the side of his chest. A wide, crimson pool had already throbbed out of it.

'It's a bad one, my lord,' he said. 'We should bind it at least. Maybe add stitching, but even then, I fear...'

'It should be cleaned first!' the girl called Melinda stated, glancing from man to man.

'Hold your tongue, wench,' De Vesqui growled. 'From now, you speak only when spoken to.'

'Staunch that blood-flow!' Thurstan told Bertrand again.

'But it should be cleaned,' the girl insisted, ignoring the heavy hands that now grabbed her arms as though simply having a view made her dangerous. 'Or the wound will become infected.'

Thurstan glanced at her, torn. He was sure he'd heard it spoken in other armies and on other battlefields that a key to surviving serious wounds was the rapid cleansing of them. 'Bring me the blade that struck him!'

The offending weapon was presented, a Turkish *jambiya*, so sharp that it had flashed into and out of Pandulf's body in the blink of an eye. It was barely stained red, let alone with dust or other filth.

'If there's any dirt in there,' the girl added, 'the blood might bring it out.'

He glanced at her again, distracted by the strange logic.

'Thurstan, in God's name!' Bertrand stammered, struggling to stop the blood from gurgling between his fingers.

'The flow needs to be curbed,' Thurstan decided. 'Bind the wound. Bring hot coals.'

'My lord,' the girl pleaded. 'If his innards are damaged, cauterising it won't save him. The poison will spread through his body. It needs to bleed a while at least...'

'A while?' he replied, incredulous. 'We're standing in a sea of the damn stuff.'

Only now did she look around, flinching as it struck her how far across the courtyard the tide of Pandulf's blood had already spread. Even Bishop Hubert, who'd retreated to a distance of ten or so yards, was still edging backward, jowls quivering with disgust.

De Vesqui snorted with scorn. 'Going so soon, your grace? When there's work for you here?'

'There's more work for *her*, surely?' William des Roches pointed from his saddle.

'That's right!' Bertrand, who was more covered in gore than any of them, glared up at the girl. 'Aren't *you* the miracle worker?'

'I...' she struggled to respond, glancing again from captor to captor. 'I can't...'

'You can pray, can't you?' Thurstan retorted. She gazed at him with new fear. Doubtless, he was a terrible sight. Girt for war, patterned with other men's blood, his grey eyes like steel blades themselves in his scarred, rugged face. 'If you're chosen by God, you can damn well pray.' It wasn't really a question.

She hung her head, cowed. 'I can pray, of course.'

'Then pray for my squire.' He turned to his men. 'Bind his wound. Find a bed.'

'He'll need water too,' the girl said. 'Plenty of water.'

'Bring water!' Thurstan shouted, his company now bustling around him.

'How do you know these things, girl?' Bishop Hubert wondered.

She watched uneasily as Pandulf, wads of cloth now clamped to his side, was hoisted up and carried away. 'In the house of the patriarch, your grace, I...'

'Never mind that,' Thurstan interrupted. 'You're supposed to be a saint. Behave like one. Pray my squire back to life, and then I'll know you're true.'

'And if I can't?' she wondered, as one of the others hauled her in pursuit of the stretcher-bearers.

'Hah!' De Vesqui laughed. 'Watch and see!' He drew his sword and picked up a spike-headed mace, before snatching hold of al-Qazairi. The terrified emir squirmed and wept but had insufficient strength to resist the scar-faced 'bear knight' who now thrust him through the rest of them, until he was in view of the surrendered garrison. There, he was flung to the floor. 'First, they watch the master's brains beaten out,' De Vesqui declared. 'Then they die too. That's how *we* repay murder. Crossbows... kill them all!'

Mercadier's crossbowmen seemed eager. All their weapons were loaded, and all now raised to the level.

'Wait!' Thurstan roared, also pushing through the crowd.

The crossbows glanced back at him. De Vesqui hesitated too.

Thurstan grabbed the emir by the rags of his robes, lugged him to his feet and with a boot planted on his backside, sent him staggering towards his men. Glancing over his shoulder, he saw that Melinda had stopped halfway to the entrance where Pandulf had been taken. 'Go, girl!' he bellowed. 'Do as I say!'

While she hastened to comply, Thurstan swung back to face the prisoners, among whose number Emir al-Qazairi now cowered.

'The rest of you verminous lumps of camel shit!' he shouted. 'On your faces!'

They clearly didn't understand his words, but his gestures were plain enough. In their ones and twos, watching him warily, they lay down on their fronts.

'Tie their hands and feet,' Thurstan told the crossbowmen. He glanced at Mercadier, who'd now come alongside him. 'Can you speak anything of their tongue?'

'Next to nothing,' the infantryman replied.

'Find a way to communicate this to them. For every hour that my squire ails, two of them will be taken at random and hanged from the walls. If he expires, they all hang together. Tell them now.'

Mercadier frowned. It perhaps wasn't the easiest instruction he'd ever been required to translate, but he went forward anyway. Even De Vesqui, initially angered to have been denied his latest mass killing, nodded his approval.

—

Thurstan crossed the gory field at Fornham on foot. He was seventeen years old again, still a squire, and though he'd just participated in his first big battle, his spirits were soaring. He was hot and tired, cut and bruised even under his mail. He yanked back his coif, which a flying blade had partly cloven, the locks beneath matted with blood, though the wound in his scalp was nothing, a slashing blow that had done no real damage.

All those years on the combat square and tiltyard, harshly instructed by his father's men, had paid off. Seventeen, and he knew only pride. Cared nothing for the slaughtered forms stretching broken and dismembered to every skyline. Or for the lady's scarf with which he now wiped the blood from his own blade. Or, in truth, for those few surviving rebels kneeling bound and stripped on the narrow rural lane nearby, uttering fearful prayers as halters were placed around their necks and linked by ropes to the saddles of horses.

Close by, his father, also mounted, watched dispassionately. His own mail was scored by battle-blades, his tabard, though clearly marked with the black crow on yellow, torn and spattered red. He'd lifted his visor, the features beneath graven in rock and cold as ice. His gaze barely flickered to his son as Thurstan strode up. When the lad tried to speak, his sire merely gestured that there was other business to attend first.

Thurstan watched as the household men-at-arms, whooping and shouting, whipped their horses away, the prisoners dragging behind through clouds of dust.

'So die all who defy the king,' the earl said simply. Thurstan made no reply, diligently polishing his blade. 'Hugh de Lacy tells me you performed capably.'

The youngster glanced up, but the older warrior's gaze lay further afield, his narrow, grey eyes riveted on some distant place when normal humanity would never be found.

'It was an honour to be part of this, father.'

'There are further honours yet. This evening at the victory feast, De Lacy will knight you.'

The lad felt a surge of excitement, but knew better than to give voice to it.

'The lords De Lucy, De Bohun and De Dunstanville will witness.'

Thurstan almost swooned. Not just to be knighted, but to be knighted on the edge of the battlefield, on a day of triumph, in the presence of those other great knights who'd wrought such havoc on the king's enemies.

They would all revel when it was over. There'd be a great banquet, gallons of ale and wine. And whores. Always, his father rewarded his men with whores. They'd rut through the long dark hours, and they'd eat again, and they'd drink. They'd drink so much wine it would pour over their writhing bodies like blood...

'Bad dreams, Wildblood?' someone wondered.

Thurstan's eyes snapped open.

At first, he couldn't make sense of it. The desert heat was stultifying in the narrow guardroom. Even Bishop Hubert, who stood in the open doorway, wore nothing but a simple, knee-length shift, which was damp and crumpled. Thurstan had chosen this simple, unadorned room to rest in because it was high up. He'd hoped the air might be fresher here, but it wasn't.

He sat painfully up on the pallet with the thin mattress, soaked in sweat.

'Don't get excited, your grace.' He mopped back his sodden hair. 'It's nothing new.'

'Sorry to hear that,' the bishop said. 'But if it's no concern to you, perhaps we can start making real plans again. To be frank, we can't afford to tarry here. Now that we have the girl…'

'We'll know how useful the girl is in a day or so's time.' Thurstan swung his feet to the floor.

Bishop Hubert regarded him thoughtfully. 'Several hours have passed since you laid the law down on that, and yet no prisoners have hanged. Pagans aren't protected by the code. So, what is it? Fear of retribution should the Saracens intercept us?'

Thurstan shot him a look. 'I fear no one and nothing, your grace.'

'You just don't want to do it, is that it? You won't put men to death who are helpless? Things have certainly changed since the hill of Ayyadieh.'

Thurstan took a long draught from the bucket of water next to his pallet. 'I was acting then on Richard's orders.'

'You wouldn't have done it for yourself?' Bishop Hubert seemed interested. 'Perhaps you're not the man I was expecting…'

Thurstan glanced at him again. 'You need to trust that I'm every inch that man.'

'Oh, I've no doubt you'll kill in battle. I've seen that myself. It's a terrifying sight. But perhaps that's because you're a soldier, not a murderer.'

Thurstan rubbed at his neck. 'Not everyone would agree with that.'

'It doesn't matter what other men say. It's all to the good. We're on a sacred mission here, Wildblood. A true quest. And *this* makes you even more the right man for the job.'

He turned to leave the garret room, but Thurstan called after him.

'What is the right man for a job like this, your grace?'

The bishop gave him a semi-incredulous look. 'A warrior of God, what else? It's not so unusual. You know the Templars, the Hospitallers. My friend… To do wolf's work, it takes wolves. But good wolves, Wildblood. Not bad ones.'

Thurstan had to snort to resist scoffing at that. There was no end to the clever, self-deceiving ways that senior churchmen could excuse their own villainies. He slipped his boots on, pulling the cords tight.

Bishop Hubert watched from the doorway. 'I know something of your past.'

'None of it is secret,' the knight replied.

'You were raised in the camp of your father, Earl Ranald, but in deep antiquity, your family were native English, were they not? Saxon nobility? During the Conqueror's time, they fought against us rather than with us. Resisting Viking and Norman alike to hang onto their privilege. And to an extent, they succeeded. In later decades, the first Henry, needing fighting men on the Welsh March, transferred their powerbase from Northumbria to Radnor.'

Thurstan eyed him, wondering where all this was leading.

'Your people changed their name as well,' the bishop said. 'Did they not?'

The knight shrugged. 'During the civil war, my grandfather supported Empress Matilda. And later, my father supported her son. The Plantagenets were Frenchmen through and through, but they weren't Norman... which was one blessing at least. But it still seemed wise to have a clean sheet. A new name would conceal, if not expunge, our English past.'

'And so the Aelfricssons became the Wildbloods.' The bishop smiled to himself. '"Wildblood". A frightening soubriquet, I'd say. It certainly matched your father's reputation when he was Lord of the March.'

'There you have it.' Thurstan stood and opened the shutter. 'Our entire potted history.'

'Not quite. Your father fought all the wars the second Henry required of him. Fought them with great ferocity. In so doing, he amassed a stable of knights at Radnor that were second to none.'

Thurstan gazed out over sun-bleached emptiness. 'The household I grew up in.'

'Especially after your mother died, I understand. You were still a child, so they subsumed you completely into that violent culture.'

'As the third son, I was always bound to be knighted.'

'Your escapades during the Great Rebellion became legend. You slew and slew, they say. And you a mere youngster. And then in Ireland...'

'I think we've discussed my past enough, Lord Bishop.' Thurstan swung around.

The bishop nodded, seeing that he'd pushed the knight enough. 'You may consider yourself a barbarous man, Wildblood. A brute, a bandit with a title. But today I see you more clearly.'

'You talk as if this gives you power over me?'

The bishop pursed his lips, then shook his head. 'I said I want a good wolf. Not a tame one.' And he left the room.

CHAPTER 25

On the second day after his wounding, Pandulf showed signs of recovery. It wasn't immediate. For twenty-four hours, he'd lain milk-white and mumbling, the girl, Melinda alongside him, mopping down his brow, bidding him drink water whenever his delirium briefly broke, and when anyone glanced through the door into the small infirmary where they were ensconced, kneeling at his bedside, head bowed, hands joined in prayer.

If nothing else on that second morning, his fever at least had abated. Word was passed to Thurstan, who came and stood over them. The boy seemed to be sleeping. Not easily, but when his crusted eyes cracked open and he set them on his master, his mouth curved into a semi-conscious smile.

'How is his wound?' Thurstan enquired.

The girl peeled back the blood-stiffened dressings. 'I'll need more bandages, my lord...'

'I'll have them sent up to you.'

She revealed a jagged slit where the blade had opened the squire up, though several black sutures currently held it closed. It was moist and the flesh around it enflamed, but there was no sign of suppuration.

'*You* stitched him?' Thurstan asked.

Melinda shrugged, wiping her hands on a damp cloth. 'The blood-flow ceased on its own. I thought it was safe. I found needle and thread in a cupboard.'

'And are my eyes deceiving me or is he doing well?'

'I feel the wound wasn't as deep as we feared, my lord.'

Despite that, Thurstan was astounded by what he was seeing. 'You say you were taught these things in the house of the patriarch?'

'Occasionally, there were accidents or illnesses. An Arab physician would attend, and I would assist.'

He glanced at her again. 'An Arab?'

'Patriarch Heraclius maintained that neither race nor creed mattered when lives were at stake.' She watched him boldly. 'You disagree?'

'Not necessarily.' He looked back at the sleeping boy. 'Though it doesn't serve to think well of those we are tasked with slaying.'

'I hear you've spared the prisoners?'

'Thus far.'

She rolled the cloth and placed it in a bowl. 'If you don't mind me saying, lord, I think that was a wise decision.'

'I said "thus far". And that's all.' He headed to the exit. 'You hear me, girl? *Thus far.*'

—

'No sign of our friends?' Bishop Hubert asked, red-faced from having climbed to the south-facing battlement.

Thurstan pointed. 'Only there.'

The bishop looked out over the simmering wilderness, directing his gaze to what resembled a mound of refuse some eighty yards to the castle's south-west. The clusters of vultures indicated that it comprised the Saracen dead. The other remnants of the garrison, the living ones, their emir among them, had finally been sent away, stripped of arms and armour but supplied with a modicum of water and food and a couple of carts for their wounded. Thurstan had issued them firm orders to head south until they found a Muslim-held town or village. Whether that would be easy or difficult for them, he didn't know, but it was the third day since they'd captured St Hildegard's Tower, he felt increasingly exposed out here, and didn't want a potential enemy within. Somewhere inside him, a voice – it might have been his father's, it might even have been Bishop Belphagor's – advised that the living will always pose a threat, will always come back to fight again in some form or other, but he couldn't help thinking that enough men had died during this quest for an object that didn't even seem to exist.

That was doubtful wisdom of course, and as he wondered about it, he absent-mindedly part-drew his sword and regarded the colourless rag bound around its hilt.

'What is that thing?' the cleric wondered.

'Your grace?'

'That filthy piece of cloth. It's been on your sword as long as I've known you.'

'A scarf… a lady's favour.'

'Ah.' The bishop's countenance softened. 'Your wife? The one who died?'

'It's of no consequence.' Thurstan slid his weapon away; he certainly wouldn't be discussing his private life with this tricksy fellow. 'What of the girl?'

'I've spoken to her since she ceased to tend your squire. At length… She reiterates what she told us before. That the infidels were holding her here because she has the ability to call on God's healing powers.'

'Well… we've searched this castle high and low,' Thurstan replied, and that was true. While Pandulf was laid low, Thurstan and his men had gone through every storeroom, stable, dungeon and oubliette. 'There's nothing here even resembling the Cross, or any other icon that might have emboldened Qazairi to defy Saladin.' Despite the evidence of his own eyes, the knight struggled to give voice to his next question. 'Is it possible this girl… this *child*… can perform miracles?'

'Saint Margaret of England certainly could.'

'You mentioned her before.'

The bishop frowned. 'She was English born. A relative of Thomas Becket, but so holy that she too worked unimaginable cures and healings. Many witnesses attested to this. And yet the damn creature went to live with the Cistercians in the Abbey of Sauvebenite near Lepuy, in the Auvergne, a convent which unsurprisingly became famous across Christendom and enjoyed huge prosperity.'

Thurstan half-smiled.

'You doubt that story?' the bishop asked.

'I'm just… What was it you called me the other day, your grace? A mere soldier? I deal with what's in front of my eyes.'

'Well... on this occasion it's young Pandulf.' The bishop nodded across the castle to the eastern rampart, where Pandulf, wearing only a pair of hose and boots, his entire upper torso swathed in clean bandages, had emerged into daylight.

'I suppose the key question is should that wound have killed him, or not?'

'What's your opinion as an experienced man of war?'

Thurstan shrugged, still mystified. 'That blade was eight inches long, your grace. At that moment, I felt certain he had only minutes remaining. But I'm not a surgeon.'

'Either way, she's obviously done this before.'

Thurstan pondered. 'I can't pretend I haven't heard of miracle cures.' He was determined to give no further details about his own of course.

'And were those others genuine?'

'Some would say so.'

'It's a strange path we tread, Thurstan Wildblood.' The bishop mopped more sweat away. 'Look at this Godforsaken barrenness. Why would anyone even want it?'

'The Muslims consider it home.'

'So they say. But they stole it from the Greeks, who inherited it from the Romans, who stole it from the Jews... no one has any call on it. Except *us*. For this is where Our Saviour lived and died. And for that reason, if no other, if there's any place where miracles can happen... this is surely it.'

'And what of Coptics? Can they be trusted?'

'I know none personally. I only know *of* them.'

'There's no possibility of witchery?' Thurstan asked.

The bishop looked amused. 'Witchery? So, you doubt God's power but not the Devil's?'

Thurstan struggled to answer. For all his determination to be hard-headed, for all his cold rejection of the divine, it was increasingly hard to ignore the possibility that powers greater than Man's were at war in this raging dust-storm of a land.

'You can't have one without the other, surely?' he said.

The bishop mused. 'All I can tell you is the girl seems devout. I questioned her at length. Her answers on doctrine were satisfactory.'

'So, what do you wish to do?'

'We should take her to the king, wherever he is...'

A voice now called from one of the towers. 'Rider coming in, my lords!'

From the north, a small dust cloud was approaching.

—

The messenger was a knight of the Levant named Aldemar de Maur, and like many of his kind, he wore colourful Eastern garb over his Western mail, though at present he was caked with grime.

'Do you have any water?' he asked, dismounting. 'I've been riding hard for several days.'

Thurstan had already called for water and handed him a brimming gourd.

De Maur, who was young and fair-haired, drank deeply, then stared around the courtyard with appreciative fascination. 'Count Humphrey will be delighted you've recaptured his desert outpost. It was the first thing they took from him after Hattin.'

'I hope he's equally delighted that in one day's time we'll be abandoning it again,' Thurstan replied. 'The Saracen garrison who were evicted can walk straight back in through the open gate.'

De Maur looked shocked. 'The garrison? You didn't kill them?'

'We killed enough,' Bertrand said.

The newcomer still seemed confused.

'We didn't take this place for Humphrey de Toron,' Thurstan explained. His hard face and stern attitude were enough to prevent the young knight probing further.

'You have a message for us?' Bishop Hubert asked.

'Yes, your grace. A very important one.'

'Has Jerusalem fallen?'

'There's been no fight at Jerusalem,' De Maur said. 'King Richard retreated again.'

Groans of disbelief were heard across the yard.

'We were close,' the messenger said. 'The army was strengthened before we marched. New companies from Tyre, courtesy of Count Henry. Even some of the French came back, with Duke Hugh.'

'The last we heard, Duke Hugh was dying,' someone said, sounding disappointed.

De Maur nodded. 'He is sick and very weak. But he wanted to be there.'

'To share in the glory no doubt,' De Vesqui chuckled.

'Why did the king retreat?' Bishop Hubert asked, visibly disappointed.

'He received more grim news from England. It makes his further participation in this war very difficult.'

'Where is the king now?' Thurstan asked.

'North. He sent a letter to Saladin, advising that Jerusalem can remain in Muslim hands if some agreement can be reached that Christian pilgrims may visit.'

'In the name of God, you're lying,' Bishop Hubert said.

'I wish I was, your grace.' De Maur became very serious. 'Because it gets worse. It was the king's thinking that if we controlled the Outremer coast, in other words could bring in new armies any time we wished, the sultan would be forced to give us the terms we seek.'

'Only one coastal fortress remains uncaptured,' Thurstan replied. 'Beirut.'

'Correct, my lord. So, the king headed north and took about half the army with him. With help from Tyre, he felt he could easily besiege the port.'

'This is not the war we wanted,' Bishop Hubert moaned. 'This is not the war.'

'Tell me, De Maur,' Thurstan said. 'Will the king prosecute the siege of Beirut himself, or will he leave it in the hands of others while he departs for England?'

De Maur swilled again from his gourd. 'No one really knows. He is torn with indecision.'

'And all this time, Saladin has been strengthening,' Bertrand said.

De Maur wiped his lips and nodded. 'Which is why he's already broken the truce… and attacked Jaffa.'

Thurstan took him by the arm. 'Attacked Jaffa?'

'Yes, my lord. From two sides at once. Muslim reinforcements have come up from Egypt, but they marched inland to avoid the Ascalon road.'

'We saw them,' Bertrand said. 'We sent a warning.'

De Maur nodded. 'I believe the garrison received it, but only after the king had gone north. Levies marched from Ascalon to assist, but it isn't just the Egyptian army that now encircles Jaffa. Saladin has come from Jerusalem. He's regathered most of those Saracen companies scattered after Arsuf. In total, he has thirty or forty thousand men.'

'And there's no word at all of King Richard?' Thurstan asked.

'I know not. As I say, I've been on the road.'

Dismayed muttering followed.

'Someone take this fellow,' Thurstan said. 'Give him food and clean bedding and tend to his horse.'

De Maur was led away.

'We can't return to Jaffa now,' William des Roches said. 'Not if it's under siege.'

'Neither can we tarry in this desert,' Bertrand retorted. 'Not in high summer.'

'We could stay here at the castle,' De Verneuil suggested. 'It's got its own well, it's excellently provisioned.'

Thurstan shook his head. 'If Saladin's at Jaffa, we're behind his lines. Those men I foolishly spared will spread the word. Some force or other will be sent here.'

'Where else can we go? Ascalon?'

'If Jaffa's under siege, Ascalon will be too. If not now, soon.'

Bishop Hubert shook his head. 'This is a hellish predicament.'

'At least we have the girl,' Bertrand said.

'Which will be even more reason for Saladin to send someone here,' Thurstan replied.

'Where in God's name do we go?' Even by his normal standards when under stress, Bishop Hubert seemed flustered. 'Wildblood, you command here. What plans have you made?'

'Maybe the girl can magic us up a flying carpet,' De Vesqui snickered. 'We can travel home over the top of Saladin's army.'

The bishop glowered at him.

'We march to Jaffa,' Thurstan said decidedly.

'Jaffa?' Even Bertrand was surprised.

'Slowly,' Thurstan added. 'I know Richard. He won't sit on his arse at Beirut and let Jaffa and Ascalon be taken.'

'So why slowly?'

'Do you want to get there before the battle… or after?'

De Vesqui chuckled again. 'That's not like you, my lord.'

'Maybe not,' Thurstan replied. 'But this time we have something precious to protect.'

—

On the east battlement, Pandulf had barely noticed the commotion in the courtyard. He sat alone, too absorbed by the infinity of rock and emptiness and the huge tides of dun-coloured dust creeping across it on the endless desert wind.

At first, he didn't even notice that the girl was approaching along the battlement walk. When he did, he tried to jump up, but pain lanced through him, and he tottered against the nearest merlon before sinking back onto his stool.

'You should rest as much as you can,' she said.

'I'm… indebted to you,' he stuttered, still captivated by her dusky skin and emerald eyes. 'I understand you saved my life.'

'I did nothing.' She spoke with a strange lack of interest.

'You prayed, did you not?'

She peered over the empty waste. 'Anyone can pray.'

'Well, this is the Holy Land. I shouldn't be surprised that such things happen,' he said. 'Either way, I'm grateful you chose to honour me with this gift.'

'I didn't choose you,' she said. 'I was forced to. Your master… Wildblood, is it?'

'Thurstan Wildblood. He commands King Richard's household.'

She didn't seem impressed. 'All you Franks look the same to me. But anyway, he forced me to do it.'

'You wouldn't have, anyway?' The lad couldn't help sounding disappointed.

'What is your name?' she asked.

'Pandulf.'

'Pandulf...' She sighed. 'The castle court was filled with wounded men. Given the choice, I might have picked you out, but then I might not. Don't take that as a personal slight. It's just that I'd never met you before.'

'Even so, you'd have passed me over to help one of your Saracen captors?'

'Aren't you my captor also?'

'The difference is, with us, you're among friends.'

'I only have your word for that.'

'No one's hurt you, have they? No one's molested you.'

'None of the Saracens did that either.'

'Only because you're special... because you're holy.'

She mused. 'It remains to be seen if that stays the hand of your people.'

'*My* people? Lady Melinda... We are Christians, like you.'

'Faith is an easy shield behind which men can hide their true nature.'

'I don't understand. We've *rescued* you.'

She turned to face him. 'To what end, Pandulf?'

'I...' He stuttered again because he didn't actually know.

'The saving of your souls? Isn't that why you're all here? And is that not a form of self-seeking?'

'Look... we're pledged to restore the Holy Places and the holy artefacts.'

'And the artefacts would include me?'

'That wouldn't necessarily be a bad thing, would it?'

'I can only hope not.' She looked back to the desert. 'For I'll clearly have no say in the matter.'

CHAPTER 26

Despite the chill in the simple stone room, Thurstan's body was rank with cold sweat. He thrashed under his sodden blanket, his head thumping. Mother Turilda tried to force the foul-tasting green cordial between his lips.

'I don't... don't want it,' he stammered.

'You must drink it.' Her stern, walnut features hovered over him. 'You are not cured.'

'I want to go with her.'

'Don't be ridiculous.'

'I'm not drinking it...'

'When you came to Kirkwood Hall, they told me you were strong. A great warrior.'

'They lied.'

'Thurstan Wildblood... am I to lose two patients today?'

'I didn't ask to be your patient.'

'I shall rephrase it. Am I to lose two neighbours today? My only two neighbours?'

'My lord?' another voice said, this one speaking French, not English. 'My lord!'

Thurstan's eyes came stickily open, and the pain of the headache ebbed away. As did the dank chill of the English autumn. Bertrand was looking in under the tent flap. 'The sentries report a rider approaching.'

Thurstan's thoughts drifted. Back to Kirkwood Hall. Where he'd sat on the battlement for long hours, swathed in furs, the interior below destroyed by his own hand. He looked out over the glass-smooth surface of the lake. No strength in his body, no will to live. Another of those tiresome sisters bringing yet another green elixir.

Reality then swam back in full. Across the tent's dim, fetid interior, Pandulf had glanced up from his own bedroll, his face glistening.

Thurstan clambered upright, adjusting his sweat-damp mail; they were permanently mailed now, awake or asleep. He grabbed his sword-belt, slung it over his shoulder and went outside with Bertrand.

The tents had been erected along a dried-out wadi, with raised ground both to left and right. No one else had stirred. The only movement came from the two crossbowmen crouched on the rise to the north, both watching the approaching source of their disquiet. Thurstan and Bertrand scrambled up and hunkered down beside them. Again, all four wore Bedouin cloaks to avoid the sun glinting from their armour.

A flat plain extended westward, the sun glaring white from its windblown surface, making it difficult to distinguish the figure of the horseman plodding towards them. This far out, there should be no one travelling alone, unless it was another messenger, though that was improbable given that they'd last received information only a few days ago. The other alternative was an Ayyubid scout, which was more likely as the Saracens they'd spared at al-Yuqhar would almost certainly have spread the word that Melinda of Jerusalem was back in Christian hands.

'I see mail, my lord,' one of the crossbows muttered. 'Could be one of ours.'

Thurstan cupped his eyes. The approaching horseman was hooded, wore the usual all-encompassing travelling rags and was coated in yellow dust, but from this angle his left leg and left arm were both visible, and they were indeed mailed. It would have been unusual, even for the Mamluks, to wear full body-mail as Christian knights did.

'Doesn't mean he's a friend,' Thurstan replied. 'And we don't treat him as such until we know for certain.' They grunted in agreement. 'You know what to do.'

The rider and his horse, who by the looks of his slumped posture and the animal's slow, uneven pace, were both suffering water depriva-tion, passed by below their position. At which point, the crossbowmen stepped into view, one in front of him, one to the side, weapons loaded and levelled.

The rider reined up, startled.

'Who are you?' Thurstan called, coming down the slope with sword drawn, Bertrand a few yards to his right.

The rider visibly relaxed. 'Lord Thurstan, it's me.'

He pulled back his hood, revealing the face of Robert de Quincy, the Scot.

'What in Christ's name are you doing here?' Thurstan said.

De Quincy slid from his saddle. His beast stood quivering. 'I'm posted to your company.'

'Have you taken leave of your senses, riding at midday?'

The Scot's face was severely reddened by the sun, his forehead blistered. 'I may have become confused in the heat... Have you any water?' Bertrand handed him a leather bottle. He drank thirstily. 'My lord... my horse.'

Thurstan signalled to one of the footmen, who took the animal's reins and led it around through a dint in the high ground to the pen, where the other beasts were resting under cover and with buckets of fresh water close at hand.

'It's laudable that you came all this way back,' Thurstan said, 'but surely you'd have been better use at Jaffa?'

'Jaffa, my lord?' De Quincy looked puzzled.

'Isn't Jaffa under siege?' Bertrand asked. 'We received a message just over a week ago.'

'Things have changed again.' The Scot wiped his cracked, flaking lips. 'Jaffa wasn't just besieged. Saladin struck its outer walls in full escalade. He had overwhelming numbers. The defenders fought hard. I know because I was with them. In the end we had to pull back. The Ayyubids surged through the town. They burned most buildings to create space for their war machines. We contested every street, made them pay steeply...' He drank again. 'In the end, we were driven back to the keep. Several days passed during which we were encircled and pounded with stones and fire-pots. We'd sent a call for assistance but hadn't expected a response. Not with the king set for home. But he came anyway. My lords... the king arrived. He hadn't brought all of this host, because he came by sea. Sailed down the coast from Acre. But he himself led the charge onto the shore. Rode off the gangway at the back of his ship, the *Franche-Nef*, his best men following. They cut through the Saracens in a frenzy. We came out to join the fight.'

The Scot drank again, gulping, shaking his head. 'It was a fray the like of which I've never seen. The tide of battle went back and forth, the gardens and orchards of Jaffa reduced to blood and ruin. Again though... our numbers were still too few and we were forced back into the keep. Richard sallied out repeatedly, torching their catapults and ballistae, setting new perimeters around the citadel... and then Count Henry's advance companies from the coastal road arrived. Now the battle was even, and the king was determined to have it. I heard him say that this was the final fight, the one he'd been seeking. He raged all over that terrible field. The infidels he slew were numberless...'

'What are you saying?' Bertrand asked wonderingly. 'Saladin's host is destroyed?'

De Quincy shrugged. 'I can't say destroyed. But defeated. What remains of his army has withdrawn to Jerusalem, harassed much of the way by Count Henry's knights.'

'Did Saladin die?' Thurstan asked.

'I've no knowledge,' De Quincy said. 'The king sought a messenger, to advise you that if you have your prize, it's safe now to return.'

Thurstan and Bertrand walked back to the wadi where they'd pitched their tents. The look on Bertrand's face was almost euphoric.

'At last, God has shown His hand,' he said.

Thurstan was hesitant to cast doubt on that because happy soldiers were effective soldiers, and their own struggle was far from over yet. But it was difficult.

In all previous wars, his ears had rung with prayers, blessings and offerings to the Lord. Every force he'd marched with had done so supposedly because God willed it. And yet, horrors had always followed. In Ireland, his master, Hugh de Lacy had brutalised the populace of two towns in particular, Killeigh and Fore, wreaking even more violence than the Viking, Turgeis, who had marauded there centuries earlier. Thurstan had never understood, even then, as an impressionable lad, how the God his gentle mother had spoken of could even allow it, let alone permit it in His own name. Why hadn't He smitten those responsible? They'd even burned the abbey there, and yet Hugh de Lacy became Lord of Meath. No heavenly power struck him, or cursed his loved ones, as it had in response to Thurstan's own barbarities.

Gwendolyn's sole offence was to marry me.

The only possible explanation was that there was no God. Or no God Thurstan wanted to know. That all events were the whims of fate. Or so he'd always told himself, so he'd forced himself to believe. And yet of late, so many strange, unlikely things *had* happened.

How was he – Thurstan Wildblood, of all people – now assigned to be saviour to a saint? If there was a God, He had a strange sense of humour.

'You were right about Richard coming back,' Bertrand said.

Thurstan glanced at him. This at least he could opine on. 'I know my king.'

'Those who pronounced him Lionheart when he was only a boy were also right.'

'A good king should be remembered for more than war though, don't you agree?'

'This one will be remembered as the king who liberated a living saint from the clutches of heathens.'

'Let's not run before our horse to market, Bertrand. We haven't even got ourselves back to safety yet, never mind the girl.'

–

Bishop Hubert received the news in what Thurstan considered surprisingly sober fashion, signalling the knight to accompany him to the distant end of the camp.

He halted when they were far from all the others. 'You saw the written orders that brought us here?' he said. 'From Richard?'

Thurstan nodded. 'I did.'

'You're able to read? You read them thoroughly?'

'Of course.'

The bishop pulled out a metal tube with a leather thong attached and a cork stopper in one end. 'You wish to read them again?' He arched an inquisitive eyebrow.

Thurstan shrugged. 'I don't need to.'

'Excellent. In which case you know I have full authority here?'

'Have I indicated otherwise, your grace?'

'No. To your credit, Wildblood, you haven't. But this may be a test for you. I've made an important decision… The girl, Melinda, is not to be returned to the king.'

Thurstan frowned. 'Forgive me, but wouldn't such a decision be in defiance of those royal orders?'

'If I'm the king's representative here, empowered with full authority, I'm entitled to change the original plan if I deem it necessary.'

'But, if the girl isn't going back to the king, where is she going?'

'England.'

At first, Thurstan thought he'd misheard. 'England?'

'Think about it, Wildblood.' The bishop lowered his voice. 'The king may already be headed there, himself. But even if he isn't, even if he's still at Jaffa, all those other powers that came with us to the Holy Land are now in Jaffa too. Henry of Champagne—'

'Who's a loyal ally,' Thurstan interjected.

'So far, but what about when he's King of Jerusalem? What about the French under Hugh of Burgundy, who now the war is over has made a remarkable recovery from his illness? What about the Templars, the Hospitallers?'

'Aren't they our allies too?'

'They were… when Saladin was the foe. But Saladin is defeated. Don't you understand, my friend? When they find out who this girl is, and what she is, they won't just stand by and let England claim her.'

'My lord bishop… isn't this girl the whole of Christendom's prize?'

'Don't be naïve, Wildblood. It's unbecoming to a man of your age and experience. Look, we shed our blood to acquire her, so it should be Canterbury where she's cloistered. She can have peace and security there, and pray for the good of the kingdom, and at the same time, the pilgrims will flock to see her and pay no end of alms.'

'How foolish of me not to realise that,' Thurstan replied.

'You should also realise that if we take her to Jaffa instead, the forces of the Holy See will grind into motion. The knights of the Temple in particular will be keen to spirit her away.'

'The Templars owe much to King Richard.'

'Maybe, but we all know how rapacious they are when it comes to hoarding wealth. Look at the rewards they could win from the French if the girl was taken to Paris or Chartres. And as for the Italians... God help us, the Italians! Half the infantry in the pilgrim army are Genoans or Venetians or Pisans. There's no hope they won't all want their say. Every damn church in Italy boasts some relic or other, some sacred icon that supplicants pay mountains of gold to kneel in front of. With every other Pope a greedy Italian how could that not be the case? Archbishop Ubaldo will *demand* Rome's right to protect her. He'll say it's their *entitlement*.' Bishop Hubert reddened. 'I won't have it, Wildblood! Canterbury is not going to miss out on a treasure like this.'

'Suppose the girl isn't a saint? In truth, we know nothing about her.'

'Grow up, Wildblood. She's a saint if we say she is.' The bishop took a moment to breathe, to scrunch a towelling cloth and dab at his head and his fat, wobbling neck. 'Look, I can see you're troubled by this. But think about it. When the king told us to bring the prize back from al-Yuqhar, he was expecting the Cross, was he not? Two pieces of desiccated wood. We could have smuggled such an item anywhere we wished. No one would have noticed. But with that girl it's different. This group of men we have will talk. No doubt about it. Once they're back among friends, they'll regale all and sundry with the wondrous miracle they witnessed. A squire called Pandulf brought back from near-death.'

Thurstan was about to reply that the king's presence would surely cow all those with devious designs on pretty young Melinda of

Jerusalem, but then he remembered that the king might not even be there. He could be sailing for home at this moment.

But there were serious problems with this scheme. Practical ones.

'Your grace... we aren't provisioned for such a journey.'

'We won't all of us be going.'

'We won't?'

'Saladin's forces are broken, but that won't necessarily work in our favour.' The bishop thought on it. 'Many of his men might now be our prisoners. So, the word could be travelling already... about this miraculous girl, this saint with the bewitching eyes. So, even a company of our size will likely attract attention.'

'And if a company of our size is too large,' Thurstan asked, 'what size of company isn't?'

'A handful, I'd say. Wouldn't you? Handpicked, obviously. You may choose the best fighters among us. I suggest you take them only from those *Familia Regis* men who are currently with us. They have the prowess, but they're also sworn to the king in a way the others are not. They'll be loyal to the last, I'd imagine... or hope.'

Thurstan was still reeling from what was being asked of him. 'A lot of men have come a long way, your grace, and have had very little for it.'

'In which case it works perfectly. Because now they'll be going home again.'

'Home is the other side of the world. And with only a handful of us...?'

'As I say, pick only the best.'

'I assume you won't be coming?'

'I must return to Jaffa. If for no other reason than to explain my thinking to the king.'

'But you've just said he may not be there.'

The bishop reddened again. 'It's not the fact that I'm too cowardly, Wildblood... though no doubt nothing will change your mind on that. But what use would I actually be? You think a man of my age and shape could survive such a journey?'

'You think any of us will survive it?'

'You have more chance than me. And secondly, just because Saladin is beaten, that doesn't mean the Pilgrimage is over. Jerusalem remains Muslim. It may be that this treaty Richard offered the sultan will now bear fruit. But we have to be in the room if we wish to partake of it. I can't go home even if I wanted to. Not yet.'

There was doubtless some truth there. It was also true that the ungainly Bishop Hubert would be neither use nor ornament on such an arduous journey, and most likely would become a casualty at an early stage, though only after inconveniencing the rest of them for mile after tedious mile.

'The matter of us being poorly provisioned can't just be dismissed,' the knight said.

'You may take half of all those supplies we currently have. We can make it back to Jaffa on the rest. There's also gold for you. More than enough to see you to a safe port.'

Thurstan thought it through. Even if Beirut was still in Muslim hands, the other city ports — Acre and Tyre in particular — were safely held by Christians. So, yes, the five hundred gold bezants that Thurstan knew the bishop kept among his saddlebags would be adequate for that.

'Wildblood, I know it's a difficult thing I'm asking, but this girl may be the single best reason why we even came east.' Oddly, a note of pleading had entered the cleric's voice.

'We need *something* to show, don't you agree? King Richard certainly does. He's been the hero of this campaign. No one will deny that... except the French of course. But the acclaim of the whole world will mean nothing if we come away without victory.'

Thurstan didn't comment. Only now was it sinking in what was being asked of him.

'No one remembers the losers, Wildblood. Will all these men have died for nothing?' The bishop's voice hardened. 'It's not a suggestion, my friend. This is an order. And it comes with the king's writ, which you are oath-sworn to obey.'

'What you're asking, your grace, is staggering. I mean, a *handful* of us... we may make it to the sea and a safe harbour, but after that, what?'

'After that it won't matter. You'll be pilgrims returning to Europe.'

'Many of whose kingdoms will want this girl for themselves. Or so you suspect.'

'Hell and damnation, Wildblood!' The cleric finally lost his temper. 'Must I think of everything? *You're* the extraordinary soldier, or so they say. I'm sorry I can't chaperone you all the way to Canterbury. But as I've tried to explain, I have pressing matters. You'll do this, yes? Remember who commands you…'

The knight wasn't listening, chaotic thoughts swirling in his head.

The word 'quest' had been tossed around like flowers at a pageant these last few months. He himself had been guilty of it. A quest was any mission or task that required significantly more mettle than the average. Except that no, that was underselling it. The quest was one of the few things about knighthood that Thurstan still liked. In fact, it was the whole of knighthood. Or it should be. It was valour, gallantry and sacrifice. Though Thurstan's own father had scarcely believed in such things, he had, on one of those few occasions when he'd deigned to speak with his third son, addressed the matter, saying that it was down to each knight to find his own method of fulfilling his vows, 'to find his own quest'.

At first glance, the thing being asked of Thurstan now — nay, *required* of him — was not so much a quest as a folly, a derangement, a suicide mission. But as the bishop had just reminded him, Thurstan was commanded to it by a king.

Serve God. Serve a king. Protect the righteous. Destroy evildoers.

Knighthood in its purest form made a list of difficult demands. And yet here, maybe, was his chance to fulfil them all in one fell swoop.

'Simply being a knight won't save your soul, lad,' Hugh de Lacy had said after his knighting on the edge of Fornham field. 'But at least it can lead you to an honourable grave. All you need do now is earn it.'

Bishop Hubert, meanwhile, was still talking. He offered the tube with the cork in it. 'Here is your documentation. It doesn't just contain your signed and sealed commission from Richard, and firm instructions that you and your companions are not to be interfered with, it will serve as a passport in most lands, though obviously not Toulouse... don't even think of showing it there. Special papers are attached, which will also see you through all the Greek ports...'

'You prepared for this in advance?' Thurstan said.

'I prepared for the possibility. As I said, it would have been an easier task to smuggle the True Cross back to England.' Again, Bishop Hubert offered Thurstan the tube. 'Keep these warrants in this water-proof container and keep it on you at all times.'

Tiredly, the knight reached out, hanging the tube around his neck and tucking it away under his clothes.

'Good man,' the bishop said. 'Your sword won't always be the answer. On occasion, you must rely on plain old officialdom. There'll be glory in this for us, though, Wildblood. And riches.'

Of course, they'd been told there'd be riches in the East, but now it seemed they had to wait till they got home again. 'When do you want us to leave?' Thurstan asked.

'There's no time like the present. Choose your men quickly. Have them ready by dawn.'

CHAPTER 27

When Thurstan first broke the news that Saladin was defeated, there was open celebration, as he'd expected: cheers, laughter, mailed fists punching the air. But when he added that the company was dividing, the response was more muted, the majority listening attentively as he explained that, for the girl's safety, she would now be taken to England.

'We'd have done the same thing had we recovered the Cross,' he said. 'Have no fear. The herculean efforts you've made will not go unnoticed.'

'Who takes her back to England?' Mercadier wondered aloud. Of them all, he looked most sceptical that this mission was possible.

'I'll make no bones about it, it will be perilous,' Thurstan replied. 'So, I'm damned if I'm asking others to do what I wouldn't do myself.'

'You can't go alone, my lord,' Pandulf said.

'I'll take a handful of chosen men, but only if they're agreeable. There'll be no blame attached if they're not.'

'Just so we're clear, my lord,' Gui de Verneuil said. 'For those you pick, the Pilgrimage is over?'

'Once the girl's safely delivered, you can return to the East if you wish,' Thurstan said. 'No one will prevent you, but you'll have done your duty.'

'You will indeed,' Bishop Hubert added. 'Because those chosen will face the sternest test of all. For which you'll obviously receive the greatest reward.'

'More reductions in Purgatory?' De Vesqui laughed.

'Knight-Serjeant...' The bishop fixed him with a reproving stare. 'The mere fact you are here reduces your sentence in Purgatory. Yes, even yours. So, imagine the benefits you'll gain from any further good you do.'

'Which is why,' Thurstan said, 'if you're willing, De Vesqui, *you* are my first pick.'

De Vesqui seemed surprised. He considered. 'A timely return home? My place in Heaven secured? Full permission to kill as many pagans as I wish. How could I refuse?'

'Gui de Verneuil?' Thurstan called.

Verneuil seemed noncommittal. 'I'm only here, my lord, because as part of the *Familia Regis*, I was commanded to come here. If I'm commanded to go elsewhere…'

'It's not a command. I've explained that.'

De Verneuil blew out a long contemplative breath. 'I suppose I've had enough heat and dust. Yes, I'll come.'

The next few *Familia* knights chosen refused. They still wished to see Jerusalem, they said, or they still had hopes the East would make them wealthy. Or both. However, Brion of Sherborne was agreeable, as was Lucius la Hai and Fenan FitzOrban. After that, Thurstan asked only one other member of the royal household, Captain Mercadier.

'Who will command my men-at-arms if I leave them now?' the infantryman replied.

Thurstan shrugged. 'The king will appoint a new captain.'

'So, I lose my post? For a hare-brained scheme like this?' Mercadier shook his head. 'I don't think so. I'm staying in the East for the time being.'

Thurstan nodded. 'As you wish. In that case, I think we already have everyone we need. Pandulf… get your equipment ready. We pull out just after dawn.'

The squire nodded and scurried away.

Thurstan also walked from the meeting, but with Bertrand in close attendance.

'What about me?' the banneret asked.

'You get more out of this than most,' Thurstan replied. 'Full and permanent command of the *Familia Regis*.'

'Thurstan… this makes no sense.'

'I agree. None of it. When you get back to Jaffa, you'll need to pull the whole household together. What remains of it...'

'No, Thurstan!' Bertrand gripped his arm. 'You have to take me with you.'

Thurstan looked at him askance. 'What?'

'Thurstan, please... as a favour to a friend.'

'Bertrand, you're Knight-Banneret of the *Familia Regis*. Your place is with the king.'

'Your place is with the king too.'

'I have a written order from Richard himself.'

'You're going to need a good man.'

'The *Familia Regis* needs a good man. You want Ramon la Hors to take command? If he's even alive.'

'Thurstan, I need this.' Bertrand's entreaty became a plea. 'Taking that girl to safety... It's a worthy cause. It might be the first worthy thing I've done in my entire life.'

'You made the journey here. That itself gains you credit in Heaven.'

'Oh yes, I made the journey here. And then it was only through your intervention that I was spared participation in a mass slaughter of prisoners.'

'You faced sterner opponents at Arsuf, and you faced them fearlessly.'

Bertrand shook his head. 'Another bloodbath. Look... call me irreverent. Call me a heretic even, but I sometimes wonder if this war is really the sort of thing God wants.'

Thurstan was surprised by how pale his oldest friend in the company now seemed to be. 'You thought these Muslim armies would turn tail, melt away into the dust without a blow struck in anger?'

'I don't know what I thought. God knows. Until I went to Chateau al-Yuqhar. And found a chance to provide escort duty for a saint. A real-life saint.'

Thurstan walked on towards his tent. 'We'll be lucky if we make it halfway back to Europe. Be thankful you're not going.'

'If I go with you and die en-route, I'll be glad. It will mean the saving of my soul.'

'If you're worried about your soul, have Bishop Hubert confess you.'

'A few words of penitence. Hardly adequate for the things I've done.'

Thurstan glanced back again. 'Bertrand, I know you. You've got more conscience than the rest of us put together.' But he hesitated to turn away again. His old friend was staring at him, wild-eyed, visibly in turmoil. 'What is it?'

'Thurstan,' Bertrand said quietly. 'I came to the East because I was commanded to, but for me personally it was to expunge a grave sin. Only in the Holy City, I felt, could I do that. But I never even got there. None of us did.'

'You certainly won't get there if you go home now.'

'Getting there isn't enough.' Bertrand grabbed his arm. 'We were supposed to liberate that sacred place. You *know* this. You also know that now we never will. Not if Richard leaves.'

Thurstan regarded him carefully, and a slow understanding dawned.

Four years prior to the Pilgrimage, Bertrand, then in service in Sicily, a kingdom at constant war with the Greeks, had partaken in the sacking of one of their greatest cities.

'Was Thessalonica so terrible a massacre?' the knight-commander asked.

'It was the worst thing you've ever seen.' Bertrand glanced shame-facedly over his shoulder to check there was no one else in earshot. 'The siege was hard, but Uncle Drogo owed fealty to Count Baldwin, so he'd have done whatever was asked of him. But when that bastard Andronikos Komnenos butchered every Catholic in the city, including Baldwin's own cousin – a young woman who was raped to death with a spear for God's sake! – he ordered this army to take the most savage revenge they could. So, they... *we* did. We'd heard so much about those Greek atrocities...' Bertrand's face registered both bewilderment and horror. As he often did in times of stress, he seemed unaware that he was clutching at the crucifix under his clothes. 'Thurstan, we ran amok. Didn't just ransack the town, we killed, raped...'

'You too?'

'In truth, I can barely remember.' The banneret's head drooped. 'That first night, I drank an entire keg of brandy-wine. Was drunk out of my mind. But I know that when I woke the following morning, I was covered in blood… and none of it my own. Thurstan –' he clenched his fist – 'I know I did hideous things. My vows of knighthood were defiled…'

Thurstan was dismissive. 'If you weren't in the right mind…'

'That's an excuse. In God's name, Thurstan… We're so caught up in this martial world where everything is achieved by force. I thought a war in God's name would be different. But again and again, it didn't feel that way. That's why I didn't want you to execute the garrison of Acre. For the same reason, I revile what you did to Count Conrad… I understand it was political necessity, but it felt wrong. At odds with everything we're here for. But even then, I told myself it was all done so that we might free Jerusalem from the pagan yoke. What greater good could any man do in the cause of repentance? And then, we reneged even on *that*.'

'And this new mission… this is your soul-saver now?'

'Don't *you* see it that way? We missed out on the Holy City, then we missed out on the True Cross. But now suddenly we have the chance to save a genuine saint, and you'd deny me that as well!' He shook his head. 'Thurstan, you have to take me. You know what I'm like with a sword. It's not like I'll be no use.'

Thurstan thought long and hard. If Richard was heading for home, he'd take the *Familia* with him. Or most of them. Bertrand would have no real role in the East.

'A trusted sword won't go amiss,' he finally said.

'You're a good friend to me, Thurstan.'

'Don't rely on that. And remember, this girl's a captive and we're her captors.'

Bertrand nodded vigorously. 'So long as we deliver her out of this hellhole.'

CHAPTER 28

'I can't even imagine what England is like,' Melinda said to Thurstan. 'I was taught about it, of course, but to me it was a semi-mythical land. And a barbarous one, where it always rains.'

'It doesn't always rain,' he replied, staring ahead as they rode. 'Though... sometimes it feels as if it does.'

'How wonderful.'

Thurstan tried to ignore her flippant tone, his thoughts elsewhere. It was two days now since they'd diverted from the main company, following a crude map that Aldemar de Maur had prepared for them, along a route that would steer them well east of Jerusalem, plunging them deep into lands that were still held by Saladin.

As the Levantine knight had promised, the terrain had grown harder and drier. By all accounts, when they reached the Dead Sea, they'd find a landscape devoid of life. It was only mid-morning, a couple of hours still to go before the midday sun would drive them all under cover, but as before, they wore stained and aged Bedouin garb over their mail, while Thurstan had made Pandulf give Melinda some spare clothes of his own: hose, boots, a hooded jerkin, and a feathered cap, into which the knight had instructed her to tuck her hair. It had been a matter of practicalities, but it had also made sense to disguise the fact they had a female with them, not just to fool spies and dissuade bandits, but to reduce any temptation among his own men. For the most part he trusted them, though De Verneuil could be an oaf when the mood was on him. De Vesqui of course was another matter. From the moment they'd been saddled with Melinda of Jerusalem, he'd paid close interest to her, though not of the leering sort. As always with Pandulf's 'dark and deadly man', there'd been something more profound, even calculating in his appraisal of the girl. Though this was nothing Thurstan hadn't anticipated or was unprepared for.

'I understand that you're taking me to England for my own safety,' she said. 'Or at least, that's what you believe. But don't I have any say in it?'

'No more than I,' he replied gruffly.

'You're a knight. You must go where your master commands.'

'And you're a saint, which means your life is more valuable than mine, and the sooner we get you away from this war, the better. Surely, you don't wish to return to Saracen captivity? Because that's all you'll find in Jerusalem.'

She sighed. 'I'm not a saint, my lord. You mustn't keep calling me that.'

'You work miracles.'

'It's not me. If it's anyone, it's whoever hears my prayers.'

Thurstan didn't bother replying that this sounded saintly enough to him. But even if there was nothing holy about her, she possessed certain special gifts. For one thing, she could ride as well as any man here, which was an unexpected advantage for them, while the previous day, when they'd hunted, she'd proved herself more than proficient with the Turkish double-curved bow, potting several desert hares. When Pandulf had congratulated her, she'd told him to read nothing into it, because she wasn't a soldier, and she would never put an arrow in a man: all human life was sacred. She'd added that she'd learned that skill as a servant of the patriarch, one of her duties to provide game for his table. There was nothing mysterious about it.

They rode on, Thurstan staring ahead, increasingly discomforted that Melinda seemed intent on keeping him company at the front of the small column. Pandulf would have been much gladder to ride alongside her. The girl might be mistaken for a lad from a distance, but up close there was no possibility, not with those fine, tanned features and alluring green eyes. It was little wonder the squire was so smitten.

'What are *you* doing here, Lord Thurstan?' Melinda asked.

'Don't ask foolish questions,' he grunted. 'You know the answer to that.'

'I mean *you* specifically. What brought you to the East? Riches? You don't seem to have amassed any. Religious fervour? I see no sign of that. Or are you seeking to improve yourself? Is there some darkness behind that face of hard indifference? Some terrible thing you seek to be shriven of?'

He glanced at her. 'Enough talking. This route's unfamiliar to us and dangerous. We need no additional distractions.'

'Of course not.' She smiled graciously, turning her animal around. 'I shall leave you alone with your thoughts. And whatever it is that haunts them.'

In truth, this was the last thing Thurstan needed: a hostage with insight.

Though insight into what? His imagination? Or something else?

This girl was supposedly a saint, and yet straight away, with no prompting from anyone, she'd sensed the burden he carried, and which he couldn't seem to throw off.

It was a dream. Nothing more.

Tiredly, he pushed these fears aside, reminding himself that they had more pressing problems, such as their dwindling water stocks. He scanned the ground ahead for any sign of greenery but saw only seared and rugged emptiness. What a place this was. How had Bertrand described it?

A land of demons?

Right now, that seemed appropriate for all kinds of reasons.

–

On the third day, the heat was unendurable even in early morning, and by now there was no natural cover, men and animals wilting within a couple of hours. When they veered towards a water signpost on a heap of red boulders, they found the spring dry.

Beyond that, they descended a barren slope to the edge of the Dead Sea itself. In Thurstan's eyes, everything they'd been warned about it was true. There was scarcely any life, not so much as a prickly thorn to break the arid monotony of its shoreline. The sea itself lapped sluggishly, as if it was glue rather than water.

At which point, Bertrand drew rein. 'What in the name of God!'

On the water's very edge, a mysterious figure, brownish-white and distinctly female, stood ankle-deep and perfectly still.

Thurstan too reined up, and also wondered what he was seeing. Skin creeping, he unwrapped the cloth from the lower half of his face.

The figure stood to just over five feet, and glittered, as though made from crystals rather than flesh. And it was undoubtedly a woman, or a representation of such. The distinctive curved hips were a giveaway, even the breasts. What was more, though it was facing away, it had turned at the waist as though to look back at them, or maybe *past* them.

'Is that...' Pandulf couldn't disguise his incredulity. 'Is that... Lot's wife? You can't say she's still here! That can't be the same woman!'

Now, Thurstan fancied he could see dints where her eyes should be, a slight protuberance for a nose. One of her arms appeared to have been raised, the hand at the side of her face.

'It's Lot's wife,' the lad said again, voice querulous. 'You don't remember? She was turned to salt. She looked behind her at that city where men behaved like beasts, while God was destroying it with fire...'

'The city of Sodom,' Bertrand said in a hollow voice. 'That was its name.'

The whole group turned to look where the figure of salt appeared to be staring. It was another empty plain, scorched, strewn with blistered rocks. Great gusts of black and heated dust swirled across it.

'God smote it so hard there was nothing left,' Pandulf said. 'Not a living soul.'

'Horseshit,' De Vesqui replied, though for once he didn't add his customary scornful chuckle.

'It's a true story.' Melinda rode up alongside them. 'But that is not Lot's wife. There are other figures like this. They form naturally along the water's edge. It's just salt. There's nothing to be afraid of.'

'The Devil there isn't!' Fenan FitzOrban's steed reared as it sensed his panic. He was the closest to the crooked, glistening shape. 'This one's bleeding! *Look!*'

They stared, now seeing reddish streaks where they hadn't noticed them before, trailing down from the effigy's eyes and nostrils.

'No, my lords,' Melinda said again. 'It's just minerals... other kinds of rocks trapped in the salt. They leach their essence. It happens all along this coast...'

Before anyone could say more, hooves thundered, saltwater spurting, as Thurstan spurred his horse forward, galloping past. Sunlight glared from his yard of drawn steel as it swept down and around, and the awful shape exploded.

'You see?' He reined up in the water. 'No blood. No warning from beyond. Just salt... like the girl said. Now... pull yourselves together. We need to find shelter, or the sun alone will burn us to a crisp, never mind God's wrath.'

Even as he'd struck down at it, he hadn't been sure what would happen, but he'd had to take action. It was far too early in this journey of no-return for the rest of the party to start seeing phantoms as well.

However, a new mood had settled on the party as they picked their way along the salt-encrusted shoreline. The Dead Sea was renowned as a cursed place. Nothing lived here. No fishes, no birds. And that city, Sodom, but not just that one, its twin, Gomorrah, had both, as Pandulf said, been citadels of evil, where devils were worshipped and depraved acts made into sport. No wonder God had vanquished both with a hail of fireballs.

All the while, of course, the sea lay flat and still, its surface more like tarnished metal than water. Cakes of salt floated, while more of those eerie, twisted mannequins adorned the shore.

Well before midday, when they usually pitched camp, Thurstan had them stop beside a line of immense coastal rocks, erect their awnings and do what they could to sleep.

In the first instance, the men were too jumpy. They knew what they'd seen. A figure of salt, bleeding from the eyes and nose. None of those other shapes counted, because they'd reflected no human features, but that first one had been all too real.

'You don't think that could have been some kind of warning?' Pandulf asked Bertrand as they sat with backs to a boulder, the lifeless sea glinting in front of them.

Bertrand had just drunk down the last droplets of water from his personal supply and now chopped at the sand with his knife. 'The girl explained,' he said tetchily, his lips cracked and dry.

'What does she know? No disrespect to her; she's a native here, and we aren't. But she was a servant in a religious household. How often did she even leave Jerusalem?'

'What do you want me to say, Pandulf? Even the rocks are turning against us? In God's name, why would they?'

The lad lowered his voice to a whisper. 'Perhaps because we're taking the girl away? Maybe this is why Bishop Belphagor made Lord Thurstan invincible...'

Thurstan, who though he'd been seated with his eyes closed, had been listening, wondered if it was worth intervening, but then decided against. He was as worn and sun-stricken as the rest of them. At present, he'd rather just sleep.

'Pandulf, this is sheer madness,' Bertrand said, though he didn't seem so convinced anymore.

'If the girl really is holy, shouldn't she be here in the East?' the lad persisted. 'The best weapon Christendom has in this fight, and we're taking her somewhere else!'

'She hardly sees herself as a weapon.'

'Does it matter how she sees herself if the Devil himself is driving this? Bertrand, look how he's empowered Thurstan. He can't be defeated...'

'That's a delusion you should divest yourself of.'

'You've seen it with your own eyes. Only Lord Thurstan could get this girl back to England, to take her away from the most important war Christendom's ever fought...'

Before Bertrand could reply, Ivan de Vesqui got to his feet. 'This is hopeless,' he said loudly. 'We've covered no distance at all, and we're already dying of thirst. Do we even know if we're heading the right way?'

Thurstan opened his eyes but remained seated. 'The sun rises in the east and sets in the west. We're heading north. It's not a difficult calculation.'

De Vesqui stood with hands on hips. 'You're sure about that? We're much further inland than the last time we went north.'

Bertrand chopped sand all the harder. Thurstan stared dead ahead.

'I've a suggestion to make,' De Vesqui said. 'And I'm not just putting this to you, my lord. I'm putting it to these others. We're all sharing this peril together. Do you deny they have a stake?'

'Speak openly,' Thurstan replied. 'No doubt you'll speak out anyway if I refuse you… behind my back.'

Pandulf eyed the looming figure of De Vesqui in silence. A few yards along, Melinda stirred into wakefulness. The rest of them were also now paying attention.

De Vesqui's mouth curled upward, exposing a brownish canine. 'Seeing as there's no hope of us getting this child to Canterbury… don't give me those blank faces, the rest of you! You seriously think any of us will make it to England?'

'So, what do *you* want to do?' Gui de Verneuil asked. 'Defy the king's orders?'

'Are they the king's orders?' De Vesqui wondered. 'It seems to me these orders came from Bishop Hubert Walter. Who's not even a senior churchman.'

'He's a baron of the Exchequer as well as Bishop of Salisbury,' Bertrand retorted. 'He's also a royal justiciar.'

'Whatever he is, he's out for himself.' De Vesqui smirked. 'And whoever this girl is, whatever power resides in that pretty little body of hers…'

'Bishop Hubert considers her valuable,' Bertrand interjected.

'The Saracens felt the same,' De Verneuil said. 'They must have. They kept her safe.'

'None of that matters!' Pandulf spoke up. 'Bishop Hubert took his orders from King Richard. Commander Wildblood has written documents to that effect.'

De Vesqui snickered. 'I doubt they specify that we are to escort this girl to England. Does the king even know she exists? Didn't he think we were retrieving the True Cross?'

'They're hardly likely to specify anything,' Bertrand said. 'They'll simply be confirmation that we're engaged in royal business.'

'So, this whole thing is open to interpretation?'

Pandulf shook his head. 'Ours is not to question, my lord.'

Thurstan was determined to rest if he could. Increasingly though, it seemed there'd be less of that to be had here than he'd hoped. He was impressed by Pandulf, though. A mere squire standing up to a murderous knight like Ivan de Vesqui.

De Vesqui grinned all the more. 'That's why you'll only ever be a pauper knight, Pandulf. If you even make it to knighthood… Which you're unlikely to if we linger out here, directionless, for much longer.'

'We aren't directionless,' Bertrand countered.

'Really?' De Vesqui said. 'What do you think will happen if we *do* make it home? You think we'll see any of the wealth this living saint is going to generate? Even if King Richard intends that we should, aren't they saying John rules England now? You'll get even less out of him than you would his brother.'

'You skate on the edge of treason,' Bertrand warned him.

'To you, maybe. Not to me.' De Vesqui tapped his chest. 'I'm a survivor. And I say we pocket the wealth this creature will generate for ourselves.'

'And how do you propose to go about that?' Bertrand scoffed.

De Vesqui snorted. 'For an officer in the *Familia Regis*, Knight-Banneret, you're something of a mule-head. How do you think? Saladin is beaten. Instead, Bishop Hubert has found new enemies among our own. Take the girl home, he says, but go by secret ways. Keep her separate from the French and the Italians, and definitely from the Templars and the Hospitallers. Because he knows *they* will seize her for themselves and do exactly as he plans to. Think about it. If Bishop Hubert and King Richard can do that… why can't we?'

De Verneuil sat slowly upright. 'Keep her for ourselves?'

'Ransom her to the highest bidder. We can ask anything we want. They'll come flocking.'

'We'll be reviled,' De Verneuil replied. 'Outlawed.'

'We'll also be wealthy.'

'And suppose it's Saladin who tables the highest offer?' Bertrand said.

De Vesqui laughed. 'What difference would that make?'

'What difference?' Bertrand got to his feet. 'Are you mad?'

'I must be. To have served under you. There are times, Lord Bertrand, when I think you must be greener than this squire.' He turned to the rest. 'You really think we're doing God's work? You actually believe that by committing mortal sin after mortal sin, your souls will be saved. Just because some rodent in a mitre says it will? Don't any of you understand? We're already damned. Tell me, Gui de Verneuil, how did King Richard finally beat Saladin at Jaffa?'

'They'll say God was on his side,' De Verneuil replied.

'Aye, that's what they'll say. But what will the real reason be? Isn't it more the case that the army of Tyre was on his side? At long last?'

Still Thurstan stared out over the tepid, stagnant waters. But inside, he was seething. De Vesqui was a lethal blade, but also a mad dog. Unlike Captain Mercadier, another brigand who'd entered the royal household when Richard ascended to the throne, he'd never made any real effort to suppress his baser instincts.

'And how did the new Lord of Tyre find himself in a position to make that happen?' De Vesqui asked them all. 'I'll tell you… because Count Conrad was conveniently but mysteriously murdered. Except that maybe it wasn't quite so mysterious.'

Thurstan finally looked around.

He appraised the brawling, bearlike figure. As rogue knights went, De Vesqui was a good man to have on your side. But by the nature of who and what the fellow was, Thurstan had long suspected there'd be limits on that. And quite clearly, they'd reached them sooner than he'd hoped for.

'I'm sure there are some here who already suspect this,' De Vesqui said, thumbs tucked into his sword-belt. 'But King Richard's savagery isn't confined to the battlefield.'

Bertrand pointed at him. 'Beware, Ivan de Vesqui. Lest you say something that follows you the rest of your days.'

De Vesqui laughed, looking at the other knights again. 'Lord Bertrand wasn't involved, it won't surprise you to learn. But *I* was. Of course I was. I'm a killer, don't you know. A pitiless killer who cares nothing for anyone but himself. But there's another here like that too. And you all know who he is.'

Instinctively, they glanced around at Thurstan.

'Put the two of us together, and add a third,' De Vesqui said. 'I don't know, Knight-Captain Ramon la Hors perhaps, and even the mighty Conrad of Montferrat... well, you all know what happened.'

The astonished silence stretched out as Thurstan climbed to his feet.

'There's some truth in what you say, Knight-Serjeant,' he said, in a casual tone. 'But you know the real reason I took you with me to Tyre?' He loosened the sword at his hip. 'It's because I've always known a time would come when I'd have to kill you.'

CHAPTER 29

'So, we come to it,' De Vesqui said, with a bellicose smile.

Thurstan shrugged. 'Sooner than expected. But this place is as good as any.'

All the rest were now on their feet, Pandulf among them, numbed by shock, hardly able to speak.

De Vesqui turned to De Verneuil, Sherborne, La Hai and FitzOrban. 'Have you men heard enough to stand with me?'

'Suddenly you need assistance?' Bertrand scoffed.

'Don't worry, Knight–Banneret.' De Vesqui seemed amused again. 'Commander Wildblood goes no further than this place, and neither do you. But the rest of you get to share in the riches we draw from this. Or you get to be dead. The choice is yours.'

Pandulf was even more horrified to now see Sherborne, La Hai and FitzOrban go and stand behind De Vesqui and unharness their weapons. 'My lords!' he pleaded. 'Think what you're doing.'

They ignored him, though from their grizzled faces, they weren't happy with the decision. They seemed twitchy, weary. Hardened though they were to these battles in the desert, the harsh conditions of the last few days had maybe overwhelmed their senses. And then, of course, there'd been that eerie figure made of salt. Pandulf himself couldn't explain it. Surely it was a portent of something, and almost certainly Sherborne, La Hai and FitzOrban thought the same thing. Of course, one other still remained undecided, the one who, after Thurstan and De Vesqui, was held to be the strongest fighter in the *Familia*.

'Gui de Verneuil, come over,' De Vesqui urged him. 'Don't pretend you haven't been planning this very same thing.'

De Verneuil looked long and hard at his serjeant, and then at Thurstan and Bertrand, and shook his head. 'There's nothing personal in this, you understand… it's purely a matter of in whose service I'm more likely to perish.' When he went over to Thurstan, he added: 'I should have said: in whose service *my soul* is likely to perish.'

'Four of them and three of us,' Bertrand said. 'Why are we always outnumbered?'

'You're not outnumbered today, my lord.' Pandulf grabbed for his own sword-belt, trying to buckle it to his waist and gasping in pain.

'No.' Melinda threw a restrictive arm around him.

'This is for your protection,' he hissed at her.

'Stay where you are, Pandulf,' Thurstan said, his gaze fixed on his serjeant.

'When this is over, squire, you may retire in respect of the miracle cure this child bestowed on you,' De Vesqui said. 'Of course, you'll have to walk back to civilisation. Because we'll need the horses. You'll need more than a minor miracle then.'

'You'll need one now,' the lad retorted, tearful with outrage. 'You all will, traitors!'

'Enough name calling.' Thurstan walked out onto the salty flat between their camp and the sea's edge.

Their opponents also walked out, the two groups halting about twenty yards apart. Pandulf and Melinda remained undercover, the girl's arms still wrapped around the boy's trembling shoulders.

None had equipped themselves with helmets or shields. It was almost as if by some unconscious agreement, they sought this thing to be over quickly.

'I'll give you men one chance to save your lives,' Thurstan told De Vesqui's compatriots. 'To walk away from this, all you need do is turn over your *Familia Regis* colours and leave. I don't care where you go. I'll report to the king that you died in the desert.' There was visible unease among the rebel trio. 'Think hard on this. The alternative won't just be death, but Hell too.'

De Vesqui smirked. 'That's some threat from a man like you, Wild-blood.'

And with a furious yell, his sword in one hand, his maul in the other, he charged.

—

The two parties closed at furious speed.

De Vesqui went straight at Thurstan, his arms windmilling. At the same time, Bertrand engaged with Sherborne, De Verneuil with FitzOrban and La Hai, their blades exploding together, ringing like bells, flashing with sunlight.

Fleetingly, the seven warriors' skills cancelled each other out, but as the two groups circled, lunging, thrusting and hacking, plumes of salt were kicked up, engulfing them in eye-stinging fog, which Thurstan quickly realised would sew confusion. No sooner had he parried a massive blow from De Vesqui, the giant's maul flying from his grasp, than FitzOrban came at him from the side, aiming a two-handed swipe with his battle-axe. Half-blinded, Thurstan was just able to duck and counterstrike on the turn, at the same time ramming his shoulder into De Vesqui's barrel chest, sending him tottering. His reverse slash at FitzOrban was blocked, but he followed it with a backhand, opening his adversary's defence, and slammed a mailed knee into his groin. As FitzOrban tottered away, gagging, Thurstan whipped his bone-handled knife loose and sheathed it in the fellow's neck.

He spun back, just in time for De Vesqui's second charge.

The giant had regathered his maul and attacked like a human threshing machine. Eyes still stinging, Thurstan backtracked to the water's edge, riding blow after blow, before catching the brute's face with a lightning cross-strike, slicing his left cheek to the bone. Again, De Vesqui staggered away. In his left-hand vision, Thurstan saw that Bertrand, his eyes also filled with salt, was on the ground, Brion of Sherborne standing over him, thrusting downward again and again, Bertrand swivelling from side to side. Just beyond him, De Verneuil had slashed La Hai cleanly across the hip, sending him staggering.

Thurstan shouted at him, pointing at Bertrand, then swung again to face the looming, salt and blood-covered horror that was Ivan de Vesqui.

The giant still had both his weapons. They came down like thunderbolts. Thurstan wove and parried, but he sensed that the big warrior was tiring. The flesh on the lower left side of his face hung off in a grisly flap, the full length of his teeth and yellow curve of his jawbone exposed. Now was the time to strike, and Thurstan did, hard, severing the maul mid-shaft, then hammering his pommel into the giant's left temple, sending him sloshing knee-deep into the waters, wading in after him. De Vesqui was slow to turn, his counter-swipe easily parried, Thurstan's sword then driving into his ribs with such force that the mail hauberk was punctured, straight steel invading the body beneath.

The giant fell forward, blood seething from his clamped lips, plunging below the shallow surface. Thurstan lumbered after him, stamping several times on his submerged skull with what he hoped was bone-cracking force, before struggling back onto the shore and lurching across to where La Hai still swapped blows with De Verneuil and Sherborne with Bertrand.

Striking from behind, Thurstan severed Sherborne's left hamstring. The rebel knight spasmed in pain, as Bertrand lunged forward, back-striking the fellow's stretched throat, opening his jugular in arcs of crimson. De Verneuil also triumphed, La Hai tottering away, shrieking, one hand clasped to a jellified right eye, only to impale himself on Thurstan's levelled sword.

The three surviving knights stood panting and sweating.

Thurstan was the first to move, walking between the casualties, nudging each with his foot to ensure he was dead. When he came to De Vesqui, he stopped at the water's edge. The huge figure lay face-down under the salt-frothed surface, crimson clouds expanding around him. He pulled a piece of rag from his harness and mopped down his blade, sliding it back into its scabbard as he returned to the others. Bertrand greeted him with haggard eyes.

'We should bury them,' he said.

'The desert can have them.'

'Thurstan, these were Christian men.'

'They chose their own beds, Bertrand. They should have known they'd be lying with ants and scorpions.'

BOOK TWO

SWORD OF DARKNESS

CHAPTER 30

In Bishop Hubert Walter's eyes, the aftermath of Arsuf had been one of the worst things he'd ever seen. The heaps of meshed and mangled corpses, the hacked limbs, the eyeless, slack-jawed faces. But Jaffa seemed a hundred times worse. Firstly, because the butchery was now over a week old, the air rank with putrescence and swarming with flies. Secondly because, though the dead again were strewed to every horizon, this had once been a glorious place with its orchards and vineyards – and now was a scene of horror.

'God the Father, Son and Holy Spirit,' Mercadier said, riding alongside the bishop.

A road of sorts had been cleared up to the city gate, though the gate itself was hardly necessary as most of the new-built outer wall had been broken or burned again. All the way, they passed carts laden with corpses so steeped in blood and ordure that they were unrecognisable, though by the looks of the soldiers who'd come with the carts, many wearing the household colours of European houses, it was mainly the Christians being collected for burial.

They found the town itself reduced to ashes and devastation. Again, a flotsam of death was scattered across it. It thickened the closer they drew to the keep, a sure sign that attempts to escalade the heart of the bastion had been pressed hard.

Leaving the rest of the troop outside, the bishop rode into the bailey alone. The dead here had been removed, nuns, monks and priests now moving between rows of wounded men laid on the ground. Amid all this, Bishop Hubert was surprised to see King Richard sitting in a chair outside the main entrance. He wore loose robes, and looked weary and unkempt, his hair hanging unwashed to his shoulders. Close behind him, Knight-Captain Ramon la Hors stood on guard.

'Congratulations, sire,' the bishop said, when the king motioned that he might approach. He dropped to one knee. 'On your victory.'

'Rise,' Richard replied tiredly. 'It was a victory for us. Hardly for mankind.'

'May I ask,' the bishop got back to his feet, 'were you wounded?'

'A reoccurrence of the illness I had at Acre. Or something similar.' Up close, the king was wan and had visibly lost weight. Those like De Quincy, who'd been awed by his performance on the field, would be shocked to see him now. 'It's no surprise. As you can tell, in the last few days this place has become a pestilent hole.'

'The dead here seem mostly to be Saracen. You haven't permitted them to collect?'

'They can if they wish,' La Hors said. 'But there aren't enough of them left to do it.'

Bishop Hubert nodded. 'Our own losses?'

'Severe,' the king said. 'But there are enough of us left that we are once again the pre-eminent force in this part of the world.'

'Pre-eminent enough for you to return home, sire? For that's the rumour we heard.'

The king gave it some thought. 'The news from England and France is very disturbing. John and Philip are in open conspiracy to divide my kingdom between them. We have good men at home, but not enough, I fear. Which means that managing what remains of the Pilgrimage must fall to you.'

Despite everything, Bishop Hubert was startled. '*Me*, sire?'

'Don't worry, good priest. I don't expect you to win any battles. I think we've all had a bellyful of fighting. Saladin certainly has. He's now lost two armies. His next priority will be survival... And that, I suspect, will be hard enough for him.'

'You think he'll be responsive to further peace overtures?'

'I'd be very surprised if he wasn't. He's a good ruler to his people. He doesn't want to waste any more lives than I do. If terms can be reached, I'm sure he'll comply.'

'I fear he won't hand over Jerusalem.'

The king didn't immediately answer. He signalled La Hors to help him to his feet, and walked, the bishop tagging behind. They stepped out through an embrasure smashed in the bailey wall by catapulted missiles, and halted. The king's eyes roved the corpse-strewn wreckage of the city. 'We're all going to have to compromise, Hubert.'

Again, they walked, the king now offering his arm so the bishop could assist him. La Hors remained close at hand, a watchful guardian. His *Familia Regis* livery, doubtless cleaned since the affray, stood out brightly in that place of greyness and death.

'If you can negotiate an open door by which Christians might enter the Holy City,' Richard said. 'If you can obtain permission for Christian services to resume there... alongside Muslim services of course, there's no point asking the impossible... I think you'll find Saladin amenable.'

'You honestly believe that, sire?'

'It's happened in the past. The Muslims aren't all bent on our destruction. If our people can live together in peace, that's what we should aim for. There's been enough... enough of *this*.' They wafted at flies. 'I'll be honest, Hubert, once I heard that John was manoeuvring, I despaired. It made me wonder why I'm fighting these people here, when I have so much more pernicious enemies at home.'

'Christians can be forgiven their indiscretions, lord.'

'Some can. In any case, my initial plan was to have you negotiate a temporary truce with Saladin. So that I could go home and deal with my brother, hostilities resuming once I returned. But if a truce can be permanent, it's better. Don't you agree?'

'So, reclaiming Jerusalem is out of the question?'

'It is for me, alas. I've neither the time, nor the resources.'

'Your enemies will paint it as a defeat.'

'They paint anything I do as a defeat.'

'What of Count Henry, the new Lord of Tyre?'

'Tyre's assistance was invaluable. It shows what we might have achieved and how much sooner had Count Conrad been with us. But if Henry now has ambitions on the Crown of Jerusalem, which he doubtless has, he'll need to win it for himself.'

'And if he does, will we still have a treaty with Saladin?'

'No, but history will record who broke it.' The king gazed bleakly down the street in front of them. Again, its buildings were burned ruins, forlorn figures sitting among the ashes. Here and there, two-man teams, their mouths covered by rags, loaded more corpses onto wagons. 'Though I doubt that will happen anytime soon. Henry has a huge swathe of Outremer to administrate, and he'll need to get it under control first. Many lordships and church offices sit vacant. On which subject, were you successful in your own mission?'

'In some ways, sire, yes... In others, no.'

'Tell me more.'

'We never found the Cross. But we think we found something better.'

As they picked their way back through the hole in the wall, the bishop told the king about the girl, Melinda, her devoutly religious nature and her ability to affect seemingly miraculous cures.

'A living saint,' Richard said, sounding strangely uninspired. 'Who'd imagine it?'

'If we can get her home safely, it will reflect well on us.'

'I can't say I'm overjoyed that Canterbury's coffers will fill while mine remain empty. Though getting her back to England will be a challenge in itself. Wildblood's her escort, you say?'

'I couldn't find anyone better at the time,' the bishop said.

'There's no one better in the whole army. He's a demon with a sword.'

'It's a strange individual to put so much trust in,' the bishop admitted. 'But I had no real choice.'

'You did well. But now you must do better.' They'd reached the keep door, where they halted. 'I sail at the first opportunity. Maybe within the next couple of weeks. But we go without fanfare. Knight-Captain La Hors and a small contingent of the *Familia Regis* will escort me.'

The bishop was shocked. 'My liege! So few?'

'I'm not abandoning the army, Hubert. But likewise, I'm not marching it away again. Not yet. If Saladin is thrown down by his people, a more belligerent replacement may restart hostilities, and that would render this whole enterprise pointless. So, the army stays for the time being. But from this moment, everything relies on you.'

'I'm truly honoured,' the bishop said to himself, as the king disappeared into the shadowy interior, his chamberlains hurrying to wrap a cloak around him.

'Before you ask, your grace,' Ramon la Hors said, 'he is recovering well. A few days ago, he could barely speak.'

The bishop eyed him. 'I have no doubt the king will return to health.'

'There are some saying that it's more about his mind than his body. That he suddenly felt the cost of this war weighing on his soul and it all but overwhelmed him.'

'Which should make it all the more important our little saint is delivered home safely.'

La Hors smiled. 'Thurstan Wildblood is the man for such a monumental task.'

'Equally monumental is *your* task, Knight-Captain.'

'Don't fret, your grace. We'll get the king back to England.'

The bishop regarded him curiously. 'You don't seem unhappy. Most of us came to recapture Jerusalem. And yet now you're going home, and you haven't even set eyes on it.'

'Oh, I saw it,' La Hors replied. 'Distantly. The morning the king decided we were marching back to Jaffa, I stood on a high rock, and I saw it. A haze of dim structures behind a stone wall painted red by the rising sun.'

'And you're content that's all you'll ever see of it?'

'I go where my duty dictates, your grace. At least I can say that I saw Christ's kingdom on Earth... even though it was far, far away.'

Then he took the bishop's hand, kissed the episcopal ring, and walked into the keep.

For all the formal politeness, there was something about Ramon la Hors that Bishop Hubert mistrusted. He was a calm, measured fellow. But so was the average wolf. Especially when stalking its prey.

CHAPTER 31

'That's only the third Ayyubid patrol we've seen in the whole of the last week,' Bertrand said. 'Do we take that as a good sign?'

'Maybe,' Thurstan replied. 'They told us Saladin's host had been routed. Maybe this is the proof of it.'

They were situated atop a rocky ridge, peering through a tangle of Christ's thorn at the twenty or so Saracen horsemen crossing the plain some five hundred yards to the west. It wasn't just the scarcity of their numbers that made an impact, it was the manner of their travel. They rode slumped in their saddles, bearing arms that looked tarnished. The usual eye-catching colours of their captain's regalia were absent; it looked dingy and torn. One of those behind him wasn't just helmetless, his head was bound with bandages.

'If this is the best they have,' Bertrand said, 'we haven't got much to worry about.'

'We should work on the basis it isn't,' Thurstan replied. 'And then we won't be disappointed.'

But deep down, a spark of hope had ignited. It was now late September, and the searing summer temperatures had levelled off. In addition, once they'd moved into the lands north of Jericho, the countryside had turned greener. It wasn't just grass. There were groves of cedar trees and extensive groundcover. Spiny scrub-thorn for the most part, though anything was preferable to bone-dry sand and rock.

'Thurstan?' Bertrand asked. 'Is it true… what De Vesqui said? That we're not just keeping the girl from the Saracens, but from fellow pilgrims too? I have to ask. It's been troubling me.'

Thurstan slithered down the slope until they were out of sight of the open plain. 'You've seen the way the French have behaved on this

campaign, Bertrand. You've heard the way they're behaving at home…
while we're still waging the good fight here? Would you trust *them*?'

'The French are old enemies. But the Templars? The Hospitallers?'

'Grandmasters Sable and De Nablus are good men, but ultimately
they're Rome's fighting arm.'

'So, we're keeping her from the Holy Father as well?' Bertrand
didn't sound happy.

Thurstan had wondered how long it would take for the truth of
their mission to dawn on him. 'We have our orders,' he said. 'It's easier
just to obey them.'

–

In a tight gully, Pandulf, Melinda and Gui de Verneuil sat facing each
other, occasionally cupping hands under the thin trickle of spring
water from a crack in one of the rock-faces, and saying little of
consequence.

This was the way it had been for so many days that Pandulf had
lost count. Surely, he'd asked that very morning, they were into the
hinterlands of Tyre by now, only for Bertrand to reply that they weren't
even as far north yet as Acre.

'You should just be grateful we've made it this far,' Gui de Verneuil
had added. 'I didn't think we would.'

That was the most he'd said since they'd halted to view the roofless
shells that were the outskirts of Jericho, a city which, according to
Melinda, was abandoned by its mainly Christian population after
Hattin. They all knew the older story, of course, about Joshua's
triumph there. How, during a war with the Canaanites, he'd led his
army around the city for seven days, his priests blowing their horns,
at the end of which, the stone defences collapsed.

'It's pity you can't conjure up something similar,' De Verneuil told
the girl. 'Maybe make the sky fall on our enemies' heads.'

'I've already told you,' she had replied, 'whatever powers I call on,
I'd never direct them to do harm.'

'Then in all honesty, what use are you?'

And now, suddenly, all these days later, out of the blue, he said it again.

'What use are you, girl? If you won't kill our foes, why can't you at least provide? Call manna from Heaven. Make this spring water flow so there are full cups for each of us.'

'Don't you have enough food already?' she replied.

Pandulf watched the exchange uneasily. She was referring to the supplies they'd purloined from their deceased colleagues on the shore of the Dead Sea. From the moment they'd left that blood-spattered place, Melinda had made it clear what she thought of the brutal fight there, and those who'd participated.

'Are you saying you *can't* do these things, or *won't*?' De Verneuil asked.

'One cannot challenge the Lord. We already have enough to see us through…'

'What about gold then. I don't have enough gold.'

'My lord…' Pandulf said.

'Quiet, boy. You've already had your miracle.' The knight sat forward. 'I want mine.'

'Greed is one of the deadly sins,' the girl said quietly.

'In which case, let's not worry about the gold. I'll just have a new sword instead.' With a rasp of steel, the knight drew the longsword from his scabbard. 'You see this?' He ran a gloved finger along its wicked edge. 'It's carved its way through a dozen battles. But look at it closely. Chipped, blunted… from hacking open the skulls of countless nonbelievers. Is it greedy to ask for a replacement? I'm sure there are many more on this road I'll need to slaughter before we reach our destination.'

'My lord, I beg you,' Pandulf said, one hand creeping towards this own weapon. 'Put away your sword.'

De Verneuil threw him a glance. 'What's that? You're a squire and you gave an order to *me*, a knight?'

'I didn't give an order, I merely requested—'

'Well, I make no request of you when I say step aside. In fact, get out of my sight.' De Verneuil got to his feet, grinning. 'I have private business here.'

Pandulf jumped up, clasping the hilt of his own sword. 'Yes, I'm only a squire and it's not my place to challenge you, but if I must, I will.'

'What's going on?' came a stern voice.

Thurstan and Bertrand were advancing along the gully.

'Nothing, my lord,' Pandulf replied. 'A slight disagreement.'

'Why is your weapon drawn?' Thurstan asked De Verneuil.

The knight put the sword to his shoulder. 'Like he said, it's nothing.'

'With so few of us left, we can't afford to quarrel,' Bertrand said.

Both Pandulf and De Verneuil averted their gazes.

'You realise how far we still have to go?' Thurstan asked them. 'You understand the kind of opponents we may meet on the road?'

'What does it matter?' De Verneuil snapped. 'The boy wasn't in danger. But you need to watch *him*, Wildblood. He's a mooncalf around this so-called angel on Earth. And he's got too much mouth for a mere lad.'

And he stalked off, pushing his way past the horses.

'We can't afford to lose De Verneuil as well,' Bertrand muttered.

Thurstan looked Pandulf and Melinda over. 'From now on, we don't leave the girl alone,' he said. 'Either you or I must always be with her, Bertrand. Now, go and find De Verneuil. Make sure he knows there are Saracens in the vicinity.'

Bertrand moved off.

'My lord,' Pandulf said, 'I—'

Thurstan cut across him. 'You too!'

Their eyes met, and the lad knew that no further nonsense would be brooked today. He scurried away.

–

'Thank you, my lord,' Melinda said after a moment. 'Your friend is of a dangerous ilk.'

Thurstan, having held his helmet under the trickle of water, now drank from it. 'My friend killed his own comrades to protect *you*.' He poured the rest over his head. 'You'd do well to remember that.'

'He seemed willing enough to do it at the time.'

'Because the alternative was fighting me.' The knight gazed down at her. 'They say you are blessed, girl. Beloved of God. But they also say I am *unblessed*.'

'I don't know what that means.'

'Pray you never find out.'

CHAPTER 32

Only now did it strike Bishop Hubert that he and Archbishop Ubaldo were the first Christians of rank to enter the city of Jerusalem since the Pilgrimage had commenced.

On first approaching it, the Holy City looked much like any other in the East, except that some of its upper battlements were still in a state of disrepair from when Saladin himself had bombarded it after Hattin. Entering through the main gate, it was just like entering Acre or Jaffa, though by prior arrangement, he and Bishop Ubaldo's small escort of Norman knights were required to hand over their weapons to the Mamluk guards. Inside, the city streets were as narrow, noisy and dirty as those they'd been used to, though among the folk thronging them, there were no white Europeans to be seen. Saladin had expelled all Christians from the city, though he'd also spared their lives, which was something Bishop Hubert felt many pilgrims to the East ought to appreciate more.

But even so, Jerusalem was Jerusalem, the navel of the world.

It was impossible for shivers not to pass through him. These were the same streets where Jesus had walked and preached. It was just beyond these walls where he was crucified, died and then rose from the dead.

Physically, it was exactly as he'd imagined, comprising district after district of chaotic, flat-roofed structures built from mudbrick or sand-coloured stone, strands of laundry hanging between them, countless faces peering from windows, but also, here and there, cramped marketplaces or the relics of much more ancient architecture: Roman arches, paved walks, freestanding columns carved with Greek or Hebrew script.

As they rode slowly, gaggles of children poured from side passages, captivated by their colourful regalia. There was little hostility on show, even from the adults, though some frowned or seemed puzzled when they set eyes on the churchmen's mitres, on Archbishop Ubaldo's jewel-encrusted crozier, or the bright gold crucifix hanging from Bishop Hubert's belt.

For all that it seemed in some ways ordinary, this was still the most sacred of cities. It was here where all the hopes of the world rested. Though it was strange to consider that when they were only visiting because of a war. In Hubert's mind, there could be no lasting peace while Islam held this ancient capital. That was a given. It was indisputable. Islam and Christianity were irreconcilable opposites, who would hate each other for the rest of time.

Or so their adherents were told.

In reality, would they really? Was it such an impossible dream that men whose faith in God had taken different paths, but who still ultimately worshipped Him, could one day live peacefully? *Thou shalt have no other gods before me.* That firm instruction had been written in *Exodus*. But what if it was the same God, just with different names?

He shook these scandalous thoughts from his head.

'You seem troubled,' Archbishop Ubaldo said.

'Just reminding myself that we can't have peace at any price, your excellency.'

The archbishop snorted. 'You seriously believe that? With Richard Plantagenet scampering home like a whipped dog?'

'We still have an army.'

'And no one to lead it.'

'Count Henry—'

'Count Henry be damned. And no doubt he will be. You've heard the latest rumour? That Conrad of Montferrat was not murdered by the Assassins, but by our own people? God forgive sin, I'm repelled by the mere thought.'

Bishop Hubert had indeed heard the story. There'd been much discussion about it. He had no idea how it might have leaked out. Of course, there was no way it could be proved. So, he wasn't greatly concerned. Soldiers in garrison would always gossip.

'You are right, though,' the archbishop said. 'To make the best we can of this appalling situation, we must secure the best peace terms possible. As such, we mustn't refrain from being forceful. Remember, these are pagans. Weak, degenerate men. It may be that circumstance has contrived to hand them a victory they haven't earned and aren't yet aware of, but if we can hold our nerve, we can buy ourselves space in which another Christian army may be brought from Europe, this time under a more peerless leader, to wipe these dogs from the face of God's Earth forever.'

Their first meeting was held in a rather small audience chamber in an equally small palace quite close to the Al-Aqsa. The room was made from unadorned marble, but filled with cushions, divans, and rich oriental carpets.

Sultan Saladin himself – who never spoke directly to his guests except through an interpreter – remained relaxed and seated. He was in trim, near-athletic condition even though he was in early middle-age. He wore a white turban and a loose black robe with Islamic verses embroidered in silver thread on the sleeves. He was inordinately handsome; grey haired but with smooth, chiselled features, a well-groomed beard and moustache, and eyes that were dark pools of intellect. Almost immediately, Bishop Hubert had him for a superior standard of opponent.

This first session was very cordial and primarily about formalities. Extravagant gifts were exchanged and promises made that all negotiations would be in good faith and that both parties would work hard to establish a lasting peace.

During their first break, the bishops and their entourage were guided around the city, from the Lion's Gate to Mount Zion, averting their eyes whenever they passed a church that had been converted into a mosque, but were permitted some time on the *Via Dolorosa* and then entry to the Church of the Holy Sepulchre, which had been opened especially for them. They were even allowed to pray. Bishop Hubert felt absurdly grateful as he knelt at the dust-covered altar that at least this holiest of sanctuaries had not been desecrated. Doubtless it had been boarded up, for the Muslims had had no use for it, but there were no signs of vandalism, no damage or Islamic slogans painted, and no foul straw or excreta to indicate that any animals had been housed here.

When he quietly mentioned this to Archbishop Ubaldo, the response was dismissive.

'The political acumen of Saladin. All along he'll have reasoned that it might one day suit him to maintain the dignity of this place. Perhaps he does want peace. Especially since we've made it clear that otherwise, we will fight on until both sides are annihilated. But once he's gone, who will come next?'

The second day's meeting was more productive, or at least it began well.

Agreements were soon reached over hostage exchanges. Since Acre, both sides had been relatively merciful with those prisoners of war they'd taken. No mention was made of the slaughter of Richard's prisoners at Acre, but likewise, nothing was said about the massacre of the Templars and Hospitallers who'd surrendered after Hattin.

After this though, there was a disturbance. One of Saladin's captains entered from a side door, bowed to his master and passed a quiet message to the translator, whose face lengthened.

To Bishop Hubert, it seemed immediately ominous.

When the message was conveyed to the sultan, he passed a curt instruction. A moment later, with a clanking of chains, three more figures appeared. Two of them were Mamluk guards, but the other was a prisoner.

Bishop Hubert sucked in a tight breath.

The prisoner, whose hands were manacled, wore ragged, dirty breeches and worn-out boots. He was bare-chested, the crude bandaging wound around his torso dappled crimson on his right side. His face was grotesquely disfigured, a huge and recent gash running from his left earlobe to the left side of his mouth, the loose flesh only adhering in place because of the blood that had congealed there. And yet for all this, despite the sun that had scorched what remained of his features to crimson leather, and the crust of scabs that had once been his lips, his immense size – his oxlike breadth as well as his height – and his great unkempt mop of matted black hair, marked him out as Ivan de Vesqui.

'Your graces,' he stuttered grinning through his pain.

Archbishop Ubaldo regarded him with a mixture of bewilderment and revulsion. When the chains were released, and the fellow slumped onto his knees and attempted to crawl forward to kiss the episcopal ring, the senior cleric dug his feet into the carpet and pushed the divan backward, shouting: 'In God's name, keep this thing away!'

The sultan's guards dragged the prisoner back.

Bishop Hubert, for his part, sat taut with fear and disbelief.

'What is this?' the archbishop demanded.

'This fellow tells us he walked wounded across a great expanse of desert before one of our patrols located him, half-dead from thirst,' the interpreter said. 'He is a Christian, as you can see. But he claims to bring news that may disturb us all.'

'Is it relevant to today's discussions?' Archbishop Ubaldo asked tersely.

'Most relevant, your excellency,' De Vesqui said, the interpreter making sure to translate everything for his master. He turned to Bishop Hubert. 'It's relevant to *you*, in particular, your grace.'

Bishop Hubert treated him to a silent but furious stare.

'I'm not sure we have time for this,' the archbishop countered. 'Whoever you are, you aren't wanted here.'

'It concerns the girl-saint, Melinda of Jerusalem,' De Vesqui retorted.

At which mention, Sultan Saladin straightened up. He spoke quickly to his interpreter, who now turned to the prisoner. 'The sultan is keen to hear more.'

De Vesqui swivelled between the two groups. 'I regret to report, my lords, that she has been kidnapped by a lawless band who will now demand a hefty ransom.'

'What are you talking about?' the archbishop said. 'Who is this girl-saint?'

'You aren't aware, your excellency?' De Vesqui feigned surprise. 'I'm shocked. But I believe the sultan is aware. And I know for a fact that Bishop Hubert is aware.'

The archbishop rolled his eyes. 'What on Earth is going on here?'

The blood pounded in Bishop Hubert's veins. There was no hope he could stay silent. All gazes were soon locked on him.

Slowly, cautiously, he related the events at the desert stronghold, al-Yuqhar, and how the aim was to retrieve the True Cross, but how instead, they came away with a serving girl who seemingly possessed the power to heal.

'To heal?' the archbishop said, mystified.

Saladin listened attentively as his interpreter provided a word-by-word account.

Bishop Hubert explained how the girl called Melinda, a Coptic Christian, had been held by her Muslim captors for this same reason, but added that he saw with his own eyes how she worked an apparently miraculous cure on a young squire.

'And in your opinion, this was a genuine miracle?' Archbishop Ubaldo asked.

'No man could know that for certain, your excellency,' Bishop Hubert replied. 'But for safekeeping, I despatched the girl to Europe with a band of knights I considered trustworthy.'

The archbishop's red and excessive face flesh quivered with rage. 'Why was I not made aware of this before?'

De Vesqui sneered: 'I think, your excellency, because you would wish such a gift conferred upon Rome rather than Canterbury.'

The archbishop glared at his fellow cleric. 'So, you felt you had a Christian saint in your grasp, a living one no less, and you sought to keep her for yourself?'

'I made a judgement that England would be the safest place for the girl.'

'Safer than the Holy See? That was either a nonsensical judgement, my lord bishop, or a villainous one.'

Saladin listened intently. A hint of a smile indicated that he was enjoying his opposite numbers' disquiet.

'You haven't heard the half of it yet, your excellency,' De Vesqui said. 'We were only a few days into the journey when the girl was taken… by the very men charged with protecting her.'

'You liar!' Bishop Hubert hissed.

'I don't lie, your grace.'

'Ivan de Vesqui, you've never told a truth in your life.'

'If that's what you think of me, why would you send me on this mission?'

'I didn't send you. I sent Thurstan Wildblood, Knight-Commander of King Richard's *Familia Regis*. For reasons that pass my understanding, it was he who chose you.'

'And it was Wildblood who first laid hands on the girl and said we should keep her for ourselves,' De Vesqui asserted. 'He said that either Christendom or Islam would pay a mighty fee to get her back. And when I sought to intervene, he tried to kill me. See my wounds, your lordships? Those others who supported me weren't so lucky. He left them for the vultures. If you need further proof, I can take you to the place where it happened.'

'Am I hearing this correctly?' the archbishop said in a voice of disbelief. 'Thurstan Wildblood! Whom rumour holds was the one responsible for murdering Count Conrad!'

'Campsite tittle-tattle,' Bishop Hubert responded. 'I know not where that ridiculous tale even came from.'

Now, the sultan spoke.

'His Highness is intrigued,' the interpreter said. 'He was led to understand that Count Conrad died at the hands of the *Hashshashin*, followers of Sheikh Rashid ed-Din Sinan.'

'He *was*,' Bishop Hubert said flatly.

Saladin spoke again, at some length.

'Be under no illusion, honoured guests,' the translator said. 'There is no love lost between the Sultanate of Egypt and Syria and the court of the Old Man of the Mountain. The *Hashshashin* objected to our attempts to make peace with Count Conrad.'

Now, Bishop Hubert felt his own shoulders stiffen. 'Excuse me, Your Highness… you were negotiating with Count Conrad?'

Again, their host seemed quietly amused. It was almost as if he didn't need a translator. But still he replied in his native tongue.

'Of course.' The interpreter made a casual gesture. 'You weren't aware of this?'

A dozen emotions cut through Bishop Hubert at the same time. First it was disbelief that so obvious an explanation lay at the root of a problem that had bedevilled them for so long. Then it was anger at the sheer depth of this betrayal. Then it was despair that men would always mire themselves in self-interest, even to the detriment of the common good.

'It hardly matters now.' Archbishop Ubaldo seemed determined to be more offended that Bishop Hubert had outmanoeuvred him over the girl-saint. 'I cannot believe you deceived me like this. And not just me. The other lords of the Pilgrimage...'

The sultan spoke again.

'We assumed the *Hashshashin* slew Conrad,' the interpreter said. 'My master feels it important to state that, though he is at odds with Sheikh Rashid, it would not sit right with him to let a fellow Muslim take the blame for a crime he did not commit. The truth must be known widely.'

'Unfortunately, the truth about *that* matter eludes us all,' Bishop Hubert said.

'Not so, my lords,' De Vesqui put in. 'If I might be so bold.' He clutched at his side, making a show of weariness. 'I was a party to the slaying of Count Conrad. We wore the garb of the Assassins. And Thurstan Wildblood was our commander.'

'And now he commits this additional crime,' the archbishop said. 'Snatching this child-saint from right under your damn nose, Hubert Walter.'

Bishop Hubert pointed at De Vesqui with a shaking finger. 'At the very best of times, this fellow is a conniving brute. The last thing we should do is take *his* word as gospel. In contrast, Thurstan Wildblood is one of King Richard's most trusted henchmen. I refuse to believe he'd have any part in this girl's abduction.'

'You'd better hope not,' the archbishop retorted. 'Because if this Saint Melinda of Jerusalem, assuming she's not some figment of your devious imagination, finishes up anywhere other than Canterbury, from where she will duly be delivered to real safety in the papal court in Rome, it will be on *your* head.'

Once again, Sultan Saladin appeared to find the whole thing amusing.

CHAPTER 33

Whether Melinda of Jerusalem's powers extended to keeping the road clear of opponents was a question that occurred to Thurstan more than once. Of course, he never asked her. He was quite happy to be sullen and uncommunicative when it came to her supposed mystical nature. The only way forward at present was to put a block on all thoughts of the miraculous, preferring to lay faith in his sword.

But for all this, for a time at least, they had no need of it.

Well into October, they met no one of ill-intent. It was true they were on backroads, scant animal tracks winding through uninhabited regions. But it was still fortunate, in Thurstan's mind. The weather also favoured them. As the autumn came on, there were greyer days, and while it was never what a native-born Englishman would call cold or even cool, the strength-sapping heat had diminished. As such, at the start of the last week in October, early in the day, Thurstan, Bertrand and Gui de Verneuil found themselves riding uphill from their small camp, and on coming to the top, peering down a broad slope covered in cypress trees on the city of Tyre.

It was a beautiful morning, the sky a pearlescent blue, the sun already rising. In a short time, the metropolis spread out below would be basking in its usual oily haze. As things were, they could see most of it clearly, along with the quilt-work meadows shoreward of it, and the many roads leading out. They could also see the vast military camps to the north, and beyond it all, the endless glimmer of the Mediterranean.

The various harbours along the city's coastline, in particular the largest, the Sidonian Harbour, appeared to be excessively busy with masts and sails. Further out, innumerable ships of all types, warships, cogs and galleys, rode at anchor. Thurstan would have taken it as a sign of the inevitable exodus west now the Pilgrimage was over, had it not been for the mailed, mounted companies heading south along the road to Acre.

It was a strange time, he thought, a twilight time between war and peace. No one knew which way the balance would tilt in the days ahead, so all eventualities were being planned for.

'Don't take this question the wrong way, my lord,' De Verneuil asked. 'But is it possible we are overreacting... hiding ourselves in these hills like outlaws?'

'I was thinking the same thing,' Bertrand said. 'These are Christian-held lands. We're all now on the same side.'

Thurstan didn't reply.

Bertrand forced a laugh. 'Thurstan, these are our brothers in arms.'

'Let's hope they remember that,' Thurstan replied.

'Granted, the girl will be valuable to whoever gets his hands on her,' De Verneuil said. 'But given these enormous events, aren't there bigger things for their mightinesses to be troubling themselves about?'

Thurstan mused on it. 'Even if Richard is heading for home, the war will drag on, I've no doubt. There'll be a treaty, and then someone will break it, and then there'll be another treaty and so on... and only minor gains will be made. And the great powers who came here in such pomp won't want to be part of that. But instead of going home with tails between legs, they'll need something to shout about... Something they can present to Christendom as a genuine prize. To indicate it was worth their while coming in the first place. So, I think they *will* put soldiers on this. Especially the military orders, who'll be desperate to salvage something for the Holy Father.'

'Will word of the girl have travelled this far north, do you think?'

'It's taken us a month and a half to get here, Gui. If the word has travelled at all, it will have reached all the ports by now.'

'In which case, how do you intend to do this thing?'

'With great caution.'

–

The city itself was bustling again, though the atmosphere this time was different. Fewer soldiers crammed the streets and squares, many, presumably, having been despatched south. But the aura now was of uncertainty. No one knew anything about their new ruler, Henry of Champagne, except that he'd already ridden off to join the war.

Meanwhile, there was chaotic activity around the docks. Droves of people, it seemed, were leaving the Levant. These weren't just refugees displaced by the Islamic conquests further south. They also included military companies who weren't prepared to serve under anyone save Count Conrad. Either way, it soon became clear to Thurstan that it would be difficult finding berths on any of the ships due to depart, though by the same token, his party would be well-concealed in such a crowd, especially as they'd already taken pains to ensure they'd blend in. All their military apparel had been bundled up and was secured on the backs of their spare horses. They themselves wore civilian garb, though first he'd had them all bathe in a hillside spring and in the case of himself, Bertrand, Gui and Pandulf, trim and smarten their beards. It was essential they looked less like battle-hardened soldiers and more like merchants who'd inadvertently been caught up in the war.

In itself, it was a good plan. There were many like that in the port when they arrived.

But the other problem was more complicated: Melinda.

Their opponents would now be searching for a group of white men in the company of a sun-kissed beauty with enchanting green eyes. Therefore, to maintain the illusion that she was a lad, Thurstan bade her cut her hair very short rather than simply tuck it away. To explain her colouring, he roughened and dirtied her clothes so that she might pass as a servant. To accentuate the illusion, they loaded her with baggage when they entered the city. Even then, they made no effort to go down to the Sidonian Harbour as a group. Instead, Thurstan opted to reconnoitre on his own, leaving his companions in the farthest back room of a tavern called *The Pewter Pot*.

En-route down to the docks, another problem gnawed at him.

Many of the ships leaving Tyre would now be carrying pilgrims returning to Europe. There'd be few among them penniless, as they wouldn't have been able to buy passage, in which case the majority would have wealth with them. Which made them worth attacking. This part of the sea was already notorious for pirates, but with more money than usual abroad on the water, there'd now be even greater danger. It would be a supreme irony if he managed to get the girl out of the Levant, right from under the noses of the Christian and Muslim worlds' greatest powers, only to lose her to a band of cutthroats.

He strolled the quaysides, stepping around barrels and piles of rigging, shouldering unobtrusively through throngs of people haggling with ships' masters, who in most cases were typical sea-rovers: grizzled, salty and gap-toothed. All kinds of vessels were moored here, from cogs to caravels to fishing boats, a constant stream of people bent under baggage as they ascended gangplanks.

Thurstan's group had over three hundred bezants left of the money Bishop Hubert had provided. That would be more than enough to secure berths, but it had to be the right kind of ship. Then he set his eyes on two impressively huge carracks, both triple-masted, battle-mented along their gunwales and with towers built fore and aft. They sat away from the quayside, anchored in the middle of the harbour, but prospective passengers were already rowing out to them on skiffs. Either of those would be ideal, but then he spotted the pristine white banners, emblazoned with red crosses, billowing among their topsails.

They were Templar ships.

And indeed, on the dockside close by, knights of the Temple were busy interacting with all those clamouring to go aboard. Thurstan walked the other way, only to find several more Templars, fully mailed under their distinctive livery, threading through the crowd towards him, but constantly stopping people and asking questions. He feigned a casual air as he sidled past, overhearing snippets of conversation.

'A band of English knights with a young Arab girl...'

Thurstan lowered his head, walking on. No one picked him out, and he left the harbour quickly, hoping to disappear into the warren of taverns and shops. But now he saw other armed and armoured men making enquiries of people. Some were knights, some men-at-arms, all in the colours of different households, and by their accents, from many corners of Christendom, but again they offered the same description.

Several English knights and an Arabic beauty.

When he returned to *The Pewter Pot*, he was relieved to see that his companions were still there, pressed into the corner at the back by the many other patrons. He pulled up a stool and spoke quietly but intently, trusting that their conversation would be lost amid the ribald shouts and gruff laughter.

'So, they *are* looking for us?' Bertrand said.

'You didn't really think this fabled Christian brotherhood that brought all these people east was going to last, did you?' Thurstan replied. 'We've been fighting these Saracens for the last hundred years. But we've been fighting each other a lot longer.'

'Does Philip of France really hold such sway?' Pandulf wondered. 'He only controls a small portion of his own kingdom.'

'There were Pisans and Genoans asking too,' Thurstan said. 'They'll be motivated by reward money. But the fact the Templars are involved suggests the real driving force is Archbishop Ubaldo.'

'That's what the Templars will say,' De Verneuil sneered. 'They'll claim they're doing it for the good of the Church. Of course they will. They're warrior monks, beloved of Christ… as they never miss a chance to tell us. But we all know the bastards will keep the girl for themselves. They never hold back from filling their own coffers.'

'Keep your voice down,' Bertrand cautioned him.

De Verneuil snickered and swilled some ale.

'The Templars are now our biggest threat,' Thurstan said. 'They have more troops than we can count. Not just here, but all across Europe. Every Templar house between here and Paris will soon be on the lookout for us. Which is why I propose that we sail… in a Templar warship.'

They gazed at him askance.

'We have to consider pirates,' he explained.

'It's true,' Pandulf agreed. 'Only the foolhardiest would attack a Templar ship.'

'In addition, we'll be in the very pocket of those who seek us,' Thurstan said. 'That should be the last place they look.'

Bertrand shook his head. 'You're mad. The Templars will notice the scars on our hands and faces. They'll see through these disguises immediately.'

'There are hundreds lining up on those piers,' Thurstan said. 'We can disappear into that crowd. The one chink in our armour is Melinda.'

Melinda, who'd been sitting listening, remained po-faced. Her small cup of wine sat on the table undrunk.

'Which is why she'll be travelling separately from the rest of us,' he added. 'At least until we are out at sea.'

Pandulf looked baffled. 'I don't understand.'

'Nor do I,' Bertrand said.

'We won't be taking our horses with us,' Thurstan said. 'That means half our baggage will have to stay behind too. But there's one particularly large bolster... in which we've been carrying our utensils, our cooking pots and such. That's where Melinda will travel.'

A stunned silence followed. Even the girl's eyes widened.

'I go in the luggage?' she asked.

Thurstan glanced at her. It was a lot to ask of anyone. It would have been a lot to ask of someone considerably smaller than she. Fleetingly, it struck him that they'd heaped more than a few indignities on this child since supposedly rescuing her. Thanks to Melinda of Jerusalem, he harboured more frustrations than he could give voice to. It particularly irked him that so many men had died 'preserving' her. But it wasn't her fault. She hadn't requested any of this.

'Only until after we sail,' he replied, in as conciliatory a tone as he could muster.

She still seemed aghast at the mere prospect, forcing him to look away.

'The main danger comes when we're boarding,' he told the others. 'She'll need to go up on deck on one of our backs. Once we're out of the harbour, passengers mingling with crew... she can come out. It's likely no one will notice one extra.'

'And who's going to carry her aboard?' De Verneuil wondered.

'You,' Thurstan said. 'You're the largest. It will look less ridiculous if you're carrying the biggest backpack. Of course,' he turned to

Melinda, 'you'll need to keep still. They might have half an eye open for stowaways. You think you can do that?'

She glanced one to the other. Their faces weren't exactly implacable – Bertrand, for one, seemed highly doubtful – but Thurstan was in charge.

'I can try,' she said quietly.

'You'll need to do more than try,' Pandulf said. 'Because if they find you, your fate won't be any better than it would with us.'

'For God's sake, boy!' Bertrand blurted. 'We don't *know* that.'

Thurstan glanced at him, eyebrow arched.

'These are the Templars we're talking about,' Bertrand hurried to explain; a note of pleading had crept into his voice. 'They're good soldiers, Thurstan. And good Christians. They've been our staunchest allies these last two years. They find the girl, what's the worst that can happen? They take her to Rome or keep her in one of their own castles. She'll still be safe. And it might not even come to that. We know that King Richard and his mother have good relations with the Temple. It might even be that the Templars will do our job for us.'

'You're saying they might take her to Richard, themselves?' Pandulf asked.

'It's not impossible.'

'Not impossible, but not likely,' Thurstan countered. 'In any case, there's one thing you're overlooking, Bertrand. This task was allotted to *us*. This is *our* quest.'

'So now you're bringing pride into it?'

'I'm saying the king put his trust in *us*,' Thurstan replied. 'To do anything less than keep that trust, or die in the attempt, would be an abrogation of our chivalrous duty.'

Bertrand laughed without humour. 'Don't take this the wrong way, but when did you care about that before?'

'How dare you!' Pandulf cut in. 'Lord Thurstan's led us with great distinction.'

'He did, aye,' Bertrand replied. 'He led his men courageously and made wise decisions. But he never let his chivalrous vows get in the way. Practicalities came first. Until now. So, let me ask you...' he turned to Thurstan again, 'what's changed?'

Thurstan fought hard to avoid glaring at him.

Bertrand was an experienced sword, but his naivety about his fellow Christians was a growing source of exasperation. It sprang mostly from an honest belief in the Gospels, but also his conscience, which, wakened by his failure to find forgiveness in Jerusalem itself, now seemed to remind him daily about the sack of Thessalonica. It was all but unhinging him, helped along of course by Pandulf's incessant talk about devils. Presumably, if devils were the cause of heinous deeds, men themselves were not. It was a simplistic view, but it meant that Bertrand was seeing less fault in those Christians who'd sworn special obedience to the Church, such as the Templars, than to Thurstan himself. But now was not the time for fights, arguments or the enforcing of rank.

'If *we* deliver the girl,' Thurstan said simply, 'we get paid a fortune.'

'Aye.' De Verneuil sat back. 'Well, that's good enough for me.'

Bertrand shook his head. 'I'm sorry... I don't believe that.'

'That's a pity.' Thurstan said. 'But if that's how you feel, there's nothing to stop you leaving our fellowship. I mean, I *should* stop you. You're under obligation. But making a fuss would draw more attention to us.'

Bertrand's cheeks reddened. 'I'm *not* leaving. I wouldn't abandon you all. I just think... I think our judgement is maybe getting clouded.'

Thurstan watched him carefully. 'As I say, that's a pity.'

CHAPTER 34

They booked themselves a single room upstairs in *The Pewter Pot*. Pandulf and Melinda were then told to stay out of sight there, while Bertrand and De Verneuil took their horses and all the equipment and supplies they wouldn't be able to carry to the nearest marketplace to get as good a price as they could.

This wasn't an easy moment, having to unload many things they'd come to rely on, including changes of clothing, spare weapons, and even their helmets, shields and chain-mail. It wasn't a desperate situation. They had the money to re-quip and purchase new horses once they'd made landfall in Europe, but it still felt like folly, leaving themselves with only a couple of weapons each, and no armour of any respectable sort.

Thurstan, meanwhile, returned to the Sidonian Harbour, to enquire about passage.

'Who are you, and how many in your party?' asked the old Templar at the counting-table on the quayside. He had wizened, haggard features, long white hair and missing front teeth.

He didn't seem particularly suspicious. There'd been at least twenty people in the queue before Thurstan, and he'd spoken to them all in a similar blunt fashion.

'Myself, two colleagues and a lad,' Thurstan replied.

'Where are you headed?'

'Anywhere away from here.'

The old Templar grinned to himself, one side of his mouth turning up. There was visible scorn there, as if here was yet another of these adventurers who'd come to the Holy Land thinking to make easy wealth, and yet, when the prospect arose of actual battle, had decided that he'd already had enough.

'The *Gloriosus* leaves on the dawn tide.' He indicated the nearest of the Templar carracks, wallowing a hundred yards out on the waters of the harbour. 'She's fitted for transportation of passengers. But she's a military vessel, so it won't be comfortable.'

Thurstan shrugged as if this didn't worry him.

'Her ultimate destination is Antalya on the southern Anatolian coast. En-route, she docks at Limassol, Cyprus.'

Thurstan struggled not to show how disappointing this was. Antalya was still in the East. Technically it lay in Christian lands, but there were all kinds of reasons why the Greeks could cause problems for them.

'The cost is ten gold bezants each,' the Templar said. 'We are a religious institution, but we need to live as well.'

'Ten bezants each,' Thurstan said. 'And you only take us as far as Antalya.'

'There are many other ships in dock. Feel free to try your luck with one of those.'

Thurstan glanced again at the *Gloriosus*, making a show of being impressed by its defensive capability. Looking at it now, there was even a ballista built into its forecastle, while the various Templar knights on board, most leaning on the gunwales, talking together, would reassure anyone seeking to sail in it. In truth, Thurstan had known that the cost of any seaborne transport out of here would be daylight robbery, but it didn't matter unduly. With the bishop's gold, he could afford to meet any price they charged. That said, he wasn't in the business of letting them know he was rich.

He sighed, as if it was a difficult decision. 'I'll take it.'

The Templar became more serious. 'You pay upfront.'

Thurstan fished out a pouch, opened it and laid down the requisite coins, while the Templar dipped a quill into a pot of ink.

'Your name?'

'Reginald de Morville,' Thurstan said, hoping the irony of having merged the names of two of Archbishop Thomas Becket's murderers would be lost on him.

It was. The Templar scratched it on the ship's manifest. 'I trust you don't have any women travelling with you?'

'Why, does it cost more for women?' The Templar didn't reply to that, awaiting an answer. 'Forgive my attempt at levity. We're all men. You'll see when we come aboard.'

The Templar nodded, writing down the name Thurstan had given him and the number of his travelling companions on a smaller scrap of parchment, their ticket for travel, before handing it over.

Thurstan slid it into his pouch. 'I take it you'll feed us?'

'You'll be served one meal a day for the duration of the journey. You'll sleep wherever you can find space. Would be a good idea to come aboard now, while there's still plenty of room.'

Thurstan considered that. It might make sense to return to *The Pewter Pot* and bring the others straight back here, but that would mean Melinda needing to stay inside the bolster all night as it wouldn't be safe to let her out until the journey was underway.

'We'll be here first thing in the morning,' he said.

'See that you are. We don't wait for anyone.' The Templar eyed him. 'Just out of interest... have you obtained a letter of credit from the Temple Church here?'

Thurstan had been about to leave but now hesitated.

The old knight was referring to the Templars' unique system of providing credit for those travellers unwilling to carry large sums with them. Each of their Temple churches housed a warrior monk with banking skills. In return for the money you deposited with him, he would provide you with a letter of credit, which could be redeemed at whichever location you finally arrived in. It was a popular method of transporting personal wealth to and from the East, but it wouldn't work on this occasion. By the time they'd reached Europe, word of who and what they were would likely have got there ahead of them, and calling at any Templar stronghold would be perilous.

'I've decided against it,' he said.

'So long as you know we can't be responsible for any losses while you're on board.'

'Not even to pirates?'

'Pirates we can handle. But there are sneakthieves on every ship. Anyway, you've been warned. Move along if you please. There are others seeking passage with us.'

As Thurstan strolled the quayside, he sensed eyes on him. He glanced around, but no one in his vicinity seemed to be paying him undue attention. He relaxed a little.

'You!' someone said from behind.

He stiffened, before turning.

A younger Templar, fully mailed and resplendent in his colours, his longsword at his hip, came along the quay towards him. Some distance behind his shoulder, the old knight seated at the table was staring after them.

'Me?' Thurstan said.

'You're English, are you not?' The Templar had a blond beard, short blond hair and very blue eyes. By his accent, he hailed from a northern land, perhaps Denmark. 'We're under orders to watch for a group of fighting men in company with a young woman. The woman a Levantine. Dark-skinned, green-eyed.'

Thurstan was unnerved. Plenty men who'd witnessed Melinda's curing of Pandulf had headed back to Jaffa from Chateau al-Yuqhar, and doubtless offered detail about what had happened. But surely none had got close enough to see that her eyes were green? Something else had happened since.

'What's that to do with me?' he asked.

'These men are English born.'

'There are many Englishmen in the Holy Land.'

'I've just been told that you bought passage on the *Gloriosus*... for yourself and a group of others.'

'That's true.'

'Who are you?'

'Reginald de Morville. I was serjeant-at-arms in the foot company of Archbishop Baldwin. On his death, we transferred to the house of the Prince of Antioch. But he didn't wish to fight Saladin, so...'

'Yes, yes, I didn't ask for your life story. You haven't seen those people I describe? I imagine you English stick together.'

'You imagine incorrectly. We English hate each other more than we hate you Danes.' Thurstan gave a crooked smile. 'For the crimes you committed in our country in the days of our forefathers. Though I'm sure, given your religious vows, you can find it in yourself to apologise for that now.'

The Templar appraised him coolly. 'You're clearly not a simpleton, my friend. So, my advice is don't behave like one.'

He turned and walked away.

–

'The problem is you have the look and bearing of a soldier,' Bertrand said. 'They were never going to be fooled that you were some civilian.'

They sat together in the bare, rather cramped space that was the upper room they'd rented. It was similar to the one Thurstan had stayed in previously, though this time it had a view down across flat-topped roofs towards the harbour rather than the Cathedral of the Holy Cross.

'I think it was because I showed no interest in taking their credit,' Thurstan replied.

Pandulf pondered. 'I suppose only someone who had nothing to steal would turn his nose up at that.'

'Or someone more likely to kill the robbers than be robbed,' Bertrand said.

'Did anyone follow you back?' De Verneuil asked.

'I didn't see anyone. Though they were suspicious.'

'So, what do we do?' Pandulf wondered. 'Surely it's unwise to go aboard?'

'Where else do we go?' De Verneuil asked.

'Isn't there another port further north?'

'Beirut,' Bertrand replied. 'But it's still held by Saladin, and even if it wasn't, it's seventy miles from here, and we've now sold the horses and most of our supplies.'

De Verneuil scratched at his beard. 'If the Templars are onto us, I don't think they'll wait till we go on board. More likely, they'll strike tonight. That ship's going to Asia Minor, and over there the girl will be harder to claim back.'

Thurstan pondered. Potentially, it was another of those no-win predicaments, but there was no doubt in his mind that if they required Melinda to remain in the haversack for an unreasonable length of time, she might pass out through suffocation. She could finish up moaning, struggling; it would give them away too easily.

It would also, as he'd already considered, be hard on her. Incredibly so.

'We treat tonight as though we were camping outdoors,' he decided. 'Take it in turns to watch. Go aboard at dawn.'

'This feels like the most incredible folly,' Bertrand groaned. 'Firstly, that the people we're hiding from are the people we'll be looking to for protection. Secondly, that we're hiding from the Templars at all.'

'We've already had this conversation,' Thurstan reminded him.

'We reached no conclusion that I can sleep easy on.'

'In that case you can stay awake. You have first watch.'

–

'So, tomorrow I'm to be bagged and delivered to the ship like a packet of dried goods,' Melinda said, joining Pandulf at the window.

He started. Having replaced Bertrand only half an hour ago, he was still dazed with sleep and rubbing at his eyes. The townscape outside lay silent and silver-lit by the moon, the hour so late that barely a light twinkled from any of its many apartments. Even so, he hadn't heard her stealing up on him. She pulled a stool over and sat down, wrapping herself in her cloak. Even in moonlight, the very short hair suited her, though there were many in Europe who'd object to a girl dressing as a boy, whatever the reason.

'It's just till we get on board,' he said, though in truth, he wasn't sure how it would work. Melinda was no more than five foot three inches at the most, and of very slight build, but she'd be folded up like a blanket. And it would still be quite a burden even for a giant like Gui de Verneuil to be lumbered with. 'And, well it's for your own...'

'For Heaven's sake, Pandulf, please don't say it's for my own good.'

'I don't suppose you'd see it that way. But where else would you go? You've no home here now. You've no home anywhere. And I suspect you realise that because you've made no effort to escape.'

'I'm still being taken by force. Whatever tragedy my life descended to before, this business makes you a kidnapper.'

He looked away. 'I can't deny it.'

'Don't fret,' she said. 'I understand the power structure here. When it all comes down to it, you're a servant. You do as you're told, or the consequences may be dire. And yes, it's also true what you say... I am a conundrum.'

'A conun...?'

'I don't know where I belong in this world. Now that Patriarch Heraclius and his house are no more.' She clasped her hands, looking out over the sleeping city. 'But I wasn't always indentured. Would it surprise you to learn that I am descended from Italian nobility. My great grandfather was a minor baron from Lombardy, who first came east on the Great Pilgrimage of 1096, and whose children and grandchildren intermarried with Coptic Christians from Egypt.'

Pandulf listened with interest.

'Alas, my own father was a gambler who in due course lost everything,' she said. 'Our country estate, our townhouse in Jerusalem... In the end, he left us in debt to the patriarch. So, I wasn't born a servant. I became one by default. At twelve years old.'

'That would explain your very obvious education,' he replied.

She eyed him again. 'Not my horsemanship? Not my skill with a hunting bow?'

'Those were mysteries too. I never really believed a serving girl would have that role in a noble house. But more endearing by far—'

She smiled. 'Endearing?'

'Is the way you talk so well. You're forthright. You... well, you have opinions and you're not afraid to voice them. Where are the rest of your family now?'

Her smile faded. 'Scattered to the winds. When Saladin took Jerusalem, many were taken prisoner and made slaves.'

'They might have been freed,' he said.

'Some of those captured were freed. Those who could pay ransom. A significant number could not, of course, my family among them. And they were enslaved, which means they'll most likely be dead by now.'

'I'm sorry you've known such suffering.'

'*You've* been kind to me at least. That, I appreciate.'

'Melinda, I wish you'd be friendlier to the others.'

She seemed taken aback. 'I'm hardly hostile.'

'I know, but you're so aloof with them. You may not think it, but your protection is their sole purpose. You heard Lord Thurstan. It's the whole of their quest.'

'Yes, I've heard a lot about this business of quest.' She looked thoughtful, though he suspected she was unimpressed by the notion, which galled him a little. 'If I understand correctly,' she said, 'when a knight embarks on a quest, he seeks some distant goal – the Holy Grail, perhaps – and must overcome unimaginable hardships in the process.'

The squire did his best to explain. 'Each knight seeks – or *should* seek – to perform courageous, exemplary deeds in the service of honourable men. That is the basic quest of knighthood. But other knights, *elite* knights, go further. They also impose a personal quest on themselves and are often oath-sworn to pursue it. You mention the Grail. An unobtainable treasure, which cost the life of Arthur's most valorous companion. Did it ever really happen? Was there a real Round Table? A knight called Galahad, who lost his life on the Grail quest? Who can say? But it serves as the perfect illustration of a mission no ordinary man could accomplish. A goal, whatever it may be, which only those knights who are striving for perfection must undertake to reach.'

She seemed to be concealing a smile. 'You put it well. But it sounds more like a dream than reality.'

'But that's the whole point. The knight's quest is a lifelong challenge. Usually because the knight's life is sacrificed in the process. That's how difficult it is.'

She sighed. 'I suppose I should be flattered. But being friendly, as you put it... Well, that may become *my* quest. An impossible goal.'

247

'Melinda, you have to stop thinking this way. These knights are sworn to this cause, but it involves horrible dangers.'

'And I should be grateful, is that what you're saying?'

'Whatever you think of their manners, your safety is their main concern.'

'You talk about them as if they're all of one mind.'

Pandulf was puzzled. 'They're all still here, are they not?'

'Yes, but your master claims that he's only doing this for pay.'

'He said that, but Bertrand doesn't believe him, and neither do I. In Lord Thurstan's case, it's firmly about the quest. I'm certain.'

She considered. 'Perhaps I agree. For some reason best known to himself, this professional killer you serve is genuinely devoted to his mission. In contrast, Gui de Verneuil is not.'

'Gui wants the money. But Bertrand shares Lord Thurstan's position.'

'I'm not sure about Lord Bertrand either,' she said.

'What do you mean?'

'Oh, Pandulf...' She patted his cheek. 'There are times when your innocence is almost sweet.'

He recoiled, stung, but then paused as he heard a brief scraping sound, like boots scuffing on wood and stonework.

He stood up.

The city lay motionless. He scanned the opposite roof, which was about twelve feet away, but it was empty. The same applied to the alley below. And then he heard it again. Melinda did too. They glanced upward... just as a black, shapeless blob descended below the casement's upper rim.

They backed slowly away as the dark form elongated downward, as stunned as they were bewildered. When it assumed the silhouette of a man, Pandulf groped for his sword-hilt, but his sword was elsewhere, propped up next to the mattress, now occupied by the sleeping Bertrand.

'My... l-lords,' he managed, but it came out a stutter.

They backed away further.

The intruder was now fully in view, hanging by his arms. He arched his body at the waist, swung back and forth, and leapt, landing inside the room. At which point, Melinda tripped backward, landing on her bottom with a yelp. The featureless intruder dropped to a half-crouch, drawing a curved dagger.

Pandulf goggled in frozen disbelief.

Then something whipped past his ear, thudding into the intruder's face.

The impact was shocking, the stricken figure crumpling down immediately. Pandulf turned and in the moonlight saw Thurstan sitting upright on his mattress, the crossbow levelled at his shoulder.

'I...' the lad stammered. 'My lord, I...'

A hand clamped his mouth.

'Some watchman you are,' De Verneuil mumbled.

Thurstan leapt up and across the room, tossing Melinda out of his way. Bertrand, who clearly *had* been asleep, came groggily after him. They turned the dead figure over. He was clad entirely in black, including the lower half of his face. When they tore that covering off, bearded Arabic features greeted them. The stiff fletchings of the crossbow bolt tufted from his left eye-socket. Thurstan ripped again at the black garb, exposing a white tunic underneath, tied at the waist with a blood-red sash.

'Assassins!' Bertrand looked dazed. 'The Assassins are here!'

Creaks now sounded from the passage beyond the door.

Many creaks, as though made by multiple pairs of booted feet.

CHAPTER 35

In that split second, the wisdom of having stripped themselves of all properties save the bare essentials became apparent. They snatched the two or three items of baggage they still had, the men buckling their swords to their waists, Thurstan sheathing his knife at his back, hoisting the crossbow and throwing the bag of quarrels over his shoulder.

De Verneuil overturned the bedframes, pushing them up against the door. Pandulf meanwhile ran to the window. 'It's twenty feet down to the alley,' he hissed. 'We should tie bits of clothing together. Our cloaks and such. We can make a rope.'

'There's no time,' Thurstan replied, as the first impact on the door sounded.

Initially, it was a shoulder being applied softly, attempting to push the door open rather than break it down. The single bar at the top held but began to strain as the pressure from the other side increased.

Bertrand stood with hand on sword-hilt. 'How many, do you think?' he asked tightly.

'I've never met these bastards before,' De Verneuil replied, 'but I've heard they come in cohorts. So, more than we can manage.'

Thurstan glanced at Melinda, who stood rigid. For the first time since he'd met her, her face was written with fear. And he understood why. Previous Muslim lords had seen the value in keeping her alive. But the Assassins, as religious extremists, had a different priority: the destruction of Shia Islam's enemies. In light of that, a Christian 'saint' would have no hope of surviving them.

The pressure on the door relaxed. Silence followed, before an enormous blow landed on the wood. The door bowed inward, a screw flitting loose.

'My lord,' Pandulf protested. 'We must do something.'

'Watch the window!' Thurstan said. 'Anyone else tries to come in, kill him before he gets his feet over the sill.'

The lad withdrew to the window. Thurstan turned, searching the room. Then spied a long, wooden board fixed to the left-hand wall, running the entire length of its base, which made it about twelve feet long.

'Bertrand, over here! Gui, guard the door!'

The two knights complied, Thurstan and Bertrand both drawing their steel and jamming their blades behind the skirting board, twisting and turning the handles. With a cracking and crunching of plaster, it detached. Thurstan carried the plank across the room, balancing it flat on the sill and then pushing it over the alley. It just about reached the parapet on the far side, creating a flimsy but serviceable bridge.

'Melinda,' he said. She stumbled towards him, eyes bulging under her boyish fringe. He took her hand in a firm grip and, throwing one arm around her waist, lifted her up so that she was standing on the plank. 'Over you go. Quickly but carefully. It won't take much vibration for it to slip free at the other end.'

Another blow landed on the bedroom door. Melinda needed no second telling and – hugging herself in her cloak – walked outward along the plank. She was no weight at all, though she wore riding boots, and proceeded with only dainty steps so the length of wood barely moved as she made it to the other side. There was another flat-topped roof over there, though there were no sounds from the darkened rooms below, so clearly no one heard when she alighted.

'Pandulf,' Thurstan said. 'You next.' He grabbed the lad's arm before he climbed up onto the sill, meeting him eyeball to eyeball. 'If the rest of us don't make it, it falls to you to take the girl to Canterbury. You understand?'

The squire swallowed and nodded. Thurstan released him.

Pandulf's journey across the woodwork was noisier. He was carrying bags and furnished now with his sword, so he walked with awkward, uneasy steps, arms outspread. The plank bounced and sprang and at one point shifted dramatically so that at Thurstan's end, one corner of it overhung the abyss, forcing the knight to grab hold of it.

'Bertrand!' Thurstan said. The banneret backed towards him, his sword still drawn. 'The same goes for you. If anything happens to me, you see the girl to Canterbury, yes?' Bertrand's eyes had fixed on the door, on which blow after blow was raining. 'You hear me?'

Bertrand nodded as he backed up onto the sill, then turned and balanced his way out. Thurstan watched, holding the plank in place. Bertrand was larger and heavier than Pandulf but moved more smoothly. He made it to the other side safely.

'Gui,' Thurstan said.

De Verneuil was standing by the door with sword drawn. 'You go next,' he said. 'I'm bigger than you. That rotten piece of wormwood is likely to break underneath me... that'll be the death of both of us.'

'At times like this, Gui, I don't value men prepared to die for the mission as much as prepared to fight for it. Now, get your arse over here and across this damn bridge!' Another impact blasted the wood, a whole section of door battered through. Dark figures milled behind it. *Go now, Gui de Verneuil!'*

Cursing, De Verneuil sheathed his sword, crossed the room, slapped Thurstan on the shoulder, then leapt up and commenced crossing. Again, Thurstan held the plank, his attention divided between his comrade and the bedroom door, which finally splintered apart as black shapes forced their way through. He shoved his foot into the crossbow stirrup, drew the string back, loaded a bolt and levelled it. He glanced again through the window. Seeing that De Verneuil had made it to the other side, he turned back again.

They were into the room.

He triggered the weapon, the bolt hitting the one at the front in the throat, dropping him to his knees, the Assassins behind tripping over him.

Thurstan jumped up onto the plank and, refusing to look down, started across. It felt loose and springy, and though he only had twelve feet to go, it was the longest twelve feet of his life. He didn't even risk looking back, though he could hear the chaos in the upper room, as they kicked the bedframes aside.

The woodwork slid sideways under his feet.

He paused, icy sweat stippling his body.

He was still six feet from safety, his companions standing watching. 'Go!' he shouted, pointing. 'The Sidonian Harbour is that way!'

They retreated across the roof, but not speedily.

Behind him, the commotion in the room grew. He shuffled forward. With another grating sound, the plank shifted again.

'Sweet Jesus,' he muttered, and with a start, realised that this was the first time he'd called on Christ's help for as long as he could remember. 'Sweet Jesus!'

The plank came loose and fell.

But Thurstan had already thrown himself forward, landing with both feet on the parapet, where he'd have overbalanced backward had Pandulf not scuttled up and caught him by the belt, pulling him down onto the flat. Thurstan grabbed him in a half bearhug, then pushed them all on. As they went, he stopped and turned, foot in the stirrup, drawing back the crossbow string again, loading another bolt. He glanced up. A dark-clad figure had appeared at the window.

Thurstan loosed, hitting his target square in the chest. Then ran.

He didn't like using the crossbow. It went against all his chivalrous vows. But he needed to remind himself that these were pagans, and pagans must feel the wrath of God any way it came to them.

'Quickly!' Again, the others had stopped to wait. Again, he pushed them.

They reached the far side of the roof, which dropped twenty feet to a second street. As before, there was no obvious way down. Then an arrow whistled past on an upward trajectory. A second followed, only narrowly missing.

'They're all around us!' Pandulf exclaimed.

Thurstan reloaded the crossbow, leaning over the parapet, scanning the area below. A figure flitted across, moving from one recessed doorway to the next. Thurstan loosed, but he wasn't a good enough marksman to hit a fast-moving target. The quill bounced from the road's surface, and in response, from some other concealed position, another arrow slanted up at them, again missing closely.

Thurstan led them along the edge of the roof.

Around a corner, a ladder was propped up from a balcony below. At Thurstan's urging, Melinda went down first, followed by Pandulf, Bertrand, De Verneuil, and then himself. Before he descended, he scanned the rooftops behind them. Black shapes were zigzagging across them, too many to count.

At the foot of the ladder, the balcony ran north for sixty yards, passing several apertures, some shuttered, some with curtains. Thurstan peeked continually over the balustrade, but even though they'd come down a level to get here, the adjacent road appeared to be sloping downhill, so it was still too far below to jump. However, just ahead, there was an open hatch in the floor, with another ladder dropping through it.

This time Thurstan went first – into pitch darkness.

They were indoors again. He turned in a circle, hefting his crossbow like a club while the others descended behind him. As his eyes attuned, he saw cloth hanging on the left. Pulling it aside, an entrance led outdoors. This time, a second wooden bridge, a trifle sturdier than before, more like a solid wooden beam, led a good fifteen yards over what appeared to be an open-air yard.

Thurstan grabbed them one after another, pushing them onto it.

As before, Melinda went first, Pandulf behind her, then Bertrand, then De Verneuil, and lastly, Thurstan himself. Only for another arrow to whisper down at them. It struck De Verneuil in the right thigh. He gasped and slumped to one knee. Thurstan, edging up behind, saw that it had sunk half its length.

'God's blood,' De Verneuil swore through gritted teeth.

'Keep going!' Thurstan dragged him to his feet. 'We're easy targets here.'

De Verneuil stumbled on. Another arrow flickered past, a black flash in the dimness, but no one was hit, and they made it to the far side, where, one by one, they barged through a half-open shutter into a blacked-out room that was stuffy and by the sounds and smell of it, crammed with sleeping bodies.

Thurstan thrust past the others, coming hard against a shutter, which rattled loudly. Cries of alarm sounded from a nearby bed.

He ignored them, yanking the shutter open, stepping outside again. A ledge ran leftward. They were still about twenty feet up. Again glimpsing shadowy movement on the parapets overhead, he shuffled sideways. The others followed. Another arrow flitted down, hitting the stonework close to Pandulf's head.

When they reached another aperture, Thurstan stepped through, the others behind. They were in a corridor. Again, it smelled rank, indicating that people were sleeping beyond the various doorways leading off it. There was also a reek of smoke.

'Hurry.' He ushered them along but waited on De Verneuil.

The injured knight came in through the outer door awkwardly. He turned haggard eyes on his commander, twisting his body, to show that he'd been struck by another arrow. This one had transfixed his right shoulder. The breath dragged in his throat. When he put his right foot down, his blood-sodden boot squished.

'Keep moving,' Thurstan said again, bringing up the rear.

They progressed along the passage, seeing a smoky torch suspended in an iron wall-bracket. Before they reached it, an assailant landed on Thurstan's back. Thurstan tottered forward, a wiry arm locked around his throat, steel rasping from a hilt. But before the Assassin could plunge the blade into the unmailed body, De Verneuil grabbed the torch and smashed it into his cloth-covered face. The wrappings caught, and the Assassin's head was suddenly swathed in flame. He threw himself off and blundered sideways, hitting the corridor wall. As he spun back, Thurstan met him with such a blow to the side of his head that his neck broke.

'Should've let him burn,' De Verneuil muttered as they stumbled on.

They'd lost sight of the other three, but a curtain hung askew ahead, admitting moonlight. A yard short of it, another masked figure sprang into their path. He slashed at them with a *scimitar*.

Thurstan blocked it with his crossbow, the curved blade lodging in the flight groove, then drew his knife and rammed it home. The Assassin sagged against them, blood gurgling through his facecloth. Thurstan shoved him sideways, pitching him down the staircase he'd ascended from, where he struck a comrade making his way up. The pair of them fell together, tumbling and clattering.

Thurstan yanked the curtain aside and thrust De Verneuil through, onto a flat roof much broader than those others they'd traversed. Beyond it, their companions had already progressed onto the next roof along. They hurried in pursuit, but the wounded knight was tottering, struggling to breathe. Thurstan looped an arm around him.

'Go without me,' De Verneuil gasped. 'I can't make it much further.'

'We're almost there,' Thurstan said.

'Almost where?' The casualty laughed but flinched with agony. 'It's a mile to the port from here.'

'Yes, but it's all downhill.'

'Thurstan… leave me.'

Thurstan ignored that, but then they reached the edge of the roof and saw that the only way to the next one was by jumping the gap between them. It was five feet or so. A healthy adult could do it easily, but De Verneuil – half his body slicked with blood, his face gleaming with sweat – shook his head.

From all directions now, they were coming. Black-clad figures advancing over the adjacent rooftops. And then Thurstan heard the clangour of steel on steel, and looked ahead to see Bertrand and Pandulf engaged with the enemy, blades flashing with moonlight as two more Assassins danced around them. Even as he watched, a third elite warrior vaulted up from a hatch about thirty yards to their left.

'Leave me,' De Verneuil croaked again. 'I'm not finished yet, but you have to go.'

Thurstan squeezed his uninjured shoulder, backed away ten yards, and ran, leaping over the gap, and landing cleanly. As he did, the third Assassin, who'd appeared on the next roof, veered towards him, a *kilij* in either hand.

Thurstan drew his longsword.

It was a perilous procedure, fighting with blades when you weren't mailed, but one way or the other, it was usually quick.

Not so this time.

Over several moments of cutting and fending, Thurstan realised that he was facing a skilled opponent. Only the Assassin's eyes were visible, two narrow gleaming buttons, as he leapt and pirouetted and struck with acrobatic ability.

Ahead, the other pairs were still engaged. Pandulf was staggering, clearly exhausted. Thurstan knew that if he didn't help soon, his squire was doomed.

CHAPTER 36

Gui de Verneuil made his way back along the edge of the roof, a snail-trail of gore behind him. But he almost laughed when he came to the top of a ladder slanting down to a lower roof, which appeared to be made from straw. He swung himself over the edge, though his right arm was near enough useless.

Commencing a clumsy descent, he was so awkward that he fell at roughly halfway, striking the thatch, which shattered under his weight. He continued downward amid dust and splinters, landing in a narrow stable space, where a single horse had been stalled. It neighed and snorted. De Verneuil, who'd jolted the arrow even deeper into his thigh, could only roll onto his side and lie shuddering, agony scything through him. He knew though that he had to get moving again, and hauled himself to his feet. The horse might be a Godsend. Even in the dim cracks of moonlight, he could see that the beast was saddled and bridled.

Seizing the animal's reins, he tried to drag it outside one-handed. But the horse didn't know him, plus it was already distressed, so it resisted, digging its hooves in.

'Of all the stupid, stubborn beasts in the whole damn Levant,' De Verneuil gasped, eyes stinging with grimy sweat, hot blood soaking every part of his body.

He pushed the stable door open and stumbled outside alone. The street lay in moonlit stillness.

A mile to the port but all downhill…

'I am Gui de Verneuil. Knight of the *Familia Regis*… and no man can stop me.'

Boldly, but stumbling, he set out on foot.

The Assassin's cranium gave with a crunch.

Thurstan, having feinted to the left, then to the right, had finally lurched through his guard, driving his longsword down, pommel first. As his opponent dropped, he spun and saw that Bertrand had also triumphed, though he was visibly fatigued, leaning on his sword, which still stood in his adversary's midriff. Their one remaining enemy was easily getting the better of Pandulf but was distracted to see his two comrades fall. He backed away as Thurstan ran at him, raising his curved steel to fend off the longsword, only to get a knife in the guts, which the knight drove to the hilt, then ripped leftward.

'Gui?' Bertrand asked, hobbling towards him, bloodied across the left cheek.

'I don't know.' Thurstan glanced back onto the previous roof. There was no sign of De Verneuil, but several more Assassins were crossing over the roof towards them at speed. 'But we'll find him.'

De Verneuil was halfway along the empty street when another arrow struck him from the left, penetrating all the way to its feathers. He juddered where he stood, biting on his bottom lip, determined that he wouldn't go down… there was nothing on Earth that could take Gui de Verneuil down.

Another arrow struck from the right. Again, it made clean, deep impact.

He tottered onward, his longsword dragging through the dirt, but when a third arrow struck him, this time from behind, he sank to his knees. The archers, three more Assassins equipped with double-curved bows, emerged from darkened recesses. They advanced, loosing more shafts, each time hitting their mark. He knelt upright, defiant, attempting to laugh, though only blood burbled from his mouth. He withstood another two volleys before tilting over onto his side. The trio of archers stood over him, so pleased with their work that they didn't notice another man with a sword coming around the corner ahead.

–

Thurstan charged on silent feet, longsword twirling. One of their heads lifted from its neck before the other two realised. But it was too late for them as well. A downward stroke clove one from shoulder to breastbone, while the other was kicked in the groin and, as he doubled over, hit mid-spine with a dagger blow that parted the vertebrae.

'Th… Thurstan,' came a whispered voice.

Thurstan scampered over to where De Verneuil had rolled partly onto his back. So many arrows stuck out from him that it was astonishing he still breathed. One of the wretched things had even punctured his left eyeball, not deeply, but sufficient that the shaft moved up and down and side to side as the dying man's eyes rolled in their sockets.

'Confess…' he stammered. 'I confess…'

Thurstan dropped to one knee. 'I'm sorry, my friend… there's no priest here.'

'Confess… me.'

'Me?'

'I beg you…'

De Verneuil lifted a shaking, blood-slick hand. Thurstan clasped it, though his mouth was dry. What could *he* say? And how could *he* say it? A beast of slaughter, solely invincible because a devil had bestowed it on him. But the mutilated face implored him.

'Do you regret your sins?' Thurstan asked him.

'I… I do,' De Verneuil stuttered.

'Tell God you are sorry for having offended Him.'

'I…'

That one remaining eye glazed over.

Thurstan rose to his feet. He looked at the pile of butchered corpses. Yet more of his gruesome work. His stomach lurched and for a moment he thought he'd be sick. What hope was there? For him? For any of them? Why were they here? How in the name of sweet Jesus Christ and the Virgin Mary's milk could they ever find their way out?

A renewed clangour rose from an adjoining street. More cries of rage. Thurstan turned to run back, but then a hefty snort drew his attention to an open door, where a saddled horse stood regarding him.

It watched with curiosity as he approached but displayed no hostility.

'I don't know who sent you, friend...' He took it by the reins, stroked it by the nose. 'God or the Devil... But you might just be a lifesaver.'

–

He entered the square at a thundering gallop.

One of the Assassins circling Pandulf and Bertrand was hit full-on by the flying steed, his body sent cartwheeling. Others darted from its path, but Thurstan veered around and with furious strokes, sundered their skulls. Another one running had been carrying a bow and a quiver of arrows and tossed them as he ran. Bertrand caught the bow, nocked an arrow, aimed, and loosed. The shaft pierced the fellow's head like a turnip.

Thurstan rode furiously after the one remaining, his animal rearing, a mighty hoof clubbing his target to the ground. Amazingly, the fellow got up. Blood and brains streaming down his *ghutra*-covered face, he again tried to run, tottering sideways.

To be stabbed in the heart by Pandulf.

A painful silence descended.

Thurstan wheeled the horse to face the others, who gazed at him unblinking.

Melinda, who'd been standing rigid, praying, looked around, askance.

Thurstan dismounted, noting that lights had appeared in several windows. They shouldn't tarry. He helped the others snatch up those few bits of baggage they'd dropped, only to hear a protracted, agonised moan. The Assassin who'd been run down by Thurstan's horse lay on his side. By the looks of him, he could barely move. Blood leaked through his *ghutra*, but his eyes rolled towards them as Melinda dropped to her knees.

'Don't even think of praying this fellow well,' Thurstan warned her.

She gave him a reproachful look. Surprisingly, the casualty then spoke to them, though his words were garbled by the blood-soaked cloth. Melinda hooked the scarf down. Even then it was difficult, the felled warrior unable to move his mouth properly, though she understood the gist of it.

'The whole sultanate of Egypt searches for us,' she translated. 'Sultan Salah al-Din and the Old Man of the Mountain... that is the Nizari spiritual leader. He says they have put aside the differences you drove between them with your murder of Count Conrad...'

Bertrand groaned. 'How could they know about that?'

Thurstan shrugged. 'It doesn't matter now.'

The injured man's eyes fixed on them with an eerie gleam.

'He says your death will come soon,' Melinda said. 'All our deaths.'

'Tell him that his will come sooner,' Thurstan replied.

'He says he is going to a better place. He doesn't fear death for he has died doing God's work. But your death will be worse. For you are a great sinner. Even your own people pursue you. The greed of the Franks is limitless.'

She paused, unwilling to continue.

'The rest,' Thurstan said.

'He says that every Christian in the sultanate seeks a lion's share of the wealth the girl-saint will provide. But none will succeed. And all the tongues of men will wag with the joy of it when the Sword of Darkness dies on the blades of his own kind.'

'Sword of Darkness?' Pandulf repeated slowly.

'Where is he hurt?' Thurstan asked.

She relayed the question. The Assassin flinched with pain as he responded.

'He says his back is broken.'

'It's unbecoming to watch a man suffer.' Thurstan's sword swept down, severing the casualty's head. 'On your feet, Melinda. We're for the harbour.'

'But how did they find us?' Bertrand asked. 'How do they even know about us? It's not just the Assassins. He said they *all* know.'

'All that matters now is we get away from here.'

'Thurstan, think about this. If the word has travelled widely, there's no possibility we can make it home.' Bertrand indicated the scattered corpses. 'We can't go through this in every town we come to...'

'Bertrand, I've already given you leave to part company with us if you wish.' Thurstan saw that Melinda was still kneeling beside the headless body, hands joined. 'On your feet, girl! Gui de Verneuil died because of you.'

'My lord!' Pandulf remonstrated. 'Melinda's prayers might have saved us...'

'Arrows would have been better!' the knight retorted.

'I don't have a bow,' Melinda said, standing up. 'We sold them all.'

Thurstan grabbed up one of the Assassins' double-curved composites and handed it over, along with a quiver of black-feathered arrows. 'Now you do. Conceal these weapons in your baggage but keep them with you. And if you need to shoot arrows into other men's flesh to save our skins, you'd better damn well do it. Or I'll leave stripes on that back of yours that a whipped dog couldn't imagine.' He turned on the rest of them. '*All of you! Move!*'

CHAPTER 37

There was a broad misconception among Northern Europeans, few of whom had ever travelled beyond their own countries, that the Mediterranean lands basked in glorious sunshine throughout the year. Few knew that Mediterranean winters, while not as harsh as northern winters, could be testing for those who weren't prepared. King Richard was as well-prepared as possible, in that he'd set sail from Acre at the earliest opportunity, October 9, even though that would take him well into the storm season. The immediate problem this presented was that it meant his vessel would need to stay close to the coast, which would lengthen the voyage considerably, and at the same time increased the possibility of attack from onshore.

At first glance, this secondary threat seemed unlikely.

Richard had embarked in the *Franche-Nef* – his huge, three-masted battle-carrack, which was painted bright crimson and sported a massive, intricately carved dragon head for a prow, while the three-lions banner streamed magnificently from the topmast. There was surely no one in the world who didn't know that this very distinctive ship was the personal transport of Richard the Lionheart and his elite *Familia Regis*.

Here though, lay the real concern… at least, in the view of Henry von Sickingen, a Rhineland-born knight of the *Familia*, who had now served Richard for several years. Throughout the first leg of the voyage, Von Sickingen had expressed concern that there weren't enough of them, because Richard, guilt-stricken about having departed the Levant with Jerusalem still uncaptured and determined not to weaken the force left behind, had insisted on travelling with only six of his personal knights. Though there was a full crew on board, and in addition to that, ten men-at-arms trained and equipped to fight as marine soldiers in the fashion of the ancient Greeks, Von Sickingen was not convinced this was adequate.

'My main fear, sire, is that, even if some of those principalities we pass don't recognise your warship, they might consider the mere presence of a vessel like this a provocation.'

They stood by the bulwark on the *Franche-Nef*'s castellated quarter deck, while half a mile away, significantly sized cavalry units were visible, weak autumn sunlight glinting from their helms and spear-tips as they shadowed the vessel along the shore. It was anyone's guess which potentate they belonged to. The king made no initial reply. He stood wrapped in a cloak, watching the hostile force.

'You're overreacting, Von Sickingen,' Ramon la Hors replied. The knight-captain commanded the small escort Richard had brought with him and from the beginning, had defended his master's itinerary. 'They might outnumber us, but they can hardly reach us on horseback, and we haven't passed a port containing any craft that could menace us.'

All this was true. As warships went, the *Franche-Nef* was an armoured masterpiece. It had catapults both fore and aft, and was loaded with ammunition: stockpiles of huge, specially forged lead grenades, which only needed to be heated and then could be flung in blazing arcs, smashing and burning the timbers of any craft that came close. To both port and starboard, there were inbuilt scorpions: huge, broad-range crossbows based on an old Roman design, which could launch twenty shafts each at a time. On landing during the battle of Jaffa, one of these alone – in a single volley – had felled a dozen Ayyubid horsemen waiting on the beach.

But Von Sickingen remained nervous. 'No disrespect is intended, my liege... No ship could be better outfitted to survive a long and dangerous voyage than the *Franche-Nef*, but we'll need to put into harbour somewhere. That, I fear, is where our limited numbers may be a problem.'

'My liege, you have six of the finest swords in the world,' La Hors said. 'No one could match you.'

'I agree, Knight-Captain,' Richard replied. 'But our friend Von Sickingen is correct. We are not well enough provisioned to sail all the way home. Besides, as you're doubtless aware, it was never my intention to sail such a huge distance. And that has now been rendered impossible, anyway.'

La Hors said nothing to that. The additional weeks added to the journey had ensured they would not reach the Atlantic until midwinter at the earliest, a time of year when no vessel could risk that great western ocean. Consideration had already been given to their breaking the journey somewhere in southern Francia, but it was obvious to Von Sickingen, and he'd said this several times already, that they could not do this in the *Franche-Nef*. It would immediately proclaim Richard's presence, and one of his oldest foes, Count Raymond of Toulouse, would pounce on them like a panther.

'It struck me, sire, that an Italian port might be safer,' Von Sickingen said. 'You have friends in Sicily.' This was a direct reference to King Tancred of Sicily, whom Richard had signed a treaty with before sailing onward to the Holy Land. 'Tancred would be honoured to have you as his guest for the winter.'

The king didn't immediately reply, and only belatedly did the German realise why. Richard had been a huge figure when he'd first arrived in Sicily. Moreover, his actions there had been demonstrative of a monarch for the ages, capturing several castles and the city of Messina in order to force the initially recalcitrant Tancred to the negotiating table. To return there in *this* fashion would cast him as a diminished figure, especially given that his war in the East had not concluded decisively.

'We can seek an Italian port further north,' Von Sickingen suggested. 'Somewhere like Rimini. Perhaps we could winter in San Marino, then, when the spring comes and the Alpine passes are clear, take a western route overland, avoiding the lands of potential enemies like Leopold of Babenberg, and re-entering Aquitaine through the Auvergne, far from Philip or Count Raymond's reach. After that, Normandy and England.'

'But that means we still head north along the Adriatic,' La Hors said. 'For a time, we'll be in Venetian waters. Would that be wise?'

Von Sickingen gave it some thought. In truth, it would not be.

The Venetians were the ultimate mercenaries. They'd followed Richard's orders when he had an army at his back, but with the Pilgrimage a failure – for yes, that was how Richard's foes would depict it – and all sense of Christian unity broken, things were now different. If they learned he was close by with only a small escort, they'd doubtless see opportunity in it for themselves.

'We need to change vessels,' the king said abruptly.

'My lord?' Von Sickingen was surprised.

'We've reached a point now where the advantages of this great craft are outweighed by the disadvantages. We need a vessel that is less conspicuous. Something in which we can put to shore whenever we wish and never attract attention.'

'Forgive me, sire,' La Hors ventured, 'wouldn't that feel rather... *ungrand*.'

'It would, Knight-Captain. But there are times when pride is an expensive luxury even for a king.' Richard looked grim. 'Let's hope my pride on this occasion has not undone us already.'

–

'At least the weather's favouring us,' Pandulf said, standing on the quarter deck, staring out over the calm blue waters lying between Tyre and Cyprus.

The *Gloriosus* cut along steadily, its canvases banging and timbers creaking. The breeze was cold, of course, as it should be in late October, but, with scarcely a cloud overhead, there was no sense of the impending doom that usually haunted land-lovers whenever they were forced onto the waves. Even pods of dolphins appeared, their black fins slicing the surface alongside them.

Melinda made no response, eyeing the western horizon, her features drawn and tired. They'd been over a week at sea, and after the first two or three days, once the sickness had worn off, those unused to ocean travel had felt the pressure of the uncomfortable conditions on board. The ones billeted on the open deck were frequently left wet and cold by squalls of rain, while those below were in cramped, smelly confines, which they shared with mice, rats and other vermin.

The one meal a day the Templars had promised, and which they'd paid so handsomely for, came in the form of a single bowl of meat stew, served promptly each noon, along with a hunk of bread, the latter of course, growing dryer and staler as the journey progressed.

But at least, as Pandulf had said, there'd been no storm to terrorise them.

'If you're so unhappy, why didn't you make a noise in the bag, when Lord Thurstan carried you on board?' he asked her. 'Why don't you go to those Templar knights now and tell them who you are?' He indicated the one or two Templars currently on deck.

'You'd allow that?' Melinda asked.

'I'd have to try and stop you, but you could resist me, and it would become an incident, and they would want to know what was happening, and then you could tell them everything.'

She looked out to sea again. 'And then more people would die.'

'That is true. Lord Thurstan will not relent. He will kill men if they try to take you from us.'

She glanced the length of the ship. Thurstan was visible amid the chaos of passengers and crew, leaning on the starboard bulwark, lost in thought as the sea rolled by. 'I'll be honest, Pandulf... I've never quite known anyone like him. His ferocity with a sword is terrifying. But it's not just that, it's his willingness to take other men's lives. It's as though they mean nothing to him at all.'

'He has come through dark times,' the squire said.

'Pandulf, we all have.'

'I don't just mean hardship. I mean...' he struggled to put it into words, 'when you're raised to be a knight, you have one key role. And that is to slay enemies. Not just your own enemies, but the enemies of your overlord. And the enemies of your faith.'

'Isn't that what everyone is doing back there?' she said. 'Putting blades in those who don't think as they do? Who don't believe in the same God.'

'But that's what all those Christians who came here were told they could do. Nay, what they *should* do... if they wanted to find reward in Heaven. It's the same thing those Muslims believe who came up from Egypt and Arabia.'

'That doesn't excuse it...'

'It *does* excuse it,' he insisted. 'Because this isn't something they hope for, it's what they absolutely believe. Because time and again, their holy men have told them.'

'I don't think Lord Thurstan believes it,' she said, still watching her guardian knight.

'No,' Pandulf said, 'but he believes in the quest. And that's all you need to know. So, go on. It's your choice.' He pointed again at the nearest of the Templars. 'Talk to them. Tell them who you are. I won't interfere. Then they can take you back east... to that cauldron of violence we've just discussed, where the war will keep going until one side is triumphant, but only after a toll of deaths we can hardly guess at.'

She regarded him with interest. 'I didn't realise you'd thought so hard on it.'

'Don't be fooled.' He couldn't help but be sullen with her. 'I'm only stating the obvious. You want the truth, I'm glad to be leaving the East.'

That wasn't entirely true, of course. He still felt that by removing this 'saint' from the war, it was defeating the purpose of having her. But he was mildly vexed by her disdain. Yes, she was a captive, but she wasn't the only one being pulled from pillar to post.

'You wish to leave the East even though there's now a treaty?' she asked.

'That treaty won't last. If King Richard doesn't come back, someone else will. And then it will all commence again, and our two armies will fight like jackals, and civilians will die in their hundreds alongside them. At least in our company, we'll die before you do. Though I can't promise that won't happen a lot sooner than we anticipate. If you go over to the Templars, for example.'

She mused on that. 'Is it warm in Canterbury at this time of year?'

'At this time of year, no. But they have many braziers and entire forests of firewood. And having seen the state of Bishop Hubert, I doubt you'll go short of food. Alternatively...' Pandulf got up to leave, 'you could jump over the side. Take your chances with the dolphins. You want my opinion, that might be your best option.'

269

CHAPTER 38

When it came to swapping his mode of transport, there were several factors King Richard needed to consider. First, he must adopt a low profile. In addition, he needed means by which to continue travelling once he'd landed in northern Italy. This meant that he and his companions must be able to take their horses with them, which negated the possibility of finishing the sea voyage in something small and simple like a fishing boat.

In the end, on the island of Corfu, the king introduced himself to the Greek governor, who, keen to make a name for himself in the world, was more than pleased to play host for a day or two, and provide a mooring for the *Franche-Nef*, a security that Richard offered to pay handsomely for. In addition, the king was given a berth on a small galley, which also had room for his six companions from the *Familia Regis*, though not the ten marines who'd accompanied him from the Levant, not if the knights wished for adequate space to be made in the hold for their horses. That the king now had even less armed protection ought to be compensated for – or so he and Ramon la Hors calculated – by the fact they'd be sailing under no recognisable colours. With a bit of luck, they could journey unnoticed all the way to Rimini.

But no such luck came.

Four days after departing Corfu, one of the tempests that had been sweeping the central Mediterranean rolled northward into the Adriatic. At first, its strong south-westerly winds pushed them onward along the Dalmatian coast at speed, but gradually the sky darkened, the sapphire sea transforming into heaving grey mountains. The wind intensified steadily, pushing them ever north-east, their sails bellying.

Down in the hold, the horses shrieked. When surf crashed across the deck, pouring in torrents through the hatches, the animals were driven to a frenzy, clattering about, breaking their tethers. In its madness, one galloped up the sloped companionway to the upper deck, where it tore madly around, buffeting men out of its way like skittles. As it bolted for the starboard bulwark and attempted to leap, Bertram de Verdun, one of the king's favourites, grabbed at its reins to try and stop it, and he too was hauled over into the boiling foam. Richard, like the rest, was too busy braced against whatever solid fixture he'd found for the shock of this to strike him. Also like the rest, he was drenched to the bone and green-faced with vomiting out what little sustenance remained in his body.

The Lionheart, the master siege-breaker, the Lord of the Desert, the single greatest warrior to take the English throne since the days of Athelstan, was as helpless as a child, barely able to think as his hair and beard ran with brine.

'Lord king!' Von Sickingen yelled, clambering up alongside him. 'The ship's master says we must change course... put ashore before it's too late. The nearest land is east of here. We've no choice.'

In the noise and fury, the king's companion was almost incoherent, but the king could do nothing but nod and jam his back all the harder against the forecastle bulkhead, his thoughts filled with prayers for their deliverance.

–

Cyprus no longer belonged to the Knights Templar, but there were still plenty of them visible in Limassol harbour, distinctive in their white tabards with the scarlet crosses, walking the quaysides or manning the battlements of the fortified church at the harbour's edge. Guy de Lusigan was officially the new Lord of Cyprus, but the Templars themselves were under no obligation to leave. They'd been his allies in the East and given that transfers of power were often occasions for anarchy, had been asked to stay on here as peacekeepers while the former King of Jerusalem installed himself and his new administration. Whatever the actual truth, it made going ashore an impossible thing to countenance for Thurstan, who again stood at the *Gloriosus*'s starboard, keeping a wary eye on several groups of the infamous warriors as they strolled.

Many passengers were disembarking, seeking a continued passage west rather than taking their chances with Antalya, which was only one of many entry points to the Empire of the Greeks – although there was no guarantee that any new-arrivals, as foreign nationals, would even be allowed past its customs gate. Not without first handing over a hefty fee. Others simply felt that diverting north was heading in the wrong direction, and would delay their journey home all the more, while a third group were simply nervous that the Greeks would be hostile to them; the current Greek Emperor, Isaac Angelos, was no lover of this third great Pilgrimage to the Holy Land, mainly because the German contingents had caused him endless trouble as they'd marched eastward through his realm.

'Can I make a last appeal to you,' Bertrand said. 'That we reveal who we are to these Templars? Right now. Voluntarily. We can trust in the goodness of their vocation. Yes, they'll take the girl off us. But she won't be harmed. If anything, she'll be much safer than where we intend to take her.'

Thurstan moved away along the bulwark. 'I'm not having this conversation again.'

'We shouldn't be at daggers drawn with the best friends we have in this part of the world.'

'In case you hadn't noticed, Bertrand, we aren't at daggers drawn. And there's no need for us ever to be. So long as we remain incognito.'

Bertrand sloped dejectedly away. Thurstan continued to watch the harbour, which was a riot of colour and noise. If it wasn't the seagulls swooping overhead, it was the market stalls all along the quaysides, their holders shouting in a hundred different languages as they haggled with throngs of customers. Skiffs navigated between the many ships, laden with vendors offering exotic fruits, rich silks and assorted hand-crafted oddments, while others contained ornately dressed and painted courtesans, the men in charge of them calling up to the sailors, who shouted down in admiration.

He watched as Pandulf made his way back up the gangway. He'd seen no harm in one of their number going ashore, just to replenish their personal supplies. If anything, it might have seemed odd if one of them didn't. When Pandulf came aboard, he opened a sack he was carrying, showing among other items, a couple of fresh loaves, some apples and grapes, and three sealed gourds of wine.

'I take it there was no trouble?' the knight asked. 'No one asked any questions, gave you a curious look?'

'No one, my lord. But it's very crowded. I think the king himself would go unnoticed.'

'Very well. Stow these items for now. We'll make a meal this evening, after we've set sail.'

–

Pandulf found Melinda on the tween deck, where they'd partitioned off a small section for themselves with hanging sheets of canvas. Still disguised as a lad in hose, jerkin and feathered cap, it was now her turn to watch the bags, which were heaped beside a porthole. She leaned there on her elbows, gazing into the hubbub of the harbour.

'I brought you something.' He reached into the sack, pulling out a smaller bag made from white linen and opening it. 'See... fresh figs. Lord Thurstan doesn't know about these. I brought them for you especially.'

'He'll be angry.'

'He won't even know if we eat them now.'

She looked outside again. 'I'm not hungry.'

'God almighty, girl! What am I going to do with you?'

'Don't blaspheme.'

'How can I not? I had to watch my spending so I could bring a gift for you. In doing this, I took a risk that Lord Thurstan might enquire where the rest of the money had gone. And he still might. And now you turn your nose up. I mean, look at these...' He held up two generous handfuls of plump purple fruit. 'Figs don't get riper than these.'

She sighed. 'Seeing as you went to all that trouble.'

He hunkered down, pushing several figs into his mouth, one after another. 'Whatever I do, I can't make friends with you.'

Melinda sat too and commenced eating. If she'd genuinely had no appetite before, she'd suddenly discovered one. Her mouth was soon covered in purple juice. 'We're friends. Of a sort.'

'Of a sort,' he snorted.

'You want to be my lover. Is that it? Have you done so much for me that I should lay down in gratitude?'

Pandulf flushed. 'I didn't mean that.'

'That's how it sounded.'

He handed her the bag. 'Here, have them all.' He sat with arms folded. 'Now *I've* no appetite.'

'I'm sorry... I know you didn't mean that.' She pushed the bag back to him. 'And I'm grateful.'

He recommenced eating. After several days of privation on board ship, these figs were as sweet and succulent as he'd ever known. 'For what it's worth, I understand why you hate us. You must feel a long way from the safety of home.'

'Well...' she dabbed her lips with a cloth, 'as you've told me a dozen times, I no longer have a home. And if I'm honest, travelling the world is probably better than occupying a stone cell in St Hildegard's Tower.' She got back to her feet and looked through the porthole. 'So, this is Cyprus? I've heard of it, but I've never been here.'

'Neither had I until the Pilgrimage. It was a Templar enclave. Still is, I suspect. Lord Thurstan's being extra careful, but everything he said about hiding under their noses... so far, it's coming true.'

'And when we reach this place, Antalya?'

Pandulf couldn't help being worried about that. 'It's difficult to be sure what awaits us there.'

'Well, whatever it is...' Melinda sat down again, 'Lord Thurstan will cut a path through it with his great shining sword.'

'It may come to that, yes.'

'Even though this Eastern empire, which once was Roman but now is Greek, is largely made up of Christians?'

'Christendom is no crucible of peace, Melinda. My former master, Hugo FitzOsbo, was convinced the Pope only sent our warring elements east to drain them out of Christian lands.'

'Your former master was a fount of wisdom. You should have stayed with him. You'd have learned good things instead of how to make war in the most frightful way.'

'He was a warrior too.' Pandulf's thoughts drifted back to an event two years previous, though it seemed a lifetime ago now. 'He was fighting at Acre, when he was engulfed by blazing oil while ascending a siege tower.'

Melinda visibly cringed.

'I saw it, Melinda… with my own eyes. I've seen many horrible things since. But trust me, that is no way for any man to die.'

She couldn't seem to respond. Just watched him.

'What you said earlier…' Suddenly, he was hesitant. 'About do I want to be your lover. It would be wrong of me not to admit that I've thought of nothing else since I first set eyes on you. I don't mean that in an unpleasant way. I mean… I'd love you to be my intended, if you know what I mean.'

'Your intended?' Melinda sounded astonished. 'Surely, you aren't serious?'

'There,' he groaned. 'You're offended again.'

'I'm not offended. Pandulf. As a serving girl, even in the patriarch's house, I was very used to powerful men, and sometimes even women, eyeing me in predatory fashion, and occasionally putting their hands where they shouldn't. That, I found offensive. In contrast, you've been polite, even gallant. But Pandulf…'

'You could do worse,' he cut in. 'When we make it back to England, I'll be knighted. Lord Thurstan holds a great estate in the north. I could be more than a household knight. I could have my own fief.'

'Pandulf… they won't let you marry me.'

He knew this, of course. It was hopeless.

He sighed. 'I just wanted you to know that if you do catch me staring at you, my intentions are not impure.'

'I appreciate that, but… even if it was possible, my devotions lie elsewhere.'

That confused him. 'Where?'

'Oh, Pandulf. Isn't it obvious? I only have dim memories of my time as the daughter of nobility. Most of the life I remember, I spent in prayer and spiritual contemplation. I'd had duties as a servant, I worked long hours... but at the same time, I was indentured to a Church household, to an episcopal prince no less, an elevated servant of God. In addition, I was never more content than when praying in the chapel or contemplating the sacred mysteries. It became inevitable, I felt, that when my father's debts were paid, I would enter an order.' She paused, as though unsure how to continue. 'I don't think I can ever provide what you want, Pandulf. Even if it was within my power.'

'Which it isn't, and never will be,' someone else cut in.

They looked round, shocked that Bertrand had slipped in past the canvas sheet without them hearing. Now, he stood at the porthole, peering pensively out.

'Forgive me for eavesdropping,' he said in dull monotone, 'but you were being so earnest with each other, I didn't have the heart to interrupt. The plain fact is, Melinda... You command celestial powers.'

'But I don't know if I do,' she replied.

'We're all witness to it. And for that reason, your life is not your own.' He laid this out for them simply and without emotion. 'When we reach England, the Church will need to appraise you. It could take months, even years. And even if they judge you a fraud, they'll never admit that. The world will know too much. Supplicants will flock from far and wide. Begging your prayers... and offering donations. Why would your keepers ever allow you to leave?'

'For God's sake, my lord,' Pandulf muttered.

'Your intentions are good.' Bertrand glanced at the lad. 'Even noble, I'd say. But don't delude yourself. For us, Saint Melinda of Jerusalem is nothing more than a package we must deliver. Forgive me, my lady, but it's better you know the truth.'

'I know it already.'

Bertrand nodded at the boy. 'He clearly doesn't.'

Pandulf stuttered. 'I just hoped—'

'We all had hopes,' the knight interrupted. 'When we were given this assignment, we all thought it our key to the Kingdom of Heaven.'

The squire regarded him worriedly. 'And now you're not sure?'

'You know my position. We sail on the evening tide, our destination the Anatolian shore. I don't know how much progress we'll make from there, but if we make any, it will doubtless be over another pile of corpses.'

'Are the Greeks so bad?'

'It isn't the Greeks,' Bertrand said, 'though they dislike us plenty enough. It's their ruler, Emperor Isaac. A vain, weak man... but vengeful. I take it Lord Thurstan hasn't mentioned that Isaac was formerly the brother-in-law of Conrad of Montferrat?'

Pandulf felt a pang of fear.

'Conrad later divorced Isaac's sister, Theodora,' Bertrand said. 'But the two potentates remained friends. In which case, if word that we are travelling has got as far as Isaac's court, it won't just be young Melinda he'll be interested in apprehending. And in that event, our fate – as in yours, mine and Lord Thurstan's – will be considerably worse than hers.'

CHAPTER 39

The shipwreck could have been far worse. They'd all known worse or at least had heard about it. Fortunately, when the galley had finally been driven inshore, it had grounded on a sandbar rather than striking rocks, and there it had wedged, continually pounded by the high seas, which had been no comfort for those on board, though at least they'd known it would recede in time, which, when it did, left them beached in the midst of desolation.

The sandflats, in many areas still under inches of water, stretched away to all horizons save the one at their backs, where the grey line of the sea bisected the sky about a half-mile distant. The air was cool, a stiff breeze cutting past them. The crew, having made imaginative use of sailcloth and several broken spars, had erected a flimsy structure just leeward of the great leaning hulk, and here had got a small fire going and were cooking broth in a kettle. King Richard partook, along with his three remaining knights, the other two, Ramon la Hors and Henry von Sickingen, having ridden respectively north and east.

Von Sickingen was the first to return, some half a day after he'd departed. He dismounted and eagerly accepted a bowl of broth, his damp cloak swathed about him.

'It would appear, my liege, that we have come ashore in the Gulf of Trieste, in the realm of the Count of Merania.'

Richard bit on his lip. This was not good news, the counts of Merania being vassals to Leopold of Babenberg, the Duke of Austria, who had left the Pilgrimage in a rage after Richard had flung his banner down from the battlements at Acre.

'He's no friend to us,' Von Sickingen said, stating the rather obvious. 'But at present, sire, we've no reason to assume he knows we are here.'

Richard eyed the ship's crew, who were mumbling among themselves. It was likely that most of them didn't even speak French, and in any case, if even one among them was minded to give word that the King of England was stranded here, he was in no position to do it yet. Even so, Richard walked away from the shelter, his knights following.

'We face a difficult decision,' he said. 'We could continue north along the coast, but that will bring us into the orbit of the Venetians, who we don't feel we can trust. The alternative is to go eastward, veering northward once we're far inland, but heading deeper and deeper into Leopold's domain. Either route is fraught with peril.'

There was a long silence.

'My view, sire, for what it's worth,' Von Sickingen said, 'is that we go north along the coast. We're incognito. There's no reason why we can't enter Venetian lands as simple travellers. The Doge doesn't know you personally, so even if you were seized and taken to his court, we could lie about who we are.'

'Maybe it won't even come to that,' Amand de Cournai, a knight of Anjou, suggested. 'We might pass through unnoticed.'

'Aye,' said another. 'And then what? We go west through the lands of the Lombards, which brings us into Burgundy, where Philip's agents will be waiting to seize us. Or maybe through the Alps? Except that it's now December... so how will we fare then?'

'Winter is the biggest threat,' Richard agreed. 'Most of the Alpine passes will already be closed. Our best option is to head north, into the heart of Austria, and from there turn west, with the ultimate aim of seeking refuge in Bavaria, where my cousin, Heinrich of Saxony has many allies. It should be open roads all the way, plus there'll be towns, villages, inns...'

'But my liege!' De Cournai protested. 'You must pass for days and days through Leopold's lands before you reach Bavaria.'

'There is also the matter of the emperor himself,' Von Sickingen warned.

Henry Hohenstaufen, the sixth of that name in the long list of Holy Roman Emperors to date, Henry the Cruel to those who'd fallen foul of him, would also consider Richard an enemy thanks to his allegiance with Tancred of Sicily, plus his family ties to the House of Welf, a dynasty of German princes long opposed to the Hohenstaufen.

The king cinched tight his damp, ragged tunic. His frame had emaciated somewhat since those halcyon days at the commencement of the Pilgrimage. Even his tawny hair and beard bore strands of grey, though he was only thirty-five years old.

'Sire!' one of the other knights warned.

From the north, a single rider was approaching.

They all of them glanced at the rag-wrapped bundle propped up inside the shelter. Their weapons. But it soon became apparent this rider was a friend.

'La Hors,' Richard said, walking forward.

The knight-captain swung down from his horse. 'I bring hard tidings, sire. You're within the reach of Leopold.'

The king nodded. 'We must trust to God that he's not yet aware of our presence.'

'I'm afraid God has disavowed us. Again.'

La Hors accepted a bowl of broth and drank it down in a gulp, scraping the interior of the dish with his woollen-gloved fingertips and licking them.

'Speak,' Von Sickingen urged him.

La Hors looked grim. 'There are mounted patrols headed this way. The closest are about a mile north. But they wear the white-and-crimson crest of Duke Leopold.'

'More than we can fight?' one of the other knights asked.

La Hors smiled at the mere thought. 'Many more.'

'That decides it,' Richard said. 'We head inland.'

'My liege, wouldn't it be better to go south?' one of the others wondered.

'Turn tail and run?' La Hors said, sounding shocked.

'We're exhausted,' Von Sickingen said wearily. 'And once they got wind of us, and these men will tell them who we are, let's not fool ourselves,' he jabbed a thumb at the crew, 'they'll overhaul us easily.'

The king agreed. 'We are too exposed out here. Inland, at least there'll be cover. Get together what baggage you've managed to save. And be swift. We must ride like the wind.'

By all accounts there had been storms further west. Severe ones. So, in some ways they'd been fortunate to take a ship like the *Gloriosus*, which was headed north. The passage had been a relatively peaceful one, the sea calm, the skies clear if cold. Several mornings they awoke to see frost on the masts and rigging.

'This feels more like home,' Bertrand muttered disconsolately.

'We're a long way from home yet,' Thurstan replied.

Each day now, he strolled the upper deck, lost in complex thoughts. The ship wasn't as full since they'd left Cyprus, so there was plenty of space for this. Conversely, it meant that he came more and more to the attention of the five or six Templars on board. Apparently, they had a cabin of their own, but during daylight hours, when they weren't at their private devotions, they were mostly to be found grouped on the forecastle, talking idly. The Danish Templar, who Thurstan had crossed words with on the docks in Tyre, seemed unusually interested, watching him with ever deepening suspicion. For his part, Thurstan ignored the fellow. Now that they were heading back to Europe, albeit by a circuitous route, his thoughts strayed constantly to what he would do when they returned to England. It all depended on how well King Richard was received there. If Prince John was in arms, no doubt funded and supplied with extra troops by Philip of France, the king might have a difficult time re-establishing himself. A full-blown civil war could already be raging.

Thurstan, as Knight-Commander of the *Familia Regis*, would be required to fight for the king, though he would have done that anyway. Prince John was a rodent, a schemer, a trickster and an unrepentant oath-breaker. Most dangerous of all, though, he was unintelligent, a blunderer who overestimated himself. Richard had only grown into the role of king since his coronation, and up until now he'd been more interested in fighting foreign wars than administration of his realm, but he was a better option than John by far.

Even so, it struck Thurstan hard that there had to be more awaiting him in England than another military camp.

Kirkwood Hall?

Should he return there?

He'd sworn that he never would. It was far to the north, several weeks' travel from the frenetic politics of England and Normandy. Of course, it was close to the Scottish border, which meant that it wasn't always peaceful. Many a reiver clan would venture over the border, looking to burn villages and steal cattle, so quite often, as a tenant-knight of Cupthorne Abbey, he'd be called on by its prioress, Mother Turilda, to draw steel in defence of her people. But for most of the time it was quiet, the pine-clad hills soaring, the multiple lakes mirroring the enormous sky.

'I have no reason to live,' he told her, as she walked with him along the shore of Kesewik Lake, gentle wavelets lapping at their feet.

In the days following his illness, he'd barely been able to stand. Even after recovery, Mother Turilda had linked arms with him to hold him upright. Fortunately, she was a sturdy woman for all her great age, lean of build, with a face like a wizened monkey, but with wiry limbs and, of course, those strong, knotty hands.

'Many who lose their loved ones think the same,' she replied. 'Gradually though, they realise that God won't tolerate that. He has a plan for every one of us. We must proceed with it, or else His anger will be fierce.'

'God's plan for me has so far been tumultuous,' he replied. 'Longswords stained with blood. Burning towns under smoke-black skies.'

'Then there is all the more reason for you to persevere.'

'You mean keep ploughing forward until my chance for redemption comes?'

'What else?'

Behind them, Kirkwood Hall, an austere granite keep inside a simple curtain wall, stood on a low rise at the lake's northern end, overlooking the stockaded settlement that was Kesewik itself. The fortress was all but empty now, most of the servants having died from the same illness that had claimed Gwendolyn and had almost claimed him. There would be no future there, that was certain.

'If I go south again and rejoin the king's house, as I fear I must, for duty calls, the only future is more battles and slaughters. They say he plans to invade the East.'

'Ah yes.' The prioress frowned. 'A holy war.'

Thurstan was surprised. 'You doubt the value of such?'

'The Holy Places need rescuing... or so I'm told.'

'Reverend Mother... you sound dubious.'

'I know nothing of these things, Thurstan. I'm just a silly, muddle-headed old woman. I'm far too busy managing the Honour of Cupthorne...'

'There's nothing muddle-headed about you, Reverend Mother. Your knowledge of herbal lore pulled me back from the brink.'

'In that case, you may add providing medicinal care to my list of baronial duties.'

'Once I'm strong enough, I'll rejoin the Familia Regis,' Thurstan said decidedly.

'If that's where your destiny awaits you.'

'It'll be Hell,' he said, 'but I'm no good for anything else.'

'We'll see about that,' she replied. 'One man's road to Hell can be another man's route to Heaven...'

It seemed perverse of course to imagine, or even harbour hopes, that you could seek salvation through violence, but memories of Mother Turilda and her words of wisdom only kindled this line of thought. She hadn't meant that you could win God's favour by going out in the world, wreaking butchery. She hadn't even been impressed by the notion of a holy war. But she'd clearly believed that under Thurstan's battle-scarred hide, there was a man worth saving. Could *this* be the route to that? The preservation of this girl–saint, who even doubted herself that she was any such thing? Especially when their main opponents now, it seemed, were the Knights Templar?

How had that come about? How would that win the Lord of Hosts' approval? Particularly when they'd be preserving this girl to suit the wiles of Bishop Hubert Walter? Yes, Thurstan was obeying the king. As his duty demanded. But just because kings were Heaven-sent, did that mean they were incorruptible?

Hah! Do you really need to ask yourself that?

He tried to shake it from his mind. It was all too confusing. He was a knight. It was that simple. He would fight and die where his overlord commanded. That was his role... his quest. It wasn't as if God loved him anyway.

He was distracted from this morass of confused thoughts by the Danish Templar, again watching him brazenly from the forecastle. For the first time, Thurstan felt a stir of unease. Previously, he'd believed the fellow was seeking to cow him, continuing their disagreement from Tyre by trying to stare him down. Alternatively, as Bertrand had said, it might just have been Thurstan's soldierly aspect. Perhaps he cut too imposing a figure to be taken seriously as an ordinary traveller.

Either way, the following morning, when they were one day and one night from Antalya, he saw the fellow in conversation with the ship's master, and handing him a small scrap of scrolled parchment, which was promptly passed to a cabin boy, who then climbed the mainmast to the crow's nest, where a cage of messenger birds was kept. Thurstan attempted nonchalance as he stood by the bulwark, but in truth, his eyes switched constantly to that teetering topmost section of the ship, where the cabin boy, having now freed one of the birds and fastened that tiny scroll to its claw, released it. It flew away, heading due north.

When Thurstan went back down to their private space on the tween deck, Bertrand stood by the porthole, where he seemed to be permanently posted these days, Melinda and Pandulf lying asleep amid the baggage.

'If Melinda makes any effort to go topside today, stop her,' Thurstan said quietly.

'Is there a problem?' Bertrand wondered.

'I'm not sure.'

'We put ashore tomorrow. Why restrict her movements now?'

'I have an uncomfortable feeling.'

Bertrand looked frustrated. 'That's all?'

Thurstan eyed him, again irritated by his friend's growing reticence about the mission. 'What do you mean "that's all"?'

Bertrand's face coloured. 'Nothing. It's just that we're all tired. And now it's December... winter, Thurstan. And we have no idea what lies ahead of us.'

'Just assume it will be nothing good. Then you won't be disappointed.'

CHAPTER 40

That night, Thurstan sat under the porthole while the others slept, watching, ears straining for any suspicious sound. Only in the early hours, with a milky light leaching over the mist-covered sea, and the great featureless landmass of Anatolia looming, was he unable to keep his eyes open any longer and so woke Pandulf, charging him with standing guard until the rest of the ship came to life.

However, the knight didn't drift into sleep quickly. Troublesome thoughts plagued him. If the Templars on this ship had decided that he and his companions were these same felons now being sought by their brotherhood in the East, why didn't they simply attack? Yes, he had a reputation with a sword, but these were Templars, highly trained themselves, and they outnumbered him. If they didn't want a fracas on the boat, why didn't they simply creep down here during the night and bind him while he slept, or better yet from their perspective, finish him off before he woke?

Maybe his fears were unfounded, and yet he knew what he'd seen. That messenger bird had not been bound for nowhere.

Later that morning, he made casual enquiries among fellow passengers about the status of the Templars in Antalya. It was a Greek city, after all. Did they have any kind of power there, or were they classed as outsiders themselves? An old Jewish man with a long beard and a skull cap, a spice merchant called Simon who regularly travelled the region, advised him that the Templar banking system was used as widely by the Greeks as by non-Greeks. The Knights Templar didn't discriminate. For their usual commission, they would provide protection and credit to anyone so long as they were heading to or from the Levant. As such, there were Templar houses dotted across the Greek states, though he conceded they were not so common as in Outremer or the rest of Christendom. He felt certain there was a small Templar house in Antalya. They were not the authority there, of course, but their assistance could be called on by the port's governor, if needed.

Thurstan repaired to their quarters, where he relayed this information.

'Is this supposed to worry us?' Bertrand asked.

'In a couple of hours we'll be sailing through the harbour gates,' Thurstan said. Already, they could hear the ringing of bells and shouting of the crew as the vessel subtly altered course, new sails unfurling to take account of the coastal cross-breeze. 'It's not impossible that our friends on the upper deck are awaiting reinforcements before they make their move.'

Pandulf was wide-eyed. 'Why would they need reinforcements?'

'Oh, Pandulf!' Melinda said. 'Between you, you slew over half a dozen Assassins.'

'So, what do you propose?' Bertrand replied.

'Leave everything here,' Thurstan said. 'All our luggage. As we approach the harbour, we go topside together.'

'With no one to watch these items?' Pandulf asked.

'No one,' Thurstan affirmed. 'You wear only the clothes you're standing in. Plus, your swords and sword-belts. Ensure the scabbards are fastened closed.'

Bertrand was grim-faced. 'You really think this is going to happen?'

'I hope it won't, but we must be ready.'

'If you're right, leaving all this baggage here will avail us nothing,' Pandulf said. 'By the time we dock, it will already be too late.' When Thurstan gave no answer, he added: 'Perhaps we can cut one of the skiffs loose?'

'There'll be no time for that,' Melinda replied. 'They'll see you.'

'We're just being cautious,' Thurstan said. 'If nothing happens, all well and good. We can return down here, collect our things and go ashore with everyone else.'

'And if it does?' Bertrand asked.

'Just do as I've said,' Thurstan replied. 'And hurry. We need to go topside.'

—

'Leopold's men are everywhere,' Ramon la Hors said, weaving his way back into the thicket of pines where Richard and his other four companions were waiting on horseback.

'This is absurd,' Von Sickingen replied. 'How are they able to pinpoint us like this? And how did they know we'd landed on this coast?'

'One of their beach patrols must have found the ship,' La Hors said. 'Those seadogs will have served us up.'

'Yes, but just to find that boat they'd have needed to be searching *this* area.'

The knight-captain shrugged. 'It's a mystery, I agree. But they've come well prepared. Leopold's numbers have been boosted by members of the Siegfried Order.'

'Siegfrieders?' Richard said, trying not to show how uneasy that made him.

The Order of Siegfried was an infamous sell-sword company, many thousands strong. In so many ways, it was a typical *routier* band, only larger and better resourced than most. Multinational in composition, the Order was allegedly available for hire to any potentate who could pay its notoriously high wages, but in truth, it was the *de facto* private army of the German Emperor. In Frederick Barbarossa's absence on the Pilgrimage, it was expected to keep order in the Empire and enforce his interests. Doubtless, it had now undertaken a similar role on behalf of his son.

'I honestly thought we'd get further inland than ten miles,' De Cournai said.

'What kind of landscape awaits us?' Richard asked.

'If we continue north-west,' La Hors said, 'it's mostly low valleys, thinly treed.'

They relapsed into thought. None of that boded well for cover.

'Will our religious insignia not protect us?' De Cournai wondered.

On the king's instructions, they'd all of them ensured that they were wearing their pilgrims' scrips and their cloaks with the crosses sewn at the shoulder over their ordinary travelling clothes. In normal circumstances, this would have granted them a certain degree of safety, as any Christian interfering with a known pilgrim travelling to or from the Holy Land was automatically excommunicated.

'That may be why they've summoned the Siegfrieders,' Von Sickingen said. 'Such a threat won't worry them.'

This was undeniable. The Order of Siegfried contained no knights, only men-at-arms, because many of the tasks it undertook went against the chivalrous code. As such, they were, in the eyes of most, a godless rabble, used mainly to terrorise recalcitrant populations rather than fight in actual battles, their black mantles, black chain-mail and black full-head helms an enduring symbol of their vicious nature. Wherever they deployed, rampage and atrocity occurred freely, which was one reason why they'd never been sent on Pilgrimage, as the knightly orders in the Holy Land would never have tolerated such ignobility.

'At the very least we should rearm ourselves,' La Hors said.

Richard sighed. He'd hoped all along that they could traverse this region overlooked as non-military, but that guise was becoming unsustainable.

'Only your swords for the time being,' he said. 'Concealed under your cloaks. But keep them in reach.'

They proceeded warily through the lightly wooded realm. For the most part, it was leafless and desolate, patches of December snow glinting between the scabrous trunks. They halted when they came to a road. It was rutted and muddy but ran south-east to north-west. They waited a dozen yards back, while La Hors scouted along it. He returned after two hours, sipping from a bottle of water.

'There's a cottage about half a mile along,' he said. 'An old woodsman's dwelling, I think, though it's deserted now. You can shelter there, sire. But I wouldn't stay too long. There's a crossroads another half-mile further on. There, I encountered a monk travelling on a donkey. He didn't have a word of French, but he understood enough Latin to inform me the road heading west leads ultimately to a town called Labacum, known locally as Ljubljana.'

'Ljubljana is where we need to go,' Von Sickingen put in eagerly. 'It sits on the highway into Bavaria.'

'It isn't so straightforward,' La Hors countered. 'Half a mile along that westward road, I spotted another party of Siegfrieders. Along with some horsemen wearing Leopold's crest. Thirty or forty in total.'

'What were they doing?' Richard asked.

'Camped by the roadside, sire.'

The king pondered. 'We could leave the road and continue through the forest. We haven't seen them scouring the woods and thickets yet.'

'These are woods and thickets we don't know,' De Cournai replied. 'We could blunder into a swamp.'

'The woods peter out beyond the crossroads I mentioned,' La Hors said. 'My liege, if you'll permit me… I've had a thought.'

The king nodded.

'You should keep one attendant by your side… I'd suggest Von Sickingen, as he speaks German and knows this part of the world better than the rest of us. We others meanwhile, will ride to the crossroads clad in our *Familia Regis* finery, and from the point where the woodland becomes open moor, ride forward at full tilt. Any pennons we have left, we fly. We even blow our horns. The Siegfrieders will pursue. There's nothing surer. Of course, they won't know that you aren't with us.'

The king mused. 'And the road to Ljubljana will be left open.'

'It may. In the meantime, I suggest we rest in this cottage I found. Just for an hour or so. There's grass along the road's edge, so the horses can eat. There's also a stable at the back, with a barrel attached, which is filled with rainwater… so they can drink. Once we're rested, we commence our stratagem. Von Sickingen, you should ride with us as far as the crossroads. But wait there, hide yourself… return for our lord when the chase is on.'

'What will the outcome be for the rest of us?' De Cournai wondered.

'Why should there be any outcome?' La Hors said. 'We aren't the king, so they'll get no ransom for us. But we *do* wear the crosses of pilgrims… once there's nothing to be gained from it, even the Siegfrieders will be loath to impede us further.'

'We'll be stripping the king of almost all his protection,' Von Sickingen argued.

'*You're* a good swordsman, are you not?' Richard asked him.

The German knight blushed. 'I have some reputation, sire.'

'As do I,' Richard replied. 'We can stand together if needs be.' He turned to the others. 'We must be honest with ourselves, gentlemen. The odds we face are onerous. They can crush us by brute force alone. So, we need to be cautious and cunning, which is why, Knight–Captain La Hors... your plan sounds good.'

La Hors nodded.

The king urged his horse onto the lane. 'Come, we're in need of rest. Let's find it while we can.'

CHAPTER 41

'Before you ask, I can swim,' Melinda told Thurstan, as they ascended the ladder to the main deck. 'I presume you've already confirmed this with Pandulf and Bertrand?'

'They can swim to the extent any man can paddle about in warm, shallow water,' he said. 'I'm not sure they can swim to the extent they may need to. But as I say, it's only a *may* at present.'

'I doubt that,' she replied.

The girl was sharp, Thurstan had to give her that.

The *Gloriosus* swung handsomely towards Antalya's Grand Harbour gate. It was no actual gate of course, but a huge gap encompassed on the east side by a great headland, which ended in a promontory of barnacle-encrusted boulders with a stone tower erected on it, the open upper section of which housed an immense flaming brazier, and on the west, though this was half a mile away at least, by a man-made stone boom, which protruded far into the ocean and again was surmounted at its southernmost tip by a tall tower with a permanently tended beacon fire on top.

At the harbour's far shoreward end, there were innumerable piers and quaysides, with uncountable numbers of boats and craft already moored there. Beyond those, flat-roofed shops and houses, indistinguishable from those they'd seen in Tyre, Acre and Limassol, rose tier upon tier, while further inland loomed the misty, snow-capped massifs of the Taurus Mountains.

While Bertrand and Pandulf stood nonplussed, Thurstan leaned over the starboard bulwark to scan the moorings ahead. On their right, the east-side lighthouse tower passed by no more than two hundred yards away. He couldn't see anything landward on the approaching waterfront that might alarm him, but in truth, he couldn't see much.

Adjusting his sword-belt, he clambered on top of the bulwark and ascended a portion of rigging. This gave him a better view, and for the first time now, he spied noticeable movement along the eastern dock-side, which, given that it was mostly clear of other vessels, presumably meant this was where the *Gloriosus* would tie up. He squinted at the figures milling there. Doubtless, there'd be porters, baggage-handlers and such, and yet he wasn't convinced these were the only men he was seeing. He glanced again at the starboard headland as it receded behind them. The ship was travelling smoothly, its sails full. More and more passengers were coming up onto deck, coated, hooded and scarfed, carrying their luggage, eager to be onshore.

He stared again at the eastern docks, and now was certain that he could pick out red crosses on white tabards.

Many of them.

The messenger bird had reached its destination.

He climbed from the bulwark and stared lengthways down the ship. The Danish Templar stood prominent on the forecastle, watching him.

Thurstan turned to the others. 'We've reached several points of no-return on this journey so far. But whether we survive this next one is in the hands of God. Melinda?'

She nodded, hoisted her small backpack onto her shoulders, and clambered onto the bulwark, clinging to the rigging. Pandulf and Bertrand watched her, puzzled. As such, neither noticed Thurstan reach under his tunic and bring out the leather pouch containing their money. It was now much depleted of course, but still clinked with bezants, more than enough to see them on for countless more miles of travel. Which was why he emptied out a handful, and then shouted at the top of his voice: 'Gold for all!'

He flung the coins along the deck, a second handful following immediately, and then a third. Pandulf tried to grab his wrist. But already the deck was in chaos, crewmen and passengers scampering around, pushing and shoving as they struggled to grab their share. On the forecastle, the Danish knight stood stiff with disbelief.

'Melinda!' Thurstan said again.

The girl nodded. And leapt from the bulwark.

'Great God!' Pandulf reached after her, though it was too late. Thurstan grabbed the squire by the belt, hoisting him up and over the bulwark as well.

'Have you gone mad?' Bertrand cried.

Thurstan stood rigid, hand on sword-hilt, glaring down the ship as the Danish Templar and his cohort fought their way towards him but were constantly hampered.

'Come with us, or stay here, it's your choice,' he retorted.

'I... I...' Bertrand also gazed along the teeming deck. The Templars were close. A couple had drawn their swords.

'Christ almighty!' The banneret also turned and vaulted over the bulwark.

Thurstan went last.

It was a fifteen-foot drop to the rolling foam. When he struck it, the shock to his system was almost overwhelming, although they'd been cold on deck, so it wasn't an instant transition from extreme heat to extreme chill. For seconds, he descended into a green void filled with bubbles. Above him the immense keel of the *Gloriosus* cast an obsidian shadow, but already the vessel was veering away, sunlight spearing down in its place.

Encumbered by his waterlogged clothes and those few items of baggage he'd stuffed into his harness, but still thinking to check that his sword was secure in its scabbard, the document tube around his neck, and the money pouch tucked back into his belt, Thurstan kicked upward. At the same time, he struck eastward, and when he broke the surface, sucked in a chestful of air and commenced a hefty, arm-over-arm crawl towards the headland, which seemed farther away than he'd expected. Not so much a couple of hundred yards now as eight or nine, and in the huge swell of the sea that was a monstrous journey. But it was that or death. For all of them.

The other three were just ahead, kicking up foam as they floundered forward. In front of them, huge waves broke on the base of the lighthouse tower, fountains of surf filling the air. No one made a sound. No one could. The backwash of the waves struck them repeatedly, slapping their faces, filling their noses with brine. But desperate people can achieve incredible things. Thurstan knew this. He'd seen it many times on campaign.

The next few minutes though, seemed like hours.

His physical prowess coming to the fore, he pulled slowly ahead of the others, which had to be a good thing, he thought, for if he could find a purchase on solid ground, he could be their anchor. When he struck the rocks, the lighthouse towering over him, teetering it seemed in its steeple-like height, he gashed his knees and elbows, but was able to dig his fingers among the shells and kelp, and haul himself upward, from where, twisting around, he could offer a hand.

Melinda came up next, eagerly taking his grip, though shivering violently. Next came Pandulf, Bertrand shoving him from behind as he too scrambled ashore. Thurstan led them hurriedly upward, over boulders covered in thick, slippery wrack, surf still breaking heavily over them. When they finally reached a point where the rocks were dry, Thurstan glanced back across the harbour. The *Gloriosus* was already far away. He fancied figures clustered its stern, watching. Figures bearing crimson crosses on white. 'This way,' he told the others, picking his way southward, looking to round the headland itself.

'This is madness,' Bertrand muttered, breathless. 'Sheer madness.'

They moved in single file along a narrow ledge, rounding the spit of the headland, the harbour falling out of sight behind them.

'Well done everyone,' Thurstan said. 'That took real courage.'

'You hardly gave us a choice,' Bertrand replied, sounding embittered.

—

The cottage was much as La Hors had described, built from timber with a roof of thatched sticks, though most of these were rotten with mildew and sagged inward. The interior was bereft of furnishing and the floor made of dirt, while the windows were covered with loose, misaligned shutters. One thing they didn't expect to find was a large iron cooking pot suspended over a rock-built hearth. It was rusted around its rim, but save for a few twigs and leaves, empty and clean. When they'd sluiced it out with water from the rain-barrel, they decided to use it to prepare some food. They'd bagged several rabbits and a partridge during their journey from the coast, while among the few supplies they'd salvaged from the ship was a sack of turnips and carrots, so once they had a small fire going, it wouldn't take long to cook a simple stew. King Richard himself, having only ever eaten food that others had prepared for him, volunteered for the duty. He even removed his cloak and wrapped it around his waist like a chef's apron.

Meanwhile, gusts of sleet blew past the exterior, plastering the sides of the trees, adding further white streaks along the woodland floor. It was deathly cold, far more so than earlier, which was a clear sign they'd forged their way into the interior.

'Maybe the Siegfrieders will retreat from this?' Von Sickingen said to La Hors, as they peered past one of the ill-fitted shutters. 'Opt for the fire-lit comforts of a great hall?'

La Hors seemed unsure. 'I think the prize is too big. Plus, they have Leopold's men with them. The mad Austrian bastard could never have dreamed he'd have a chance to get the King of England in his clutches.'

'I'd love to know how he found out we were here.'

'When we discover whose tongue wagged, we'll plan something special. In the meantime, it's about survival.'

Von Sickingen couldn't dispute that.

The two of them joined the queue while the king distributed the thin and rather tasteless stew, each man slurping several mouthfuls from the same ladle, which they'd found hanging from a hook in a dusty corner.

'Just around now anything tastes good,' De Cournai remarked, smacking his lips. The king eyed him. 'Forgive me, sire. It's wonderful, excellent… but I'm no judge of fine cuisine.'

'Cleary.' But the king treated himself last of all, and he too pulled a face.

The meal done, La Hors and the group who'd provide the diversion opened their baggage and took out their mail-coats and leggings, and their *Familia Regis* colours.

'Which direction do you intend to ride in?' Von Sickingen asked.

'Directly north,' La Hors replied. 'With your permission, sire?'

The king inclined his head with reluctant approval.

It was mid-afternoon by the time the men were fully equipped, the horses groomed and resaddled. La Hors led his troop at a canter along the narrow track, which, the sleet having ceased, was now freezing into ruts and ridges. Von Sickingen, still dressed in his pilgrim's garb, rode about sixty yards behind. As planned, they'd left the king in the cottage, frustrated and silent, clearly feeling unmanned, but firmly in control, his Hot Duke days far in his past.

As they approached the crossroads, La Hors and his men broke into a gallop, icy mud flying from their hooves, Von Sickingen holding back. They reached the crossroads unmolested, but with perfect timing, because right at this moment, a company of mailed horsemen was approaching eastward along the road to Ljubljana, the red-and-white Babenberg banner above them. Those at the front wore open-faced iron caps, and the distinctive Babenberg colours, but those at the rear, and there were many more of these, were in the black mantles and full-head helmets of the Order of Siegfried.

Von Sickingen veered off the track, halting his beast and dismounting amid a clutch of holly trees, where the cover was still good. He watched tautly as the enemy patrol, having immediately sighted La Hors and his men, also hit a gallop. Cautiously, he clambered forward through the prickly foliage. From his new position, he could see La Hors and his men bolting over the crossroads, through the narrow belt of trees beyond and then out onto an open sweep of moorland. Undaunted, their pursuers swerved off the road, riding at their heels.

He hurried on through the frozen undergrowth, reaching the road to Ljubljana, which when he peered westward was empty. Stumbling across to the northern verge, from where the land sloped down, he saw that a Wild Hunt was taking place. La Hors and his men, already much diminished, had spread out, which was only sensible if they wished to avoid being struck by missiles. The chasing horde of Siegfrieders, now seemingly ahead of Duke Leopold's men, had done the same, and were riding after them at furious speed.

Hastening back, the German knight leapt into his saddle, regained the road and galloped for the cottage. The king emerged from it as he slid to a halt outside.

'My liege, we must leave.'

Richard nodded, returning indoors.

They could carry only the barest essentials, but there were still several bolsters that needed fastening among their saddlebags. It took several minutes to sort these from the rest. Then Von Sickingen went out through a rear door to fetch the king's horse from the stable. At which point he heard the thunder of hooves on the lane.

Alarmed, he scampered back outside. Unable to see the road from the rear of the cottage, he dashed indoors, where the king stood with sword drawn – just as the front door was kicked inward from its decayed hinges.

The first of them to come in evidently held senior rank in Duke Leopold's guard. He was fully mailed and wore a broad-brimmed helmet, and a red-and-white surcoat. He also carried a mace, which he wielded threateningly.

'Lower your swords, my lords,' he said in German-accented French. More of his men pushed into the room behind him. 'We're under orders to take you alive… if that proves to be possible.'

Beyond the Austrian soldiers blocking the doorway, Von Sickingen could see the closed steel visors of the Order of Siegfried.

'You're outnumbered,' the Austrian officer said again. 'You must realise.'

'Who are you?' Richard asked him.

'I am Count Meinhard of Gorz, servant to Duke Leopold of Austria. You, of course, are Richard Plantagenet.'

'You're sure of that?'

Count Meinhard's soft cheeks and plush white whiskers gave him the air of a man who'd risen without hardship. But now he smiled coldly. 'I know it for a fact.'

'In which case, you must also know that to lay hands on pilgrims from the East is an offence against God.'

The count's expression hardened. 'We have our duty…'

His men-at-arms advanced with crossbows levelled.

'You'll be excommunicated,' Von Sickingen warned them, both he and the king pointing blades.

'For taking you into protective custody?' Count Meinhard affected an injured tone. 'When these woods are filled with bandits, bears, wolves?'

'My lord,' Richard said, 'you really think that after everything we've been through, some pampered popinjay like you can waylay us? You and your boy soldiers, whose mysterious absence from the Pilgrimage must be explained by either cowardice or weakness of faith, or both.'

Count Meinhard tinged pink. 'That's an amusing accusation, coming from the one who left his army behind.'

Richard didn't rise to the bait. There were now eight or nine crossbows ranged against them. Several Siegfrieders had also pushed through; they too wielded crossbows.

Von Sickingen chose this moment to jump in front of the king. 'The back door, sire... flee! Your horse is waiting.'

Richard retreated towards the rear entrance.

'That would be a wasted effort,' came another voice.

The fugitives spun round, to find Ramon la Hors standing there, still in his *Familia Regis* garb, but with visor lifted.

'Stand with us, La Hors!' Von Sickingen shouted. 'The king needs us.'

But La Hors's sword hung at his hip. 'The king,' he said, 'should surrender.'

Two more Siegfrieders came through the back door behind him, their crossbows also loaded and levelled, but not on him, on Richard and Von Sickingen.

'What is this?' the German knight shouted.

'This is your survival guarantee,' La Hors replied. 'I've vouched for you both... assured Count Meinhard that you'll put away your swords.'

Von Sickingen was too baffled to make sense of it. 'Where are the others?'

'Feeding the Austrian crows,' La Hors sighed. 'I regret that. It didn't need to happen. When I peeled away across the moor, they could have done the same... before the quarrels flew.'

'*You* betrayed us, Ramon?' Von Sickingen stuttered. 'You changed sides in the moment we needed you most?'

'He was never on our side to begin with.' Richard spoke with eyes narrowed. 'You guided us to this very position, did you not, Knight-Captain?'

Von Sickingen was staggered. 'You're with our enemies?'

'Enemies... friends?' La Hors shrugged. 'Horns on the same scrawny goat called Poverty. You were always a devoted knight, young Henry, but your wisdom is lacking. All that matters in the end is personal wealth. When we first went east, we were promised lands, titles. But now we are heading home, none of us any richer.'

Von Sickingen regarded him with glassy-eyed hatred. 'You're a traitor. Not just to the king but to God...'

La Hors laughed. 'The king failed.'

'*Liar!* Peace was made with Saladin. The door to Jerusalem is open.'

'I don't care too much for peace.' La Hors switched his focus to Richard. 'No disrespect, my liege, but I couldn't just head home with pockets empty. As such, I sent a message to Duke Leopold after we'd docked at Corfu, explaining that we were bound for Rimini but would likely put ashore for supplies before then. Of course, our shipwrecking was the ideal outcome. From there, under a pretence of scouting, I was able to contact Leopold's men and tell them exactly where their prize would be.'

'You purposely led your companions to their deaths!' Von Sickingen said.

La Hors shrugged again. 'Add them to the long list of companions I've lost since this mindless adventure commenced. I take no responsibility for those, and certainly none for these.'

Von Sickingen threw a haggard glance at the king, and then at the crossbowmen.

'I sought only to lead them away,' La Hors added. 'I gave them every chance to surrender.'

'Gallant of you.' Von Sickingen seemed tearful. 'I wonder what Satan will make of it...' He whirled on his former colleague, arcing his longsword over and down. But La Hors had drawn his own steel, and with two swift strokes, parried the blade, and struck deep into Von Sickingen's unguarded chest.

The pain shot through the German's middle like ice, all the way from front to back. He even heard the metal grating through his spinal structure. He dropped to his knees, hot blood splurging from his mouth. 'Lord... king...' he clawed at his sovereign, then toppled forward, the dirt floor hitting his face, only vaguely aware of Richard roaring and launching himself forward, sword on high... and the Siegfrieders leaping onto him, wrestling his weapon loose, pinioning his arms behind him.

'You think you'll be paid for this treason, you can think again,' he heard the king snarl. 'These Siegfried murderers serve the German Emperor, not Duke Leopold.'

'I advise against irking us further, Lionheart,' Count Meinhard replied haughtily. 'You're no king here.'

'There'll be a reckoning for this, Meinhard!'

'Not for us.'

The angry, struggling group moved away, kicking up dirt behind them – full into the empty eyes of Henry von Sickingen, who saw and heard no more.

CHAPTER 42

The next few days involved untold difficulty. Initially concerned that they'd freeze to death in their wringing-wet clothes, Thurstan had them climb into the loft of a barn on the outskirts of the main city. Here, they stripped off their sodden garb, hanging it from the rafters overhead, and then buried themselves in straw. Outside meanwhile, Templar horsemen ranged along the narrow, crooked streets.

No one had seen them yet, but for how long could they remain concealed?

'We need to get to the higher ground,' Thurstan told Bertrand. 'With December upon us, they won't be expecting that.'

'Will we survive up there?' Bertrand replied. 'Thurstan... it's cold, and we're hungry.'

Thurstan knew there was no arguing with this. Even when their clothes were dry and they'd dressed again, they weren't adequately protected against the chill. In addition, they'd been unable to bring any food with them, which meant they were famished. He resolved these problems by sneaking out under cover of night, and stealing whatever he could lay hands on, whether that be garments from washing lines: a woollen cloak, hooded and with sleeves, for himself, a knee-length tunic for Bertrand, and a short cape each for Pandulf and Melinda. Or items of food: a fresh-baked loaf cooling on a kitchen window, or two sacksful of nuts and dates, which had been loaded into a storehouse for the coming winter.

It was all gratefully received, though not without hints of guilt.

'So, now we've become thieves?' Bertrand said on the third night.

'It's that or death,' Thurstan replied.

'But we don't need to steal.' The banneret shook his head. 'We don't need to do any of this…' Before he could say more, they heard the scuffling of booted feet on the ladder leading up to the hatch. Thurstan jerked upright, grabbing his sword, but as the hatch, lifted, it wasn't a Templar helmet that came into view, but the face of a bearded man wearing a fur cap. He stared uncomprehendingly at the knight, before dropping from sight, shouting.

'Quickly!' Thurstan said.

They grabbed what few belongings they still had, crossed an open section of the barn by balancing along a beam and opened a pair of loft doors, ten feet below which lay the roof to a small outhouse made from interwoven sticks. The man who'd found them was now out on the street, shouting, his voice shrill with panic. Though night had descended, other voices responded. One by one, Thurstan swung his companions down by the hands, so they only had a few feet to drop onto the outhouse roof. Pandulf and Melinda managed it without difficulty, but Bertrand, who was heavier, went clean through. In fact, the whole of the flimsy roof collapsed under his weight, the other two falling as well. Thurstan clambered down via a rope suspended from the hay derrick overhead.

The outhouse contained nothing but sacks of grain, which broke Bertrand's fall, and now was filled with swirling dust. Thurstan bade them cover their mouths as he unbarred the door and opened it to an inch.

Local people, possibly already on alert due to the recent thefts, dashed about everywhere, some carrying torches.

'We join this crowd the first chance we get,' Thurstan said. 'Try to blend in. These are just townsfolk. They won't know for sure who they're looking for.'

'But when the authorities arrive?' Pandulf asked. 'They may have Templars with them. Even our friends from the ship.'

'Agreed.' Thurstan regarded their thin, frightened faces. 'That means we can't tarry, but we go out in ones and twos. Pandulf and Melinda, you two first. Behave as young lovers do. Hand-in-hand. Head towards the mountains. We'll meet you outside the town.' They nodded. 'Do it discreetly,' he added. 'Talk to no one but make as if you're searching for the scoundrels who've been raiding the kitchens and laundry yards.' He opened the door to half a foot. 'Go now.'

They sidled through. Thurstan closed it again, then turned to Bertrand, taking the money pouch from his belt and handing it over.

Bertrand looked at it, puzzled. 'What's this?'

'I'm the one who locked gazes with the fellow who found us,' Thurstan said. 'So, I'm more likely to be spotted on the street than you. That means there's more chance I'll have to fight. If I'm cut down, take the opportunity to escape and rejoin the others. This money won't buy you passage all the way to England, but it'll get you a considerable distance. From there, use your ingenuity to find other means.'

'Thurstan!' Bertrand grabbed his arm. 'You can't ask this of me!'

'You're a knight, aren't you? You're sworn to the quest.'

'But this whole thing is madness. Even with you to lead us, we'll never make it. It's impossible to conceive of the distance and dangers still in our way. You expect *three* of us to succeed? A mere three?'

Thurstan shook the hand loose. His vision had now adjusted to the dimness of the shed. Bertrand looked as weary and haggard as any man he'd seen, and was wildly whiskered, his hair a shapeless mop. He was also white as a ghost.

'You *must* do this, Bertrand,' he said simply. 'We're nothing to these people but thieves and renegades. We'll be lucky if they only hang us.'

'We can still surrender to the knights of the Temple. At least then the girl will be safe.'

'That may be our last resort,' Thurstan conceded. 'If for no other reason than to save her life for Christendom. But we aren't at that stage yet.'

In truth, Thurstan still had no intention of handing Melinda to the Temple. He'd send her back to England alone if it came down to it, rather than break his oath. But thus far on the journey, they'd already committed crime after crime – hopefully in a higher cause, but who knew? – so, it didn't make much difference now if he lied to his friend to gain cooperation.

Bertrand seemingly felt better on hearing this. He nodded, tucked the money pouch under his tunic, then leaned against the door, opening it an inch again.

'There are still many people,' he said. 'I hear horses coming.'

And indeed, the bass drumbeat of approaching hooves sounded. At the same time, a muffled shouting sounded inside the barn. The fellow who'd found them had clearly waited until he had enough confederates to go up there again.

'Go,' Thurstan said.

Bertrand slipped out into the pandemonium.

Thurstan waited, listening.

Several horsemen thundered past. Whether they'd be Templars or mounted guards from the governor's palace, it wasn't possible to say. Already though, he was thinking that their steeds might come in useful. There was no realistic hope that he and the other three could venture into the Taurus Mountains on foot, not in winter, especially as they didn't even have a map. So any advantage he could find had to be seized on.

He glanced back out through the narrowly open door. Firelit figures ran excitedly, many now carrying improvised weapons such as spades and hatchets, but there were also spears on view and curved Greek *parameria*. It would make no difference now whether he concealed his own sword. Some of these panicking townsfolk might notice that it was a straight blade with a cruciform hilt, the weapon of a Christian knight, but given this level of commotion – many clearly thought that bandits had attacked – it was still unlikely they'd know who they were looking for.

The Templars would, of course. But none of them were in sight.

Thurstan stepped out, closing the door behind him. He stood rigid for a moment. More and more townsfolk seemed to be running and shouting. Just to his left, beyond the outhouse, the great angular structure of the barn was filled with firelight. No doubt they now searched its capacious interior, digging through the hay, dragging dust-thick sheets off heaps of old farming equipment.

He commenced walking. If memory served – because it was too dark to see for certain – the Anatolian uplands dominated the horizon to the left of this position. So, that was where he headed, sidling between ramshackle buildings. Swimming from the *Gloriosus* before she docked, they'd already been outside Antalya's inner defences when they came ashore. Which meant that this was the shanty part of the city. The shops and dwellings had been thrown together cheaply, in a chaotic jumble, with only narrow, noisome alleys between them. It wouldn't have been a safe place to traverse at the best of times, especially at night, but most of its occupants had now been drawn to the barn, so he was able to travel several hundred yards, turning down another crooked passage, before someone accosted him.

A burly fellow, bald-headed and bearded, carrying a hefty club, emerged from the shadows and grabbed the corner of Thurstan's cloak. The knight spun, felling him with a single blow of his fist. He squatted over the groaning form, checking for anything useful, but all he wore was a leather doublet, food-stained pantaloons, and well-worn boots. He also reeked of onions and sweat. A common backstreet ruffian rather than some local watchman.

Thurstan took the club, a knobbly-ended piece of wood, and a broad-bladed hunting knife, which the fellow had worn at his waist, and which would replace the trusty bone-handled blade he'd lost while swimming from the *Gloriosus*, before hurrying on. Now that he was further from the fire-lit main street, he was able to see the black ridge of the mountains on the star-spangled sky. He hurried down a passage towards it, and as he did, a cry rose to his rear. A woman. No doubt, she'd come across her husband or lover, or whoever the bearded, bald-headed oaf had been.

Thurstan flattened himself against the wall, glancing back. Nothing was clearly visible, until a flickery orange light shifted into view. A firebrand, held aloft by a horseman. Sweat speckled the knight's face. In the wavering glow, he glimpsed dark mail, and a white mantle with the blood-red insignia of the Templars. There was an audible exchange of Greek as the rider spoke with the woman. Thurstan waited, tense. Her husband could have been assaulted by anyone, of course. But the brute had been a brawny type, and well-armed. No run-of-the-mill footpad could have floored him so easily.

Evidently, this was the Templar's line of thought, for he raised a curved horn to his lips, and blew a single, prolonged blast.

Thurstan ran, attempting to go light-footed, but collided with a barrel, which crashed over. Another thirty yards, and a figure looked down from overhead, holding a lantern. An angry shout followed.

Hooves pounded as the Templar galloped along the alley.

Thurstan burst out into a broad square. Three or four passages led in different directions. The horn sounded again to his rear, another replying to it from somewhere to his right.

He took the passage on his left but didn't venture far. On the left-hand side of it, there was a rock-built wall, which came to shoulder height. He vaulted up and over it, landing knee-deep in a stinking pile of trash, and hunkered down to listen as the horseman thundered by on the other side. Rising up again, he waded forward, an eye-watering fetor engulfing him. It looked and smelled like household refuse, and now that his vision was again adjusting, he saw that it expanded for dozens of yards. He'd sought sanctuary in the city's rubbish dump.

It didn't matter. He continued across, at times sinking to his hips. Finally, he reached the next boundary wall. He scaled over it, landing catlike in a second narrow alley. He squatted. On his left, the way seemed clear. But on his right, he spotted another of the Templars, perhaps fifty yards away, waiting on horseback, his shield on his left arm, his lance tilted upward.

Shield and lance? They weren't taking chances.

Trusting to the shadows, Thurstan watched on until the Templar jerked his reins, and his animal walked forward out of sight. He padded up there, halting just before the alley entrance, listening. There was no obvious sound, so he chanced a peek.

The Templar was perhaps forty yards off. He'd halted his beast again and now conversed with another of his brethren, this second one also girt for war.

Thurstan glanced further around, seeing that they were on the town's outskirts. To his left, a wider street veered away between more lopsided structures, lines of hanging laundry zigzagging back and forth across it. But at the far end, it opened into apparent nothingness, just the amorphous blackness at the base of the looming mountains. Countryside.

He looked back towards the Templars. The torchbearer had joined them, the trio conferring together.

A detailed plan was now forming in Thurstan's mind. He scurried off to his left. As he did, he drew his sword, cutting down the first line of washing, yanking the damp garments from their pegs, throwing the pegs aside, keeping the rope.

When he came to the end of the street, it was exactly as he'd hoped.

The road continued beyond the town, but as a rugged track heading straight towards the mountains. The halfmoon shone down over sweeps of barren land strewn with boulders. But some thirty yards ahead, two trees, both twisted and leafless, stood one to either side of it, roughly on a level with each other. Rushing to the one on the left and scrambling up it, he looped one end of the rope around its trunk at around ten feet from the ground, tying it in a solid knot. Jumping down and crossing over, he looped the other end around the tree opposite, but in this case ensuring that it was loose, draping it over a chewed-off stub of branch, to keep it level. The main section of rope he allowed to droop down until it lay on the road surface.

He turned to the town, cupped a hand to his mouth and shouted: 'Knights of the Temple, beloved of God… It is I, Thurstan Wildblood. I am the one you seek. Come and find me. If you dare.'

In almost no time, hooves were rumbling. He retreated into the blackness on the right, crouching down, waiting. Almost before he could blink, three riders loomed pell-mell out of the darkness. Leaping back to his feet, he yanked on his line, drawing it upward, pulling it taut between the two trees.

The trio of horsemen struck it at the same time, each one across the neck or the upper chest. In all cases they were catapulted backward from their mounts, their animals neighing with terror, almost losing their footing as they collided with each other and veered away in alarm.

Thurstan dashed forward, club in hand. Of the three riders now strewn on the road, two were still helmeted, though the one who'd been carrying the torch was bare-headed, his helm having been torn clean off. He was the one Thurstan cudgelled first. The other two, he had to unfasten their neck straps and yank the helmets off himself. The first of these was too groggy to resist, but the second, though stunned by his fall, tried to get up, grappling with his assailant.

'Forgive me, friend.' Thurstan shoved him back down. 'But I've no time for this.' Thankfully, another single blow was all it took.

He found the first of the horses standing not too far away. While walking over there to collect it, he spied another. When he returned to the road, the two animals in tow, he saw that the third had got there ahead of him. Along with Pandulf, Bertrand and Melinda.

It was the squire who'd led it there.

Bertrand, meanwhile, had sunk to his knees, eyes fixed on the three unmoving forms.

'Are they dead?' he asked quietly.

'I hope not,' Thurstan replied. 'But I can't be sure.'

Pandulf looked equally horrified. 'My lord... these men weren't pagans.'

'If they had been, the question wouldn't even arise. We can't waste time here. Take a horse each. Whatever's in the saddlebags is ours. Melinda, you will ride with Pandulf.'

The girl nodded, expressionless, seemingly dazed by their rapid change of fortunes.

But Pandulf still seemed shaken. 'Where are we going?'

'By the looks of it,' Thurstan said, 'north.'

'What lies north?'

'It's the opposite direction from Antalya.' Thurstan mounted up. 'That's all we need know at present.'

CHAPTER 43

The track winding into the Anatolian high country soon became a path, and in due course even this petered out. It was a wild land indeed. Vast swathes of mountain rubble interspersed with clutches of pine trees, upwardly tilting heathland streaked with snow leading steadily towards the white-capped escarpments of the Taurus massif. After several days ascending into these windswept climes, Thurstan might have thought they'd be free of pursuit, but this was never the case.

It was on the first day, as he looked backward from a rocky promontory, that he saw a party of Templars perhaps half a day behind. Even at that distance, they were distinctive in their heraldic garb. That first time he saw them, there were ten or so. The next time, on the second day, they were only five. Evidently, they'd been splitting up as they progressed, some of them following different routes, but they were considerably closer now.

'Templars,' Pandulf said glumly. 'They have a willpower that can't be broken.'

'Thankfully, the same can't be said for their bodies,' Thurstan replied, ushering them onward.

On the morning of the third day, their pursuers were even closer. But their number had shrunk now to two. Thurstan and his party watched. Just in front of them, the land fell away in a sheer drop of forty or fifty feet, then levelled off slightly before tilting downward again at a gentler gradient. It was this lesser slope that the two Templar horsemen were currently toiling their way up. Left of this position, the downward slope was even gentler. Still steep, but passable. It was by this path that Thurstan and his companions had ascended to this point, a plateau of sorts, though there were additional levels of higher ground ahead, a narrow gully winding uphill between bluffs, before losing itself in misty pinewoods.

'They're very close,' Melinda commented.

No one responded; it was apparent to all that if they remained here, they'd have the Templars' company within an hour.

'How can they still be following us?' Pandulf said.

'Thurstan made it personal,' Bertrand replied. 'By attacking three of their men and stealing their horses.'

'I didn't ask why, I asked how. Since when did they teach woodcraft and trail-finding in the Templar academies?'

Bertrand had no answer to that. Thurstan though, was fascinated to see one of the two riders dismount, pick something up and show it to his compatriot, before thrusting it under his sword-belt. He nodded to himself. As he'd suspected, there'd been more to this pursuit than met the eye. He moved away from the cliff edge. 'Pandulf, you and Melinda go up through the gully. Conceal yourselves in the woods.'

'What do you and I do?' Bertrand asked.

'For some reason, of all the foothills in this mountain range, these particular Templars are keen to investigate this one. But that must end. We can't keep pushing the horses.'

'So… we fight them?' Bertrand looked astonished. 'Thurstan, these men are Templars. They'll be disciplined, trained…'

'Which is why we must tackle them from behind.'

Bertrand's face lengthened all the more. 'From behind?'

'There was a crossbow among the saddlebags on the horse you took, no? A bag of bolts?'

'Thurstan… one can't use a crossbow against fellow Christians. And to attack knights any other way than from the front would be a crime against chivalry.'

Thurstan regarded him long and hard. He shouldn't have had to explain that at present all they had were their weapons and their wits, that this was now the business of survival. And in truth, he didn't think that he needed to. Sad though that made him.

He signalled for the two youngsters to go. They did so, Pandulf looked unhappy to be excluded from the coming fight, Melinda strangely impassive, as if the worst thing that threatened her was a change of ownership. Which in truth, it was.

'Thurstan, listen.' Bertrand spoke with a tone of pleading. 'These Templars are not our enemies. All they want is what's best for the girl. Even now, who knows…? They might be coming to offer an armed escort.'

Thurstan grabbed his horse by the reins. 'With luck they'll head up the gully… That'll mean we can take them from overhead.'

'This is so wrong.'

'First, we put our horses out of sight.' Thurstan moved from his own horse to Bertrand's, helping himself to the crossbow and the sack of bolts that hung among its bolsters, slinging the latter over his shoulder. 'If you won't use this, I will.'

'Thurstan…'

Thurstan glanced at him. 'I've a question for you, Bertrand. Why didn't you stay on the ship?'

'What do you mean?'

'You've made your feelings about this mission plain from the start. So, why didn't you stay on the ship?'

'Well… you are my friends.'

'You'd have been among friends if you stayed on board.'

Bertrand stared at him in puzzlement, but also with fear.

'Do you deny it?' Thurstan asked.

They locked eyes for several moments, and then Bertrand went for his sword. Thurstan swung the crossbow first, its heavy wooden stock clunking against the side of his friend's skull. Bertrand's knees buckled and he crumpled to the ground.

Thurstan knelt on top of his insensible form, placing fingertips at the side of the neck. A steady pulse was notable. Bertrand's eyelids fluttered. He breathed slow and heavy, but at least he breathed.

Satisfied, Thurstan yanked the cords from his friend's boots, using the first to bind his hands behind his back, the second to bind his ankles. Then he heard something, a clink of mail. He jumped up, scrambling to the edge of the high ground. The two Templars were ascending the gentler path on the left. They'd dismounted and were leading their horses, so the going was slow – they puffed and grunted and leaned forward, but they were already halfway up. Thurstan slung the crossbow and its missile bag over his shoulder and taking both his and Bertrand's horses by the reins, led them towards the mouth of the gully, but then diverted right, picking his way over a landslide of rocks.

Once out of view, he tied the two animals to a small, stunted tree and left the crossbow alongside them as he doubled back. Hefting the bound and unconscious Bertrand over his shoulder, he carried him the same way, dumping him next to the horses. He didn't go back a second time but grabbed the crossbow and clambered up the rocks onto the flatter ground overhanging the gully. Here, he lay down to wait. As he did, he tugged the drawstring back and loaded a feathered quarrel into the flight groove.

From below and to his left, he heard hoofbeats. He couldn't see beyond the gully itself, and he didn't want to risk standing. But now the voices of two men came into earshot, breathless after their hard climb in chain-mail.

He couldn't help hoping that one of them might be the Danish knight who'd become suspicious of them on the *Gloriosus*. The fellow had had a job to do, but he'd been a mite too insolent in his manner. He was probably that way with everyone: a swaggering bully, whose guilt-free mistreatment of others was fuelled by the self-righteousness he drew from serving in a holy order.

Meanwhile, that 'holy order' factor was a difficult one for Thurstan to contend with. These men had carried the torch for Christ in the darkest of places. While a multitude of other pilgrims had travelled to the East and then gone home again, these warriors of God had remained, holding fortresses, protecting travel routes, fighting endless battles on land and sea. And they were worthy opponents. Thurstan had seen that for himself.

These Templars are not our enemies...

'They are today,' he muttered, and yet it tore at his conscience to think that in a very short time, he'd be unleashing crossbow bolts on them.

At the very least, it struck him that he owed them a fair fight. Though it wouldn't exactly be fair. Two of them, both mailed, while he stood alone and unarmoured.

The duo of mounted figures appeared at the lower end of the gully.

Thurstan hunkered down, but not so far that he couldn't see them as they proceeded.

They too, it seemed, had identified this chokepoint in the land as a potential ambush spot. They'd even put their helmets on. He edged forward on his chest, peeking down. Despite the helmets, their visors were lifted and their faces came into view. He didn't know either of them, though on reflection, that might make it easier. It would haunt his conscience less. He placed his hand on the crossbow.

One was so young that he couldn't have been knighted long before joining the order. He had a fresh, clean-shaved face and very fair hair, which hung almost to his shoulders. The other was older and sturdier, with a thickset body, broad shoulders, and a dark beard, and he eyed the overhanging parapets with growing unease.

He is the first you must kill, a whispering voice said.

Thurstan almost looked round, for half a second convinced that someone had stolen up behind. Earl Ranald again? Bishop Belphagor? There was no one there, of course. The advice had come from inside his own head. And it had spoken the truth. The more dangerous of the two must die first.

They were almost now on a level with him. He'd let them pass, then shoot them from their saddles.

These Templars are not our enemies...

'They are today,' he mumbled again.

As the two targets passed by below, he rose to his feet, taking aim. This would be the easiest work he'd ever done in the business of killing. And maybe for that reason, the old wound burned in the middle of his hip in a way it hadn't done for days, he swore, lowered the weapon again, ran along the edge, and with a roar, leapt down at them.

Fair fight it is! he told himself, hitting the bearded one in the back with both feet, knocking him clean from the saddle.

It broke Thurstan's own fall also, so, as he landed, he rolled and jumped back to his feet. But the bearded Templar had been hurt. He was down on hands and knees, hunched in pain. Thurstan kicked him full in the face, sending him sprawling onto his back.

The other meanwhile, was fighting to control his horse. His companion's mount had already bolted up the gully. The second wished to follow it, but as Thurstan lurched towards him, the horseman drew his steel. He wheeled his animal in a half-circle and struck down at his assailant, who blocked it with his own blade. The Templar's sword deflected downward, slicing into his own left thigh.

He shouted in pain, jerking on his reins.

It was too much for the terrified animal, which broke into a gallop, thundering down the gully, its passenger swaying as he lost control and then, when they were out on the open ground again, possibly because he feared the terrified brute might charge over the edge, leaping from the saddle, landing hard on his injured leg.

Thurstan hastened down on foot, confronting him close to the cliff edge.

'You can survive this,' he said simply. 'Walk away. Don't come back.'

But the young Templar, despite his wound, stood ready. He'd discarded his dented helmet, but his shield was raised, his sword hefted. The fair hair was smeared in strands across his red, sweaty face.

'You think I'd do that?' His accent was Germanic. 'How could I kneel before God when my time comes?'

'Continue with this folly, and you'll be doing that very soon.'

'So be it!'

They engaged, blades flashing.

Though he was carrying a shield while his opponent wasn't, the young Templar steadily backtracked under the hail of precision blows. He responded as best he could, hacking and parrying with fury, but one deft thrust, and his face was opened to the cheekbone. A second, and his shield was sundered. Only the arrival of his companion, who now came stumbling down the gully towards them, prevented the inevitable. He too had removed his helmet, but his face was a mask of dirt and blood.

Thurstan backed away, as the two of them came at him side-by-side.

'You'd be the dog we were warned about,' the older one hissed, his accent Italian. 'A knight of the English retinue, but a soulless killer... inspired by a demon.'

'You believe every faerie story you're told?' Thurstan replied, circling.

'Only those better attested to than others.'

'Then come and find out for yourself.'

The bearded knight threw himself forward. The clangour rang across the hillside. Thurstan cut and parried, then caught him under the beard with a right-handed punch, sending him tottering backward. Howling, the younger Templar charged. Thurstan met him with a two-handed stroke. The youngster tried to block, but his own sword flew back into his face, splitting his nose lengthways. He gagged and stumbled, scarlet mist erupting.

Thurstan swung back to the older one. This fellow struck harder and faster, but he was dazed, and Thurstan met his attack with ease, taking a chunk from his shield, before swinging again to the youngster, who now struck blindly. Thurstan counterstruck, ramming his sword-tip into the young Templar's throat. The youngster's chain aventail bore the worst of it, but more blood appeared, and the wounded man clutched at it, gagging.

They were now on the cliff's very edge. Thurstan parried another flailing blow, struck his opponent's belly with the pommel of his sword, then stepped around him and slashed the back of his already wounded thigh. The young Templar squealed as his leg gave, his body pitching over, bouncing down the rock face to the sloping grassland below.

With cries of anger, the older Templar lumbered forward. Again, he struck with skill and force, but Thurstan blocked every blow, hacking another piece from his shield, and then ripping the mail on his left shoulder. Gore welled up underneath, but the Templar strove on, striking, counter striking. Thurstan ducked and wove, then caught him point-on beneath the collarbone. The Templar's mail proved its worth; the sword didn't slide clean through, but it made its mark, and he staggered backward, ashen faced, before slumping onto his buttocks.

He gestured with his blade, but Thurstan kicked it from his hand. A second kick caught the point of the fellow's chin, the back of his head hitting the earth. He lay groaning, his wounded chest heaving.

A pounding of hooves now sounded from the gully, out of which Pandulf emerged on horseback. Melinda was close behind, also mounted. By the looks of it she'd sequestered the Templar horse that had fled up towards the pinewood.

'I told you brats to stay hidden!' Thurstan shouted.

'I heard sounds of combat,' Pandulf protested, drawing rein. 'I'm your squire. I couldn't just hide in some wood.'

Melinda stood in her stirrups. 'Where is Lord Bertrand?'

'*Lord* Bertrand!' Thurstan snorted contemptuously. 'Sleeping off the price of his pride.'

A rasping chuckle drew his attention back to the Templar.

'Pride?' the fellow said, red froth fizzling between his teeth. 'You and that vainglorious king of yours epitomise pride? You think you can have this girl-saint all for your own? You think you can cheat the Church?'

'Does it matter where she is?' Thurstan retorted. 'So long as she's safe in Christian hands?'

'Safe?' The Templar chuckled again, though clearly it pained him. 'Do you know where you are? Do you have any idea where you're taking her?'

'We'll work our way back to England. You can be sure of that... and if you're the best they can send after us, with very little difficulty.'

'England...' Another chuckle, more bloody froth. 'You haven't heard? How your beloved king, the so-called Lionheart, fell into enemy hands?'

A trickle of ice ran down Thurstan's spine. He jammed his sword-tip against the casualty's throat. 'What are you talking about?'

'How he was waylaid. By a scheming German duke. How he now resides in a dungeon, in chains... for the rest of his days. England is a realm of chaos. There'll be no safety there for her. Nor even for you.'

'My lord, can this be true?' Pandulf asked.

'You're lying.' Thurstan leaned harder on his sword, pressing its point into flesh.

'Why would I?' the Templar gasped.

'You'd say anything to make us leave her with you. And yet look at you... I doubt you can even stand.'

'At least my soul is clean. At least I'm not damned to hellfire...'

Thurstan leaned on his sword again, forehead beaded with sweat. The Templar held his breath, fresh blood emerging through his aventail.

'My lord, please!' Pandulf cried.

But it was another voice he heard above all others.

'Live by the sword, Thurstan Wildblood,' Mother Turilda said on that final day at Kirkwood Hall.

'And die by it?' he replied grimly. *'That could only be a good thing.'*

'No. You become its slave. And swords can't distinguish between good and evil.'

This puzzled him. 'Wasn't it you who said this could be my road to Heaven?'

'God made you a warrior...'

'I rather think my father and his knights...'

'No,' she said firmly. *'Your father and his knights taught you the skill. But the fierceness of spirit was a gift from your real Father. Be sure you don't abuse it, Thurstan Wildblood. You came here out of shadow. Pray you don't fall back into it.'*

'Lord Thurstan!' A warning cry. From Melinda.

The Templar had pulled another weapon from under his mantle. An old-fashioned seax, a half-foot of edged steel. He lunged, knocking Thurstan's blade aside. But not quickly enough. Not before Thurstan snatched out the knife he'd stolen in Antalya, and drove it home.

CHAPTER 44

When Bertrand came round, he looked dazed and pale-faced. He rubbed at the points on his wrists where the cords had bound them, though those cords had now been removed, then glanced up from the rock against which he had been dumped.

Melinda and Pandulf stood close by, clutching their respective horses by the reins. Directly in front of him, though, was Thurstan, who regarded him bleakly, still unsure how best to address the miscreant. Instead, one by one, he flipped gold bezants at him.

'Recognise this money?' Thurstan asked.

Bertrand seemed confused. 'What are... what's happened?'

'Because *I* do. It's ours. Or rather, it *was* ours. Until, mysteriously, I found it in the purse of this fellow over here.'

Thurstan stepped aside, revealing the body of the bearded Templar.

'I found *this* on him too.' He tossed a gold crucifix forward. It had a ruby centrepiece. 'I always thought that had personal value to you, Bertrand. Seems I was wrong. Or was it that you knew you'd be getting it back? Maybe you expected to get the coins back too, though I doubt that. The coins weren't just markers, were they? To show our enemies which way we were heading. They were payment for preservation of your skin when you were finally caught...'

'Thurstan, listen...'

'And a sign you were prepared to impoverish us, to make our journey continuously harder.'

'Thurstan...'

'You damn conniving Judas!' Thurstan snarled, his anger at last breaking. 'You betrayed us all!'

Bertrand pointed. 'And you betrayed God!'

Clearly unable to bear it any longer, Pandulf gave his reins to Melinda and came forward. 'My lords, my lords, please...'

'Stay out of this!' Thurstan barked.

'Thurstan...' Bertrand had now got to his feet, though he was wobbly. 'This has gone on long enough.'

'Did you reach this decision on the *Gloriosus*? Was that why the skipper suddenly and mysteriously decided to send a messenger bird ahead of us?'

Bertrand returned his stare boldly.

Thurstan approached him. 'You don't deny it?'

'Stay back...' Bertrand reached for his hip – to find an empty scabbard. 'Stay back, I said.'

Thurstan smiled. 'I'd break you with my bare hands, but you're a knight.' He tossed the captive's sword forward. 'And a knight deserves a fighting chance.'

Slowly, he drew his own blade.

'My lord!' Pandulf protested. 'This is Bertrand! There must be some misunderstanding.'

'There's no misunderstanding,' Bertrand said. 'Admit it, lad, you've been having doubts too. Where in God's name are we?' He threw his arms out. 'Where are we even going to? We're still in the East, for Christ's sake. The kingdom of the Seljuk Turks lies only beyond these mountains. And all the while, good men, warrior monks who could help us, and above all, who could save this girl for Christendom, are being eluded and ambushed, and even slaughtered. In God's name, Thurstan, think what you're doing! There's no hope we three can get the girl back to England. In Jesus's name, we're still a thousand miles from Europe.'

'Pick up your sword,' Thurstan told him.

'My lord, wait.' Pandulf inserted himself between them. 'Let us think this through.'

Thurstan didn't speak this time, just grabbed the squire by the corner of his cloak and flung him out of the way.

Try as he wanted to, he couldn't bring himself to forgive such treachery as this. If it hadn't been for Bertrand, they'd be sailing west by now. They could have wintered in friendly lands and finished their journey in the spring. Now, who knew what they were facing.

'Grab your sword!' he said again.

Reluctantly, but squaring his jaw and straightening his back, Bertrand picked up his weapon. They circled each other. Pandulf continued to protest, begging them to desist, until Melinda put a hand on his shoulder. She wore a sad but resigned expression.

'Did this one really deserve it?' Bertrand wondered, sidling past the fallen Templar.

'Ask yourself.' Thurstan swished his blade. 'You brought him here.'

Bertrand had now come close to the cliff edge, where the horse that had belonged to the younger Templar stood pulling at chunks of grass. He regarded Thurstan grimly. Then lunged for the horse, grappling with the Templar crossbow suspended among its saddlebags, unhooking it and swinging it around.

Thurstan lurched towards him, but Bertrand, no mean warrior himself, had already loaded a quarrel and levelled it.

'So much for your chivalrous ideals,' Thurstan said, halting.

'You're wrong, Thurstan. I'd never loose an arrow at a Christian knight. But today is an exception. Too much hinges on this. The girl must be saved for God and Holy Mother Church… and you can't do it. So, go! Grab your booty and leave this place! Or die.'

Thurstan smiled. 'Obviously, I choose death. That should be easy for you. You've been toying with the idea the whole distance. You've grouched at every decision I've made. You've objected and argued. *You* wish to be the hero of this saga.'

Bertrand shook his head. 'I've told you, that isn't it.'

'You seek to escort her to the door of St Peter's yourself.' Thurstan advanced again. 'By that time adorned in Templar garb, no doubt.'

'Thurstan… *stay back*!'

'You'll save your soul and be a hero into the bargain.'

'I warn you!'

'Don't warn me, Bertrand. Shoot. Except you won't. Because you're not the hero you imagine. You're too weak.'

'My God, don't provoke me!'

'Provoke you? I've given you every chance. I gave you the chance to ride away, more than once. I even said let's do it the knightly way... sword-to-sword.'

'The knightly way, aye. Me against you?' Still levelling the crossbow, Bertrand swung up into the saddle. 'That'd be fair. Mortal man versus one who fights with the Devil's power...' He wheeled the animal around, his back to the gulf. 'Know this. There are Templars all over these hills. And I'll be back with them. And we'll take charge of this saint on Earth and protect her properly. You meanwhile can go to the pits of Sheol for all I care...'

At which point he gasped and stiffened, dropping his bow.

Thurstan lurched towards him but halted again as he saw the second missile fly.

Like the first, it struck Bertrand from behind, but this time toppled him from the saddle. He landed on his front, two crossbow bolts jutting from his spine. He trembled as he lay there, making a mighty effort to look up at his former companions. Then his head fell forward. The others jerked towards him, but Thurstan shouted at Pandulf and Melinda to keep back, before going forward himself at a crouch, placing fingers at his friend's neck and then in front of his gaping mouth. A thin trickle of blood emerged from it, but there was no breath.

He crawled on to the cliff edge.

Below, three figures were grouped around the broken form of the Templar who'd fallen. One was on horseback, the other two dismounted, one of them kneeling, but one – clearly the one who'd loosed the fatal bolts – rapidly drawing his string back and inserting another missile. All three wore leather coifs and mail-coats and over the top of those, the heavy brown mantles with the emblazoned red crosses of the Templar serjeants-at-arms. Men of no breeding, they could never be knighted, but they'd sworn vows all the same, and served their noble masters as mobile infantry, providing fearsome support in battle. Of course, they understood nothing of chivalry, hence they'd shown no hesitation in loosing crossbow shafts at a fellow Christian.

It was a courtesy they'd receive in kind.

Thurstan took Bertrand's bow, checked the bolt was in place, then rose up and took aim. The trio below, presumably thinking they'd been facing a single opponent, froze in shock. Thurstan loosed at the mounted serjeant first, as he, if they broke in flight, would be quickest to escape.

The horseman clamped a hand to his left eye and, as his mount shied away, fell from the saddle.

The other two stared at him, dumbstruck, before Bertrand's killer raised his own weapon and shot back, the bolt winging upward. Thurstan stepped sideways, and it flickered past. Reloading himself, he took aim again, striking his second target in the knee. The bowman cried out, staggering, dropping his weapon.

The unscathed member of the trio climbed to his saddle, but Thurstan's next shot caught him in the middle of his back. He arched in pain, his animal cantering wildly. Thurstan bided his time, waiting for the opening to come, then loosed again, striking the same fellow a second time, knocking him to the ground like a game bird.

The one remaining hobbled away, dragging his crippled leg behind him. Again, Thurstan took his time, choosing his moment. When he launched his final shaft, it flew true, hitting the target squarely in the nape of his neck.

'I know,' he said, walking back to the others, looking at Melinda in particular. 'We could just have ridden away. With no turncoat to leave clues behind us, we could have eluded them. But when lessons are needed, it's best they're taught firmly. From here on, anyone thinks they're going to follow us, they'll know it will cost them.'

CHAPTER 45

'Why did you call out to Lord Thurstan?' Pandulf asked. 'To warn him, I mean?'

Melinda shrugged tiredly.

For several hours, they'd been driving on into the Taurus foot-hills. They were better equipped now, having stripped their most recent opponents of everything they'd been carrying: both Thurstan and Pandulf were fully mailed, and had spare weapons and horses, their bolsters were crammed with food and drink, they had blankets, utensils, feed for their mounts, and extra furs and sheepskins to wrap themselves against the chill. Less reassuringly, they were now advancing through a fathomless forest, dark and icy firs closing from all sides, making it difficult even to calculate the time of day.

'That Templar might have wounded him badly,' Pandulf persisted, genuinely puzzled that she'd helped her captor. 'Hamstrung him. Maybe even killed him. If he'd managed that, your ordeal would be over.'

'Over?' Melinda shook her head. 'I'd have exchanged one master for another.'

'We all serve masters, Melinda. Lord Thurstan too.'

She glanced around. While she and Pandulf rode ahead, leading their pack-animals, Thurstan travelled behind, an alpha wolf trailing at the rear, which allowed them a little space in which to converse.

'The truth is I don't know,' she said. 'Perhaps because he's taken huge pains to protect us.'

'You're becoming used to his leadership, you mean?'

She thought on it. 'When I first met him, I dismissed him as a professional killer, a casual slayer of men. I still consider him the hardest, coldest man I've ever met. And yet… *you're* very loyal to him.'

Pandulf reddened a little. 'He saved my life.'

She glanced at him with interest. 'How so?'

'When…' The lad glanced over his shoulder. Thurstan was still a way back. 'When Hugo FitzOsbo was killed, Lord Thurstan didn't need to adopt me as his squire. It was an act of charity. God knows what my life would have been without it, or how short.'

'He's made up for that by shortening many others.'

'You never saw him as King Richard's knight-commander. He was popular among his rank and file.'

'It doesn't surprise me that he's a soldier's soldier.'

Pandulf shook his head. That was too simplistic a categorisation. 'He shared privilege with them as well as hardship. In judgements, he was firm but fair.'

'The true measure of a man, Pandulf, is not how his supporters see him, but those who oppose him.'

'I thought you just said you no longer saw him that way.'

'Well…' She shrugged again. 'One must admire his perseverance. It's an impossible task he's been set. It's killed all his men already. Yet he struggles on with it manfully, which shows great fealty to his king. Which also should be admired.'

'He's also safeguarding a saint on Earth,' he reminded her.

She gave a half-smile. 'He doesn't believe that, Pandulf. You know *that* at least? He doesn't believe in saints or angels, or anything else sacred.'

'I don't know if it's quite like that. It's more… it's more that he thinks God cheated him.'

She glanced at him again. 'God cheated him?'

'For taking his wife when he did.'

'He was married?' She looked thoughtful. 'I see.'

'When Richard took the cross, William Marshal, who was royal champion, left the *Familia Regis* to join the Council of Regency. And Lord Thurstan, who was the Marshal's lieutenant, was promoted to commander. He was also rewarded for his service with the hand of an heiress, Gwendolyn of Adelard, who brought as her dowry a place called Kirkwood in Cumberland. A tenancy of the Abbey of Cupthorne.' He hesitated, wondering if he was being too fulsome with such personal information. 'I'm... I'm told my lord was happy there. For the first time in his life. Until Lady Gwendolyn took ill and died. According to Bertrand, Lord Thurstan left the north and never returned.'

She thought about this. 'When we smartened ourselves up to enter Tyre, I noted that he washed that piece of cloth he always keeps tied around the hilt of his sword. Once the grime and blood had gone, I realised that it was a lady's scarf. His wife's?'

Pandulf wasn't so sure. He'd noted the scarf too, several times, but had always considered it a memento of some tournament. Lord Thurstan had apparently won many.

'Surely, he'd keep something to remember her by?' the girl said.

'He tries not to remember. According to gossip in the *Familia*. He's put it all behind him. I suppose it hurts too much.'

'That's a sad tale,' she conceded, 'but one can't take the loss of loved ones out on others.'

'You've only seen this side of him because of our circumstances.'

'A great man should rise above all circumstance.'

'I didn't say he was a great man,' Pandulf replied, 'but he isn't an evil man either. It would have been far worse for you if you'd ended up in the clutches of Ivan de Vesqui.'

She sighed. 'I suspect it's a case of better the devil you know.'

He glanced sharply at her. 'Why would you say that?'

Melinda looked puzzled. 'It's merely a saying.'

'Do... do you know things?' he asked tentatively.

She frowned. 'Know things?'

'I...' He struggled to rephrase it, not daring to enquire if there was anything more to what she'd just said – perhaps because God or one of his angels had whispered it to her in a dream. 'I mean, do you... hear...?'

'Voices from Heaven?' she finished for him. 'Because of my saintly status? Do I *know* Thurstan to be a creature of the Devil because the Lord of Hosts told me?'

His inability to answer was answer was enough.

She rode on. 'You're now wondering how I know that Lord Thurstan supposedly belongs to Satan?'

'How could you?'

'Again, it's no miracle, Pandulf. Bertrand told me on board the *Gloriosus*. He told me all about Thurstan's fever dream and the Bishop of Hell.'

'Did he mention the wound that healed like an upside-down cross?'

'Like the symbol of St Peter, you mean?'

'Symbol of...' This had occurred to the lad also. The inverted crucifix wasn't always a demonic sign. But taken with everything else? 'So, none of this concerns you?'

She shook her head. 'Would I ride with him if it did?'

'Does that mean...?'

'Does that mean I know he isn't, or that I ride with him because I don't know anything, because I'm a mere mortal... like you?'

He reddened, frustrated again that she thought him foolish.

'Pandulf, you're a sweet and innocent boy,' she said. 'At times, I wish I was a saint, so as to avoid disappointing you...'

'Or even so that you could summon a legion of angels to stand in our defence,' Thurstan cut in, having ridden up from behind. He drew rein, turning in the saddle as he scanned the endless ranks of evergreens.

Pandulf looked too but saw nothing untoward. 'Is something wrong, my lord?'

Thurstan seemed uncertain. 'It may be nothing.' He spurred his horse onward. 'But we're not out of the fire yet. From here on, we stay close together and we all of us stay alert.'

–

They continued for hours up a gentle slope, the pinewood showing no sign of thinning. A light snow had now fallen, leaving a glimmering white carpet, while palls of frozen mist drifted between the straight, silent trunks.

Melinda gazed around. It was so alien to her, this land of rock, ice and shadow. The cold too. It was relentless; no matter how many layers she put on, it bit deep. And then there was the eerie stillness. It was easy to remember the age-old tales she'd learned as an infant, about far-distant Europe, with its ogres, werewolves and witches. Faerie tales, she reminded herself. Childhood fancies. And yet here in this place, with her sole guard a knight supposedly cursed by a genuine demon, they felt all too real.

'For how long do we head north, my lord?' Pandulf asked.

'The Templars still lie behind us,' Thurstan replied, watching the encircling woods like a hawk.

'Even after what happened down below?' The squire sounded surprised.

'Especially after what happened below,' the knight said. 'You think a few deaths will dissuade them? They've died in their thousands since their foundation, and still they're in the East, fighting the good fight.'

Melinda agreed with that much at least. The Knights Templar, with their strange, stiff manners and polite but unfriendly attitude, had been part of everyday life in the Kingdom of Jerusalem since 1118. Long before her own birth, of course. Long before the birth of almost anyone still alive today.

'They won't give up on us, Pandulf,' she said quietly. 'As long as they can track us, we're in danger.'

'But surely,' the lad argued. 'With Bertrand gone...'

'We rode across the snowline some time ago,' Thurstan replied. 'Which means they won't need a line of trinkets to follow. So, we're not so much riding north as riding where the forest lies.'

By her own admission, Melinda knew little about the waging of war, but again this seemed like a sensible strategy. For as the pine-wood deepened, the settled snowfall diminished, until it lay only in patches, their hooves then crunching on acorns and frosted twigs. But as the trees grew closer and tighter, casting an eerie, greenish darkness where once there'd been daylight, the mist thickened too

– and it was around then, towards the end of that first day, when she thought she began glimpsing *things*. Shaggy upright forms moving just beyond her eyeline, which, whenever she looked properly, melted out of sight. She whispered a warning to the others, but they'd seen things as well. When the horses became skittish, they all knew they weren't imagining it.

'Ride close to each other,' Thurstan advised quietly. 'Shields to your left and right.'

They'd loaded their spare animals with all the Templar supplies and equipment they could, but all had agreed, even Thurstan, that it would be too serious a sin to display Templar colours when they weren't Templars themselves. In light of this, Pandulf protested about the shields, which carried painted-on Templar devices, but Thurstan signalled for silence.

They rode on nervously, sensing more movement in the half-hidden trees. Still though, there was no attack. Melinda wondered if the Templar insignia on the shields was having this effect, and if so, how long it would last for. But more and more often, whenever she jerked her head around, she spied hairy, brutish figures withdrawing into the icy vapour.

When they were next in open space, Thurstan rode back to the pack animals, and returned with three helmets. 'I should have made you wear mail,' he told her, handing one over. 'But this will be better than nothing.'

'It will sit on me like a bucket,' she replied.

'It's the business of survival.'

'I appreciate your concern, my lord.'

Helmeted, she supposed that she felt moderately safer as they proceeded, though it frustrated her that her vision was now reduced to a narrow slot. In due course, when the woods seemed suddenly quieter, she lifted the visor. Thurstan meanwhile took the opportunity to ride back again to the pack animals. This time when he returned to Melinda's side, he handed her a mail-coat, a coif with aventail, and a double-curved hunting bow with a quiver of arrows.

'From here on, my lady,' he said quietly, 'you will earn your keep. And I don't mean shooting hares and squirrels.'

There might have been more argument from her, but again they heard movement from half-glimpsed sources. The menacing presence had returned, if it had ever gone away.

Pandulf helped her don the mail, and after that, she rode with an arrow nocked on the string. The squire meanwhile drew his sword and rested it across the pommel of his saddle.

'One thing I've learned already,' he said in a transparent attempt to be reassuring. 'Men don't seek to die. There are fanatics in every horde. Assassins and Knights Templar, who'll willingly embrace martyrdom if their calling bids them. But the vast majority seek to live. Often, this means that greater numbers don't always count for much. That armies, once broken, will run. That many who've just seen blood for the first time will skulk at the back for fear the next might be their own.'

'And yet you sound nervous,' she replied.

He gave a weak smile. 'That's the case with men. But who's to say these are men?'

Frustrated, Melinda removed her helmet.

'That may be a mistake,' Pandulf warned her.

'If I keep it on, this bow will be useless. It may be useless anyway. Another hour and it'll be night.'

'I'd say we should stop and make camp now, but I'm fearful the fire would burn with a blue flame.'

She glanced at him, confused. 'I don't understand.'

Pandulf swallowed. 'There's an old tradition in England... It comes down to us from the Danes, that in the presence of spirits, fire burns with a blue flame.'

'I see.' Her eyes roved back across the mist-shrouded firs. 'You fear we face a supernatural foe?'

'Don't you?'

The pair of them looked sharply left. It wasn't possible to be sure, but again it seemed that a shaggy, shapeless something had just withdrawn from sight.

'I'm sure such stories are only for children.' Melinda wasn't at all sure about that, but was determined not to give in to fear. 'In

Outremer, our Muslim servants would tell stories of the *djinn*, evil spirits of the desert, who would waylay lone travellers. But I knew no one who'd ever experienced this. The Muslims said this was because they prayed to *Allah*, and he would protect them.'

'Alas,' Pandulf replied, 'I don't think we enjoy our God's favour enough for that.'

'I thought that winning God's favour was the whole purpose of this mission.'

'We killed Templar knights. The servants of Rome. God's right hand on Earth.'

Melinda shook her head. 'I've never heard of God sending monsters to inflict punishment. Much less at Christmastide.'

'Christmastide?'

'It must be close now. God would not send evil powers in the holy season.'

'There are others who would,' he muttered.

'Pandulf, cease this!' she scolded him, still watching the trees. 'Your imagination is overwhelming you.'

But she too felt disconcerted. When Bertrand had spoken to her on the ship, he'd admitted that initially he believed the whole business of Thurstan's devil to be nonsense, but in time, as the knight-commander's chosen course seemed to run contrary to the interests of the Church, he'd come to fear that his friend had been… 'unblessed'. That was the term he had used. Was that possible? Surely, if there were some who were blessed, there were others who were unblessed?

Again, her gaze flickered from tree to tree, their phantom outlines dissolving as the mist crept in closer. Alongside her, Pandulf darted glances left and right.

Melinda was devout in her beliefs. But she'd never seen anything miraculous here on Earth and had never expected that she would. 'My kingdom is not of this world,' the Lord had said. But did that mean mysterious powers weren't present?

How could she assume so when she herself supposedly possessed them?

But then, God working miracles was one thing. The Devil doing it was another.

No, she told herself, Lord Thurstan had not traded his soul for invincibility. In the short time since she'd lost her freedom, even before then, she'd known several wild and terrible men, and while she had no doubt that Lord Thurstan could destroy any one of them in single combat, there was still something about him. As Pandulf had said, he wasn't evil. She was strangely certain of this.

Yet that didn't discount the possibility that he'd come into contact with evil.

It wasn't so outlandish an idea. And it didn't necessarily mean that he'd been tainted.

Melinda eyed their guardian knight as he rode past them again. For the last hour now he'd been patrolling the length of their cavalcade, such as it was, moving from front to back, his shield proudly displayed, his longsword drawn. Whatever his sins, there was no lack of courage there. And whatever meant to come at them out of the mist, he would fight it to the very end, and that would be a virtue in any man.

'You know, Pandulf, your master may be a champion because he was always a champion,' she said. 'Maybe he's simply had cause to demonstrate it more in recent days.'

The squire glanced at her, agitated. 'And his crimes against the Templars?'

'Were they crimes? Christian men have done wrong for centuries, and it's often fallen on other Christian men to stop them.'

'But these were Templars.'

'A designation invented by Man, not God.'

Pandulf looked to his front. 'I'm surprised you're defending him. *You*, of all people.'

'I probably have more reason than most to hate him. But just at this moment, I'm glad he's with us rather than against us.'

Before they could speak further, Thurstan drew rein alongside them. He was as grimly serious as they'd ever seen. 'There's a hummock just ahead on the right,' he said. 'It's dry ground, so we can camp. I'll build a fire at the top, and if needs be, we can make a stand.'

'If we build a fire, my lord,' Pandulf said, 'won't we be seen for miles around?'

'They already know we're here, lad.'

'What are they?'

'Who knows. But trust me when I tell you… they aren't our friends.'

CHAPTER 46

They found the small hillock and once they were on top of it, its rounded summit the only part treeless and maybe thirty yards across, they tied the horses up, and Thurstan cut evergreen branches and dried brushwood, so that, within a short time, a hearty blaze was sending spirals of sparks into the winter night. It would make them visible, he realised, but it would also cast light into the trees around them, which was something of an advantage. He instructed Melinda to collect all the loose, heavy stones she could find, while he and Pandulf took fishing twine from one of the Templars' bolsters and strung it between the trunks on the lower slopes beyond the light, hanging it with utensils, so that it would clatter if disturbed.

'My lord,' Pandulf said nervously. 'My lord, I asked you this before... *what* are...?'

'Just men, lad. Like us.' Thurstan's eyes speared the vapour. 'Nothing more.'

'Didn't the Danes used to talk about mist-things?'

'You won't hear any Danish spoken till we reach Constantinople,' Thurstan replied.

'But what of Bishop Belphagor?'

'Still letting that nonsense eat away at you?'

'I know you believe it too.'

The knight shrugged. 'Even if I did, why would he seek to impede us now?'

'Because, though you denied the Church their saint, you're still taking her to safety.'

'And following that logic, Bishop Belphagor's next vengeful move would be to denude me of my new, Samson-like powers? Is that not so?'

The lad's face fell as he realised that his master was humouring him.

'Maybe he will,' Thurstan added. 'Either way, we'll know in the next few hours.'

—

It wasn't even that long.

Twenty minutes after Thurstan lit the fire, by which time he was restocking it with fresh evergreens, the flames dancing high again, they heard renewed movement in the encircling fog: rustlings, gruntings, the shuffling of heavy feet through frost-dried mulch.

Melinda did everything she could to fight down those childhood fears of ogres and trolls and other kinds of monsters.

'Prepare yourselves,' Thurstan said, his crossbow loaded.

They stood at different points around the fire, Pandulf close to the horses, but all of them equidistant from each other, forming a triangle, their eyes locked on the woodland murk. Each had their weapons ready and piles of stones at their feet, though at present they could only imagine, not actually see, the humped, fur-clad beings moving beyond their firelit perimeter. Melinda stood especially stiff, a single arrow nocked, the quiver at her hip. As well as the warm clothing she'd donned, she was encumbered by mail, something she'd never worn before. Thurstan had bidden her ensure the coif was up.

At least he hadn't made her wear the helmet, she thought; its restricted vision would hamper her archery. Not that this pleased her. She'd always told herself that she'd never willingly participate in war.

'Pandulf tells me you think these beings are merely men?' she called to the knight. 'That there is nothing of the supernatural about them?'

'That is my earnest belief,' Thurstan replied.

'Then I must warn you that I may hesitate. To kill is a dreadful sin.'

He glanced round at her. 'Even when your life may depend on it?'

'Our lives are fleeting, a test of our worthiness for Heaven.'

'Then let me put it a different way...' He turned his back on her again, watching the woods. 'These people are brigands... they plan to attack us because they want what is ours. Is that not a sin of covetousness? Before you answer, consider this: when they see you are a woman, they may spare your life, but not your virtue. As for Pandulf and I, we will certainly die because they'll see no other way. If you can work to prevent all that, would it not also be a sin to renege on it?'

Melinda had no answer. There was turmoil inside her. Of course, it would be a sin. One had a duty to assist other souls in peril.

Then, with a *swish* of air, a heavy stone was launched out of the darkness. It swooped towards Pandulf, who fended it off with his shield.

'Easy,' Thurstan counselled. 'Don't respond yet. We only have so many missiles... We can't afford to waste them.'

Another stone hurtled from another direction. It *thwacked* into the flames, a gout of fresh sparks erupting.

'We are easy targets framed on this fire!' Pandulf shouted.

'We'd be equally easy in darkness,' Thurstan replied. 'Only then we wouldn't be able to see them to fight back.'

–

Thurstan squinted into the gloom, but the blackness was all encompassing. The horses meanwhile were increasingly frightened, whinnying, yanking on their tethers. And then the first jangle of utensils sounded. He swung around, took aim and let fly. The bolt whipped into the blackness; there was a *thunking* impact and a grunt of pain. As he reloaded the crossbow, more stones flew in. One struck him on the shoulder, but his mail absorbed it. Another clattered from Pandulf's shield. Melinda yelped as a hefty one narrowly missed her head.

A second clank of cutlery sounded from the other side of the fire. 'Melinda!' Thurstan hissed.

'I can't see anything,' she protested.

More clanking, this time on Pandulf's side. He readied his sword and shield, but another stone was flung – this one especially large. It struck the corner of his helmet. He dropped to one knee.

'Pandulf!' Thurstan shouted, turning again.

And now, finally, he *saw* them. Two dark, cumbersome forms, great hairy brutes ascending through the fiery shadows towards the groggy squire.

Thurstan loosed another bolt. It struck one in its oxlike shoulder, and the creature flinched and grunted, but it continued upslope. Pandulf was back on his feet now and struck the first with his shield, but he only caused it to stumble. The second, he swiped at with his sword, but his arm was captured mid-flight, and then they both were onto him, bearing him down, snarling like beasts.

Thurstan took aim again, but was then seized from behind, an enormous foul-smelling hybrid of man and animal enveloping him in its powerful arms. He tottered into the camp, before flicking his body forward, flinging the abomination over his head, so that it landed full in the crackling flames. Its fur ignited, its entire form immediately ablaze. Shrieking, it blundered into the night, tumbling down the hillside.

As Thurstan got back to his feet, another one loomed out of the darkness, the fanged upper jaw of a wolf where his face should be, its eyes no more than hollow sockets.

The knight was transfixed. When he raised his crossbow, he saw that the bolt had fallen from the groove. Instead, he swung it like a club, bludgeoning the beast-man's head so hard that the timber stock broke. Seemingly only dazed, it came on again, another one close behind. Thurstan drew his sword, and swept it two-handed, chopping through the first one's midriff, though the blade caught itself in the mangled mass of flesh and fur, while the second beast looked to be wielding a club of its own, something more like half a tree trunk. As it raised it to smash it down on Thurstan's helmet, something black and speedy flickered through his vision and stood quivering in the creature's upper chest.

Thurstan glimpsed the fletchings of an arrow as the thing toppled backward. He spun around. Melinda had already strung a second goose-shaft and now loosed it at Pandulf's assailants, whose numbers had increased to three. Another clean shot, the arrow thudding into the breastbone of a creature pounding the lad's shield with a stone. With inhuman gurgles, it fell off him. The other, which was raking at the lad's chest with a blade, but was struggling to penetrate his mail, reared up – this one also wore a portion of wolf skull on its head, and it was here where the arrow hit it, cleanly, through the empty eye-socket.

The beast-man threw himself backward and bounded downhill, knocking his other compatriot against one of the horses, which, in its fright, back-kicked him brutally, sending him flying.

Melinda swung back to Thurstan, and loosed another missile. It flashed past him, striking another would-be opponent.

He glanced over her shoulder as the monstrous form capered away.

'Everyone to me!' Thurstan called, backing towards the flames. 'Melinda, cover your own quarter. That's the only direction where they're so far unscathed.'

Melinda, stood wide-eyed, before turning to the face the woods on her own side. Pandulf, meanwhile, had got to his feet. His helmet had come off and he looked bruised and battered, his face gouged several times. Links were missing from his mail, but the layers of leather and felt underneath had held firm.

On the lower slopes, shapeless figures hauled off those foes killed or wounded so grievously that they couldn't get away on their own. Thurstan watched them, knowing he had no choice but to permit it. They couldn't stop them if they wanted to.

'Saint Melinda of Jerusalem,' he said, as an eerie silence now fell. 'More like Mistress Lethal. We should rechristen you.'

'I'll never forgive myself,' Melinda replied.

'For saving your companions' lives?'

'For taking the lives of others.'

'What… are they?' Pandulf stammered.

'Men,' Thurstan said. 'As I told you.'

'But what manner of men?'

Before anyone could reply, a great howling commenced in the trees.

'God help us,' the lad breathed. 'First men... if that's what they were, and now wolves!'

'Not quite,' Thurstan said. 'Get as close to the fire as you can. We need open space around us.'

But in truth, they were close enough. The blaze had diminished since they'd last fed it, many embers now scattered, but its heat was immense. Their backs were already singeing, their sweat-filled hair drying out and stiffening. More and more lupine voices took up the howling, until soon there must have been hundreds of them out there, and again, the small party was pelted with stones.

'Wolves don't heave rocks,' Thurstan said from behind his shield.

'The question stands,' Pandulf said. 'What manner of men are these?'

'Men who clearly feel they must call for additional forces,' Thurstan replied.

'Dear Lord, aren't there enough of them already?'

'The next attack will overwhelm us.' Thurstan's gaze lingered on the entwined boughs overhead. 'We need to distract them away from here.' He crossed the camp to the tethered horses, shoved the money pouch under his belt, and with three strokes of his sword, cut the animals loose, shouting and slapping their flanks.

He barely needed to, the entire group galloping away down the hillside. The howling dwindled, replaced by shouts and guttural cries.

'That will draw some of them off,' Thurstan said. 'You two... into the trees.'

The youngsters complied without argument, sheathing their weapons, their panic driving them upward through the thick, spiky branches.

'You men have what you what!' Thurstan called into the darkness. 'If you want us too, come and get us... but it will cost you dear! This, I promise!'

Highly likely they didn't understand French, if they understood any tongue of civilised men, but he felt certain his import was clear. Then he too turned and scrambled up into the nearest pine, though he purposely chose a different one from Pandulf and Melinda. One winter, as a boy, he'd evaded a pack of real wolves by climbing a tree in the forest of Radnor and waiting them out. But these weren't wolves. However they appeared, they were men, and it wasn't impossible that they'd try to set fire to the trees. They'd have Satan's own job, doing it, of course. One would be difficult, but it would be even harder to torch two.

'Melinda!' he called, straining his voice to be heard over the dirge. 'Any one of these devils enters the camp, approaches the fire… you shoot him dead, you hear?' She didn't reply. 'Melinda!' he called out again, angry.

'I hear you,' she replied, sounding vexed.

'And while you're at it, now would be a good time to pray for a miracle.'

'She's already praying, my lord,' Pandulf's voice came back.

Below them, the howling dragged on.

'I would pray too,' Thurstan said to himself. 'If I thought anyone would listen.'

CHAPTER 47

When day finally broke, it was brighter and clearer than they'd been used to. It was still bitingly cold, but the mist had ebbed away, sunlight streaking a forest floor again turned white by frost, except for the area below them, which was blackened by fire and spattered with crimson.

Stiff with cold and fatigue, begrimed by smoke, they slowly and painfully clambered down.

'I see our latest batch of supplies has taken leave of us,' Pandulf said.

'At least we're alive.' Thurstan prowled what had once been their perimeter.

Melinda struggled to say anything. She was numb, and not just with fatigue. Pandulf approached her warily.

'We wouldn't have won that fight without you,' he said.

'Did we win it?' she wondered.

'As, Thurstan said, we're—'

'Yes, we're still alive. *We* are, at least.'

'You'd rather it was them and not us?' Thurstan asked.

'No,' she replied. 'But I won't pretend I enjoyed the role I played.'

'For God's sake, girl!' He sheathed his sword, unbuckling it from his waist and hanging it on his back. 'No one enjoys it, but like it or not, you have a duty to live.'

'At the expense of others?'

'We do what we must. But if it troubles you, take it up with God. It's in His name that we're all here in the East in the first place.'

They set off walking. The knight had a point, she supposed. They'd none of them come here simply to be martyrs, but to liberate the Holy Places. And wasn't it God Himself who'd sent those entities against them the previous night? Maybe He hadn't sent them, but He hadn't held them back… in which case did He seriously expect they'd be uninjured. But then she realised that she was thinking like a warrior, and she hated herself for what she'd become. There was never any victory in killing.

–

They headed north-west. More by fortune than design, the forest thinned out. There was more snow, but there were also half-frozen streams, from which they were at least able to drink. Thurstan advised Melinda that if they saw any game, she should shoot. But the landscape was strangely quiet. In England, there'd be bird calls even in winter. They'd hear the coughing of stags, the distant *chip-chop* of axes as woodsmen cleared land.

'I can't help thinking that we're still not alone,' Pandulf said, hefting his shield, which now was dented and bloodstained. His other hand was tight on his sword-hilt.

'You're not wrong,' Thurstan said, spying movement.

Left of them, ten or so fur-clad figures, carrying spears and clubs, were moving parallel through the trees.

'God's breath,' the lad muttered.

'How many arrows remain?' Thurstan asked Melinda.

'Fourteen,' she said. 'There were more quivers on the horses, but they're now gone.'

'Why don't they just attack?' Pandulf wondered.

'We also have company on the right,' the girl said.

A similar line of shaggy figures was visible on that side as well. They too were keeping their distance, but more and more brute shapes were emerging from the woods behind them.

'It'll come soon enough,' Thurstan said.

The pinewood, meanwhile, opened out further. Soon, there was only sky above them. They fell into single file as they ploughed through snow-caked bracken.

'Have they herded us to this place?' Pandulf asked.

Thurstan was wondering the same. The bracken was now waist-high, and he had to draw his sword to hack open a pathway. The enemy could easily be concealed at close quarter. Melinda, positioned between the two men, nocked an arrow, but when Thurstan glanced back at her, her mouth trembled, and her eyes were moist with tears.

'Be ready,' he said.

'To what end?' she replied. 'If we're going to die here, why take more lives?'

'Good Lord!' Pandulf said.

Some thirty yards further on, the rest of the forest horde had grouped in front of them. A great press of them, maybe thirty or forty barred the fugitives' path. They wielded a range of crude weapons, from cleavers to mattocks to heavy stones.

Those on the left and right began to encroach.

'I'd hoped it wouldn't come to this.' Thurstan turned to look at the youngsters. 'It was a reasonable gamble that once they had our baggage, we'd be left alone. But not so.'

Pandulf was ice-pale, while Melinda hung her head; of the two of them, she seemed more resigned to her fate. The arrow was no longer nocked.

With animal-like howls, the fur-clad phalanxes closed in from all three sides. They too were hampered by the snowy vegetation, but they came through it forcefully. It struck Thurstan fleetingly that they'd have been far better doing as he'd feared they would: placing their stronger warriors close at hand, concealed. It put question-marks against their intelligence. But now that he saw them up close and in daylight, they weren't as terrifying as they'd been in the darkness.

Beneath their rancid hide costumes, he saw stringy frames, faces that were shrivelled, grizzled, ingrained with forest dirt. If only there hadn't been so damned many of them. And then, there came a sudden baying of horns, and from the left, two horsemen rode into view.

The trio stared, bewildered.

Their initial impression was of two handsomely clad knights. Both wore full, gleaming body-mail and flowing, colourful raiment, one decked in a chessboard pattern of blue and white, the other in chevrons of green and gold. Their steeds, huge thoroughbreds each, wore matching livery.

Thurstan in particular was thunderstruck.

These were the sorts of riders he'd expect on a tourneying ground in Europe, not here in Anatolia. Certainly not on the wild slopes of the Taurus mountains. Nevertheless, the two knights' arrival was welcome. As they veered round the edge of the bracken field, continually blowing their hunting horns, the shaggy folk broke and ran. There was no hesitation. They scattered in all directions, plunging away through the frozen vegetation.

'It's like God has sent us angels,' Pandulf said.

But if that was the case, they were ruthless angels indeed, for the two knights now put away their horns, hefted their shields and lowered their lances. On the flatter ground, they hit a furious gallop, bearing down on the fleeing beast-men, each of the two most laggardly immediately speared through their backs. The knights then drew handweapons: the one in blue and white a longsword, the one in green and gold a chain-mace. With deft horsemanship, they veered in and out of the hairy folk, striking fiercely but cleanly whenever a target came in reach. Even then, the beast-people made no attempt to stand and fight. A couple might have flung spears or lobbed stones, but to no avail, and any who broke their stride were ridden down, the two gorgeously clad steeds rearing, striking hammer blows with their ironshod hooves.

In next to no time, maybe a dozen of their victims lay gashed and trampled, in most cases dead, and all the while Thurstan and his companions watched as the mad pursuit went on, the horsemen calling to each other in cheerful voices as they struck and slashed and cut the stragglers down, finally pursuing the rest into the shadows of the woodland.

Thurstan stood stock-still. Many times, he'd seen for himself how the heavy cavalry charge, the preferred way to fight for most Christian armies, could decimate its opponents before the infantry even engaged. At full pelt, it was nigh-on irresistible. And yet this minuscule version of it had still been an eye-opener. It didn't say much for the beast-men, and yet these two knights – two men alone – attacking them with such ferocity and yet at the same time, in joyous, near-sporting fashion, had left the English knight wondering what it was that he'd just witnessed.

And not a little unnerved by it.

'We need to leave,' he told the others. 'Right now. While the way is clear.'

They nodded, all three plodding away through the bracken, again unsure where they were going, but knowing only that they must vacate this open space. Just ahead, they spied what looked like a natural road that had formed between the approaching bulwark of trees and the steeply rising rocky ground on its left. It was uneven and covered in snow, but it was a gap, and they could pass along it. But they weren't far along, walking hard but their legs already cramping because once again the ground was elevating, when they heard a rumble of hooves behind.

Thurstan's sword was already drawn, but before he could spin around again, a cheery voice sounded. 'Welcome, strangers!' it hailed them in French.

They had no choice but to stop and turn. The two knights cantered up the snowy track in pursuit, their weapons sheathed. The one in blue and white had already removed his helmet, revealing a youthful face under a mop of soft fair hair. When he drew rein alongside them, they saw that he was clean-shaved and handsome, with intense blue-green eyes.

'Apologies that you fell foul of our local vermin.' Again, he spoke in French, his accent of the East, though not as strong as Melinda's. He smiled as he looked them over, briefly eyeing Thurstan's longsword. 'Though it appears you took an account of them yourselves.'

'You were there last night?' Melinda said, surprised.

'Alas, no. Had we been, I fear none of that unpleasantness would have happened.'

'There are several funeral pyres back there in the trees,' the knight in green and gold said. He too had removed his helm, revealing equally young and appealing features, though he was grey-eyed and dark of hair, his beard and moustache neatly trimmed.

'We had no choice but to fight,' Pandulf replied.

'Of course,' the fair-haired knight said.

'Who are you?' Thurstan asked.

'My name is Echthra,' the beard replied. 'And this is my younger brother, Kakia. We are knights in service to our sister, Countess Aimatochysia, who rules these lands.'

'A Frankish countess?' Thurstan said. 'In the Anatolian uplands?'

Echthra and Kakia exchanged amused glances. 'You think you're the first Westerners to come here?' Echthra asked. 'In this great age of pilgrimage?'

Thurstan was still suspicious, but the point was valid. Baronial families from Europe had erected strongholds all over the Greek-held lands west of the Bosphorus, the ones they collectively knew as 'Romania', so why not here in those to the east?

'Your own names?' Echthra enquired.

'Bertrand du Voix,' Thurstan said, saying the first thing that came into his head. 'A knight of Normandy.' He could only hope that out here in the East, they wouldn't take note of his English accent. 'Retainer to Count Robert of Dreux. This my wife, Marietta, whom I met and married whilst in Outremer... and my squire, Eadric.'

'Is that a Templar shield, I see?' Kakia spoke with curiosity, eyeing Pandulf.

The squire shrugged. 'When in danger, one uses any means of defence one can find.'

'Yet you're not Knights Templar yourselves.' It was a statement rather than a question.

'The boy won the shield,' Thurstan replied, discomforted that he and his friends were still on foot, while these two unknowns remained mounted. 'In a contest of arms.'

Kakia gave a doubtful smile. 'A Templar willingly surrendered his colours?'

'It's a complicated story.'

The silence between them stretched taut, only for Echthra to wave it away. 'Worry not. There's no love lost for the Temple of Solomon here. Whatever happened between you and the Soldiers of Christ is your own affair.'

345

'We're grateful for your help,' Melinda said, though her tone was doubtful.

The knight nodded. 'We're glad to be of service. Where are you bound?'

'At present,' Thurstan said, 'Constantinople.'

'Indeed?' Echthra replied. 'You realise you're headed in completely the wrong direction?'

'We are,' Thurstan said. 'But as you've already inferred, we ran into trouble on the road.'

Echthra nodded. 'Then it's even more a good thing that you met us when you did. My sister will welcome you grandly. All Christian travellers are welcome at the chateau. You may bathe, eat, rest and warm yourselves by the Yuletide fire.'

'So, it *is* Christmas?' Pandulf said.

Echthra looked surprised. 'You weren't aware that today is Christmas Eve?'

'We lost count of the days,' Melinda explained.

'No matter. We recovered a couple of your horses. At least you can now ride.'

'Is it far?' Thurstan asked.

'An hour's journey.' Echthra nodded to his brother, who wheeled his animal around and cantered back along the trail. He then saw the open cuts on Pandulf's face. 'You're wounded. No matter, my sister, Aimatochysia, will tend to that for you.'

'Your sister must be very gracious,' the lad replied.

'She is long in the habit of receiving strangers. Ah…'

Kakia returned, leading two of the horses they had lost the night before.

'I fear your baggage will have been pillaged,' Echthra said.

'At least we're alive,' Thurstan grunted.

'Even so, it's a crime for which those Zoódis scum will pay.'

The threesome mounted up, Thurstan selecting one horse for himself, Pandulf and Melinda sharing the other. It still bothered the English knight that they were taking these two handsome strangers at their word. Yet he was tempted by what they were offering. A

Christmas fire and a warm bed? When the alternative was trudging on through these mountains with only two mounts between them.

'Who are the Zoódis?' Melinda enquired, as they rode eastward.

'The costumed brutes who assaulted you,' Echthra replied. 'An outlaw clan, hated by all, who only survive here because of the remoteness of the region.'

'How did they come to be so bestial?' Thurstan asked.

'They brought it on themselves,' Kakia said. 'With their filthy, incestuous habits. Their health is poor, their intellect non-existent. They're descended from a murderous man and wife, who were hunted across the sultanate of Rum many years ago, the man under sentence of impalement for his crimes. When they came here, the sultan's soldiers gave up the chase. They managed to hide themselves in the mountains, where they then produced more children and grandchildren than a whole nest of rats.'

Echthra took up the tale. 'What you see now are several generations of their offspring. Inbred vermin who offer nothing of value. Halfwits and cripples existing as bandits and scavengers.'

'And as such, we hunt them for sport,' Kakia added. 'As you may have seen.'

'We did,' Thurstan said.

'Countess Aimatochysia is renowned for her hospitality but also her dedication to the rule of law,' Echthra explained. 'She has sworn to drive all brigands from her lands.'

Thurstan thought back on the massacre he'd witnessed. 'I'm impressed it took only two of you to set them running.'

Echthra smiled again. 'As I said, they are degenerate and diseased. Any opponents on horseback are more than they can manage. Had you known, I dare say you yourselves could have driven them from the field.'

'Though, I wouldn't recommend putting it to the test,' Kakia said jovially. 'We had an advantage, for neither Echthra nor I have ever yet met our match in combat.'

Echthra drew rein and pointed ahead.

'Here we are, friends. Chateau Apelpisia.'

They gazed ahead, three things immediately striking Thurstan with awe.

Firstly, the immense gorge that lay across their path. It was at least two hundred yards across, and easy to imagine that it plunged to perilous depth. Secondly, the bridge that spanned it. This was an extension of the road they now followed, though less broad, about ten yards in width. No stonework was visible; it was made entirely from timber – one beam laid after another, each fastened to the next with iron bands, and yet suspended by two complex masses of inches-thick ropes bound and knotted around huge timber frameworks anchored into the bedrock of the cliffsides. It looked sturdy enough, and yet only secondary ropes provided safety barriers on either side. For anyone fearful of heights, it would be a difficult experience. Thirdly, the land on the other side: more dense pine forest, this time ascending tier upon tier until at the apex there was nothing but barren crags and deep ravines, and atop those, perched on a toothlike pinnacle, seemingly growing out of the very granite of the mountain, a castle.

Thurstan had expected some kind of fortification – where else would an influential countess live? – but something more in keeping with the architecture of this region than this. It lacked any complex ornamentation. There were no machicolations along its parapets, no conical-roofed towers. Instead, it had the harsh exterior of a simple baronial stronghold: a sheer outer wall, austere battlements, a faceless inner keep with only arrow-loops to admit light.

'Pray, don't be alarmed,' Echthra shouted, gallivanting ahead. 'The bridge looks horrendous, but it's perfectly sound.'

He rode out onto it, setting it swaying slightly, though it still looked heavy and solid. As further proof, he spurred his horse forward, galloping across to the far side. Kakia went too, whooping as he followed. The bridge's timbers thrummed and thundered and it swung visibly, but there was no obvious sign of weakness. Even so, when the three travellers ventured onto it, they did so slowly and on foot, leading their nervous animals by the reins. Thurstan himself stole a single glance downward, seeing the narrow thread of a river, filled with rocks, perhaps three hundred feet below.

'Countess Aimatochysia sounds very cordial?' Pandulf said, as they crossed.

'Not to the Zoódis,' Melinda replied.

'That Zoódis rabble would have killed us,' Thurstan reminded her.

'We should be thankful it was Echthra and Kakia who came along,' Pandulf added with a hint of irony. 'Because after all, they've never yet met their equal.'

CHAPTER 48

After a torturous uphill climb along a narrow, rocky track, enclosed again by snowy pines, they reached the castle's entrance. Thurstan was surprised to see its outer gate standing open, its portcullis raised. The rest of the stronghold, with its lofty towers and faceless walls, looked indomitable, in which case an open gate was surely an oversight, though he'd already seen how Countess Aimatochysia and her two brothers dealt with the region's undesirables, so maybe their reputation was defence enough.

In the courtyard, they left their horses in the care of a boy who looked close to being a simpleton and ascended a covered timber staircase to the keep's main entrance. The castle itself was built from crude stone, though the buildings in the inner court were of simple wood and thatch. And yet things were markedly different inside the keep.

They entered a grand hall, lit by an enormous fire and innumerable smoky candles. It was warmly carpeted, its walls decked with weapons and lavish tapestries, while the high ceiling – so high in fact that it could barely be seen – was hung with heraldic flags. The atmosphere was strongly martial, but there was comfort there too.

The servants in Chateau Apelpisia moved about quietly and unobtrusively. With the exception of one tall, solemn fellow with cadaverous features, whom Echthra referred to as Kopek, they were mostly female, wearing dark, plain clothing, their hair tied in scarfs. Like Kopek, they were serious, sombre types, who spoke together barely at all, though even as the guests were led into the great hall, several women were already in the process of setting a banquet table, arranging multiple high-backed chairs, placing huge candelabra along it at regular intervals, but also dishes, napkins and cutlery, the latter not just comprising knives but forks as well, an Italian affectation, which prior to Outremer, Thurstan had only seen on rare occasions. At Echthra's bidding, one of the women showed the three guests up several flights of granite staircase, saying there were comfortable apartments and fresh changes of clothes awaiting them.

'I can't believe it,' Pandulf said. 'It's almost as though we were expected.'

Thurstan too was compelled to wonder about their change of fortune. It was difficult to believe that, a couple of hours earlier, they'd been marooned in a desolate forest, cold, grimy, exhausted, and encircled by grisly folk intent on butchering them.

The entrances to their two apartments were on the same corridor, and apparently, or so Echthra had said before they'd come up, they'd find a bath-chamber at the far end. Only when Thurstan and Melinda were ensconced in their own quarters, which were richly furnished, more tapestries on the walls, thick hangings over the casements, a blazing hearth and an immense four-posted bed, did they address the matter of their so-called marriage.

'Don't fret yourself.' Thurstan stripped off his gauntlets and furs and unlaced his hauberk at the neck. 'I won't be seeking conjugal rights.'

Melinda assessed the room disbelievingly. A bundle of folded but fluffy towels sat on the bed. 'Such comforts,' she observed.

'And yet still you seem sad?'

'You know why, my lord.'

He stood in front of the fire, warming his hands. 'You don't consider that you too were a victim down there on the mountain? Placed in peril with no option but to resist?'

She chewed her bottom lip. 'When the Zoódis came at us in the open, just before Lord Echthra and Lord Kakia intervened… the desire to loose arrows came on me again. I know I spoke piously beforehand, but I did not want to die.'

'If only death was all you'd faced. There could have been rape, torture… you'd have done well to feather as many of those animals as you could.'

'But that's the point, Thurstan. They weren't animals. They were men, and now we know they were men in a dreadful state... men depraved by circumstances, who own nothing and have been forced to make the wilderness their home.'

'Haven't you just described your own position?'

She pondered as she sat on the bed. 'I still think it's wrong to kill.'

'Of course. But sometimes it can't be helped.'

'But only in extreme times... when there's no other alternative.'

'We agree on that, at least.' He arched his back. 'Now, we should take full advantage of this lapse in our misfortune... apparently there's a bath-chamber down the passage. I've never heard of such a thing indoors, though I'd imagine that among the Outremer elite it isn't so uncommon.'

Her lack of response implied that this was a matter she hadn't thought twice about.

'I'd ask you to show me how this bath-chamber functions,' he said. 'I'd imagine there's some kind of cistern, maybe a sluice. But I expect that learning to kill is sinfulness enough for one day, so I won't now require you also to be naked in a steamy room with a lusty fellow such as me.'

He glanced at her, but she didn't detect the humour, instead staring at the flames on the hearth. 'If it's like the bath-chamber in the patriarch's house, it's a simple mechanism. But I will go first.' She stood and grabbed herself a towel. 'If there's any complication, I can tell you about it on my return.'

He nodded. She moved to the door and opened it but then turned again.

'Thurstan... this devil that supposedly haunts you? Do you attach any credence to it?'

He watched her warily. She watched him back, with deadly seriousness.

'Last night,' he said, 'very briefly... I wondered if in leaving the Levant, I was finally shaking loose from his power, and so he'd sent demons to stop us. But now, as you see, that wasn't the case. And if he has any power, if he exists at all, he hasn't prevented us finding life-saving sanctuary here.'

'No.' She seemed relieved by that. 'Of course not.'

When they came down to dine that evening, they felt better. A hot bath was always a Godsend, even to Thurstan, who hadn't experienced them often, while the change of clothes they'd each found waiting on returning from the bath-chamber made them feel less like interlopers and more like honoured guests. Thurstan now wore a maroon tunic with a scalloped cape, green hose and leather, calf-length boots, while Melinda looked resplendent in a graceful fitted gown of gold and yellow thread, a bright blue cloak and a white linen veil and wimple. Pandulf came behind, as any good squire or page should, wearing a russet tunic, grey hose and ankle-fitting shoes.

Echthra and Kakia, who awaited them, had also changed, both now in similar blue-and-gold finery. The banquet was almost set, partly with shimmering glassware, another luxurious reminder they were still in the East, but it was also tricked out with Christmas greenery. The food itself was a sight to set any man salivating: great trenchers heaped with slabs of smoking beef, fresh baked loaves and pies, cooked fowl, bowls of figs and dates. However, the main event of the evening commenced when Countess Aimatochysia herself arrived, her handmaids scuttling fussily around her.

Her beauty was so entrancing that it left Thurstan tongue-tied.

Her raven-black hair was thick and lush, piled on top of her head and held in place with a golden band; when loosened, it would doubtless fall to the small of her back. She had the smoothest features: fine porcelain cheekbones, a small, cherubic mouth, her lips stained the most vivid shade of red, her eyes a penetrating violet-blue. Her hourglass physique was sumptuously clad in a long, full gown, of deepest scarlet, with a beautifully embroidered cape at her shoulders. Like her brothers, she dripped with gold and silver.

She said nothing at first, merely smiled and nodded courteously as the guests were introduced, then, rather primly, with no great extravagance, took her place at the table. The others were seated directly opposite, facing her, while Echthra chose a chair to the left of his sister, Kakia to the right.

'My dear guests,' the countess said, her tone silky smooth, 'I fear my darling brothers' ineptitude as hosts knows no bounds. I would have come to you sooner, but only late this afternoon did I receive word that we had visitors.' Her two brothers sat smiling, unabashed. 'We've now been formally introduced, but please, my friends, tell me a little more about yourselves… in your own words.'

Thurstan again relayed the fake names that he'd given to Echthra and Kakia.

'Lord Bertrand and Lady Marietta,' the countess replied with fascination. Her violet eyes were captivating. 'You are most welcome in this house.'

'Thank you sincerely, Countess,' Thurstan said. 'The road has been hard.'

'Forgive me asking…' she indicated to a servant that her guests' goblets needed filling, 'but, if you're returning to Normandy, you have strayed far from the normal path.'

'We sailed from Jaffa to Cyprus, and thence, supposedly, Crete,' Thurstan explained. 'After that, we should have proceeded to Sicily. Unfortunately, not far out of Limassol, our ship was set upon by pirates. We three put to sea in a coracle, which in time brought us ashore on your southern coast. But we lost everything in the process.'

'You were well enough equipped to defend yourselves last night,' Echthra commented. 'At least for a time.'

Thurstan sipped his wine, which, while he was no expert, was both sweet and refreshing. 'I regret that we've already had several difficult encounters in Anatolia. The pirates left us with almost nothing, but there were others, inland, who still sought to interfere with us… It didn't always go well for them.'

The countess arched her finely drawn eyebrows, then clapped her hands and gave a delicate, delightful laugh. 'These are harsh lands, and there are many rogue elements. But I'm thrilled that you fought your way to safety. Now, in some recompense, I hope, you may rest with us here for as long as you desire, and we will feed and clothe you, and re-equip you for your journey when you're ready to resume.'

'You're incredibly kind,' Melinda said, dabbing at her eyes with a napkin.

'Pray, don't thank me, Lady Marietta. Pilgrims returning from the East are beset by all kinds of ill-fortune. One sometimes wonders what the celestial powers are thinking. But maybe the solution to that riddle is found in the likes of us, who consider it our duty as fellow Christians to do what we can to alleviate the pain and distress of those who are lost.' But now the noblewoman sat back to regard her female guest with additional interest. 'My dear child, you're a bubbling pot of emotion. Please, don't be upset. You're safe here.'

Melinda sniffled and wiped away her tears. 'Apologies, my lady. But I think I can speak for the oth— For my husband as well as myself... When I say that such generosity of spirit... such all-round hospitality is more than any of us could have hoped for.'

Countess Aimatochysia looked sad. 'You've seen more hardship than your husband has admitted to, haven't you, child?'

'Marietta came from a titled family,' Thurstan cut in, concerned that Melinda's emotional state might expose more about them than it should. 'But after the fall of Jerusalem, she was made a slave.'

The countess was visibly horrified.

'It was Lord Bertrand who rescued me,' Melinda said.

'And then married you? How romantic. And now, Lord Bertrand, you return to your ancestral home?'

'We do, my lady, yes.'

'Have you been to Europe before, Lady Marietta?'

Melinda dabbed again at her tears. 'Until now, I've never left the Levant.'

'Alas... once you pass the Italian lands, it's a dreary place. Especially in winter. Though the winters here can be cruel too, as you're no doubt aware.'

'If I might be so bold, Countess,' Thurstan said, 'I'm fascinated by your presence in this wild place. How does a Greek stronghold like this have the air of courtly France? How is it that you and your brothers speak French so well?'

'My dear Lord Bertrand...' She seemed amused. 'French is our first language.'

'Forgive me,' he said, 'I assumed… Greek.'

'We speak Greek,' Echthra replied. 'As administrators in this region, we must. But our family's traditions are important to us.'

'You must realise that we are of French descent,' the countess said. 'Our esteemed ancestor was Father Peter of Achères, the famous Priest of Amiens.'

Indeed? Thurstan thought.

'The one they called "Peter the Hermit"?' Melinda said, surprised.

'Most knew him by that name,' the countess replied. 'In time he simply became "The Hermit". A vagabond priest, but beloved by God, he brought a peasant army to the East, and armed with nothing but faith, made his way barefoot to Jerusalem, where he led the first wave of pilgrims over the Holy City's walls.'

Thurstan didn't immediately respond, because he wasn't entirely sure that Peter the Hermit had truly been beloved by God. In reality, the man was a fanatic who led his pauper army to annihilation, but not until it had robbed, pillaged and raped its way across Christendom, massacring entire Jewish communities in the Rhineland. It only reached Jerusalem after joining the real army, led there by Godfrey of Bouillon. All this had happened a century ago, but stories persisted that, even after the capture of the Holy City, it was the Hermit's continued incendiary preaching that incited his new friends to destroy its population.

Countess Aimatochysia frowned. 'You seem disturbed, Lord Bertrand?'

'Just intrigued, Countess.' He sipped more wine. 'It's a riveting tale. But I can't help wondering how a priest sworn to poverty could have founded a noble house.'

Kakia barked with laughter. 'Welcome to the Empire of the Greeks. Here, anything can be purchased.'

'My great grandfather carried huge riches away from Jerusalem,' the countess explained. 'Though all had been justly claimed, of course.'

'Of course,' Thurstan said.

'Our family now has military obligations in return. You may not realise it, my friends, but we are close here to the border with Rum.

At some point, the Seljuks will come, and when they do, my brothers and I, and all our followers, will fight.'

She imparted this news with a strange air of fatalism, as though the outcome of such an event was already decided and would not be positive. Yet it didn't darken her mood. She continued to engage politely and wittily with her guests, but most of all was keen to know about events in the outside world.

'Speaking as a soldier, Lord Bertrand,' she said, 'how would you say the war against the infidels is going? Are we Christians fighting well?'

Thurstan, who was starting to feel a little tired, gave it measured thought. 'I'd say the successes are piecemeal, Countess.'

'I'm sorry to hear that.'

'After King Richard arrived, we won most of the battles, but here in the East, the Muslims are closer to home than we and can always summon legions of reinforcements.'

'We can't just kill them all?' Kakia wondered, an odd, cold smile on his lips.

Thurstan shrugged. 'I fear it's difficult, if not impossible, to kill an idea.'

The host family's stoicism clearly ran deep, for if they'd been hoping to hear something that might reassure them about their own position, they evidently hadn't done, and yet they seemed unperturbed.

'Forgive me,' Thurstan said, 'if...' Suddenly, his eyelids felt heavy. From out of nowhere, torpor was stealing up. It was hard to concentrate; those other voices in the room became muffled. 'Forgive... if these aren't... the tidings you hoped...'

The entire chamber swam.

'Are you unwell, Lord Bertrand?' Countess Aimatochysia asked.

'I think... it must...' Thurstan stumbled both in thought and word. 'I think... the journey... we slept very...'

He glanced at his companions and was surprised to see both Melinda and Pandulf slumped in their chairs, heads drooped. He looked at the goblet of wine in front of him, and then at his hostess, her violet eyes gleaming like gemstones through the blurry glow of the candelabra.

The next thing he knew, servants were advancing from the shadows.

'Such a shame,' he heard his hostess say. 'Such a crying shame.'

This time, her laugh wasn't quite so delicate. Or so delightful.

CHAPTER 49

Thurstan fought as hard as he could against the narcosis that gripped him. But in vain. His body was a ton-weight, his limbs lifeless append-ages. The best he could do with his eyelids was flutter them as several people manhandled him out of his chair.

'Take him below,' a male voice instructed. It sounded like Echthra.

The next thing Thurstan knew, he was being carried. The warmth of the firelit hall receded, and then he was in a colder, darker place. There was grunting and a scuffling of feet as he felt himself descending a steep stairway. He made another effort to struggle. If he kicked out or managed to grapple with them, he was sure he could overwhelm these wretches of servants, but again, no part of his body responded, his vision no more now than a narrow, smeary crack. He had the idea there was a firebrand below, leading the way, and maybe one behind, the reflections of its flames flickering on a right-hand wall of wet bricks. On his left meanwhile, he fancied there was a black void. When the grunting and cursing of his captors didn't fill his ears, he heard a frenzied snarling and slashing down there, and a wild, furious barking.

'Patience, my friends,' someone called from behind him. This time, he thought it was Kakia. 'You'll get your usual share of leavings.'

–

Chateau Apelpisia only had one dungeon passage, owing to the sheer difficulty its original founders had had in burrowing into the bedrock of this near-unassailable peak. That said, though dimly lit by smoky torches, it was a good two hundred yards in length, and there were many cells opening off from it, little more than cubby holes in truth, separated from the passage by thick iron bars.

Lady Marietta's inert form was carried down to the far end over Kopek's shoulder. Once here, he took a key from the wall and opened the very last of the cells. Inside, there was a rectangular wooden table. He laid her on it on her back, then brought a torch in from outside, to light the five half-melted tallow candles on a stone shelf. Their greasy stink was terrible, though no worse than the other rancid odours pervading this subterranean place. The light they issued was an eerie shade of green, but it made no difference to the unspeaking manservant, who'd done this so many times before.

First, he dragged the girl's boots off, pushed her skirts up past her thighs and belly, and then, taking a knife from his belt, cut away her underclothes, leaving her lower half naked.

Next, he spread her legs apart and lifting the right one first, pulled down a chain from the pulley system overhead, clasping a metal cuff around her ankle. When he'd done the same with the left, he turned a wheel on the wall, cranking the mechanism on the ceiling again, Marietta's legs widening apart.

Echthra had now come to the cell's entrance. He was naked save for a pair of leather breeks held in place by a steel-studded belt, and gleaming all over with sweat. He mopped back his wringing hair and took a long draught from his flagon of wine.

Kopek bowed to his master and walked away along the corridor.

Echthra was about to select from the range of blood-caked cutting tools suspended from hooks on the wall, when a throat was cleared out in the passage behind. He turned, to find Kakia, still dressed, standing by the cell entrance.

'What do we do with the knight?' the younger sibling asked.

Echthra placed his cup on the shelf. 'Where is he?'

'Come and see.' They went down the passage together. Thirty yards along, the cage door stood open on the cell in which their male guest's fully clothed but deeply unconscious body had been dumped.

'His private papers confirm that he's who we suspected he was,' Kakia said. 'The one they call Wildblood.'

Echthra shrugged, satisfied if unsurprised.

'But that means he's a dangerous beast,' Kakia added. 'Shouldn't we just kill him?'

'Under no circumstances,' Countess Aimatochysia said, as she glided along the passage towards them, her gorgeous scarlet brocade replaced by an immodest gown of black leather, cinched at the waist, but open from the navel to the neck, her ample cleavage pushing it outward. She'd unbound her hair, which hung in dense black tresses. Her eyes glittered violet and her mouth shone blood-red.

'He's no use to us here,' she said, 'but he'll be no use either to the court of Isaac Angelos if we deliver him dead. The Greeks will like nothing better than to make a show-trial for the murder of Count Conrad, and if the execution of Andronikos Komnenos is anything to go by, they'll dismember the miscreant alive over a period of days. They'll also pay handsomely for that privilege.'

Smiling, Kakia closed Thurstan's cell door, locked it and hung the key on the wall, before ascending to the higher levels. Once they were alone, Countess Aimatochysia exchanged a voluptuous kiss with her younger brother, Echthra, and then returned along the passage herself, to where another cell stood open. Inside this one, the young squire introduced as Eadric, though no doubt his real name was different, hung naked in his shackles, still deeply unconscious. She appraised him, as she fingered a row of hand-held torture devices suspended on the wall.

Echthra meanwhile went back to Marietta's cell, where she still lay on the table, her legs indecently spread. He downed his flagon of wine in a gulp, then reached for a pair of shears. Their purpose once had been the slicing of fleeces from the backs of sheep, but through years of practice, the children of Chateau Apelpisia had educated themselves in the many other interesting uses that everyday implements could be put to.

He expanded the shears and snapped them closed. At first it was an effort. They were glutinous with congealed gore, but this tangible remnant of some former guest only added to the enjoyment. Besides, their blades would be sharp enough underneath. All the items down here were honed to perfection.

And then, rather to his own surprise, Echthra dropped the shears. It was not by intent, or even carelessness.

Suddenly, it was a struggle to manipulate his own fingers.

Echthra muttered in confusion but could only form incoherent words. And then the cell tilted, the candlelight twirling. He reached for the table but missed it, and when he fell, struck it hard with the side of his head, which sent him spinning into unconsciousness far more speedily than any cup of drugged wine would have done on its own.

—

Melinda propped herself up on her elbows. Swiftly, she extricated her feet from the hanging stirrups, her ankles having proved too slender for the metal clamps to lock tightly around. She didn't just have her elfin shape to thank for that. Her captor's swaggering overconfidence was partly responsible, not to mention the impression she'd deliberately given that she was nothing more than a weak and weepy girl. Neither Echthra nor Kakia had imagined that, once she was insensible, she'd be any kind of problem.

And of course, at no stage in reality, had she been insensible, or even close to it.

She rearranged her skirts and climbed from the table. Despite being free, she was shaking: the fear and filth in this place, the horror of what had almost been done to her. But all that mattered now was getting herself and her friends out.

She pulled her boots on and approached the open cage door. The main corridor appeared to be deserted. She glanced back to where Echthra lay prone, and then at the hideous tools arrayed on the wall.

Sweat beaded on her forehead as she peered back along the corridor.

Never in her life had she been so glad that she didn't touch strong drink.

For that reason alone, she'd brought a leather water bottle down to the banquet, but for fear that she might offend her hosts had kept it concealed in a pocket inside her cloak. Her intent had been to continually but covertly water her wine, but she hadn't even commenced this pantomime when she noticed something peculiar: almost as soon as they'd entered the hall, while Thurstan and Pandulf had stood in slack-jawed appreciation of the feast that greeted them, to Melinda, something was missing from the great chamber. Religious paraphernalia. These people had promised they were celebrating Christmas and had made great play of the assistance they provided to fellow Christians. Yet nowhere did she see a crucifix or icon. The tapestries depicted dragons, griffins, knights in battle, but no members of the Holy Family, no saints, no pilgrims en-route to the Holy Places. Perhaps because she'd considered that in itself strange, she'd thought again on their hostess's curious name, and how it had seemed familiar to her. And then, in a flash, she'd been struck by a fleeting memory of her lessons in Greek when she was still only a child.

Aimatochysia, in its truest form of translation, meant 'Bloodlust'.

She'd wondered if she was mistaken. Surely, she was? But maybe not, because the meanings of other Greek words were by then coming back to her.

Did Echthra not translate as 'Spite', and Kakia as 'Malice'?

It wasn't just unlikely, it was impossible, ridiculous. But the real sense of horror had dawned when she'd recognised the meaning of the word, Apelpisia.

'Despair'.

Chateau Apelpisia meant 'Castle Despair'.

Yet again, it seemed preposterous but at the same time was undeniable. These could not have been their hosts' real names, but even if they were nicknames, they were nicknames their owners were happy to go by.

What in Heaven did *that* mean?

From that moment, she'd undertaken not to drink any wine, for at least one of them must retain a level-head. The first thing she did was covertly empty her water bottle under the table, and from then on, whenever her goblet was replenished by the servants, she'd craftily pour its contents into the bottle. When Thurstan and Pandulf had succumbed to their intoxicants, she too had feigned unconsciousness.

It was still a miracle, though, that Echthra, led fleetingly from the cell by his brother, had given her that window of opportunity in which to free herself, throw away his wine and refill it with her own.

The plan had been made on the hoof, in the midst of grave fear. She could scarcely believe it had worked. And yet they weren't out of this place yet.

When they'd brought her along the passage the first time, she'd been playing dead. With eyes firmly closed, she hadn't seen through the bars into any of the adjoining cells. Now she did and it was an effort not to scream with horror.

In the first one, a nude corpse was suspended upside down over a brass tub. It was difficult to tell what sex it was, for so many body parts had been chopped away. Congealed gore streaked the pitiful form and filled the tub almost to the brim. In the next one, a gruesomely blackened body was strapped to a wheel. Underneath this one lay the charred relics of a fire. All along the passage, on either side, it was the same, the remnants of tortured, eviscerated humans – invariably they were young people, both male and female – fastened into painful and degrading contraptions. It was perhaps a small mercy that most, if not all, appeared to be dead.

By the time she reached Thurstan's cell, her cheeks were running with tears, her shoulders heaving. In this one at least, the prisoner was so far unharmed, the knight lying slumped against a wall. Not exactly unconscious, he twitched feebly but seemed unable to lift his head.

Melinda grabbed the key from the hook, only to hear a female voice from a little further along the passage. It was gentle, soothing, but it was undoubtedly Countess Bloodlust.

'There, my pretty, my sweet. I'm glad it only took a small amount of my special wine to put you to sleep. That's the appeal of the young, you see. You're soft, unformed. But it wouldn't do for me to commence my work alone. There'd be no point. You need to experience it with me. So, the time is now, my pretty. My little chick. Come back to me... that's a good boy. Come back to me.'

Melinda crept another three cell doors along and gazed through the bars at an appalling scene: the young squire, stripped naked, hanging spread-eagled against the far wall. In his case, he appeared to have been bound with ropes to a series of rings in the brickwork. The countess stood with back turned, her blue-black hair tumbling, leaning against him, crooning, patting him softly on the cheek, though in her other hand she wielded a pair of pincers, their iron teeth glowing red as she'd just lifted them from a bucket of hot coals.

'Time to wake up,' she said again. 'Come now, my sweet. We can't start the festivities without you.'

Scarcely able to think clearly, Melinda stepped quietly into the cell behind her, reaching for a length of hanging chain and bunching it in her fist. The gentle clinking of metal links distracted the mad countess, but she didn't look around before Melinda struck her – as hard as she'd ever struck anyone or anything – not on the back of the head, as she'd intended, but on her right temple. The blow jarred the girl's arm and shoulder, but her captor-in-chief hit the dungeon floor like a sack of sand.

Melinda had no clue how long she'd be unconscious for, but at least she'd bought them some time. She dashed back into the corridor to Thurstan's cell, which she now unlocked. He lay as he had before.

'Thurstan! Thurstan!' She grabbed him and shook him. 'Thurstan! You must wake up! You must!'

Thurstan groaned and gestured, but it was feeble.

'Sweet Jesus, help me,' she muttered, hooking her hands under his armpits and hauling him bodily out into the passage. '*Pater noster in Caelo, sanctificetur nomen tuum...*'

Even in ordinary clothes, he was a deadweight. Thurstan wasn't especially tall or even broad, but he was solid, a fighting man, all bone and muscle. '*Adveniat regnum tuum... fiat voluntas tua...*' Lugging him such a distance, it was all she could do to breathe, let alone pray. '*In terra sicut in Caelo... panem nostrum quotidianum da nobis hodie...*'

By the time she reached the end of the passage, she was exhausted, but determination to save her friends' lives drove her on. They would escape this pit. This charnel house.

Of course, if the passage had been difficult, the stairway, which was narrow and agonisingly steep, was all that and worse. She panted and sweated as she lugged him upward, but the desperation spurred her on. Even if she made it to the top, where would she go then? Was there any hiding place in this castle where her friends would have time to recover? Could she make it outside without being discovered? There was surely only minuscule chance of doing that alone.

'*Et dimitte nobis debita nostra… sicut et nos dimittimus debitoribus nostris…*'

Halfway up, the stair was perilous going, the treads worn and wet. Water dripped from overhead, while to the right lay some kind of terrible abyss, down in the depths of which she heard a ferocious snarling, growling and barking.

'*Et ne nos inducas in tentationem… sed libera nos a malo…*'

It seemed impossible that she could make it to the top before someone else came down. A few minutes more and she had managed it, but the whole of her body ached, every joint and muscle strained to breaking point.

Here, an arched portal led out into a bare stone passage. Lungs heaving, her once fine clothes clinging to her sweaty form, Melinda peeked out. The passage ran fifty yards to the right, where beyond an open doorway, firelight danced, but only twenty yards to her left, where it ended abruptly at a curtain made from heavy black cloth.

Shuddering with effort, she dragged Thurstan into a sitting posture and left him just inside the stairway door. He muttered again and shook his head slightly. It seemed that he was coming round, though only slowly. Leaving him be, she crept on catlike feet to the fire-lit entrance and found herself staring into the main hall. A single person was visible: Kakia, Lord Malice himself. He stood by the table, knifing hunks of smoked beef, shoving them into his mouth at the same time as swilling wine. He was distracted by the food, but there was no way to get past him without being noticed.

She returned to her insensible companion, again drawing only a mumbled response when she whispered to him. Frustrated and frightened, she went the other way. Before she reached the curtain, there was a second passage on her left. Down at its far end, she saw snowflakes swirling past an upright aperture. Highly likely that was no more than a window, or a door onto a lower battlement, but there was just a chance, albeit slim, that it was a way out. Returning to the stairway, she took Thurstan by his armpits again and hauled him in that direction. However, when she reached the adjacent passage, one of the countess's female servants had emerged from a room partway along it, and was standing with her back turned while she locked it.

Frantic, Melinda yanked the black curtain aside and pulled Thurstan's body behind it, swiftly drawing it closed. There she waited, breathing as quietly as possible. Voices approached on the other side. One female, the other male – the latter sounded like Kopek. They spoke together in some language she'd never heard before, their footsteps then receding.

Wiping her sweaty forehead with a sleeve, Melinda turned and looked behind her. And saw that they had stumbled into some kind of miniature chapel. It was vaulted, so it gave that impression, though everything else in the room was new to her: the central stone altar for example, which was covered in runic symbols and dead flowers, red flames burning atop candles that smelled like human fat balanced in the middle of it. Most eye-catching, of course, was its centrepiece: an upright human corpse nailed and chained to an inverted cross, with a goat's skull where its head should be.

CHAPTER 50

It was all Melinda could do not to fight her way back through the curtain. Instead, she averted her eyes and clamped a hand to her mouth. Even then, it took several seconds to calm down – her breathing coming so hard and heavy that she feared this alone would give her away.

When she plucked up the courage to look round the curtain, the corridor directly ahead and the corridor adjacent both lay deserted. Again, she took Thurstan by the armpits, and with strength now fuelled by horror and disbelief, lugged him towards the snow-filled aperture. Before she reached it, though, she already had a sinking feeling. She could see a row of merlons beyond it, snow piling on top of them. It was a battlement after all. Perhaps there'd still be a staircase down, maybe connecting with a postern gate, but increasingly that felt unlikely. The whole purpose of this structure was impregnability.

When she hauled Thurstan outside, her worst fears came to pass.

She laid him on the soft white carpet, hurried to the merlons and looked down through the gap between them. The drop on the other side was precipitous. Not just to the foot of the castle's outer wall, but down the cliffside too, three hundred feet at least. The pine-covered crags below were partly hidden by the swirling flakes.

She looked left. The battlement walk continued around the exterior, vanishing from sight. It was the same on her right; she ventured in that latter direction first, hoping against hope, but some thirty yards on, instead of finding a stairway down, the heavy stone defences made a sharp turn and closed the walkway off.

A cul-de-sac.

She stopped, shoulders sagging.

'I can't allow you to leave,' a voice said from behind. 'My family are all I have.'

Shocked, she spun around.

Kakia stood there. He still wore the same cheery apparel as before and was unarmed save for a dagger at his belt. Absurdly, it struck her what a striking young figure he made, with his handsome looks, his blue-green eyes and fair hair, especially as he almost seemed sad to be confronting her. Of course, it was impossible to divorce him from everything else that she'd seen here.

'You worship Lucifer?' she asked, voice shaking.

'Not I. My sister and her servants. My brother… sometimes.'

'Why?'

He sighed. 'Who can explain it? I think Aimatochysia seeks a reason for why she's the way she is. As for Echthra… he just enjoys the way he is.'

'And you condone all this?'

'As I say, my family are all I have.'

'Your family come first, whether they're right or wrong?'

He shrugged. 'Is that not the way of your Christian kingdoms? What crimes have your leaders committed in the East, and yet still your Church and people cheer them on.'

'To a greater good.'

He smirked. 'Spoken like a true zealot.'

'If you're genuinely better than your brother and sister, turn your back while we leave.' Her voice became an entreaty. 'Please. You don't even need to help us. Just don't hinder us.'

'No one leaves Chateau Apelpisia. You're the closest anyone has come to that, and you can only have managed this by causing injury to my kin.' He drew the dagger from his belt, and advanced towards her. 'In which case, I can't be merciful. Though at least I can spare you the suffering. Open your collar, show me your throat… it'll be over before you know it.'

Melinda backed to the nearest merlons. 'Don't come near me.'

'You're not the stuff martyrs are made of?'

'Once I thought I was. Now, I'll resist you… I'll fight.'

He nodded. 'Very admirable. Who encouraged this change of heart?'

Thanks to the softness of the fresh-fallen snow, he clearly hadn't heard Thurstan closing from behind. Only realised he was there, in fact, when a hefty set of bunched knuckles slammed hard into the nape of his neck.

'No one that matters to you,' Thurstan said.

The young man staggered, almost blacking out where he stood, making it an easy thing for the knight, even in a shaky state himself, to hustle him to the merlons, hook one arm under his crotch, then tip him up and out through the nearest embrasure, dropping him from view.

'Didn't he boast that he's never yet met his equal?' Thurstan peered down the castle wall after him. 'Where he's going now, I imagine there are plenty.'

Melinda threw herself onto him, hugging him. 'Thank God.'

'Easy, girl. I'm not exactly steady as a rock.'

She backed away again. 'These people are in league with the Devil.'

'I can't say that surprises me. Where's Pandulf?'

'Still in the dungeons. The countess plans to torture him.'

'And Lord Echthra?'

'I don't know. I drugged him, but that was some time ago.'

'Show me.'

No sooner had they stepped back into the passage leading to the hall than Kopek emerged casually from behind the black curtain.

Before the startled fellow could react, Thurstan seized him around the head and threw him against the closest wall. The impact was skull-splitting, but just to be sure, the knight flung him at it again, and again, and after that, as the black-clad underling lay twitching and frothing at the mouth, kicked his head several times further. Until he twitched no more.

Melinda hung back, hands over her face.

'Just remember,' Thurstan said, steering her on by the elbow. 'He was complicit.'

'I know… but it should still be for God to decide.'

'God's deciding right now.'

When they came to the top of the stairway, the blackness of a chasm yawned below. Thurstan halted, feeling under his tunic and swearing. 'Damn tube of warrants has gone. Without that, we can't just walk out of here.'

'They took everything we had,' Melinda replied.

'In that case, I need a weapon.'

'There are weapons in the great hall.'

He nodded and they continued along the passage. The great hall remained deserted. There was no sign of the other servants.

'Watch every corner,' Thurstan said as they crossed the vast room to the hearth, alongside which hung a particular longsword that had captured his eye earlier. Its straight, steel blade glinted blue down its edges; its iron pommel and cross-guard had been worked with silver and gold, its jewelled hilt bound with jet-black velvet.

'*You're* a good-looking devil, and no mistake.' Thurstan took it down, weighing it in his hand. He twirled it in a flourish, backward and forward. Melinda watched the rest of the hall, nervously.

'They were going to sell you to Emperor Isaac,' she said as they headed back.

Thurstan nodded. 'So, they know who we are?'

'The news has travelled.'

He looked thoughtful. 'From here on, we must be cleverer.'

'From here on?' As the horrors in this awful place had unfolded, she'd managed to blot out the reality that, even if they escaped this living nightmare, the terrible journey would go on, that the majority of it still lay ahead.

'What do you expect?' he replied. 'We give up because we've met stiff opposition?'

'I don't know what I expect, my lord.' She tried not to sound as weary as she felt. 'I never expected any of this, that is sure.'

'Always expect the worst. That way, there'll be no unpleasant surprises.'

'That's the creed of the doomed.'

'We're all doomed, Melinda. One way or another.'

At the top of the dungeon stair, they heard the savage beasts yowling and snarling in the void below. Thurstan paused to listen. 'Dear God...'

'I've seen what they do to people,' Melinda said. 'I dread to think what they've done to their dogs.'

As Thurstan led them down, Melinda explained about her own escape, but couldn't account for the whereabouts of her surviving captors. However, when they entered the dungeon corridor, it was suspiciously quiet. Thurstan advanced, Melinda tagging close behind. For the first time, Thurstan now saw the atrocities in the barred alcoves, but dealt with them with his usual rationale. If the victims were unknown to you, it served no purpose to cry. If they were known, it would make avenging them all the sweeter.

When they reached Pandulf's cell, the boy hung as before, but he was moving now, groggily turning his head. Countess Aimatochysia still lay motionless.

Thurstan squatted beside her. She was breathing steadily, but her eyes were fast shut. 'You hit her?'

'I had to,' Melinda said.

'It wasn't an admonition. What did you hit her with?'

'A chain.'

'It's done the trick.' He extricated the pincers from the countess's grasp. 'I'll never understand why foul deeds always seem worse at the hands of the beautiful.' He tossed the implement away. 'Untie the boy. Perhaps use your cloak, yes? Make him a loincloth. He's suffered enough without adding embarrassment.'

Melinda nodded. 'Where are you going?'

'This won't take long.'

He continued along the passage, sword ready. When he reached Melinda's cell, it was empty. Echthra had vanished. Disappointed, he returned.

Pandulf was now on his feet, albeit leaning against Melinda, who had one arm round his back. She'd wrapped her blue cloak around his loins, but the lad still seemed oblivious. He wore a docile, near-bovine expression.

Thurstan glanced back out into the corridor. It was still clear.

'I'll take him.' He wrestled the lad from her and threw him up over his shoulder. At the same time, he handed Melinda the sword. 'Take this, if you will.'

'Can you carry him?' she wondered, locking the cell behind her, the countess still inside it. 'A few minutes ago, you were in a stupor.'

'We may as well find out.' Thurstan set off towards the foot of the stair, though the lad felt heavier than expected. He found himself lurching rather than striding.

'Thurstan?' Melinda said, concerned.

'All is well,' he replied irritably, though if the drug was still undermining his strength, he didn't want to chance that treacherous stair in total darkness. 'Bring one of these torches. We need light.'

She did as he asked, its red reflection capering ahead as they commenced the climb. Thurstan's face was soon dripping. When he sensed the void on the right, and heard the ravening beasts, it had a dizzying effect.

So much so that he almost didn't see the figure waiting halfway up.

Only Melinda's frightened yelp drew his attention to it. He halted.

Five steps above them, Echthra blocked any further ascent. He still wore his leather breeks and steel-studded belt. But he'd thrown on an old peasant shirt and now stood with longsword in hand.

'You will pay,' he said, 'for the harm you have done.'

Thurstan lowered Pandulf to the steps. The lad had regained consciousness but was too fuddled to stand unaided. The knight didn't speak, just held his hand back to Melinda.

'Thurstan,' she whispered, 'you're not fully recovered...'

He snapped his fingers, and she placed his sword-hilt there.

'Ah.' Echthra seemed pleased. 'You mean to make a contest of it.'

'I hear my friend gave you a full draught,' Thurstan said. 'That means we're both in a drowsy state. The odds should be even.'

'I wonder.' Echthra smiled. 'I've heard much about you, Wildblood. One can't fail to be impressed that you made it this far.'

'You're sure we're who you think we are?' Thurstan replied. 'You know how many pilgrims are heading for home?'

'Not so many with a lady's scarf tied on the hilt of their sword.' Echthra smiled all the more. 'Yes, indeed. A rare lapse on your part? Or is that rag so important to you that it can *never* be removed?'

'Your ears aren't fit for such personal information.'

His opponent shrugged. 'Either way, you wield a different weapon now.' He nodded at the sword from the hall. 'That one belonged to my father. He once used it to behead a hundred hostages, when Sheikh Zengi refused to make payment.'

'Today, it serves a better cause.'

'*You*, you mean?' Echthra laughed. 'So, you're a good man now?'

'I wouldn't go that far.'

'You see I have the higher ground?'

'That won't make any difference.'

'So, there's no point in me retreating upstairs, offering you an open space, an even surface?'

'None whatsoever.'

'You're very confident, Wildblood.'

'So confident,' Thurstan replied, 'that even if you offered me the road, I'd refuse. You are a lesson, Lord Echthra, just aching to be taught.'

This time the handsome fellow's smile split him ear to ear. His teeth were pearly-white, but his dark hair was a sweat-soaked mop hanging over eyes of madness.

His sword came down with such force, it might have butchered a bullock.

Thurstan parried, sparks flying. In return, he struck at his opponent's legs, but Echthra swept the blade away, responding with a furious roundhouse. Thurstan leapt backward, descending a couple of stair-treads, the soles of his boots sliding on the greasy stone. For a grotesque moment, he tottered over the abyss.

Echthra, whose blows were fast and sure, aimed for his neck.

Thurstan parried again. Fleetingly, it left his foe open. He lunged, striking point-first into the midriff, but his blade failed to pierce the steel-studded belt. And now he was feeling torpid again, weakness seeping through him, neck and shoulder muscles tightening, vision blurring. It had to be the same for his opponent, but it was true that Echthra held the higher ground.

And it *would* make a difference.

Further blows rained down. Thurstan deflected one after another. But his feet slid continually. He tottered on the edge of the gulf, the roaring and yowling echoing in its depths. Helpless to do anything else, he sank to one knee.

Echthra descended, chopping at his adversary's guard, two-handed. And yet, his blows seemed lighter, less accurate. His wits too were scattering. His fourth or fifth blow half overbalanced him.

'Melinda!' Thurstan gasped, reaching behind. 'The light!'

The staff of the torch was placed in his hand. He glanced up. Echthra stood shaking his head, mopping his eyes. He raised his steel for another butchering blow, but seemed sluggish, unfocussed. Thurstan was sluggish too, too much to raise his blade.

But not his torch.

Which he touched by its flaming end to the hanging hem of Echthra's shirt.

The fellow's upper half ignited.

Suddenly, he was a man of straw. His shrieks turned ghastly as the flames enveloped him. He dropped his weapon, tearing at the garment. Thurstan took a final massive swing at him, steel biting through his foe's left knee-joint, the limb buckling, the entire body toppling sideways... and dropping, blazing, into the blackness below.

By their increased snarling and slavering, the beasts appreciated the treat, overcooked or not.

'Not so chivalrous, my lord,' Melinda said, helping Thurstan to his feet.

'Chivalry is a two-way thing, my lady. You heard him say it... he had the higher ground.'

'You allowed him the higher ground.'

'He shouldn't have accepted it.'

CHAPTER 51

If what remained of the castle servants hadn't been in hiding before, they clearly were now. As the fugitives searched high and low for their property, they saw no one, though as it occurred to Thurstan that some of them might have left, might even have gone in search of help, he urged Pandulf and Melinda to be quick.

The two men had now recovered quickly from their stupor, the seriousness of their predicament perhaps assisting with this.

'We've been a couple of days in this wilderness,' Pandulf said. 'I haven't seen any other fortifications, or dwellings. I'm sure they have armed retainers, but they must be far from here.'

'The fact remains that our presence is known about,' Thurstan replied. 'We can't dally. We must stay on the move.'

It was the early hours of Christmas morning, and snow was still falling. A fresh layer gathered on the battlements, in the courtyard, in the surrounding forest, though it wasn't so deep that it would cause them difficulty. They found their own clothes in trunks in the apartments they'd used, while Thurstan's all-important royal documents, having been read through quickly by their captors, were scattered on the bed. Their mail and weapons they located in an armoury just off the passage to the black magic altar. Here, they recovered everything they'd lost, and even took extra items they might need: another crossbow and a bag of quarrels, several bushels of extra arrows for Melinda's hunting bow. Aside from Pandulf, who was still almost naked, Thurstan forbade them from re-attiring themselves, or even re-mailing.

'There'll be time for that later,' he said. 'Before anything else, we must leave.'

He was even hesitant about taking food from the table in the great hall, where most of it still lay untouched.

'I'm famished,' Pandulf complained.

'We know the drink is tainted,' his master replied. 'And you want to chance the food!'

'You said, yourself… Lord Kakia was eating it.'

'The servants might have poisoned it since,' Melinda said. 'They've had several opportunities since we got free.'

That decided it. They left the banquet, though they paused before ignoring the food in the larder, of which there was plenty. It seemed unlikely the servants would have damaged that stock, as they themselves would need to eat once their enemies had departed. But as Thurstan said, it was better not to take a chance.

'We have our own markswoman, and now she has all the missiles she'll need,' he said. 'We can hunt.'

They found the two horses they'd retrieved after the fight with the Zoódis in a stable off the courtyard. But here, they met their first resistance, the idiot stable lad rising from under a pile of straw and charging them with a pitchfork. Thurstan parried the blow with a sweep of his arm and felled the lad with a punch.

'Weren't his brains addled enough?' Melinda wondered.

'He lives,' Thurstan replied simply.

'He's hurt.'

'He'll be hurt more if the countess's supporters arrive here and find him the only living male in the castle with no sign he resisted.'

'The rules of this game are hard, my lady,' Pandulf added. 'But you couldn't have been expected to realise that.'

Melinda said nothing, but by her expression, she clearly felt that she *should* have realised.

Further problems arose when they found that the two animals had been stripped of their saddles and other accoutrements, and there was no trace of them in the stable block. It was obvious that they neither had time to go through the entire stronghold again, nor to wait until the stable lad recovered enough to help them, assuming he'd even know what they were talking about, which was unlikely.

'It's not a disaster,' Thurstan said, taking them into the next outbuilding, where there was a sizeable four-wheel cart. 'If anyone's keeping watch for us, they'll be looking for a knight and his squire escorting a saintly girl. Not two male peasants delivering farm produce. If we fill this with straw, Melinda can hide, while you and I, Pandulf, can drive.'

It helped that there was adequate tack to tether the two horses to the cart. Pandulf took charge of this, while Thurstan and Melinda stowed their belongings in the back and heaped on the straw. They even found an oil-lamp on a hooked stand, the lower section of which slotted into a pannier alongside the driver's bench. Thurstan lit it with a candle, and now they had firelight by which to travel.

'Would any peasants be working on Christmas Day?' Pandulf wondered.

'No one will,' Thurstan replied. 'Which also means there'll be no one to see us for a good twelve hours or so. God willing, we'll be far from here by then.'

Almost ready, they donned those furs and fleeces they had to hand, their longer-term plan to change into full peasant clothing when they were safely away from here. Melinda concealed herself under the straw, the two men ascending to the driver's bench and driving out across the courtyard, now a pristine field of white. It was the same story beyond the outer gates, which they saw as they descended the hillside. Pandulf watched the trees; the spaces between them were silent, snow-filled grottos, the only movement the ceaseless fluttering of flakes.

He huddled into his furs. 'Do we even know which direction to take, my lord?'

'For the moment, it's wherever this road leads us.'

If it hadn't been for the gap it made between the trees, that road would barely be visible now, its white blanket steadily deepening. That smothering hush of a snowy winter's dawn lay over them, the grey light of morning rising to their rear.

At which point a ferocious scream split the frozen air.

Both drivers turned to look behind.

Still only several hundred yards downhill from the castle, the lowering monument to evil dominating the skyline, they saw that a figure on horseback had emerged in front of it. A figure wielding a blazing torch. Even from this distance, they could see that the figure's upper body was mailed. They could also see, from its shape, that it was female. It wore black skirts and a heavy black cloak, while a mane of black lustrous hair hung past its shoulders. She ululated after them again, a furious, lingering war cry, raising her torch high as an entire horde of additional figures appeared alongside her. Four-legged, snuffling round for a scent, and one by one, as they detected it, setting up a hideous chorus of yowls, snarls and barks.

'Lord help us,' Pandulf whispered.

Melinda raised her head from under the straw to peak over the cart's tailgate – just as the hellish pack came charging downslope, baying like things possessed. Thurstan snapped the reins, whipping his two horses into a gallop, the cart bouncing and jolting, the lantern swinging crazily. Whenever they turned a bend, its wheels locked and slid. Even then, the horses, terror-stricken by the sounds of the chasing pack, needed no encouragement, reaching full speed as soon as they were able.

'Are those dogs?' Pandulf shouted, horrified. 'I've never seen anything like them.'

Thurstan snapped the reins harder, the white ribbon of the narrow road twisting and looping. Despite this, the most fleet-footed of their pursuers were soon alongside them, and they were the ghastliest things the knight had ever seen: enormous, gambolling brutes, black and grey in colour, more like wolves than dogs, and yet not sleek, not handsome. Their heads were huge and bullock-shaped with immense jaws and slablike, bone-shearing teeth. Ropes of drool flew from thick, wobbling jowls still crimson from the meal they'd made of Lord Echthra.

'How many?' Thurstan shouted over his shoulder.

Pandulf clung on as he turned on his seat. Melinda knelt upright, rigid with fright. Neither immediately responded.

'Damn it, how many?'

'Thirty...' the girl stammered. 'No, forty... Maybe fifty.'

Thurstan gazed on ahead as the perilous downhill road meandered. He glimpsed the two pack leaders, one to either side of the vehicle.

They yowled again, froth spurting, deep-set eyes flashing hatred. No normal pack would try to take down a galloping horse, let alone two running side by side. But if one of the horses became lame, or if the wagon broke an axel or sprung a wheel, which was easily possible on this road at this speed, there'd be no stopping them.

Another straight stretch opened ahead, descending steeply.

It was a deathly prospect covered in snow, but at least they picked up speed.

'Pandulf, take the reins!' Thurstan shouted.

The lad nodded dumbly, clutching on tight as the leather grips were handed over.

The knight now glanced around, the road behind entirely filled with fearsome hounds, blood dabbling their maws.

Countess Aimatochysia rode at their rear, but a good hundred yards back.

With one hand latched onto the wooden rim behind him, Thurstan straddled over it into the cart's bed. Flake-filled wind whipped him, all sense of balance teetering, the wooded hillside swirling past. But the next thing, he was down in the straw, scrabbling under it for the sword that his tormentors' father had once wielded. He drew it from his scabbard.

'Get down!' he ordered Melinda.

One of the foremost and largest of the beasts had made a mighty effort to come pounding up. It was monstrously powerful, easily six feet in length. It leapt, a frenzied death-defying attempt to land in the rear of the cart.

Thurstan met it head-on, ramming the blade between its slavering jaws. It almost yanked the weapon from his hand as it fell dragging behind them, but the blade came free, slick with gore. The slain beast bounced over and over in the snow, several pack members tumbling over it, others halting to wheel around and tear at the carcass. But not all. Thurstan rocked backward as a second animal leapt. It landed full on him, a colossal mass of bone and black, matted fur hitting him in the face, savage teeth grizzling at his scalp.

He heard Melinda scream, before twisting his body to the right and hurling it both from himself and the vehicle.

'Here!' He ferreted through the straw, pulled the double-curved bow out and handed it to her. She nodded, rummaging among their kit for the arrows.

'*My loooord!*' Pandulf shrieked.

Thurstan spied a sharp, steep turn in the road ahead.

'Slow the horses!' he shouted. 'If we roll this thing, we're dead.'

The lad lugged on the reins as hard as he could. The horses, still panicking, resisted, but they were tiring too and acutely aware their hooves were slipping and sliding, and the slowdown commenced. Thurstan glanced back as the pack gained. But now Melinda loosed her first arrow, another beast going down, crashing head over heels into the snow-filled underbrush. This time, the others ignored it, pursuing madly as they sensed they were closing the gap.

Pandulf shouted another warning as they veered around the bend, skidding sideways, snow hurtling into everyone's faces, the cart tipping onto two wheels. Thurstan threw himself to the left, to rebalance it, and a moment later they were speeding downhill again. But with the horses having slowed, another of the pack-leaders took its chance, striking at their rearmost hooves, drawing blood from a fetlock.

Thurstan dug through the straw, pulling out the crossbow. It was an advanced model, an Eastern design as opposed to the simpler, Western ones he was used to. At first it confused him, but then he saw the crank-handle with which to draw back the bowstring. He fitted a quarrel into place, leaned over the cart's rim, where the front-running dog was ripping at the right runner's rear shank, and loosed.

The quarrel thudded home.

Yowling in pain, the brute fell out of the chase.

Behind him, Melinda was drawing more arrows, loosing repeatedly.

Her first shot missed, but the second struck clean, dropping yet another pursuer. More of its companions turned on it. The third caught a hound in mid-air. This too had leapt, but she transfixed it through its middle. Yet still they came, two dozen of them, and now they were right at their rear, the right-hand horse struggling with its injury.

'Can you hit the countess?' Thurstan shouted.

'She's too far back,' Melinda replied.

It was true. The countess, having seen the damage being wrought on her pack, had receded in their wake.

'More dogs, then,' he said. 'Thin them out. Put the beasts down.'

She complied, loosing shaft after shaft. Some flew wide, though most hit targets, more brutes going nose over tail in the snow. But now the slope was lessening, and their maimed horse was struggling all the more, and they were losing speed. Thurstan, having tried to help with his crossbow, only to find that he lacked the skill unless it was at close range, cast the weapon down and grabbed his sword again.

Melinda shuffled backward as another beast leapt. He met it with steel, cleaving its skull. Another bounded up, but the girl had repositioned herself, her arrow winging into it in mid-air, sending it crashing into the trees.

The sloped road now levelled out and they were running on the flat. The injured horse was in a desperate state, sweat-lathered, limping abominably, the cart travelling skew-whiff, dredging through snow rather than skating over it.

But then, astonishingly, at this critical moment, the pack seemed to lose heart.

Thurstan watched incredulously as, one by one, they gave up on the chase, slowing from a charge to a canter, snarls and slashings replaced by whimpers of uncertainty. When he glanced ahead, he saw the reason.

They were approaching the gorge.

He could have laughed. Many times, he'd known dogs baulk at crossing bridges, even footbridges over minor streams. Meanwhile, the horses, drained and whinnying, pumping out gallons of smoky breath, were too terrified to feel any qualms, and didn't break stride as they trundled onto the creaking structure.

Of course, whether the bridge would take the weight of a loaded cart was another matter.

The three passengers sat frozen and silent as they crossed, the vehicle slowing down as the horses sensed they were no longer being followed. Far below – several hundred feet at least – Thurstan could again spy the glimmer of moving water, the black teeth of jutting rocks. The timbers groaned and protested, but as they approached the other side, he peered behind, and on the far side saw the pack milling confusedly, still unwilling to cross, the mounted Countess Aimatochysia finally arriving among them.

'God be praised,' Pandulf exclaimed as they rode up onto solid ground again.

'Halt us here,' Thurstan said.

As the lad reined the horses to a standstill, the knight lifted the lantern from the hook over the bench and leapt down. Melinda climbed down as well, staring back across the gorge. Thurstan joined her.

The grey of dawn, heightened by the whiteness of the snow, ensured there was sufficient light for them to watch as the countess kicked her mount back and forth among her frightened pack, shrieking at them in some foreign tongue. Whatever language it was, it contained a magic of sorts, because gradually, at first individually but then in twos and threes, the beasts commenced slinking across the bridge.

Thurstan opened the door to the lantern, blew on the oil-flame and thrust in a fistful of straw. The straw caught. He wrapped a bundle of rag around it, the flames flaring, then carried it to the timber framework on the cliff's edge, where most of the guy-ropes had been fastened.

One after another, he lit them.

Melinda might once have raised an objection, but now she simply watched the pack as they straggled across the chasm, coming on faster and faster, still on their bellies but bloody-faced, snarling, drooling.

One after another, meanwhile, the ropes blackened and unravelled.

Yowling once more, refocussing on their targets, the hounds at the front broke into a gallop – just as the bridge sagged downward, the cables snapping and lashing, timbers twisting, stakes shifting out of place.

The roadway in the sky flipped sideways, before dropping.

With fast diminishing shrieks, the hell-pack was pitched into infinity.

Pandulf, having tied up the horses, came and stood next to Thurstan. They watched with fascination as, on the far side, the deranged noblewoman leapt from her horse, coming to the cliff edge and hurling incoherent curses.

'It's a good thing we don't believe in demons,' Thurstan said.

'She must be mad,' the squire replied.

'Mad or merely bad, it's not our concern anymore.' Thurstan turned away.

'Wait!' Melinda said.

He looked back. The countess hadn't noticed, but figures were emerging from the snowy woods behind her. Humped, hulking figures clad in shaggy animal hides, armed with brute weapons.

When Countess Aimatochysia realised, her shrieks changed in timbre. From uncontrolled wrath to purest terror. But it was too late. The Zoódis fell on her with gusto. She kicked, screamed and fought, to no avail, for they numbered a dozen at least as they carried her away.

EPILOGUE

A sky the colour of ice arched over endless ranges of jagged crags, clutches of night-black forest tucked between them, strands of grey cloud hanging frozen.

Thurstan surveyed it wearily, before pushing back from the high point, through leafless tangles and descending into the hollow where Pandulf and Melinda waited beside their meagre fire. The youngsters huddled in their furs and picked at greasy bones. They looked pale and pinched, not just with cold, but with hunger for thus far that Christmas Day they'd dined once, on a single squirrel that Melinda had shot.

The girl glanced up and saw the look on Thurstan's face.

'Is the road ahead hard?' she enquired.

'In truth?' He felt at his hip, which was aching dully. 'It barely exists.'

'Maybe we should wait here a while?' she suggested. 'It may not look so bad when we're rested.'

Thurstan unbuckled his sword-belt, wrapping the bejewelled weapon and its scabbard in rags. 'We need to put distance between ourselves and Castle Despair. Finish your victuals and pack up.'

'We haven't seen anyone else the whole of Christmas Day,' Pandulf protested.

'The countess didn't see the Zoódis... but they saw her.'

Pandulf and Melinda got to their feet, pulling up their hoods and scarfs.

'Surely we haven't come through all this to die at the hands of degenerate ruffians?' the lad said. He spoke with what he clearly hoped was confidence.

'Thurstan is right, Pandulf,' Melinda replied. 'Why risk losing the chance we've made for ourselves?'

'If you think so.' The squire got what few belongings he had together. 'But I've no doubt we'll survive. We must. We're in the presence of powerful forces. We surely accept that now? How else have we lasted so long?'

'Mostly through cold steel,' Thurstan said. 'Quench the fire.'

Pandulf did as instructed, and they moved through the trees to where the cart awaited them, the two horses nosing at what remained of a pile of fodder.

'That's how you disposed of the mad countess,' Pandulf said. He glanced at Melinda. 'I'm thinking of those other occasions. Cold steel didn't save my life in that desert stronghold.'

'Neither did I,' Melinda said tiredly.

'You nursed me back to health.'

'In truth, I did very little.'

'You prayed over me.'

'I did that, yes.' She loaded her belongings into the bed of the vehicle. 'It's gratifying to learn that I was listened to. But Pandulf… you may need to consider that you're stronger and more determined to live than you realise.'

'And Lord Thurstan's cure?'

'How can you doubt that Lord Thurstan is strong?' she said.

'That wound he suffered would have killed an ox.'

'You brats talk about me as if I'm not here,' the knight grumbled, checking the horses.

'Apologies, lord,' Melinda said, suddenly seeming thoughtful 'But in your case… maybe it *was* a miracle. And yet maybe it owed nothing to this thing you fear.'

He glanced round at her. 'You mean a miracle of *God's* devising?' If laughter ever came easy to him, he'd have laughed now. 'When I've done nothing but decry Him for years?'

'God has uses for all of us,' she said, climbing on board.

'But the devil my lord saw in his dream,' Pandulf said.

'Devils can be used too.' She glanced at Thurstan. 'Perhaps only *you* could escort me away from the East?'

Pandulf frowned. 'Into lifelong captivity? Far from any place where you could do good? Why would that be God's will?'

'Enough of this,' Thurstan grouched. 'Pandulf, get aboard.'

The squire did so, settling on the bench, while his master pondered the route ahead. After crossing the gorge, they'd diverged from the main road, but couldn't just plough on through the wilderness, not with a four-wheel wagon and an injured horse, and not while maintaining a pretence that they were en-route to market. As such, they'd resumed their journey on an unmade cart-track, two meandering furrows at present frozen solid and covered in snow, which now wove off ahead of them, tilting dangerously sideways and then descending into dark, snow-clad woods.

'What good would I do in the East, Pandulf?' Melinda asked him, still thinking on it. 'What role would I really have played? Except perhaps to give those armies of men who hate each other for no reason they understand yet another reason to keep slaughtering?'

Pandulf still looked confused. This was clearly a concept he hadn't grappled with previously, though if Thurstan was honest, neither had he.

'You're saying they'd fight over *you*?' the lad said. 'As well as the Holy Places?'

'Why not?' She mused. 'There can never be peace if one side has an advantage over the other.'

'And what if your abduction leads to a Church schism?' Thurstan wondered.

'Better a schism than a war without end,' she replied.

'Melinda,' the knight said slowly. 'You've seen what I do and how I do it. How can that be God's will?'

'The Lord moves in strange ways.' She knelt up against the cart's rim, her enthusiasm growing. 'But there were few other options with those Luciferians at Chateau Apelpisia. I'd go further... if you were really in thrall to a devil, Lord Thurstan, would those creatures... who were even named after sins, not have welcomed you? Would your dark

387

master not have driven you to embrace them in return? Would your so-called master not have attended the feast in person? To celebrate the triumph of evil?'

Thurstan felt a faint stirring of memory: that conversation with Bishop Hubert outside the keep at Jaffa, when fleetingly he'd entertained thoughts that he might not be damned after all. What was that other thing the bishop had said?

To do wolf's work, it takes wolves. But good wolves, Wildblood. Not bad ones.

Was it possible? he wondered.

The girl made a kind of sense. He'd never admit it, but at times, his seeming invulnerability in battle felt unnatural even to him. His speedy recovery from the elixir at Castle Despair had also been instrumental in their survival.

'That's right, my lord.' Pandulf turned eagerly on the bench. 'There was no triumph of evil this day. You saw Lucifer's acolytes as enemies. You slew them.'

Aye, I slew them. Because slaying is what I do. It's what I've always done. And where did slaying figure in the teachings of Jesus Christ?

But again, Thurstan wondered about it. Mother Turilda thought she saw something in him, did she not? *God has a plan for every one of us. We must proceed with it, or else his anger will be fierce.* She'd even said that God had made him the warrior that he was. But then she'd never really known the extent of his anger towards the Almighty. And even she had been concerned that when he'd opted to go back to war, there was a danger he might... how had she put it?

Fall back into shadow.

No, it was no miracle of God's that had saved him on the plain of Arab-el-Ghawarneh. It was no miracle at all. Just his own brute strength.

Pandulf meanwhile, was still talking. 'Maybe that's part of the reason God's spared you? To mete justice to those murdering wretches back at that castle.'

Thurstan looked at him askance. 'Listen to yourself, boy. Mete justice? *God's* justice?' He couldn't pretend that the thought didn't elate him, but it was sheer nonsense. 'I'm the Sword of Darkness, haven't you heard? I've even found myself a sword that's famous for the evil it did. Perhaps it called to me? Isn't there an old saying that like attracts like?'

There was a brief silence, but then Melinda rummaged in the straw, digging out the bejewelled sword from the great hall and unwrapping it. 'If you're concerned this sword is evil, my lord, sanctify it.'

Thurstan had been about to climb up but now stared at her in disbelief. 'What?'

She dug into the straw again, lifting out his other sword, indicating the tattered scarf tied around its hilt. 'Take this memento and bind it to the new sword.'

'Are you mad?' he whispered.

'Why not? If that scarf's a memento of your dead wife, Gwendolyn, who you clearly loved a great deal, then it can only be—'

'It wasn't Gwendolyn's,' he said abruptly.

Both Pandulf and Melinda fell silent, the latter somewhat abashed, as Thurstan climbed sour-faced to the driving bench. He snapped the reins and they jolted forward.

'We need to make ground before dark,' he said gruffly. Then he added: 'It *was* a memento. You're right about that. But of the first major battle I ever fought. Fornham, during the Great Rebellion.' He gazed dead ahead as they travelled. 'I took it from the sword-hilt of a knight I killed. The first knight I ever killed, as it happened. I never knew his name or where he came from... or who the lady was who gave him her scarf before he rode to war.'

'All this time, you've revered it,' Pandulf said, shocked. 'And it's nothing but loot? A trophy?'

Thurstan said nothing, eyes fixed ahead.

'No.' Melinda poked her head between them. 'I don't think that's it.'

'You think you know me, Melinda,' Thurstan warned her. 'But you don't...'

'I know you well enough.' She reached between them, now holding the aged scarf, which she'd evidently pulled loose. 'This is a sign of your regret, is it not?'

Shouting and yanking on the reins, Thurstan brought the animals to a halt.

He sat there stiff-backed, seething. Or trying to. Because no real anger came. The matter of the scarf, and the emotions it stirred, had gnawed at him for years.

'Regret for the opponent you slew?' Melinda ventured. 'This man you didn't know? Whose lady would never see him again?'

'I... I didn't wish to see it trampled in the mud.' Thurstan tried to shrug. 'It clearly meant something to him... and he was a worthy opponent, so...'

'So, now it's your daily reminder that there's a cost to these things.'

'At the time, I wouldn't countenance such thoughts...'

'But you took it all the same. Even back in those terrible days when you'd learned nothing but war, when you were young and unrestrained, and even deadlier and crueller than you are now... you felt bad enough to remove this heirloom to a place of safety, and have it with you always, to keep his memory alive... and you consider yourself a wicked man? Easy meat for devils and demons?'

He turned slowly to look at her. 'I've slain hundreds since then.'

'In battle. To serve your lord and save the lives of your comrades.'

'I had prisoners killed.'

'Which Bertrand said damaged your soul,' she replied. 'Because you *didn't wish* it. You even spared *him* that same dishonour. The first time I laid eyes on you, my lord, you were wild with concern... for the life of someone else. Your squire.'

Thurstan couldn't reply. Saint or not, this young woman had vision. The green depths of her eyes peered into him, seeing much more than he'd ever admitted, even to himself. She produced the sword from the castle, the wicked implement that had shed so much innocent blood, and tied the fallen knight's scarf around its hilt.

'This is no longer a sword of darkness, Thurstan Wildblood,' she told him. 'And neither are you.'

'We... we need to go,' he stuttered turning to his front, snapping the reins.

'You've said that already,' Pandulf said, sounding equally affected by what he'd just witnessed. 'But... go where?'

Thurstan wondered too. After everything they'd been through, their entire company was whittled down to its last three souls, and they weren't even out of Anatolia yet.

'England.' Melinda settled back into the straw, concealing the sword. 'Where else?'

Thurstan stared ahead again. 'You said it yourself. It's a long way.'

'And you said that this is your quest. And now we know it's a Godly one.'

The knight pondered that possibility with fascination. Incredulity, even.

Good wolves, Wildblood. Not bad ones.

Maybe it was God who guided that javelin…

'So… England?' Pandulf said.

'On the basis that we're unlikely to find friendlier shores any time soon…' Thurstan snapped the reins. 'England it is.'